OM
THE SECRET OF
AHBOR VALLEY

OM
THE SECRET OF
AHBOR VALLEY

BY
TALBOT MUNDY

PILGRIMS PUBLISHING
◆Varanasi◆

OM THE SECRET OF AHBOR VALLEY
Talbot Mundy

Published by:
PILGRIMS PUBLISHING

An imprint of:
PILGRIMS BOOK HOUSE
(Distributors in India)
B 27/98 A-8, Nawabganj Road
Durga Kund, Varanasi-221010, India
Tel: 91-542-2314059, 2314060, 2312456
Fax: 91-542-2312788, 2311612
E-mail: pilgrims@satyam.net.in
Website: www.pilgrimsbooks.com

PILGRIMS BOOK HOUSE (New Delhi)
9 Netaji Subhash Marg, 2nd Floor
Near Neeru Hotel, Daryaganj, New Delhi 110002
Tel: 91-11-23285081
E-mail: pilgrim@del2.vsnl.net.in

Distributed in Nepal by:
PILGRIMS BOOK HOUSE
P O Box 3872, Thamel, Kathmandu, Nepal
Tel: 977-1-4700942, Off: 977-1-4700919
Fax: 977-1-4700943
E-mail: pilgrims@wlink.com.np

First Published 1924
Point Loma Second Edition 1993
Copyright © 2004, Pilgrims Publishing
All Rights Reserved for India , Nepal, Sri Lanka, Bangala Desh and Pakistan.

ISBN: 81-7769-246-1

Printed in India at Pilgrim Press Pvt. Ltd. Lalpur Varanasi

INTRODUCTION

It was in 1923, as the house guest of Katherine Tingley on Point Loma, a suburb of San Diego, California, that Talbot Mundy began work on a novel which was to be set in India and have, as background, much of the Indian philosophy he had imbibed during his years there. When the manuscript was finished he sent it to his literary mentor Arthur Sullivant Hoffman, editor of *Adventure,* one of the most popular magazines of adventure of its day. In April 1924 Mundy wrote to publisher Bobbs Merrill: "I've heard from Hoffman who says 'The Secret of Ahbor Valley' is another *Kim.* He adds it is much the best book I have ever written . . . I go on record here and now that it is a marvel that Hoffman bought the story. It breaks all *Adventure's* rules including a spiritual theme . . ."

Several titles for the book had been suggested, but finally all parties settled on *Om: The Secret of Ahbor Valley.* It was a perfect title, for *Om* was not only the nickname of his hero Ommony but was, significantly, the Sanskrit root mantra of creation.

Mundy was happy with his work. On Labor Day, 1924, he wrote to Bobbs Merrill: "I have read proofs now Lord knows how many times . . . usually a nerve racking and disgusting process. But at night, nearly midnight, when I turned the last page over, dowsed the lights and started for the attic, I felt a solid feeling in me that I had been reading a real book. It did not seem in the least as if I had written it."

Talbot Mundy was actually born William Lancaster Gribbon on April 23, 1879, in Hammersmith, London, England. He was the eldest son of a prominent London businessman. He was sent to Rugby School, the famous English boarding school of *Tom Brown's Schooldays* fame, but the death of his father, when Mundy was fifteen years old, had a detrimental effect on his ability to concentrate on his lessons and he left school the following year. Strong family connections with the Anglican Church caused his mother to suggest that he train for the Anglican priesthood. The boy answered this by running away to Germany where he joined a travelling fair. He never returned home to live.

Followed those adventures in India, South Africa, Portuguese East Africa (now Mozambique) and British East Africa, which gave him background experience to draw on in his creative work. In 1909 he was in New York and writing for *Adventure* magazine, which launched him into almost immediate popularity. In 1914 his first book *Rung Ho!* was published to wide critical acclaim. Forty-two books rapidly followed, but with the publication of *King of the Khyber Rifles* in 1916 his reputation as a bestselling author had been assured.

For many years now, however, the work which both Mundy and his critics considered his finest and most enduring masterpiece has been out of print. I am delighted, therefore, that Point Loma Publications has seen fit to rectify that oversight, and deeply conscious of the honor of being asked to contribute an introduction to this new edition of *Om: The Secret of Ahbor Valley*, a classic of modern literature.

In India Mundy had become fascinated by Indian occult teachings and, following his arrival in America, he had dabbled for a while with Christian Science. In 1922 he moved from New York to San Diego, and on meeting with the Theosophist leader Katherine Tingley (1847-1929) he found a philosophy which was part of the path — the Middle Way — which he had already begun to tread. He became a member of the Universal Brotherhood and Theosophical Society and was soon contributing regularly to *The Theosophical Path*, and in a few short years rose to be a Cabinet Officer of the Society. He remained in his Point Loma home in the environs of San Diego until 1928.

Om was serialized from October 10 to November 30, 1924, in *Adventure*. In the October 10 issue Mundy contributed a 2,000 word article containing background information about the Mahatmas, Ahbor Valley and Ancient Wisdom. The book edition was published in November 1924. British, Swedish and German editions were soon to follow. In autographing a copy to Katherine Tingley, Mundy wrote: "What wisdom it contains was learned from you, and its unwisdom is my own."

Critical praise was immediate on both sides of the Atlantic. Letters poured into *Adventure*, others came via Bobbs Merrill, and still more were sent to *The Theosophical Path*, which published extracts in the February and April 1925 issues.

Gottfried de Purucker reviewing it in *The Theosophical Path* (December 1924) said: "There is not another work in modern literature like this book, it sets a mark and blazes a trail which others and less capable writers indubitably will try to follow and to attain . . . We must have more books like *Om*."

Iverson L. Harris, Katherine Tingley's private secretary and attorney for the Theosophical Society, felt moved to write a personal note to Bobbs Merrill on December 30, 1924: "The story relates to the adventures of conquering souls. It will surely live. Through the medium of its wonderful adventure mystery, thoughtful parents and teachers will be glad to introduce young minds into realms of lofty thought and splendid ideals made real by the hand of one who has obviously traveled at least some distance along 'The Middle Path'."

In Britain, where Hutchinsons published *Om* in January 1925, the *Times Literary Supplement* recorded: "Critics . . . have called it a second Kim." The book went into an immediate second edition and six editions had been issued before the Fall of that year. The prestigious literary newspaper *The Yorkshire Post* commented: "If there had been no Rudyard Kipling, Mr. Talbot Mundy might have gathered a lot more fame than has yet fallen to his lot. He is our most fascinating portrayer of India as it appeals to the romantic and adventurous."

In fact, Mundy found the comparisons with Kipling somewhat odious. Although Kipling had been a favorite author of his in his early years, Kipling had become increasingly jingoistic. His works supported the British imperialist idea and portrayed India through European imperial eyes with the Indians appearing in his books as no more than colorful native caricatures. Not so Mundy's view of India. He was always questioning the imperial ethic, and saw empire as a thing of transcience. This attitude caused the *Times Literary Supplement* to accuse him of being anti-British. But Mundy did not simply portray Europeans in imperial triumph against a bizarre native background. He showed humanity absorbed with all its complex problems in terms of utter realism. Rather than *Om* being another *Kim* some critics have unequivocally stated that *Om* is a far better book than *Kim*. This is certainly the view of the former British High Court Judge and authority on Buddhism, Christmas Humphreys. Mr. Humphreys rates Mundy among his favorite writers and has quoted from several of his novels in his own works on Eastern philosophy.

In presenting this new edition of what, in my opinion, is Talbot Mundy's outstanding literary achievement, a work of romance, high drama and adventure and deep philosophy, what better than to turn to the opinion of Katherine Tingley who helped to inspire its creation. Writing in *The Theosophical Path*, January 1925, she stated: "It contains a genuine and powerful message of Brotherhood. In the wise utterances and quaint sayings of the old Lama, the book marks a new epoch in the history of fiction."

— Peter Berresford Ellis

London, July 1980

PUBLISHER'S NOTE

The centenary last year of the birth of Talbot Mundy serves as appropriate stimulus for Point Loma Publications to present another edition of this his best of books.

This edition also brings to the publishers a unique measure of inner satisfaction as the manuscript itself was written just a few minutes' walk from our own offices; and though that creative writing was begun over half a century ago, members of our staff still nourish a distant memory when Talbot Mundy, as a guest of Katherine Tingley, would read a chapter of an evening to a group of friends there.

Another realization cannot be overlooked: today such a book, combining outward adventure and inner mystic learning along that eternal path called by some the Middle Way, may well be received with greater understanding than when first published. Despite explosive signs of world disruption and almost universal undiscipline, the call from many for more Light sounds clear, the longing for a truer vision of the Reality beyond the illusion of the passing scenes is more prevalent. In *Om, the Secret of Ahbor Valley* the discerning will find rays of light that are both provocative and revelatory.

CONTENTS

EVOLUTION

Tides in the ocean of stars and the infinite rhythm of space;
　Cycles on cycles of æons adrone on an infinite beach;
Pause and recession and flow, and each atom of dust in its
　　　place
　In the pulse of eternal becoming; no error, no breach
But the calm and the sweep and the swing of the leisurely,
　　　measureless roll
　　Of the absolute cause, the unthwarted effect—and no
　　　haste,
And no discord, and nothing untimed in a calculus ruling
　　　the whole;
　　Unfolding; evolving; accretion; attrition; no waste.

Planet on planet a course that it keeps, and each swallow
　　　its flight;
　Comet's ellipse and grace-note of the sudden firefly glow;
— Jewels of Perseid splendor sprayed on summer's purple
　　　night;
　　Blossom adrift on the breath of spring; the whirl of
　　　snow;
Grit on the grinding beaches; spume of the storm-ridden
　　　wave
　　Hurled on the north wind's ice-born blast to blend with
　　　the tropic rain;
Hail and the hissing of torrents; song where sapphire rip-
　　　ples lave
　　The crest of thousand-fathom reefs upbuilt beneath the
　　　main.

Silt of the ceaseless rivers from the mountain summits
　　　worn,
　Rolled along gorge and meadow till the salt, inflowing
　　　tide

Heaps it in shoals at harbor-mouth for continents unborn;
　Earth where the naked rocks were reared; pine where
　　　the birches died;
Season on season proceeding, and birth in the shadow of
　　　death;
　　Dawning of luminous day in the dying of night; and a
　　　Plan
In no whit, in no particle changing; each phase of becoming
　　a breath
　　Of the infinite Karma of all things; its goal, evolution of
　　MAN.

OM

CHAPTER I

"COTTSWOLD OMMONY . . . IS NO MAN'S FOOL"

IF you want views about the world's news, read what
Cottswold Ommony calls the views papers; there is plenty
in them that thoroughly zealous people believe. But remember the wise old ambassador's word of caution to his
new subordinate: "And above all, no zeal!" If you want
raw facts devoid of any zeal whatever try the cafés and the
clubs; but you must sort the facts and correlate them for
yourself, and whether or not that process shall leave you
capable of thought of any kind must depend entirely
on your own ability. Thereafter, though you may never
again believe a newspaper, you will understand them and
if you are reasonably human sympathize.

There used to be a café in Vienna, where a man might
learn enough in fifty minutes to convince him that Europe
was riding carelessly to ruin; but that was before 1914
when the riders, using rein and spur at last, rode straight
for it.

There is still a club in Delhi, where you may pick
up odds and ends of information from over the Pamirs,
from Nepaul, from Samarkand, Turkestan, Arabia and
the Caucasus, all mixed up with fragments from the olla
podrida of races known collectively as India. And having
pieced them all together you may go mad there, as comfortably as in Colney Hatch, but with this advantage:
that nobody will interfere with you, provided you pay
your bills on the first of the month and refrain from sitting
on two newspapers while you read a third.

3

It is a good club, of the die-hard kind; fairly comfortable; famous for its curry. It has done more to establish empire, and to breed ill-will, than any other dozen institutions. Its members do not boast, but are proud of the fact that no Indian, not even a Maharajah, has ever set foot over its threshold; yet they are hospitable, if a man knows how to procure the proper introduction (no women are admitted on any pretense), and by keeping quiet in a long-armed chair you may receive an education. You may learn, for instance, who is and who is not important, and precisely why. You may come to understand how the old guard, everywhere, inevitably must die in the last ditch. And, if you have it in you, you will admire the old guard, without trying to pretend that you agree with them.

But above all, you may study the naked shape of modern history as she is never written—history in the bathroom, so to speak. And once in a while, you may piece together a dozen assorted facts into a true story that is worth more than all the printed histories and all the guide-books added together. (Not that the club members realize it. They are usually bored, and almost always thinking about income-tax and indigestion, coupled with why in thunder so-and-so was fool enough to bid no trumps and trust to his partner to hold the necessary ace.)

When Ommony turned up at the club after three years in a forest he produced a refreshing ripple on a calm that had grown monotonous. For a week there had been nothing to discuss but politics, in which there is no news nowadays, but only repetition of complaint. But Cottswold Ommony, the last of the old-time foresters (and one of the few remaining men in India whom the new democracy has not reduced to a sort of scapegoat rubber-stamp), stirred memories and conjecture.

"*His* turn for the guillotine! He has done too damned well for twenty years, not to have his head cut off. I'll bet you some babu politician gets his job!"

"You'll have to make that bet with Ommony, if he's mad enough. Didn't you hear poor Willoughby was killed?

That leaves Jenkins at the head of Ommony's department, and they've hated each other since Jenkins turned down Ommony's younger sister and Ommony told him what he thought about it. Not that the girl wasn't fortunate in a way. She married Terry later on and died. Who'd not rather die than have to live with Jenkins. Willoughby always considered Ommony to be a reincarnation of Solon or Socrates, plus Aristides crossed on Hypatia. Willoughby—"

But everybody knew the ins and outs of that news. A fat babu in a dirty pink turban that would have scared any self-respecting horse, driving a second-hand Ford, with one eye on the Punjabi "constabeel" at the street crossing, bumped into and broke the wheel of Willoughby's dog-cart, setting any number of sequences in motion. The horse bolted, tipped out Willoughby, who was killed under a tram-car, and crashed into Amramchudder Son and Company's open store-front, where blood from the horse's shoulder spoiled two bales of imported silk. A law-suit to recover ten times the value of the silk was commenced against Willoughby's estate that afternoon. (Mrs. Willoughby had to borrow money from friends to carry on with.)

The babu put on full speed, naturally, and tried to escape down a side-street, of which there are as many, and as narrow ones in Delhi as in any city of its size. He ran over a Bengali (which nobody except the Bengali minded very much), knocked down two Sikhs (which was important, because they were on their way to a religious ceremony; righteous indignation is very bad stuff when spilled in the street), and finally jammed the Ford between a bullock-cart and a lamp-post, where the pride of Detroit collapsed into scrap.

The owner of the bullock-cart, a Jat with a wart on his nose, which his mother-in-law had always insisted would bring bad luck (she said so at the trial later on, and brought three witnesses to prove it), was carrying, for an extortionate price, a native of a far-northern state, who had recently arrived by train without a ticket, and who knew how to be prompt and violent. The man from Spiti (which is the name of the northern state) descended from his perch at the rear of the cart, picked up a spoke that the collision had broken away, and hit the babu with it exactly once between the eyes. The babu died neatly without saying anything; and a hot crowd of nine nationalities, that was glad to see anybody die with politics the way they had been for a year or two, applauded.

The man from Spiti vanished. The "constabeel" arrested the owner of the bullock-cart, who turned his face skyward and screamed "Ayee-ee-ee!" once, which was duly noted in a memorandum book for use as evidence against him. Seventeen onlookers, being questioned, all gave false names and addresses, but swore that the Jat with the wart had attacked the babu; and a *wakil* (which is a person entitled to practise law), who knew all about the Jat's recent inheritance from his uncle, offered legal services that were accepted on the spot. Presently, in the jail, a *jemadar* and two "constabeels" put the Jat through a hideously painful third degree, which left no marks on him but did induce him to part with money, most of which was spent on a debauch that ended in the *jemadar* being reduced to the ranks since the *wakil* objected on principle to sharing the loot of the Jat with any one and therefore righteously exposed the *jemadar's* abominable drunkenness.

Meanwhile, the native papers took the matter up and proved to nine points of decimals that the incident was wholly due to British arrogance and the neglect of public duty by an "overpaid alien hegemony," demonstrating among other things that the British are a race "whose crass materialism is an insult to the spiritual soul of India, and whose playing fields of Eton are an ash-bed from which arise swarms of Phoenixes to suck the life-blood of conquered peoples." (Excellent journalese conceived on the historic principle that if you make sufficient smell you are sure to annoy somebody, and he who is annoyed will make mistakes, which you may then gleefully expose.)

The Sikhs who had been knocked down by the Ford accused the "obsequious servants of alien tyranny"—meaning the police—of having tried to prevent them from attending their religious ceremony; the fact being that the police had taken them to the hospital in an ambulance. The entire Sikh community in consequence refused to pay taxes, which set up another sequence of cause and effect, culminating in a yell of "Bande Mataram!" as three or four thousand second-year students, who were not Sikhs, rushed foaming at the mouth into the Chandni Chowk (which is a business thoroughfare) with the intention of looting the silversmiths and putting the whole city to the torch. A fire-engine dispersed them; but the stream of water from the hose ruined the contents of Chanda Pal's drug-store.

Chanda Pal called in an actuary who possessed a compound geometrical imagination, and sent in a bill to the government that is still unpaid; and, having failed to collect immediately, he wrote to a friend who was an undergraduate at Oxford, with the result that a Member of Parliament for one of the Welsh constituencies asked at Question Time whether it was true that the Viceroy of India in person had high-handedly confiscated without compensation all the drugs in the Punjab; and if so, why?

The answer from the Treasury Bench was "No, sir;" but the foreign correspondents omitted to mention that, so the French, Scandinavian and United States newspapers had it in head-lines that "British in India inaugurate new reign of terror. Goods confiscated. Revolution threatened." A bishop in South Africa preached a sermon on the subject; thirty-seven members of the I. W. W., who were serving a term in San Quentin, went on a sympathetic hunger strike and were locked up in the dungeon; and a Congressman from somewhere in the Middle West wrote a speech that filled five pages of the *Record*. Stocks fell several points. Jenkins stepped into Willoughby's official shoes.

However, clocks continued ticking. Roosters crowed.

The sun appeared on schedule time. And Willoughby's funeral was marked by dignified simplicity.

Except that he hugely regretted his friend Willoughby, Cottswold Ommony cared for none of these things. He sat near the electric fan in a corner of the club smoking-room, aware that he was being discussed, but also quite sure that he did not mind it. He had been discussed, on and off, ever since he came to India. He looked quite unlike Hypatia, whatever Willoughby may have thought of his character.

"Willoughby overrated him," said somebody. "You can't tell me Ommony or any other man is such a mixture of marvels as Willoughby made out. Besides, he's a bachelor. Socrates wasn't."

"Oh, Ommony's human. But—well—you know what he's done in that forest. It was raw, red wilderness when he was sent there. Now you can stand on a rock and see ninety miles of trees whichever way you care to look. Besides, dogs love him. Did you see that great dog of his outside? You can't fool that kind of dog, you know. They say he knows the tigers personally, and can talk the jungle-bat; there was only one other man who ever learned that language, and *he* committed suicide!"

"All the same—he's not the only man who's done good work—and I've heard stories. Do any of you remember Terry—Jack Terry, the M. D., who married Ommony's young sister? One of those delightful madmen who are really so sane that the rest of us can't understand 'em. Had weird theories about obstetrics. Nearly got foul of his profession by preaching that music was an absolute necessity at child-birth. Wanted the government to train symphony orchestras to play the Overture to Leonori while the birth takes place. Perfectly mad; but a corking good surgeon. Always dead broke, from handing out his pay to beggars—broke, that is, until he met Marmaduke. Remember Marmaduke?"

"Dead too, isn't he? Wasn't he the American who endowed a mission somewhere in the Hills?"

"Yes, at Tilgaun. Marmaduke was another madman—ab-so-lutely mad—and as gentle as sunrise. Quiet man, who swore like a trooper at the mention of religion. Made his money in Chicago, slaughtering hogs—or so I heard. Wrote a book on astrology, that only ran to one edition—I sold my copy for ten times what I paid for it. I tell you, Marmaduke was madder than Gandhi. They say he left America to keep the elders of the church he belonged to from having him locked up in an asylum. The mission he founded at Tilgaun caused no end of a stir at the time. Surely you remember that? There were letters to the *Times,* and an archbishop raised a shindy in the House of Lords. Marmaduke's theory was that, as *he* couldn't understand Christianity, it was safe to premise that people whose religion was a mixture of degraded Buddhism and devil-worship couldn't understand it either. So he founded a Buddhist mission, to teach 'em their own religion. No, he wasn't a Buddhist. I don't know what his religion was. I only know he was a decent fellow, fabulously rich, and ab-so-lutely mad. He persuaded Jack Terry to chuck the service and become the mission medico—teach hygiene to men from Spiti and Bhutan—like teaching drought to the Atlantic! Jack Terry married Ommony's sister about a week before leaving for Tilgaun, and none of us ever saw them alive again."

"*Now* I remember. There was a nine days' scandal, or a mystery, or something."

"You bet there was! Terry and his wife vanished. Marmaduke was carpeted, but couldn't or wouldn't explain, and he died before they could make things hot for him. Then they gave Ommony long leave and sent him up to Tilgaun to investigate—that was—by gad! that was twenty years ago—Good lord! how time flies. Ommony discovered nothing; or, if he did discover anything, he *said* nothing—he's a great hand at doing that, by all accounts. But it leaked out that Marmaduke had appointed Ommony a trustee under his will. There was another trustee—a red-headed American woman—at least I heard she's red-headed; maybe she isn't—named Hannah Sanburn, who has been running the mission ever since. She was not much more than a girl at the time, I remember. And the third trustee was a Tibetan. Nobody had ever heard of him, and I've never met a man who saw him; but I'm told he's a Ringding Gelong Lama; and I've also heard that *Ommony* has never seen him. The whole thing's a mystery."

"It doesn't seem particularly discreditable to Ommony. What are you hinting at?"

"Nothing. Only Ommony has influence. You've noticed, I dare say, he always gets what he goes after. If you asked me, there's an even chance he may 'get' Jenkins, if he cares to."

"That's notorious. Whoever goes after Ommony's scalp gets left at the post. What's the secret?"

"I don't know. Nobody seems to. There's Marmaduke's money, of course. Ommony handles some of it. I don't suggest fraud, or any rot like that; but money's strange stuff; control of it gives a man power. Ommony's influence is out of all proportion to his job. And I've *heard* —mind you, I don't know how true it is—that he's hand-and-glove with every political fugitive from the North who has sneaked down South to let the clouds roll by during the last twenty years. They even *said* Ommony was on the inside of the Moplah business. You know the Moplahs didn't burn his bungalow,—they say he simply asked them not to—can you beat that—and it's a fact that he stayed in his forest all through that rebellion."

Ommony was restless over in his corner. His obstinate jaw was only half-concealed by a close-clipped, graying beard, and there was grim humor on his lips. Having done more than any living man to pull the sting out of the Moplah rebellion, hints to the contrary hardly amused him. He was angry—obviously angry. However, one man claimed casual acquaintance and dropped into the next chair.

"Expecting to stay long in Delhi?"

"I don't know. I hope not."

"Care to sell me that wolf-hound?"

Ommony's reserve broke down; he had to talk to somebody:

"That dog? Sell her? She's the sum total of twenty-years' effort. She's all I've done."

The inquisitor leaned back, partly to hide his own face, partly to see Ommony's in a more distinct light; he suspected sunstroke, or the after-effects of malaria. But Ommony, having emerged from his reserve, continued:

"I don't suppose I'm different from anybody else—at least not from any other reasonably decent fellow—made a lot of mistakes, of course—done a lot of things I wish I hadn't—been a bally ass on suitable occasion—but I've worked—damned hard. India has had all the best of me and—damn her!—I haven't grudged it. Don't regret it, either. I'd do it again. But there's nothing to show for it all—"

"Except a forest. They tell me—"

"A forest, half-grown, that corrupt politicians will play ducks and drakes with; a couple of thousand villagers who are now being taught by those same politicians that everything they've learned from me is no good; a ruined constitution—and that dog. That's all I can show for twenty years' work—and like some others, I've had my heart in it. I think I know how a missionary feels when his flock walks out on him. I'm a failure—we're all failures. The world is going to pieces under our hands. What I have taught that dog is all I can really claim by way of accomplishment."

That particular inquisitor lost enthusiasm. He did not like madmen. He withdrew and considered Ommony in a corner, behind a newspaper, *sotto voce*. Another not so casual acquaintance dropped into the vacant chair, and was greeted with a nod.

"You've been absent so long you ought to see things with a fresh eye, Ommony. D'you think India's breaking up?"

"I've thought so for twenty years."

"How long before we have to clear out?"

"The sooner the better."

"For us?"

"I mean for India!"

"I should have thought you would be the last man to say that. You've done your bit. They tell me you've changed a desert into a splendid forest. D'you want to see it all cut down, the lumber wasted and—"

Ommony pulled out his watch and tapped his finger on the dial.

"I had it cleaned and repaired recently," he remarked. "The man charged me a fair price, but after I had paid the bill he didn't have the impudence to keep the watch for fear I might ruin it again. India has a perfect right to go to hell her own way. Surgery and hygiene are good, but I don't believe in being governed by the medical profession. Cleaning up corrupted countries is good; but to stay on after we've been asked to quit is bad manners. And *they're* worse than breaking all ten commandments. Besides, we don't know much—or we'd have done much better."

"You think India is ripe for self-government?"

"When things are ripe, they fall or decay on the tree," said Ommony. "There's a time to stand aside and let 'em grow. There's such a thing as too much nursing."

"Then you're willing to chuck your forest job?"

"I *have* chucked it."

"Oh! Resigned? Going to draw your pension?'

"No. Pension wouldn't be due for two years yet, and I don't need it. India has had the use of me for twenty-three years at a fair price. I'd be satisfied, if she was. But she isn't. And I'm proud, so I'll be damned if I'll accept a pension."

Ommony was left alone again. That news of his resignation was too good to be kept, even for a minute. Within five minutes it was all over the club, and men were speculating as to the real reason, since nobody ever gives any one credit (and wisely, perhaps) for the motives that he makes public.

"Jenkins has succeeded Willoughby. Ommony knows jolly well that Jenkins has it in for him. He's pulling out ahead of the landslide—that's what."

"I don't believe it. Ommony has guts and influence enough to bu'st ten Jenkinses. There's more than that in it. There never *was* a man like Ommony for keeping secrets up his sleeve. You know he's in the Secret Service?"

"That's easy to say, but who said so?"

"Believe it or not—I'll bet. I'll bet he stays in India. I'll bet he dies in harness. I'll bet any money in reason he goes straight from here to McGregor's office. More than that—I'll bet McGregor sent for him, and that he didn't resign from the Forestry without talking it over with McGregor first. He's deep, is Cottswold Ommony —deep. He's no man's fool. There's no man alive but McGregor who knows what Ommony will do next. Anybody want to bet about it?"

The remainder of the conversation at the club that noon rippled off into widening rings of reminiscence, all set up by Ommony's arrival on the scene, and mostly interesting, but to stay and listen would have been to be sidetracked, which is the inevitable fate of gossips. There was a story in the wind that, if the club had known it, would have set all Delhi by the ears.

He who would understand the Plains must ascend the Eternal Hills, where a man's eyes scan Infinity. But he who would make use of understanding must descend on to the Plains, where Past and Future meet and men have need of him.

CHAPTER II

OMMONY did go straight to McGregor but he and Diana, his enormous wolf-hound, walked and club bets had to be called off because there was no cab-driver from whom the *chuprassi** could bludgeon information.

Neither his nor Diana's temper was improved by the behavior of the crowd. The dog's size and apparent ferocity cleared a course, but that convenience was not so pleasant as the manners of twenty years ago, when men made way for an Englishman without hesitation—without dreaming of doing anything else.

The thrice-breathed air of Delhi gave him melancholia. It was not agreeable to see men spit with calculated insolence. The heat made the sweat drip from his beard on to the bosom of a new silk shirt. The smell of over-civilized, unnaturally clothed humans was nauseating. By the time he reached an unimaginably ugly, rawly new administration building he felt about as sweetly reasonable as a dog with hydrophobia, and was tired, with feet accustomed to the softness, and ears used to the silence, of long jungle lanes.

However, his spirits rose as he approached the steps. He may have made a signal, because the moment the *chuprassi* saw him he straightened himself suddenly and ran before him, up-stairs and along a corridor. By the time Ommony reached a door with no name on it, at the far end of the building, the *chuprassi* was waiting to open it—had already done the announcing—had already seen a said-to-be important personage shown out with scant ex-

---

*Uniformed doorkeeper.

15

cuses through another door. The *chuprassi's* salaam was that of a worshiper of secrets, to a man who knows secrets and can keep them; there is no more marrow-deep obeisance in the world than that.

And now no ceremony. The office door clicked softly with a spring-lock and shut out the world that bows and scrapes to hide its enmity and spits to disguise self-conscious meanness. A man sat at a desk and grinned.

"Sit. Smoke. Take your coat off. Sun in your eyes? Try the other chair. Dog need water? Give her some out of the filter. Now—"

John McGregor passed cigars and turned his back toward a laden desk. He was a middle-sized, middle-aged man with snow-white hair in a crisp mass, that would have been curly if he had let it grow long enough. His white mustache made him look older than his years, but his skin was young and reddish, although that again was offset by crow's-feet at the corners of noticeably dark-gray eyes. His hands looked like a conjurer's; he could do anything with them, even to keeping them perfectly still.

"So you've actually turned in your resignation? We grow!" he remarked, laughing. "Everything grows—except me; I'm in the same old rut. I'll get the ax—get pensioned some day—dreadful fate! Did you have your interview with Jenkins? What happened? I can see you had the best of it—but how?"

Ommony laid three letters on the desk—purple ink on faded paper, in a woman's handwriting. McGregor laughed aloud—one bark, like the cry of a fox that scents its quarry on the fluke of a changing wind.

"Perfect!" he remarked, picking up the letters and beginning to read the top one. "Did you blackmail him?"

"I did."

"I could have saved you that trouble, you know. I could have 'broke' him. He deserves it," said McGregor, knitting his brows over the letter in his hand. "Man, man, he certainly deserves it!"

"If we all got our deserts the world 'ud stand still."

Ommony chose a cigar and bit the end off. "He's a more than half-efficient bureaucrat. Let India suck him dry and spew him forth presently to end his days at Surbiton or Cheltenham."

McGregor went on reading, holding his breath. "Have you read these?" he asked suddenly.

Ommony nodded. McGregor chewed at his mustache and made noises with his teeth that brought Diana's ears up, cocked alertly.

"Man, they're pitiful! Imagine a brute like Jenkins having such a hold on any one—and he—good God! He ought to have been hanged—no, that's too good for him! I suppose there's no human law that covers such a case."

"None," Ommony answered grimly. "But I'm pious. I *think* there's a Higher Law that adjusts that sort of thing eventually. If not, I'd have killed the brute myself."

"Listen to this."

"Don't read 'em aloud, Mac. It's sacrilege. And I'm raw. It was at least partly my fault."

"Don't be an idiot!"

"It was, Mac. Elsa wasn't so many years younger than me, but even when we were kids we were more like father and child than brother and sister. She had the spirituality and the brains; I had the brute-strength and was presumed to have the common sense; it made a rather happy combination. As soon as I got settled in the forest I wrote home to her to come out and keep house for me. I used to trust Jenkins in those days. It was I who introduced them. Jenkins introduced her to Kananda Pal."

"That swine!"

"No, he wasn't such a swine as Jenkins," said Ommony. "Kananda Pal was a poor devil who was born into a black art family. He didn't know any better. His father used to make him stare into ink-pools and all that devilment before he was knee-high to a duck. He used to do stunts with spooks and things. Jenkins, on the other hand, had a decent heritage and ditched it. It was he who invited Kananda Pal to hypnotize Elsa. Between the two of them

they did a devil's job of it. She almost lost her mind, and
Jenkins had the filthy gall to use that as excuse for
breaking the engagement.''

"My God! But think if he had married her! Man,
man!''

"True. But think of the indecency of making that
excuse! I called in Fred Terry—''

"Top-hole—generous—gallant—gay! Man, what a delightful fellow Terry was!'' said McGregor. "Did he really
fall in love with her? You know, he was recklessly generous
enough to—''

"Yes," said Ommony. "He almost cured her; and he
fell in love. She loved him—don't see how any real woman
could have helped it. But Jenkins and Kananda Pal—oh,
curse them both!''

"Amen!'' remarked McGregor. "Well—we've got what
we want. How did you hear of these letters?—Just think
of it! That poor girl writing to a brute like Jenkins to
give her mind back to her. So that she may—oh, my
God!''

"I saw Kananda Pal before he died. That was recently.
He was quite sorry about his share in the business. He
tried to put all the blame on Jenkins—you know how rotters
always accuse each other when the cat's out of the bag. He
told me of the letters, so I went to Jenkins yesterday and,
having resigned, I was in position to be rather blunt. In
fact, I was dam' blunt. He denied their existence at first,
but he handed 'em over when I explained what I intended
to do if he didn't!''

"I wonder why he'd kept them," said McGregor.

"The pig had kept them to prove she was mad, if any one
should ever accuse him of having wronged her,'' Ommony
answered. "Do they read like a mad-woman's letters?''

"Man, man! They're pitiful! They read like the letters
of a drug-addict, struggling to throw off the cursed stuff,
and all the while crying for it. Lord save us, what a time
Fred Terry must have had!''

"Increasingly rarely," said Ommony. "He had almost

cured her. The attacks were intermittent. Terry heard
of a sacred place in the hills—a sort of Himalayan Lourdes,
I take it—and they set off together, twenty years ago, to
find the place. I never found a trace of them, but I heard
rumors, and I've always believed they disappeared into the
Ahbor country."

"Where they probably were crucified!" McGregor added grimly.

"I don't know," said Ommony. "I've heard tales about
a mysterious stone in the Ahbor country that's supposed to
have magic qualities. Terry probably heard about it too,
and he was just the man to go in search of it. I've also
heard it said that the 'Masters' live in the Ahbor Valley."

McGregor shook his head and smiled. "Still harping on
that string?"

"One hundred million people, at a very conservative
estimate, of whom at least a million are thinkers, believe
that the Masters exist," Ommony retorted. "Who are
you and I, to say they don't? If they do, and if they're in
the Ahbor Valley, I propose to prove it."

McGregor's smile widened to a grin. "Men who are as
wise as they are said to be, would know how to keep out of
sight. The Mahatmas, or Masters, as you call them, are
a mare's nest, Ommony, old man. However, there may be
something in the other rumor. By the way: who's this
adopted daughter of Miss Sanburn?"

"Never heard of her."

"You're trustee of the Marmaduke Mission, aren't you?
Know Miss Sanburn intimately? When did you last see
her?"

"A year ago. She comes to Delhi once a year to meet
me on the mission business. About once in three years I
go to Tilgaun. I'm due there now."

"And you never heard of an adopted daughter? Then
listen to this."

McGregor opened a file and produced a letter written in
English on cheap ruled paper.

"This is from Number 888—Sirdar Sirohe Singh of Tilgaun, who has been on the secret roster since before my time. His home is somewhere near the mission. 'Number 888 to Number 1. Important. Miss Sanburn of mission near here did procure fragment of crystal jade by unknown means, same having been broken from antiquity of unknown whereabouts and being reputed to possess mysterious qualities. *Miss Sanburn's adopted daughter'*—get that?—'intending to return same, was prevented by theft of fragment, female thief being subsequently murdered by being thrown from precipice, after which, fragment disappeared totally. Search for fragment being now conducted by anonymous individuals. Should say much trouble will ensue unless recovery is prompt and secret. *Miss Sanburn's adopted daughter'*—get that again?—'has vanished. Should advise much precaution not to arouse public curiosity. 888.'— What do you make of it?'' asked McGregor.

"Nothing. Never heard of an adopted daughter."

"Then what do you make of this?"

McGregor's left hand went into a desk-drawer, and something the color of deep sea-water over a sandy bottom flashed in the sunlight as Ommony caught it. He held it to the light. It was stone, not more than two inches thick at the thickest part, and rather larger than the palm of his hand. It was so transparent he could see his fingers through it; yet it was almost fabulously green. One side was curved, and polished so perfectly that it felt like wet soap to the touch; the other side was nearly a plane surface, only slightly uneven, as if it had been split off from another piece.

"It looks like jade," said Ommony.

"It is. But did you ever see jade like it? Hold it to the light again."

There was not a flaw. The sun shone through it as through glass, except that when the stone was moved there was a vague obscurity, as if the plane where the breakage had occurred in some way distorted the light.

"Keep on looking at it," said McGregor, watching.

"No, thanks." Ommony laid the stone on his knee and

deliberately glanced around the room from one object to another. "I rebel against that stuff instinctively."

"You recognize the symptoms?"

"Yes. There's a polished black-granite sphere in the crypt of a ruined temple near Darjiling, that produces the same sort of effect when you stare at it. I'm told the Ka'aba at Mecca does the same, but that's hearsay."

"Put the stone in your pocket," said McGregor. "Keep it there a day or two. It's the fragment that's missing from Tilgaun, and you'll discover it has peculiar properties. Talk with Chutter Chand about it, he can tell you something interesting. He tried to explain to me, but it's over my head—Secret Service kills imagination—I live in a mess of statistics and card-indexes that 'ud mummify a Sybil. All the same, I suspect that piece of jade will help you to trace the Terrys; and, if you dare to take a crack at the Ahbor country—"

"How did you come by the stone?" asked Ommony.

"I sent C99—that's Tin Lal—to Tilgaun to look into rumors of trouble up there. Tin Lal used to be a good man, although he was always a thorough-paced rascal. But the Service isn't what it used to be, Ommony; even our best men are taking sides nowadays, or playing for their own hand. India's going to the dogs. Tin Lal came back and reported everything quiet at Tilgaun—said the murders were mere family feuds. But he took that piece of jade to Chutter Chand, the jeweler, and offered it for sale. Told a lame-duck story. Chutter Chand put him off—kept the stone for appraisal—and brought it to me. I provided Tin Lal—naturally—with a year behind the bars—no, not on account of the stone. He had committed plenty of crimes to choose from. I chose a little one just to discipline him. But here's the interesting part: either Tin Lal talked in the jail—*or* some one followed him from Tilgaun. Anyway, some one traced that piece of jade to this office. I have had an anonymous letter about it,—worth attention—interesting. You'll notice it's signed with a glyph—I've never seen a glyph quite like it—and the handwriting is an educated woman's. Read it for yourself."

He passed to Ommony an exquisitely fashioned silver tube with a cap at either end. Ommony shook out a long sheet of very good English writing-paper. It was ivory-colored, heavy, and scented with some kind of incense. There was no date—no address—no signature, except a peculiar glyph, rather like an ancient, much simplified Chinese character. The writing was condensed into the middle of the page, leaving very wide margins, and had been done with a fine steel pen.

"The stone that was brought from Tilgaun by Tin Lal and was offered for sale by him to Chutter Chand is one that no honorable man would care to keep from its real owners. There is merit in a good deed and the reward of him who does justly without thought of reward is tenfold. There are secrets not safe to be pried into. There is light too bright to look into. There is truth more true than can be told. If you will change the color of the sash on the *chuprassi* at the front door, one shall present himself to you to whom you may return the stone with absolute assurance that it will reach its real owners. Honesty and happiness are one. The truth comes not to him who is inquisitive, but to him who does what is right and leaves the result to Destiny."

Ommony examined the writing minutely, sniffed the paper, held it to the light, then picked up the tube and examined that.

"Who brought it?" he asked.

"I don't know. It was handed to the *chuprassi* by a native he says he thinks was disguised."

"Did you try changing the *chuprassi's* sash?"

"Naturally. A deaf and dumb man came. He looked like a Tibetan. He approached the *chuprassi* and touched his sash, so the *chuprassi* brought him up to me. He was unquestionably deaf and dumb—stone-deaf, and half of his tongue was missing. The drums of his ears had been bored through—when he was a baby probably. I showed him the stone and he tried to take it from me. I had to have him forcibly ejected from the office; and of course I had him followed, but he disappeared utterly, after wandering aimlessly all over Delhi until nearly midnight. I have had a look-out kept, but he seems to have vanished without trace."

"Have you drawn any conclusions?"

McGregor smiled. "I never draw them before it's safe to say they're proved. But a young woman almost certainly wrote that letter; Miss Sanburn's adopted daughter—"

"Who I don't believe exists," said Ommony.

"—is reported by 888, who has hitherto *always* been reliable, to have disappeared. She disappeared, if she ever *did* exist, from Tilgaun; the stone unquestionably came from Tilgaun, and it seems to have been in Miss Sanburn's possession, in the mission. *Ergo*—just as a flying hypothesis—Miss Sanburn's adopted daughter *may* have written that letter. If so, she's in Delhi, because the ink on that paper had not been dry more than an hour or two when it reached me."

"Have you searched the hotels?"

"Of course. And the trains are being watched."

"I'm curious to meet Hannah Sanburn's adopted daughter!" said Ommony dryly. "I've known Hannah ever since she came to India more than twenty years ago. I've been co-trustee ever since Marmaduke died, and I don't believe Hannah Sanburn has kept a single secret from me. In fact, it has been the other way; she has passed most of her difficult personal problems along to me for solution. I've a dozen files full of her letters, of which I dare say five per cent. are purely personal. I think I know all her private business. As recently as last year, when we met here in Delhi,—well—never mind; but if she had an adopted daughter, or an entanglement of any kind, I think I'd know it."

"Women are damned deep," McGregor answered. "Well; we've not much to go on. I'll entrust that stone to you; if you're still willing to try to get into the Ahbor country, I'll do everything I can to assist. You've a fair excuse for trying; and you're a bachelor. Dammit, if I were, I'd go with you! Of course, you understand, if the State Department learns of it you'll be rounded up and brought back. Do you realize the other difficulties? Sven Hedin is said to have made the last attempt to get through from the North. He failed. In the last hundred years about a dozen Europeans have had a crack at it. Several died, and none got through—unless Terry and your sister did, and if so, they almost certainly died. When Young-husband went to Lhassa he considered sending one regiment back by way of the Ahbor Valley but countermanded the order when he realized that a force of fifty thousand men wouldn't stand a chance of getting through. From time to time the government has sent six Goorkha spies into the country. None ever came back. It's almost a certainty that the River Tsangpo of Tibet flows through the valley and becomes the Brahmaputra lower down, but nobody has proved it; nor has any one explained why the Tsangpo contains more water than the Brahmaputra. Old Kinthup, the pundit on the Indian Survey Staff, traced the Tsangpo down as far as the waterfall where it plunges into the Ahbor Valley, and he threw a hundred marked logs into the river, which were watched for lower down; but none of the logs appeared at the lower end, and not even Kinthup managed to get into the valley. The strangest part about it is, that the Northern Ahbors come down frequently to the Southern Ahbor country to trade, and they even intermarry with the Southern Ahbors. But they never say a word about their valley. The rajah of Tilgaun—the uncle of the present man—caught two and put them to torture, but they died silent. And another strange thing is, that nobody knows how the Northern Ahbors get into and out of their country. The river is a lot too swift for boats. The forest seems impenetrable. The cliffs are unclimbable. There was an attempt made last year to explore by airplane, but the attempt failed; there's a ninety-mile wind half the time, and some of the passes to the south are sixteen or seventeen thousand feet in the air to begin with. I'm told carburetors won't work, and they can't carry enough fuel.—So, if you're determined to make the attempt, slip away secretly, and don't leave your courage behind! If it weren't that you've a right to visit Tilgaun I should say you'd have no chance, but you *might* make it, if you're awfully discreet and start from the Tilgaun Mission. If it's ever found out that I encouraged you—"

"You've been reeling off discouragement for fifteen minutes!"

"Yes, but if it's known I knew—"

"You needn't worry. What made you say you think this stone will help me to trace the Terrys?"

"Nothing definite, except that it gives me an excuse for sending you to Tilgaun more or less officially. I employ you to investigate the mystery connected with that stone. As far as Tilgaun you're responsible to me. If you decide to go on from there, you'll have to throw me over—disobey orders. You understand, I order you to come straight back here from Tilgaun. If you disobey, you do it off your own bat, without my official knowledge. And I'm afraid, old thing, you'll have to pay your own expenses."

Ommony nodded.

"See Chutter Chand," said McGregor, "and dine with me to-night—not at the club—that 'ud start all sorts of rumors flying—say at Mrs. Cornock-Campbell's—her husband's away, but that doesn't matter. She's the only woman I ever dared tell secrets to. Leave it to me to contrive the invitation—how'll that do?"

"Mrs. Cornock-Campbell is a better man than you or me. Nine o'clock. I'll be there," said Ommony, noticing a certain slyness in McGregor's smile. He bridled at it.

"Still laughing about the 'Masters,' Mac?"

"No, no. I'd forgotten them. Not that they exist—but never mind."

"What then?"

"I'll tell you after dinner or rather some one else will. I wonder whether you'll laugh too—or wince! Trot along and have your talk with Chutter Chand."

DECIPHERED FROM A PALM-LEAF MANUSCRIPT DISCOVERED IN A CAVE IN HINDUSTAN

Those who are acquainted with the day and night know that the Day of Brahma is a thousand revolutions of the Yugas, and that the Night extendeth for a thousand more. Now the Maha-yuga consisteth of four parts, of which the last, being called the Kali-Yuga, is the least, having but four-hundred-and-thirty-two thousand years. The length of a Maha-yuga is four-million-and-three-hundred-and-twenty thousand years; that is, one thousandth part of a Day of Brahma. And man was in the beginning, although not as he is now, nor as he will be . . . [Here the palm-leaf is broken and illegible] . . . There were races in the world, whose wisemen knew all the seven principles, so that they understood matter in all its forms and were its masters. They were those to whom gold was as nothing, because they could make it, and for whom the elements brought forth. . . . . [Here there is another break] . . . And there were giants on the earth in those days, and there were dwarfs, most evil. There was war, and they destroyed. . . . [Here the leaf is broken off, and all the rest is missing.]

CHAPTER III

"WHAT IS FEAR?"

CHUTTER CHAND's shop in the Chandni Chowk is a place
of chaos and a joy for ever, if you like life musty and
assorted. There are diamonds in the window, kodak cam-
eras, theodolites, bric-a-brac, second-hand rifles, scientific
magazines, and a living hamadryad cobra in a wire enclosure (into which rats and chickens are introduced at intervals). You enter through a door on either side of which
hang curtains that were rather old when Clive was young;
and you promptly see your reflection facing you in a mirror that came from Versailles when the French were bribing Indian potentates to keep the English out.

Every square foot of the walls within is covered with
ancient curios. A glass counter-show-case runs the full
length of the store, and is stuffed with enough jewelry to
furnish a pageant of Indian history; converted into cash
it would finance a very fair-sized bank. Rising to the level
of the counter at the rear is a long row of pigeonholed
shelves crowded with ancient books and manuscripts that
smell like recently unwound mummies. Between shelf and
counter lives (and reputedly sleeps by night) the most
efficient jeweler's babu in India—a meek, alert, weariless
man who is said to be able to estimate any one's bank balance by glancing at him as he enters through the front door.
But Chutter Chand keeps himself out of sight, in a room at
the rear of the store, whence he comes out only in emergency. On this particular occasion there were extra reasons for remaining in the background—reasons suggested
by the presence of a special "constabeel" on duty outside
the shop-door, who eyed Ommony nervously as he walked
in.

Ommony went straight to the room at the rear and found Chutter Chand at his desk—a wizened, neat little man in a yellow silk turban and a brown alpaca suit of English cut. The suit and his brown skin were almost of the same shade; an amber pin in his yellow necktie corresponded with the color of his laced shoes; the gold of his heavy watch-chain matched the turban; his lemon silk handkerchief matched his socks; his dark-brown, kindly, intelligent eyes struck the key-note of the color harmony.

Unlike so many Indians who adopt a modified European style of dress, he had an air of breeding, poise and distinction.

"There is always something interesting when *you* come, Ommon*ee!*" he said, rising and shaking hands. "Wait while I remove the specimens from that chair. No, the snakes can not escape; they are all poisonous, but carefully imprisoned. There—be seated. You are full of news, or you would have asked me how I am. Thank you, I am very well. And you? Now let us get to business!"

Ommony grinned at the gibe, but he had his own way of going about things. He preferred to soak in his surroundings and adjust his mind to the environment in silence before broaching business. He lit a cigar, and stared about him at the snakes in cages and the odds and ends of rarities heaped everywhere in indescribable confusion. There were an enormous brass Gautama Buddha resting on iron rollers, a silver Christian crucifix from a Goanese cathedral, and some enamel vases, that were new since his last visit; but the same old cobwebs were still in place in the corners of the teak beams, and the same cat came and rubbed herself against his shins—until she spied Diana in the outer shop and grew instantly blasphemous.

Still saying nothing, Ommony at last produced the lump of jade from his hip pocket.

"Yes," said Chutter Chand, "I have already seen it." But he took off his gold-rimmed spectacles and wiped them as if he was eager to see it again.

"What do you know about it?" asked Ommony.

"Very little, Sahib. To crystallize hypothesis into a mis-|
take is all too easy. I prefer to distinguish between knowl-||
edge and conjecture."

"All right. Tell me what little you do know."

"It is jade undoubtedly, although I have never seen jade
exactly like it—I, who have studied every known species
of precious and semi-precious stone."

"Then why do you say it is jade?"

"Because I know that. I have analyzed it. It is chloro-
melanite, consisting of a silicate of aluminium and sodium,
with peroxide of iron, peroxide of manganese, and potash.
It has been broken from a greater piece—perhaps from an
enormous piece. The example I have previously seen that
most resembled this was found in the Kara-Kash Valley of
Turkestan; but that was not nearly so transparent. That
piece you hold in your hand is more fusible than nephrite,
which is the commoner form of jade; and it has a specific
gravity of 3.3."

"What makes you believe it was broken from a larger
piece?"

"I know by the arc of the curve of the one side, and by
the shape of the fracture on the other, that it has been
broken by external violence from a piece considerably
larger than itself. I have worked out a law of vibration
and fracture that is as interesting in its way as Einstein's
law of relativity. Do you understand mathematics?"

"No. I'll take your word for it. What else do you know
positively?"

"Positively is the only way to know," the jeweler answered, screwing up his face until he looked almost like a
Chinaman. "There was human blood on it—a smear on
the fractured side, that looked as if a careless attempt had
been made to wipe it off before the blood was quite dry.
Also the print of a woman's thumb and forefinger, plainly
visible under the microscope, with several other finger-
prints that certainly were Tin Lal's. The stone had come
in contact with some oily substance, probably butter, but
there was too little of it to determine. Furthermore, I

know, Ommon*ee,* that you are afraid of the stone because
to touch it makes you nervous, and to peer into it makes
you see things you can not explain.''

Ommony laughed. The stone did make him nervous.

''Did *you* see things?'' he asked.

''That is how I know it makes *you* see them, Ommon*ee!*
Compared to me you are a child in such respects. If I, who
know more than you, nonetheless see things when I peer
into that stone, it is logical to my mind that you also see
things, although possibly not the same things. Knowing
the inherent superstition of the human mind, I therefore
know you are afraid—just as people were afraid when
Galileo told them that the earth moves.''

''Are *you* afraid of it?'' asked Ommony, shifting his
cigar and laying the stone on the desk.

''What is fear?'' the jeweler answered. ''Is it not recognition of something the senses can not understand and
therefore can not master? I think the fact that we feel a
sort of fear is proof that we stand on the threshold of new
knowledge—or rather, of knowledge that is new to us as
individuals.''

''You mean, then, if a policeman's afraid of a burglar,
he's——''

''Certainly! He is in a position to learn something he
never knew before. That doesn't mean that he *will* learn,
but that he may if he cares to. People used to be afraid of a
total eclipse of the sun; some still are afraid of it. Imagine,
if you can, what Julius Cæsar, or Alexander the Great, or
Timour Ilang, or Akbar would have thought of radio, or a
thirty-six-inch astronomical telescope, or a kodak camera.''

''All those things can be explained. This stone is a
mystery.''

''Ommon*ee,* everything that we do not yet understand
is a mystery. To a pig, it must be a mystery why a man
flings turnips to him over the wall of his sty. To that dog
of yours it must be a mystery why you took such care to
train her. Look into the stone now, Sahib, and tell me
what you see.''

"Not I," said Ommony. "I've done it twice. You look."

Chutter Chand took up the stone in both hands and held it in the light from an overhead window. The thing glowed as if full of liquid-green fire, yet from ten feet away Ommony could see through it the lines on the palm of the jeweler's hand.

"Interesting! Interesting! Ommon*ee*, the world is full of things we don't yet know!"

Chutter Chand's brows contracted, the right side more than the left, in the habit-fixed expression of a man whose business is to use a microscope. Two or three times he glanced away and blinked before looking again. Finally he put the stone back on the desk and wiped his spectacles from force of habit.

"Our senses," he said, "are much more reliable than the brain that interprets them. We probably all see, and hear, and smell alike, but no two brains interpret in the same way. Try to describe to me your sensations when you looked into the stone."

"Almost a brain-storm," said Ommony. "A rush of thoughts that seemed to have no connection with one another. Something like modern politics or listening in on the radio when there's loads of interference, only more exasperating—more personal—more inside yourself, as it were."

Chutter Chand nodded confirmation. "Can you describe the thoughts, Ommon*ee*? Do they take the form of words?"

"No. Pictures. But pictures of a sort I've never seen, even in dreams. Rather horrible. They appear to mean something, but the mind can't grasp them. They're broken off suddenly—begin nowhere and end nowhere."

Chutter Chand nodded again. "Our experiences tally. You will notice that the stone is broken off; it also begins nowhere and ends nowhere. I have measured it carefully; from calculation of the curvature it is possible to surmise that it may have been broken off from an ellipsoid having

a major axis of seventeen feet. That would be an immense
mass of jade weighing very many tons; and if the whole
were as perfect as this fragment, it would be a marvel such
as we in our day have not seen. I suspect it to have qualities more remarkable than those of radium, and I *think*—
although, mind you, this is now conjecture—that if we
could find the original ellipsoid from which this piece was
broken we would possess the *open sesame* to—well—to laws
and facts of nature, the mere contemplation of which would
fill all the lunatic asylums! I have never been so thrilled
by anything in all my life.''

But Ommony was not thrilled. He had seen men go mad
from exploring without landmarks into the unknown. He
laughed cynically.

'' 'We fools of nature,' '' he quoted, '' 'so horridly to
shake our disposition with thoughts beyond the reaches of
our souls!' I'd rather wipe out the asylums.''

''Or live in one, Sahib, and leave the lunatics outside!
Shakespeare knew nothing of the atomic construction of the
universe. We have advanced since his day—in some respects. Has it occurred to you to wonder *how* this stone
acquired such remarkable qualities? No! You merely
wonder *at* it. But observe:

''You have seen a pudding stirred? The stupidest cook
in the world can pour ingredients into a basin and stir
them with water until they become something compounded,
that does not in the least resemble any one of the component
parts. Is that not so? The same fool bakes what he has
mixed. A chemical process takes place, and behold! the
idiot has wrought a miracle. Again, there is almost no resemblance to what the mixture was before. It even tastes
and smells quite differently. It looks different. Its specific gravity is changed. Its properties are altered. It is
now digestible. It decomposes at a different speed. It has
lost some of the original qualities that went into the mixture, and has taken on others that apparently were not
there before the chemical process began.

''You can see the same thing in a foundry, where they

mix zinc with copper and produce brass, and the brass has qualities that neither zinc nor copper appears to contain. A deaf and dumb man, knowing neither writing nor arithmetic, could produce brass from zinc and copper. A savage, who never saw an abstraction, can produce wine from grapes. Good. Now listen, Sahib:

"Let us dive beneath the surface of these experiments. The capacity to become brass under certain conditions was inherent to begin with in the zinc and in the copper, was it not? But how so? It was inherent in the atoms, of which the zinc and the copper are composed; and, behind those again, in the electrons, of which the atoms are composed. Let us then consider the electrons.

"Suppose that we knew how to pour electrons into a receptacle and make, so to speak, a pudding of them! Could we not work what the world would think are miracles? I have made diamonds in my workshop. I believe I can make gold. What could I not do, if I knew how to manage electrons in the raw—electrons, in every one of which is the capacity to become absolutely *anything!*

"It has possibly not occurred to you, Ommon*ee,* but the more I pursue my studies the more I am convinced that there was once a race of people in the world, or possibly a school of scientists drawn from many then-existent races, who knew how to manage electrons. I think they lived simultaneously with the cave-men. We find the bones of cave-men because those were ignorant people, such as the Bushmen of to-day, who buried their dead. We do not find the bones of the scientists of that period, because they were enlightened and disposed of corpses in the fire. The *art* of the cave-men is evidence that there *was* art of a very high order, which some one presumably taught. They painted pictures in caves into which no sunlight penetrated; therefore, there must have been artificial light of a sort superior to torches or tallow candles, because otherwise the color-work would have been impossible. That is proof that there *was* science in those days, of which the cave-men could avail themselves just as to-day a lunatic may use electric light. And the fact that we find no traces at present of what we can recognize as a very high order of civilization then existent is no proof that there was none; it may have been totally different from anything with which we are familiar. Furthermore, the world has only been extremely superficially explored.

"Be patient, Ommonee. I am coming to my point. I have studied that piece of jade. Three days and nights I studied it without sleep. To me its peculiar properties appear to confirm observations—micro-photographic observations that I have made and recorded during a period of ten years. In its essence, what is photography? It is the practise, by means of chemicals, of rendering visible to the human eye impressions of objects produced by light on a prepared surface. It is necessary to prepare the surface, which we call a dry plate or a film, because we do not yet know how else to render the light-made impression visible to the human eye. But it is there, whether we make it visible or not. And what I have discovered is this: that every particle of matter has a photographic quality, which varies only in degree. You stand against a rock—and not necessarily in sunlight, although sunlight helps; your impression is indelibly photographed on that rock, as I can prove, if you have time to witness some experiments. It is photographed on anything against which you stand. Other images may be superimposed on yours, but yours remains. In rare instances, in certain atmospheric conditions, these impressions become visible without any other chemical process, although it seems to require a certain nervous state of alertness before the human eye can perceive them.

"You remember the case of the Brahman who hanged himself in a cellar not far from this shop of mine? His body hung there for a day before they found it. For weeks afterward what was supposed to be his ghost was seen—by scores of reputable witnesses—hanging from the beam. That was several years ago. There was a great stir made about it at the time, and there were letters to the newspapers stating instances of similar occurrences. There was

an investigation by experts from a research society, who
denounced the whole story as an imposture.

"However, I was one of those who saw the ghost, and I
made notes, and some experiments. Finally I photographed
it! That satisfied me. I am sure that the alleged ghost
was nothing but a photograph made on the wall, and that
it was rendered visible by certain chemical conditions, not
all of which I have been able to ascertain.

"Now then: if that is possible in one instance, it is possible in every instance. There is no such thing as an exception in nature; we have discovered a law. So take this
piece of jade: we see things when we look into it. I deduce
that they are photographic. And because no other piece
of stone that I know of has the same quality of receiving
impressions that are instantaneously visible, it seems prob-
able to me that it has been intelligently treated by some
one who knew how to do that."

"It might be a natural chemical process," said Ommony.

"I think not. Have you noticed that the strange moving
images visible *within* the stone are not the reflections of
objects? The stone is not a mirror in the ordinary sense. It
does not seem to reflect at all the objects that surround it.
I have never succeeded in seeing my face in it, for instance,
although I have tried repeatedly, in all sorts of light, from
every angle. It appears to me to reflect *thought!*"

Ommony made the peculiar noise between tongue and
teeth that suggests polite but otherwise unconditioned in-
credulity. Chutter Chand, deep in his theme, ignored the
interruption.

"I believe it reflects *character!* I believe that every
thought that every man thinks, from the day he is born
until the day he dies, leaves an invisible impress on his
mind as well as a visible impress on his body. You know
how changing character affects the lines on the palm of a
man's hand, on the soles of his feet, at the corners of his
eyes, at his mouth, and so on? Well: something of the same
sort goes on in his mind, which is invisible and what we call
intangible, but is nevertheless made up of electrons in mo-

tion. And those impressions are permanent. I believe
that somebody, who knew how to manipulate electrons, has
treated this stone in such a way that it reflects the whole of
a man's thought since he was born—just as a stone wall, if
it could be treated properly, could be shown to retain the
photograph of every object that had passed before it since
the wall was built.

"I believe this was done very anciently, and for this
reason: that if any one possessed of such intelligence and
skill were alive in the world to-day, his intelligence would
burn itself into our consciousness, so that we could not help
but know of him.

"I am of opinion that the process to which the jade was
subjected rendered it at the same time transparent; because
it is not in the nature of jade to be quite transparent normally. And in my mind there is connected with all this the
knowledge (which is common property) that the Chinese—
a *very* ancient race—regard jade as a sacred stone. Why?
Is it not possible that jade peculiarly lends itself to this
treatment, and that, though the science is forgotten, the
dim memory of the peculiar property of the stone persists?"

"You've a fine imagination!" said Ommony.

"And what *is* imagination, Ommon*ee*, if not a bridge between the known and unknown? Between conventional so-
called knowledge and the unexplored realm of truth? Have
you no imagination? Electricity was possible a thousand
years ago; but until imagination hinted at the possibility,
who had the use of it?"

Ommony returned the stone to his pocket. He was interested, and he liked Chutter Chand, but it occurred to
him that he was wasting time.

"You're right, of course," he said, "that we have to
imagine a thing before we can begin to understand it or
produce or make it."

"Surely. You imagined your forest, Ommon*ee*, before
you planted it. But between imagination and production,
there is labor. You see, what the West can't understand it

scoffs at, whereas what the East can't understand it calls sacred and guards against all-comers! I think you will have to penetrate a secret that has been guarded for thousands of years. They say, you know, that there are Masters who guard these secrets and let them out a little at a time. May the gods whom you happen to vote for be grateful and assist you! I would like to go on the adventure with you—but I am a family man. I am afraid. I am not strong. That stone has thrilled me, Ommon*ee!*"

"If you like, I'll leave it with you for some more experiments," said Ommony.

"Sahib—my friend—I wouldn't keep it for a rajah's ransom! It was traced to this place—how, I don't know. You noticed the policeman at the door? He is put there to keep out murderers! There has been a ruffian here—a Hillman—a cutthroat who said he came from Spiti—a great savage with a saw-edge tulwar! Ugh! He demanded the stone. He demanded to know where it was. If it had not been that I had a shop-full of customers, and that I promised to try to get the stone back from the man who now had it, he would have cut me in halves! He said so! I am afraid all the time that he will return, or that some of his friends will come. Oh, I wish I had your lack of an imagination, Ommon*ee!* I could feel his saw-edged tulwar plunging into me! Listen!" (Chutter Chand began to tremble visibly). "Who is that?"

Ommony glanced into the shop. There were two men, evidently unarmed or the "constabeel" would never have admitted them, standing talking to the clerk across the show-case-counter. One was apparently a very old man and the other very young. Both were dressed in the Tibetan costume, but the older man was speaking English, which was of itself sufficiently remarkable, and he appeared to be slightly amused because the clerk insisted that Chutter Chand was "absent on a journey." Neither man paid the slightest attention to the jewelry in the show-case; they were evidently bent on seeing Chutter Chand, and nothing else.

"Admit 'em!" whispered Ommony. "I'll hide. No, never mind the dog; she'll follow them in and sniff them over. If they ask about the dog, say she belongs to one of your customers who left her in your charge for an hour or two. What's behind that brass Buddha?"

"Nothing, Sahib. It is hollow. There is no back."

"That'll do then. Help me pull it out from the wall—quick!—quiet!"

They made rather a lot of noise and Diana came in to investigate, which was opportune. Ommony gave her orders *sotto voce* and she returned into the shop to watch the two curious visitors.

"Now, don't let yourself get frightened out of your wits, Chutter Chand. Encourage 'em to talk. Ask any idiotic question that occurs to you. When they're ready to go, let 'em. And then, whatever you do, don't say a word to the policeman."

Ommony stepped behind the image of the Buddha. Chutter Chand, leaning all his weight against it, shoved it back nearly into place, but left sufficient space between it and the wall for Ommony to see into an old cracked mirror that reflected almost everything in the room. Then, taking a visible hold on his emotions, Chutter Chand strode to the door and stood there for a moment looking—listening—trying to breathe normally. He forced a smile at last.

"Oh, let them in—I will talk to them," he said to the clerk in English, with an air of almost perfect, patronizing nonchalance. Only a very close observer might have known he was afraid—that fear, perhaps, in him was more than "recognition of something that the senses do not understand."

We should ascend out of perversity, even as we ascend a mountain that we do not know, with the aid of guides who do know. None who sets forth on an unknown voyage stipulates that the pilot must agree with him as to the course, since manifestly that would be absurd; the pilot is presumed to know; the piloted does not know. None who climbs a mountain bargains that the guide shall keep to this or that direction; it is the business of the guide to lead. And yet, men hire guides for the Spiritual Journey, of which they know less than they know of land and sea, and stipulate that the guide shall lead them thus and so, according to their own imaginings; and instead of obeying him, they desert and denounce him, should he lead them otherwise. I find this of the essence of perversity.

FROM THE BOOK OF THE SAYINGS OF TSIANG SAMDUP

CHAPTER IV

THE two Tibetans entered, the older man leading, and squatted on a mat which the younger man spread on the floor. Their manner suggested that they had accepted an invitation, instead of having gained admission by persistence; but Ommony, watching every movement in the mirror, noticed that the older man laid his hand on the seat of the chair he himself had just occupied—which, being old, he *might* have done to help himself down on the mat, but, being active, he almost certainly did for another reason.

Chutter Chand sat at his desk magisterially, wiping at the gold-rimmed spectacles again, waiting for the visitors to speak first. But they were not to be tempted into that indiscretion. They sat still and were bland, while Diana came and deliberately sniffed them over. The hound seemed interested; she lay down where she could watch them both, her jowl on her paws, one ear up, and her tail moving slightly from side to side clearing a fan-shaped pattern in the dust.

The old man was a miracle of wrinkles. He resembled one of those Chinese statuettes in ivory, yellowed by time, that suggest that life is much too comical a business to be taken seriously—much too serious a business to be cumbered with pride and possessions. He was a living paradox in a long, snuff-colored robe, the ends of which he arranged over his lap, leaving the hairy strong legs of a mountaineer uncovered. He helped himself to an enormous quantity of snuff from an old Chinese silver box, that he presently stowed away in a fold of his garment. The pungent stuff

40

appeared to have no effect on him, although Diana, catching a whiff of it, sneezed violently and Chutter Chand followed suit.

The young man was another ivory enigma, absolutely smooth in contrast to the elder's wrinkles, and much paler. He, too, wore snuff-colored clothes. His head was wrapped in a turban of gorgeously embroidered brown silk, in contrast to the other's monkish simplicity, and the cloth of which his cloak was made seemed to be of lighter and better material than the older man's. He was remarkably good-looking—straight-featured and calm—placid, not apparently from self-contentment but from assurance that life holds a definite purpose and that he was being led along the narrow road. There was an air of good temper and wisdom about him, no apparent pride nor any mean humility. His eyes were blue-gray, his hands small, strong and artistic. His feet, too, were small but evidently used to walking. He was in every dimension smaller than the older man, unless mind is a dimension; they appeared to be equals in mental aroma, and they exuded that in the mysterious way of a painting by Goya y Lucientes.

"Well, what do you want?" Chutter Chand asked at last in English. It was a ridiculous language, on the face of it, to use to a Tibetan; but the older man had been using English in the outer shop, and Chutter Chand knew no Prakrit dialect.

The answer, in English devoid of any noticeable accent, was given by the older man in a voice as full of humor as his wrinkled face.

"The piece of jade," he said, unblinking, ending on a rising note that suggested there was nothing to explain, nothing to argue about, nothing to do but be reasonable. He snapped his fingers, and Diana, normally a most suspicious dog, came close to him. He ran his fingers through her hair and she laid her huge jowl on his knee. Chutter Chand crossed and uncrossed his legs restlessly.

"I haven't it," said the jeweler. "Besides—er—ah— you would have to tell me your—that is—er—you would have to establish first by what right you make such a demand. You understand me?"

"I have made no demand," the old man answered, smiling. His voice was sweetly reasonable; his bright old eyes twinkled. "You have asked what I want. I have told you."

"Tell me who you are," said Chutter Chand.

"My son, I am a Lama. I am one who strives to tread the Middle Way."

"Where from?"

"From desire into peace!"

"I mean, what place do you come from?"

"From the same place that the piece of jade came from, my son. From the place to which he who desires merit will return it."

"Is the jade yours?" asked Chutter Chand.

"Is the air mine? Are the stars mine?" the Lama answered, smiling as if the idea of possessing anything were a joke made by an inquiring child.

"Well; what right have you to the piece of jade?" Chutter Chand snapped back at him. He let the irritation through without intending it and smiled directly afterward in an attempt to undo the impression. But if the Lama had noticed the acerbity, he made no sign.

"None, any more than you have," came the answer in the same mild voice. "None has any right to it. I have a duty to return it to whence it came—and a duty to you, to preserve you from impertinence, if that may be. It is not good, Chutter Chand, to meddle with knowledge before the time appointed for its understanding. He who would tread the Middle Way is patient, keeping both feet on the ground and his head no higher than humility will let it reach. Be wise—O man of intellectual desires! Destruction is in rashness."

His fingers touched Diana's collar and twisted it around until the small brass plate, on which Ommony's name was engraved, came uppermost; but his eyes continued to look straight at Chutter Chand. It was the younger man, squatting in silence beside him, his head and body motionless, whose bright eyes took in every detail of the room, not omitting to notice the movement of the Lama's hand. Except for the eyes, his face continued perfectly expressionless.

"Well—er—ah—before I answer definitely, I would like you to tell me about the jade," said Chutter Chand. "You will find me reasonable. I am not a sacriligeous person. Er—ah—can you not establish to my satisfaction that—ah —I would be doing rightly to—er—let us say, to entrust the piece of jade to you?"

"I think you know that already," said the Lama, in a voice of mild reproof, as if he were speaking to a child of whom he was rather fond. "What does your heart say, my son? It is the heart that answers wisely, if desire has been subdued. I have come a very long way——"

"*Desiring* the piece of jade!" sneered Chutter Chand— regretting the sneer instantly—driving finger-nails into the palm of his hand with impatience of himself.

"True," said the Lama. "Desire is not easy to destroy. Yet I do not desire it for myself. And for you I desire peace—and merit. May the Lord live in your heart and guide you in the Middle Way."

The jeweler moved restlessly. The atmosphere was getting on his nerves. There was an indefinable feeling of being in the presence of superiority, which is irritating to a man of intellect.

"You mean, there will be no peace for me unless I give up the piece of jade to you?" he asked tartly.

"I think that is so," said the Lama gently.

"Well; it is not in my possession."

"But you know who has it," said the Lama, looking straight at him.

The jeweler did not answer, and the Lama's eyes beamed with intelligence. The young Tibetan moved at last and whispered in his ear. The Lama nodded almost imperceptibly, turning the dog's collar around again with leisurely fingers, whose touch seemed magically satisfying to Diana.

He looked then once, sharply, at the big brass Buddha, let his eyes rest again on the jeweler's, and went on speaking.

"What a man can not do is no weight against him. It may be the hand of Destiny, preventing him from a mistake. The deeds a man does are the fruits that are weighed in the balance and from which the seeds of future lives are saved. Peace *be* with you. Peace refresh you. Peace give you peace that you may multiply it, Chutter Chand."

The Lama arose and the younger man rolled up the mat. Diana jumped to her feet. Chutter Chand made an attempt to get out of his chair with dignity; but the Lama seemed to have monopolized in his own person all the dignity there was in sight, which was embarrassing.

"Er—ah—I appreciate the blessing. Er—ah—are you going? But you haven't told me what I asked about the jade—ah—would you care to come again?— Perhaps——"

The Lama smiled, stroked Diana's head, bowed, so that his long skirts swung like a bronze bell and one almost expected a resonant boom to follow, and led the way out, followed by the younger man, who smiled once so suddenly and brightly that Chutter Chand's nervous irritation vanished. But it returned the moment they had gone. He jumped at the noise Ommony made pushing the brass Buddha away from the wall.

"Damn them both!" he exploded. "Sahib, I hate to be mystified! I detest to be patronized! I feel I made myself contemptible! I could not think! I could not make my brain invent the questions that I should have asked!"

"You did pretty well," said Ommony. "See 'em home, girl!"

Diana's tail went between her legs, but she did not hesitate; she trotted out of the shop—stood still a moment on the sidewalk—sniffed—vanished.

"Sahib, they will send some one to loot this shop of mine! Ommon*ee*——"

"Tut-tut! Those two didn't overlook one detail. The young one read my name on Diana's collar and whispered it to the Lama. The Lama knew I was behind the Buddha.

He suspected something when he felt the chair-seat and found it warm."

"Worse and worse!" said Chutter Chand despondently. "To incur the enmity of such people is more dangerous than to tamper with my snakes!"

Chutter Chand, his brain full of western and eastern science, his suit from London and his turban from Lahore, yearned to the West for protection from eastern mystery. Ommony, all English, steeped in the Orient for twenty years, had thrown his thought eastward and was reckoning like lightning in terms of Indian thought.

"They didn't suspect my presence until *after* they came in here.——Shut up, Chutter Chand! Listen to me!—— They'll have brought a man to watch outside the shop and follow any one who follows *them*. They can't have cautioned him about the dog, because they didn't know about the dog, and they would never suspect a dog of having enough intelligence. Their man will be still out there watching the shop-door. Wait here!"

He ran into the outer shop, hid behind one of the curtains at the door, and stood facing the mirror that gave him a view of the "constabeel's" back and of fifty yards of crowded street, including the sidewalk opposite. The "constabeel" appeared to be intently watching somebody, and in less than a minute Ommony picked out the individual— a tall, good-looking, boy-faced Hillman in a costume that suggested Bhutan or Sikkim—shapeless trousers and a long robe over them, with a sort of jacket on top of that. He was trying to look innocent, which is the surest way of attracting attention; and he was so intent on watching the shop-door that passers-by continually bunted into him— whereat he seemed to find it hard to keep his temper. Ommony watched him for a minute or two, and then spoke to the policeman through the curtain.

The policeman nearly gave the game away by turning his head to listen, but spat and scratched himself to cover the mistake. Ommony repeated his instructions carefully and the policeman strolled down-street. Ommony emerged

and walked slowly in the opposite direction; over the way,
the Hillman began at once to follow him, suiting his pace
to Ommony's. Ommony crossed the street; so did the policeman. Ommony turned and walked toward the Hillman;
the policeman followed suit, approaching from the rear.
Ommony came to a halt exactly in front of the Hillman,
feeling dwarfed by the man's big-boned stature and aware
of the handle of a long knife just emerging through a slit in
a robe that reeked strongly of ghee. The policeman, nervously fingering his club, halted to the Hillman's rear, six
feet away. Passers-by began to detect food for curiosity;
there were searching glances and a palpable hesitation;
there would have been a crowd in sixty seconds.

"Come with me," said Ommony, in Prakrit.

"Why?" asked the Hillman, staring at him, wide-eyed
with surprise at being spoken to in his own tongue.

"Because if you do, no harm will come to you; and if
you don't you'll go to jail."

The Hillman's hand crept instinctively toward his knife,
and the policeman made ready to swing for the back of his
head with a hard-wood club.

"Are you a fool, that you don't know a friend when you
meet one?" asked Ommony.

"I have met enemies, and women, and one or two whom
I called master, and many whom I have mastered—but
never a friend yet!" the Hillman answered. "Who art
thou?"

"Come with me and learn," said Ommony.

The Hillman hesitated, but the crowd was distinctly beginning to gather now—a little way off, not sure yet but
alert for the first hint of happenings. It grew clear to the
Hillman that escape might not be easy.

"I fear no man!" he said, turning his head and recognizing the policeman, who was hardly two-thirds his size.
He spat eloquently for the policeman's benefit, missing him
neatly by about the thickness of a knife-blade. "Whither?" he asked then, looking straight into Ommony's eyes.

Ommony led the way across the street into Chutter

Chand's shop, where he halted to let the Hillman go in first.

"Nay, lead on!" said the Hillman, stepping aside.

"No. For you have a weapon and I have none. Moreover, I have said I am a friend, and I prefer to be a living friend rather than a dead one! Go in first," laughed Ommony.

The Hillman laughed back. There was none of the solemnity about him that enshrouds the men from the Northwest frontier. Eastward along the Himalayas, where the smell of sweat leaves off and the smell of rancid butter begins, laughter becomes part of life and not an insult or indignity. He swaggered into the shop with no more argument and at a nod from Ommony walked straight through to the office at the rear.

"Krishna!" exclaimed Chutter Chand. He jumped for a corner, seized a two-handed Samurai sword, drew it from the scabbard, and laid it on the desk. "I will let my snakes loose!" he almost screamed, in Hindustanee.

But the Hillman sat down on the floor, on the exact spot where the Lama had been, and Ommony sat down in the chair facing him, motioning to Chutter Chand to resume the other chair and be sensible.

"But this is the ruffian who came and threatened me!" said Chutter Chand. "That knife of his is saw-edged! Take it from him, Ommon*ee!*"

The Hillman appeared to know no English, but seemed to have made up his mind about Ommony. Friendship he might not believe in, but he could recognize good faith. He watched Ommony's face as a child follows a motion picture.

"What is your name?" asked Ommony.

"Dawa Tsering."

"Where are you from?"

"Spiti."

"Oh, my God!" exclaimed Chutter Chand. "Does he say he is from Spiti? They are all devils who come from that country! It is there they practise polyandry, and their dead are eaten by dogs! He is unclean!"

"Who is that Lama who was in here just now?" Ommony went on.

"Tsiang Samdup."

Chutter Chand did not catch that name; or, if he did, the name meant nothing to him. Ommony, on the other hand, had to use all his power of will to suppress excitement, and even so he could not quite control himself. The Hillman noticed the change of expression.

"Aye," he said, "Tsiang Samdup is a great one."

"Who is the other who was with him—the young one?"

"His *chela.**"

"What name?"

"Samding. Some call him San-fun-ho."

"And what have you to do with them?"

Instead of answering, the Hillman retorted with a question.

"What is *thy* name? Say it again. Ommon*ee*? That sounds like a name with magic in it. *Om mani padne hum!* Who gave thee that name? Eh? Thy father had it? Who was he? How is it a man should take his father's name? Is the spirit of the father not offended? Thou art a strange one, Ommon*ee*."

"Why did you come in here some days ago and threaten Chutter Chand?" asked Ommony.

"Why not!" said the Hillman. "Did I not ride under a te-rain, like a leech on the belly of a horse, more hours and miles than an eagle knows of? Did I not eat dust— and nothing else? Did I not follow that rat Tin Lal to this *place?* Did I not—pretending to admire the cobra in the window—*see* him with my own eyes *sell* the green stone to this little lover-of-snakes? I *said* too much. I *did* too little. I should have slain them both! But I feared, because I am a stranger in the city and there were many people. Moreover, I had already slain a man—a Hindu, who drove an iron car and broke the wheel of the cart I rode in. I slew him with a spoke from the broken wheel. And it

---

*Disciple.

seemed to me that if I should slay another man too soon thereafter, it might fare ill with me, since the gods grow weary of protecting a man too often. So I returned four days later, thinking the gods might have forgotten the previous affair. They owe me many favors. I have treated the gods handsomely. And when this little rat of a jeweler swore he no longer had the stone, I threatened him. I would have slain him if I thought he really had it, but it seemed to me he told the truth. And *he* promised to get the stone back from some one to whom he had entrusted it. And I, vowing I would sever him in halves unless he should keep faith, went and told Tsiang Samdup, who came here accordingly, I following to protect the old man. I suppose Tsiang Samdup now has the stone. Is that so?"

"He *shall* have it," said Ommony.

"I think thou art *not* a liar," said the Hillman, looking straight into Ommony's eyes. "Now, I *am* a liar. If I should have said that to thee, it would only be a fool who would believe me, and a fool is nothing to be patient with. But I am not a fool, and I believe thee—or I would plunge this knife into thy liver! Who taught thee to speak my language?"

Ommony saw fit not to answer that. "Is it not enough for thee that I can speak it? Where can I find the holy Lama Tsiang Samdup?"

"Oh, as to that, he is not particularly holy—although others seem to think he is; but I am from Spiti, where we study devils and consider nonsense all this talk about purity and self-abnegation and Nirvana. Who wants to go to Nirvana? What a miserable place—just nothing! Besides, I know better. I have studied these things. It is very simple. Knife a man in the bowels, as the Goorkhas do with a *kukri*, or as I do as a rule, and he goes to hell for a while; he has a chance; by and by he comes to life again. Cut his throat, however, and he dwells between earth and heaven; he will come and haunt thee, having nothing else to do, and that is very bad. Hit him here—" (he laid a finger on his forehead, just above the nose)—"and he is *dead*. That should only be done to men who are very bad indeed. And that is the whole secret of religion.''

Ommony looked serious. "I would like to talk to you about religion—''

"Oh, I could teach you the whole of it in a very short time.''

"—— but meanwhile, I would like to know where the holy Lama Tsiang Samdup is staying.''

"I don't know,'' said the Hillman.

"You are lying,'' said Ommony. "Is that not so?''

"Of course. Did you think I would tell you the truth?''

"No. That hardly occurred to me. Well—''

Diana came in, waving her long tail slowly. She flopped on the floor beside Ommony and there was silence for about a minute while the Hillman stared at her and she returned the gaze with interest. Finally her lip curled, showing a prodigious yellow fang and Ommony laid a hand on her head to silence a thunderous growl.

"That is an incarnation of a devil!'' said the Hillman. "In my country we keep dogs as big as her to eat corpses. Devils, as a rule, are *very* evil, but I think that one—'' (he nodded at the dog) "—is worse than others. Well—I go. Say to that fool at the door that he should not offend me with his little stick, for it may be he desires to live. I am glad I met thee, Ommon*ee*.''

He waved his hand, smiled like a Chinese cherub, and walked out, ignoring Chutter Chand as utterly as if he had never seen him; and at the door he smiled at the policeman as the sun smiles on manure. The policeman did his best, but could not keep himself from grinning back.

He who puts his hand into the fire knows what he may expect. Nor may the fire be blamed.

He who intrudes on a neighbor may receive what he does not expect. Nor may the neighbor be blamed.

The fire will not be harmed; but the neighbor may be. And every deed of every kind bears corresponding consequences to the doer. You may spend a thousand lives repaying wrong done to a neighbor.

Therefore, of the two indiscretions prefer thrusting your own hand into the fire.

But there is a Middle Way, which avoids all trespassing.

FROM THE BOOK OF THE SAYINGS OF TSIANG SAMDUP.

CHAPTER V

THE HOUSE AT THE END OF THE PASSAGE

CHUTTER CHAND'S usefulness had vanished. His brain did not function now that fear had the upper hand. He could think of nothing but the Hillman's knife and of the possibility that there might be more Hillmen, who would knock down the policeman at the door, storm the shop, loot everything and slay.

"I tell you, Ommon*ee*, you have only lived in India twenty years. You do not know these people!"

He began hurriedly putting in order a mechanical system of wire and weights by which the snakes might be released in an emergency, all the while complaining bitterly against a government whose laws forbade the keeping of firearms by responsible, reputable, law-abiding citizens.

Ommony laughed and walked out with both fists in his pockets, preceded by Diana, who was a lady of one idea at a time, and that one next door to an obsession. She had "seen 'em home." Ergo, she should now show Ommony where "home" was, and he was quite satisfied to follow her. To have tracked Dawa Tsering the Hillman would simply have been waste of time, for the man would soon see he was followed and would almost certainly play a great game of follow-my-leader all over town. Moreover, the very name of the Lama—Tsiang Samdup—had excited Ommony in the sort of way that news of an ancient tomb excites an archeologist.

It was well on toward evening—that quarter-of-an-hour when the streets are most densely thronged and every one seems in a hurry to get home or to get something done before starting homeward. All cities are alike in that re-

52

spect; there is a spate before the slack of supper-time and
temple services.

The hound threaded her way patiently through the
crowd and turned down a narrow thoroughfare past fruit
and vegetable shops, where chafferers were arguing to
cheapen produce at the day's end and all the races of the
Punjab seemed to be mixed in tired confusion—faded and
ill-tempered because the evening breeze had not yet come,
and walls were giving off the oven-heat they had stored up
during the day.

There was no especial need to take precautions. Sufficient time had elapsed since the Lama and his young companion left the Chandni Chowk to convince them they had
not been followed; and in any case, the most ill-advised
thing Ommony could have done would have been to act
secretively. A man attracts the least attention if he goes
straight forward.

Those who noticed him at all admired, or feared, the dog,
and *she* paid no attention even to the mongrels of her own
genus, who snarled from a respectable distance or fled
down alleyways. Diana turned at last down suffocating
passages that led one into another between blind walls,
where death might overtake a man without causing a stir a
dozen yards away. But if you think of death in India, you
die. To live, you must think of living, and be interested.

One of the passages opened at last into a square, whose
walls were built of blocks that had been quarried from the
ancient city; (for cities surrender themselves to posterity,
even as human mothers do). The paving was of the same
material, still bearing traces of the ancient carving, but rearranged at random so that the pattern was all gone. At
the end of the courtyard was a stone building of three stories, whose upper windows overlooked it. (Those below
had been bricked up.) There was an open door in the wall,
that led into a long arched passage in which other doors to
right and left were visible. Diana ran straight to the open
door, and stopped.

Ommony began to feel now like a sailor on a lee shore,

with rocks ahead and pirates to windward. It was growing dark, for one thing. At any moment the Hillman with
the saw-edged knife and the haphazard notions about death
might approach down the passage from the rear. Forward
lay unknown territory, and a buttery smell that more than
hinted at the presence of northerners, whose notions of
hospitality might be less than none at all. He could be seen
through the window-shutters, but could not see in through
them. And he had in his pocket the lump of jade, that had
lured men all the way from beyond Tilgaun into the hot
plains that they hate. He wished he had left the jade somewhere.

It was the sound of a footstep some distance behind, that
might be the Hillman's, which decided him. He strode
forward and entered the door, his footsteps echoing under
the arch. Diana followed, growling; she seemed to have a
feeling they were being watched.

The passage presently turned to right and left in darkness, and Ommony, as he paused to consider, became
acutely conscious that his trespass was not only rash, but
impudent. He had no vestige of right to intrude himself
into the quarters of strangers, nor had he the excuse that
he did not know what he was doing. A tourist might commit such an impertinence and be forgiven on the ground
of ignorance, but if *he* should be knifed for ill-manners he
would not be entitled to the slightest sympathy. He decided at once to retrace his steps; and as he turned to face the
dim light in the doorway a voice spoke to him in English
suddenly, making his skin creep.

Diana barked savagely at a small iron grating in a door
to one side of the passage, filling the arch with echoes. It
took him several seconds to get the dog quiet. Then the
voice again:

"Go away from here! Go away quickly!"

It sounded like a boy's voice—young—educated. It was
not pitched high; there was no note of excitement—hardly
any emphasis. Diana barked again furiously, and there
was no time for hesitation; either he was in danger or he

was not; the hound said, Yes; the boy's voice implied it;
curiosity said, Stay! Common sense said, Make for the
open quickly! Intuition said, Jump! and intuition is a
despot whom it is not wise to disobey.

He reached the courtyard neck and neck with Diana, who
nearly knocked him over as she faced about savagely with
every hair bristling, fangs bared, eyes aglare. He seized
her by collar and tail and threw his weight backward to
stop her from springing at the throat of a man in dingy
gray, who paused in mid-stride, one hand behind him, in
the doorway. There was another man behind *him*, dimly
outlined in the gloom. Their faces, high-cheek-boned and
fanatical—almost Chinese—were fiercely confident, and
why they paused was not self-evident; for the man who
held a hand behind his back was armed, and with something
heavy, as the angle of his shoulder proved.

Diana saved that second. Her animal instinct was quicker than Ommony's eye, that read anticipation in the faces
in front of him. She nearly knocked Ommony over again
as she reversed the direction of effort, broke the collar-hold
and sprang past him, burying her fangs in something (Ommony knew that gurgling, smothered growl). She had
knocked him sidewise and he spun to regain his balance
while a ten-pound tulwar split the whistling air where his
back had been. He was just in time to seize the wrist that
swung the weapon—seize it with both hands and wrench it
forward in the direction of effort. The saw-edged tulwar
clattered on the paving-blocks, but the enemy did not fall,
for Diana had him by the throat and was wrenching in the
opposite direction. It was Dawa Tsering!

The Hillman's hands groped for the hound's forelegs; to
wrench those apart was his only chance, unless Ommony
could save him. A spring tiger-trap was more likely to let
go than Diana with a throat-hold. Ommony took the only
chance in sight; he yelled "Guard!" to Diana, and crashed
his fist into the Hillman's jaw, knocking him flat on his
back as Diana let up for a fraction of a second to see what
the new danger might be. He seized her by the tail then

and dragged her off before she could rush in to worry her fallen foe.

Her turn again! Struggling to free herself, she dragged Ommony in a half-circle, nearly pulling him off his feet as the man in the doorway lunged with a long old-fashioned sword. The third man seemed to prefer discretion, for he still lurked in the shadow, but the man with the sword came on, using both hands now and raising the sword above his head for a swipe that should finish the business.

There was nothing for it but to let Diana go. Ommony yelled "Guard!" again, and jumped for the saw-edged tulwar that had clattered away into the shadow. His foot struck it and he stooped for it as the swordsman swung. The blow missed. Diana seized the foe from behind and ripped away yards of his long cloak. Dawa Tsering struggled to his feet, more stunned by the blow on the back of his head when he fell than mangled by Diana's jaws; he staggered and seemed to have no sense of direction yet.

And now Ommony had the tulwar. He was no swordsman, but neither was his antagonist, who was furthermore worried by Diana from the rear.

"Guard, girl!" Ommony yelled at her, and discipline overcame instinct. She began to keep her distance, rushing in to scare the man and scooting out of reach when he turned to use his weapon. The third man possibly had no sword, for he still lurked in the doorway. Ommony ran, calling Diana, who came bounding after him, turning at every third stride or so to bark thunderous defiance.

The strange thing was that no crowd had come. The walls had echoed Diana's barks and Ommony's sharp yells to her, that must have sounded like the din of battle in the stone-walled silence. It was almost pitch-dark now, and there were no lights from the upper windows, although the glow of street-lights was already visible like an aura against the sky. The whole affair began to seem like a dream, and Ommony felt his hip pocket to make sure the jade was still there.

He paused in the throat of the narrow passage by which

he had come, sent the hound in ahead of him, and turned
to see if he was followed. He heard footsteps, and waited.
In that narrow space, with Diana to guard his back, he felt
he could protect himself with the tulwar against all-comers.

But it was only one man—Dawa Tsering—holding a
cloth to his throat and walking unsteadily.

"Give me back my weapon, Ommon*ee!*"

The words, spoken in Prakrit, were intelligible enough
but gurgled, as if his throat was choked and hardly func-
tioning. Diana tried to rush at him, but Ommony squeezed
her to the wall and grabbed her collar.

"Down!" he ordered, and she crouched at his feet,
growling.

"Aye, hold her! I have had enough of that incarnated
devil. Give me my knife, Ommon*ee!*"

"You call this butcher's ax a knife? You rascal, it's not
a minute since you tried to kill me with it!"

"Aye, but that is nothing. I missed. If you were dead,
you might complain. Give me the knife and be off!"

Ommony laughed. "You propose to have another crack
at me, eh?"

"Not I! Those Lamas are a lousy gang! They told me
I could come to no harm if I obeyed them and said my
prayers! Their magic is useless. That she-devil of thine
has torn my throat out! I doubt if I shall ever sing again.
Give me the knife, and I will go back to the Hills. I wish
I had never left Spiti!"

"I told you I am a friend," said Ommony, speering
about in his mind for a clue as to how to carry on.

"Aye. I wish I had believed you. Give me the knife."

"Do you know your way around Delhi?"

"No. May devils befoul the city! That is, I know a little. I can find my way to the te-rain."

Ommony felt in his pocket, found an envelope, and pen-
ciled an address on it in bold printed characters.

"Midway between ten and eleven o'clock to-night, go out
into the streets and get into the first *gharri** you *meet.*

*Carriage.

Give that to the driver. If the driver can't read it, show
it to passers-by until you find some one who can. Then
drive straight to that address, and I will pay the *gharri-
wallah**. If your throat needs doctoring, it shall have it."

"And my knife?"

"I will return it to you to-night, at that address."

"All right. I will come there."

"I suppose, if I had given you the knife back now, you
would have killed me with it?"

"Maybe. But you are no fool, Ommon*ee!* You had better go quickly, before those Lamas find some way of making
trouble for you."

Ommony accepted that advice, although he did not believe that, if they really were Lamas, they would go out of
their way to make trouble for any one outside their own
country. It is one thing to attack an intruder; quite another thing to follow a man through the streets and murder
him. He was glad he had hurt nobody. Dawa Tsering's
hurt was plainly not serious. There is no satisfaction whatever in violence (if it can possibly be avoided) to a man of
Ommony's temperament. He walked in a hurry along the
narrow, winding passageways and found the street again,
bought food for Diana, gave her the package to carry (for
she was temperamentally dangerous in a crowd *after* having used her jaws in action, unless given something definite
to do), and after fifteen minutes' search found a *gharri,* in
which he drove to McGregor's office. McGregor was not
there, so he pursued him to his bungalow, where he fed Diana and examined curios for fifteen minutes before deciding
what to say.

McGregor understood that perfectly. He might not
know Ommony as he knew files, the law of probabilities,
and criminal statistics; he might, from deep experience,
mistrust his own opinion; but he did know that when Ommony poked around in that way, picking up things and
replacing them, it was wise to wait and not ask questions.

---

*Cab-driver.

He smoked and watched his servant putting studs into a clean dress-shirt.

"Have you one man you can absolutely bet on, who could take a package to Tilgaun and could be trusted not to monkey with it on the way, or lose it, or let it get stolen?" he asked at last.

"Number 17—Aaron Macauley, the Eurasian, is leaving for Simla on to-night's train. He would proably want to spend a day or two in Simla, but he could go on to Tilgaun after that. He's quite dependable."

"Yes. I'd trust Aaron Macauley. I want a small box, stout paper, string and sealing-wax."

McGregor produced them and watched Ommony wrap up the piece of jade and seal it with his own old-fashioned signet-ring. He addressed the package to Miss Hannah Sanburn at the Tilgaun Mission.

"Better tell Macauley it contains bank-notes," said Ommony. "That'll give him a sense of importance and keep him from being too curious. Tell him to ask Miss Sanburn to keep the package there for me until I come."

"All right. Now what's the theory?"

"Nothing much. I was attacked just now—not serious. The man who got the worst of it will join us after dinner. I'll give you all the grizzly details then. Might possibly surprise you. See you again at Mrs. Cornock-Campbell's."

"Who is a fountain of surprises," said McGregor, smiling. "Meanwhile, how about protection? Do you want a body-guard?" It was not exactly clear why he was smiling.

"No," said Ommony, looking contemplatively at Diana, who appeared to have fallen asleep on a Bokhara rug, "I've got a more than usually good one, thanks. Observe."

He started on tiptoe for the door. Diana reached it several strides ahead of him and slipped out first, to sniff the wind and make sure that the shadows held no lurking enemy.

"If men were as faithful as dogs," he began. But McGregor laughed:

"They're not. Faith, very largely, is absence of intelligence. Intelligence has to be trained to be honest; it has no morals otherwise. Without a good Scots grounding in religion, the greater the intelligence the worse the crook."

"Oh, rot!" said Ommony, and walked out, leaving McGregor chuckling.

A certain poet, who was no fool, bade men take the cash and let the credit go. I find this good advice, albeit difficult to follow. Nevertheless, it is easier than what most men attempt. They seek to take the cash and let the debit go, and that is utterly impossible; for as we sow, we reap.

FROM THE BOOK OF THE SAYINGS OF TSIANG SAMDUP.

CHAPTER VI

"MISSISH-ANBUN IS MAD"

EVEN since the Armistice, when military glory topped the rise and started on the down-grade of a cycle, there are still worse fates than being wealthy in your own right and the wife of a colonel commanding a Lancer regiment—even if your children have to go to Europe to be schooled, and your husband is under canvas half the time. And there are much worse fates than dining with Mrs. Cornock-Campbell, anywhere, in any circumstances. To be in a position to invite yourself to dinner at her Delhi bungalow means that, whatever your occupation, you may view life now and then from the summit, looking downward. Viceroys come and go. Mrs. Cornock-Campbell usually educates their wives.

They say she knows everything—even why the German Crown Prince once cut short a tour of India; and that, of course, means she is no longer in the bloom of youth, and never indiscreet, for you don't learn state secrets by being young and talkative.

Ommony is one of her pet cronies, though they rarely meet (which is the way things happen in India). He looks such a blunt old-fashioned bachelor in a dinner-jacket dating from away before the war, the contrast he creates with modern artificial cynicism is so satisfying, and he so utterly lacks pose or pretense, that he brings out all her vivacity (which is apt to be chilled when imitation people assume manners for the sake of meals).

The talk, for the hour while dinner lasted, was of anything in the world but Ringding Lamas and the Ahbor country. Ommony was probed for epigrams, coined in the

62

depths of his forest, that should make John McGregor
wince and laugh—such statements as that "You can look
for faults or virtue. Vultures prefer ullage. Suit yourself. A man sees his own vices and his own virtues reflected
in his neighbor—nothing else! Another's crimes are
what you yourself would commit under equally strong
pressure. His virtues are greater than your own, if only
because they're less obvious. The most indecent exhibition
in the world is virtue without her cloak on!" Not polite
exactly, (particularly not to the chief of the Secret Service), but not tainted by circumlocution. And again:
"They say the fact that people work entitles them to vote.
Horses work harder than men! Soap-box nonsense! The
only excuse for work is that you like it, and the only
honest objection to loafing is that it's bad for you."

John McGregor, in the rare hours when he is not feeling
the pulse of India's restless underworld, is an addict of the
Wee Free Kirk with convictions regarding the devil.

"A personal devil?" said Ommony. "I wish there was
one! Hell breeds more dangerous stuff than that! If I
thought there was a devil, I'd vote for him. He'd clean
up politics."

John McGregor, ganglion of India's crime statistics and
acquainted with all evil at first hand, was shocked, to Mrs.
Cornock-Campbell's huge delight.

"Now, John! What have you to say to that?"

McGregor cracked a nut nervously and sipped at his
Madeira.

"He could find a host of half-baked theorists to praise
him for the blasphemy," he said deliberately, "but the
ultimate appalling circumstance of being damned is a high
price for applause."

Ommony laughed. "I'd rather be thought damned by
a man I respect than be praised by damned fools," he
retorted. "We three will meet beyond the border, Mac.
I'm looking forward to it. I can't see anything unpleasant
in death, except the morbid business of dying. *May there
be no moaning at the bar when I put out to sea.*' It looks

as if I might be the first of the three of us to take that
trip."

So, by a roundabout route, the conversation drifted to
its goal. Over her shoulder, at the piano, in the rose and
ivory music-room after dinner Mrs. Cornock-Campbell
tossed the question that brought secrets to the surface.

"John says you are going to the Ahbor country."

John McGregor's eyes glowed with anticipation, but
he crossed his legs and lit a cigarette, throwing himself
back into the shadow of an antique chair to hide the smile.

"Going to try," said Ommony. "My sister and Fred
Terry disappeared up there twenty years ago. They left
no trace."

"Are you sure?"

She went on playing from Chopin and Ommony did not
notice the inflection of her voice; he was listening to the
piano's overtones, vaguely displeased when she closed the
piano without finishing the nocturne.

"I was at Tilgaun seven months ago," she said. "Co-
lin" (that was her husband) "had to go to Burma, so I
went to Darjiling. I heard of the Marmaduke Mission, and
grew curious. I wrote, and Miss Sanburn kindly invited
me to come and stay with her. The most delightful place.
Please pass me a cigarette."

"Did Hannah mention me?" asked Ommony.

"Indeed she did. You seem to be her *beau ideal;* and
funny enough she said you, and the Lama Tsiang Samdup
must have been twin brothers in a former incarnation!
She told me you and he have never met each other, although
you are co-trustees with her under Marmaduke's will. It
sounds like Gilbert and Sullivan. I didn't see the Lama,
but I did meet some one else who is quite as interesting."

McGregor crossed his legs and blew smoke at the ceiling.

"How well do you know Miss Sanburn?" asked Mrs.
Cornock-Campbell at the end of a minute's silence. She
was watching Diana, stretched out on the bearskin, hunting gloriously in a dream-Valhalla. If she saw Ommony's
face it was through the corner of one eye.

"Oh, as well as a man can ever hope to know a very unusual woman," said Ommony.

"That doesn't go deep—does it! I admit I suspected *you* at first. Then I remembered how long I have known you and—well—you're unorthodox, and you're a rebel, but—I couldn't imagine you leaving a child nameless."

"What on earth do you mean?" asked Ommony.

"So I suspected Marmaduke—naturally. But all sorts of dates and circumstances turned up quite casually, which eliminated *him*. I was at Tilgaun a whole month before I was quite sure that Miss Sanburn is not a mother. I was almost disappointed! She is such a dear—I admire her so much—that it would have given me a selfish satisfaction to know such an abysmal secret, and to keep it even on a death-bed! However, the child is not hers. She calls her an adopted daughter, though I doubt that there are any legal papers. The girl is white. She's about twenty. The strangest part is this: that the girl disappears at intervals."

"This is all news to me," said Ommony. "Mac said something, but—"

"It isn't news you iconoclast! It's a most romantic mystery. The girl was there when I arrived. She wouldn't have been; but you know what a business it is to get to Tilgaun. I was supposed to wait for ponies and servants from the mission; they didn't come, and as there was a party of rajah's people going, I traveled with them. They were in a hurry, so I reached the mission quite a number of days before I was expected, and I met the girl on the far side of the rope bridge just before you reach Tilgaun—you remember the place? There's a low steep cliff with only a narrow passage leading out of it. She was sitting there nursing a twisted ankle—nothing serious—but she couldn't get away without my seeing her; and of course it never entered my head to suspect that she would want to avoid me. She told me her name was Elsa."

"That was my sister's name," remarked Ommony, who had an old-fashioned way of growing sentimental when that name cropped up among intimates.

"I lent her a spare pony and she rode up to the mission with me. Jolly—she was the jolliest girl I have ever seen, all laughter and intelligence—with strange sudden fits of demureness—or perhaps that isn't the right word. Freeze isn't the right word either. She would suddenly lapse into silence and her face would grow absolutely calm—not expressionless, but calm—like a Chinese girl's. It was as if she were two distinct and separate women. But she's white. I watched her finger-nails."

"Might be Chinese," Ommony suggested. "They're given to laughter, and their finger-nails don't show the dark lunula when they're pressed. Hannah Sanburn receives all comers at the mission."

"I am certain she is English," Mrs. Cornock-Campbell answered. "But as far as I could judge she speaks Tibetan and several dialects perfectly. Her English hasn't a trace of Chi-chi accent. She has been wonderfully educated. She has art in every fiber of her being—plays the piano *fairly* well—mostly her own compositions, and you may believe me or not, they're fit to be played by a *master*. And she draws perfectly, from memory. That night at supper, and afterward, she talked incessantly and kept on illustrating what she meant by drawing on sheets of paper—wonderful things —not caricatures—snap-shots of people and things she had seen. Wait; I've kept some of them. Let me show you."

She found a portfolio and laid it on Ommony's lap. He turned over sheet after sheet of pencil drawings that seemed to have caught motion in the act—yaks, camels, oxen, Tibetan men and women taken in mid-smile, old monastery doorways, flowers—done swiftly and with humor. There was a sureness of touch that men work lifetimes to achieve; and there was a quality that almost nobody in this age *has* achieved—a sort of spirit of antiquity, as simple as it was indefinable in words. It was as if the artist knew that things are never what they seem, but was translating what *she* saw of things' origins into modern terms that could be understood. The drawings were of yesterday, clothed in the garments of to-day and looking forward to to-morrow.

"She seemed to see right through you," Mrs. Cornock-Campbell went on. "I don't believe the smartest man in the world could fool that girl. She has the something within that men instinctively recognize and don't try to take liberties with. She seemed equally familiar with Tibetan and European thought, as well as life, and to know all the country to the northward. I gathered she had been to Lhassa, which seems incredible, but she spoke of it as if she knew the very street-stones, and you'll see there are sketches of bits of Lhassa in that portfolio—notice the portrait of the Dalai-Lama and the sketch of the southern gate.

"And all the while the girl talked Miss Sanburn seemed as proud and as uncomfortable as a martyr at the stake! When Elsa began to talk of Lhassa I thought Miss Sanburn would burst with anxiety; you could see she was on the perpetual point of cautioning her not to be indiscreet, but she restrained herself with a forced smile that made me simply love her. I know Miss Sanburn was in agonies of terror all the time.

"When Elsa had gone to bed—that was long after midnight—I asked Miss Sanburn what her surname was. She hesitated for about thirty seconds, looking at me—"

"I know how she looked," said Ommony. "Like a fighting-man with a heartache. That look has often puzzled me. What did she say?"

"She said: 'Mrs. Cornock-Campbell, it was not intended you should meet Elsa. She is my adopted daughter. There are reasons—.' And of course at that I interrupted. I assured her I don't pry into people's secrets. She asked me whether I would mind not discussing what little I already knew. She said: 'I'm sorry I can't explain, but it is important that Elsa's very existence should be known to as few people as possible, especially in India.' Of course, I promised, but she agreed to a reservation that I might mention having met the girl, if anything I could say should seem likely to quiet inquisitive people. And that was a good thing, because I had no sooner returned to Delhi than John McGregor came to dinner and asked me pointedly

whether I had seen any mysterious young woman at Tilgaun. I think John intended to investigate her with his
staff of experts in—what is the right word, John?"

"Worm's-eye views," said McGregor. "Not all the
king's horses nor all the king's men could have called me
off, as you did with a smile and a glass of Madeira. Thus
are governments corrupted."

"So you're the second individual to whom I have opened
my lips about it," said Mrs. Cornock-Campbell, not exactly
watching Ommony, but missing none of his expression,
which was of dawning comprehension.

"I'm beginning to understand about a hundred things,"
he said musingly. "You'd think, though, Hannah would
have told me."

Mrs. Cornock-Campbell smiled at John McGregor.
"Didn't you know he'd say just that? Wake up, Cottswold! This isn't church! It's because you're her closest
friend that you're the last person in the world she would
tell. She's a woman!"

Then there were noises in the garden and Diana left off
dreaming on the bearskin to growl like an earthquake.

"An acquaintance of mine," said Ommony. "If you
can endure the smell, please let him in. Or we might try
the veranda."

Diana had to be forcibly suppressed. The butler, a Goanese (which means that he had oddly assorted fears, as well
as a mixed ancestry and cross-bred notions of convention,
that were skin-deep and as hard as onyx) had to be rebuked
for near-rebellion. And Dawa Tsering, with his neck swath-
ed in weirdly-smelling cloth, had to be given a mat to sit on,
lest he spoil the carpet. It needed that setting to make
plain how innocent of cleanliness his clothes were; and his
reek was of underground donkey-stables, with some sort of
chemical added. (There were reasons, connected with possible eavesdroppers, why the deep veranda was unsuitable.)

"And the knife, Ommonee?" he asked, squatting cross-
legged, admiring the room. "Is this thy house? Thou art
a rich man! I think I will be thy servant for a while. Is

the woman thy wife? It is not good to be a woman's servant. Besides, I am a poor hand at obedience. Nay, return
me my knife and I will go."

"Not yet," said Ommony, studying by which roundabout route it might be easiest to elicit information. He
decided on the sympathetic-personal. The man's neck
had plainly received attention, but the subject served.
"Shall I get a doctor for your neck?"

"Nay, Tsiang Samdup made magic and put leeches on
it and some stuff that burned. Lo, I recover."

"You mean the holy Lama Tsiang Samdup? The Ringding Gelong Lama? He who was at Chutter Chand's this
afternoon?"

Ommony knew quite well whom he meant, but he wanted
to convey the information to the others without putting the
Hillman on guard. By the look in the Hillman's eye, his
mood was talkative—boastful—a reaction from the failure
of the afternoon.

"Aye, the same."

"I should have thought his *chela* would have attended
to that."

"Samding? Nay, they say that fellow is too sacred altogether. Not that I believe it; I could cut his throat and
show them he dies gurgling and whistling like any other
man! But the Lama looks after him like an old wife with
a young husband and the boy mayn't soil his fingers. Rebuke thy dog, Ommon*ee*—she eyes me like a devil in the
dark. So, that is better. *Ohe*—I wish I had never come
southward! Yet, I have seen this house of thine. It is a
wonder. It will serve to speak of, when I go back to Spiti
and tell tales around the fire."

Ommony translated for the others' benefit, and went on
questioning.

"I suppose you will return to Tilgaun with the Lama and
his *chela?*"

"May the stars and my *karma* forbid! I go under the
belly of a te-rain, as I came. To Kalka I go; and thence by
foot on the old road to Simla, where I know a man who will

pay me to carry goods to the rajah of Spiti. That is a long journey and a difficult. I shall be *well* paid.''

Again Ommony translated.

''Ask him how and where he learned that trick of riding under trains,'' said McGregor.

''Oh, as to that,'' said Dawa Tsering, ''there are few things simpler. In my youth'' (he spoke as if he were already ancient, instead of perhaps two- or three-and-twenty) ''I desired a woman of Spiti whose husband was unwise. He should have gone on a journey oftener. And he should not have returned in such haste. I wearied of his home-comings, so I lay in wait and slew him. And the rajah of Spiti, who is a jealous man—liking to attend to all the slaying in that country, which is nevertheless too much for one individual, even if he *does* have an army of fifty men —fined me three hundred *rupees*.* Where should I get such a fortune? Yet, unless I paid it, I should have to join his army and gather fuel, which is as scarce in Spiti as an honest woman. So I ran away. And after wandering about the Hills a month or two, enjoying this and that adventure, I reached Simla, where I met a man with whom I gambled, he offering to teach me a new game, not knowing we use dice in Spiti. And *his* dice were loaded. So I substituted mine. And when I had won from him more than he could pay, he offered to teach me his profession.''

''Gambling?'' asked Ommony.

''Nay. I never gamble. I take no chances. I do the gods a favor now and then, since it seems from all accounts they need it, but I never trust them. That fellow told me of the te-rains that run from Kalka southward, to and fro, and of the many *rupees* that the passengers leave in their pockets while they sleep. He supposed I would undertake the dangerous part and thereafter share the loot with him, and he showed me how to hide under a te-rain until night-fall and then—but it was *easy*. And I found out after a while where he hid the half of our profits, which he *claimed*

---

*About one hundred dollars.

as *his* share after *I* had done all the climbing in and out of
windows in the dark. So I took what he had hidden, and,
what with my own savings, the total amounted to more than
a thousand *rupees*. Then I returned to Spiti, and I buried
the money in a certain place, and went to the rajah and
lied to him, saying I had earned the amount of the fine as
a wood-cutter but that a certain one (who was *always* my
enemy) had stolen the money from me on the very first
night that I returned. So the rajah transferred my fine to
that other man, who had to pay it, and then, of course, I
had to leave Spiti again—swiftly. That other man has
many friends. But I will find a way to deal with him."

"When did you first meet the holy Lama Tsiang Samdup?" Ommony asked.

"Hah! I returned to the te-rains, being minded to make
a fortune, but the gods played a scurvy trick on me. I was
doing nicely; but on a certain night a fool of a policeman
pounced on me at an *istashun** just as I was crawling in
under the wheels. He dragged me out by the leg, and it
was not a proper time to kill him, since there were many
witnesses. So I raised a lamentation, saying I would ride
to Delhi to the bedside of a friend, and that I had no fare.
And lo, the Lama Tsiang Samdup stepped out of the
te-rain and paid my fare, praying that I would permit
him thus to acquire merit. So I rode with him to Delhi,
he questioning me all the night-long and I at my wits' end
to invent sufficient lies wherewith to answer him. And in
Delhi I being a stranger in the city, he set out with me to
help me find my friend; and, there being no friend, we
naturally did not find him, whereat the Lama wept. So it
seemed to me he was a man who needed some one to look
after him; moreover, he was certainly a very rich man.
And I had not yet thought of a way of defeating my
enemy in Spiti. Restrain thy she-dog, Ommon*ee;* I like
not the look in her eye."

Ommony put Diana outside with orders to guard the
front door.

---

*Railway station.

"How long ago did this happen?" he asked, forcing himself to look only vaguely interested as he resumed his seat.

"Oh, maybe a year ago—or longer. The time passes. I agreed to serve the Lama for a while, although he wearied me with his everlasting lectures about merit, and the Wheel, and the gods know what else. Also he keeps low company—actors and singers and such folk. When he left me at Tilgaun on his way northward I was well content to rest from him a while. He gave me money, of which he has *plenty* although he is much too careful with it; and there were good-looking girls at the mission, which is a marvel of a place with a high wall. But I saw how to climb the wall. So it came about that there was trouble between me and Missish-Anbun—she who is Abbess of the place—a bold woman, who was not afraid to stand up to me and speak her mind. Lo, I showed her my knife and she laughed at it! I speak truth. So by the time the Lama came back from the North I was a by-word and a mockery among the people of Tilgaun, who are a despicable lot but prosperous, and full of a notion that Missish-Anbun is the cause of all good fortune. And *she*, of course, being a woman and unmarried (which is witchcraft) told tales to the Lama about me when he returned; whereat he (the old fool!) was distressed, saying *he* was answerable, in that he had left me there during his absence. He spoke much about the Wheel, and merit, and responsibility. And I, who can not help liking the old fool, although I laugh at him—and at myself for eating rebuke from him—was ashamed. Aye, I was ashamed. He made me promise to perform acts of repentance—as *he* said, to offset my own sins—but as *I* think, because he had a use for me.

"And now he had Sam-ding with him, the *chela*, whom all men in that part regard as a reincarnation of some ancient prodigy who has been dead so long that his bones must have dissolved into powder. (But the priests tell just such tales, and who can say they are not true?)

"And there was much excitement over a piece of green stone. It had disappeared from somewhere up North, although none mentioned the name of the place whence it had come, but I had heard *some*thing, and the rest I saw. There had come a man from Ahbor to the mission, dying of a belly-wound, and if *my* advice had been asked he would have been left to die outside the wall, because those Ahbors are devils. *I* have heard they eat corpses, which is a dog's business, and I *know* none dares to enter their country. But Missish-Anbun is mad, and she took him into the mission, where they stitched up the belly-wound and tried to make him live. But he died, and they found the stone in his clothing, and Missish-Anbun kept it. There was much talk about the stone, for the most part nonsense; some said this, and some said that, but it was clear enough that whoever really owned the stone had set inquiries going and a rumor had been spread that there was danger in possessing it.

"I had made up my mind to steal the stone from Missish-Anbun and discover how much it might be worth to a man of some skill in bargaining; for it seemed to me there could not be much danger to *me* as long as I had my knife.—Where *is* my knife, Ommon*ee?* Presently! Well, don't forget to return it to me. That knife and my future are one.

"As I was saying, I was about to steal the stone. But a girl in the mission—one whose virtue I had satisfactory reason to suspect—forestalled me. She took the stone and ran with it toward the house of Sirdar Sirohe Singh, who is a prince of devils, and a father of lice, and no good. (He had warned me to leave Tilgaun, and I had told him who his father was.)

"And there had come a rat of a man named Tin Lal to Tilgaun, too much given to asking questions. Him I was minded to slay, because that girl, whose virtue I say was not such as others seemed to think, no longer smiled at me when I sat in the sun near the mission gate, but took more notice of Tin Lal than was seemly. Night after

night I had waited for her, and it came to my ears too
late that there was a reason, that concerned me, for the
smile in Tin Lal's impudent eye. I whetted the edge of
my knife on a stone by the image of the Lord Buddha
that is set into a niche in the mission wall.

"But the girl stole the stone and ran off with it, and
Tin Lal waited for her at a narrow place where the path
to the *sirdar's* house runs between a cliff on the one hand
and a deep ravine on the other—a place where the eagles
nest and there is mist ascending from the waterfall below.
He pushed her into the ravine and climbed down after
her, taking the stone. And then *he* disappeared. And
Sirdar Sirohe Singh, who is a dog—whose liver is crawling lice—whose heart is a dead fish, accused *me* of the
deed. There was talk of bringing me before the rajah,
and there was other talk of driving me away.

"Nevertheless, I had promised the Lama I would wait
for him in Tilgaun. I was not minded that my time had
come. Moreover, I am one who keeps promises. So I
slew the loudest talkers—very secretly, by night; and
after that there was not so much insolence toward me
when I passed up and down the village.

"*Ohe*—but I was weary of Tilgaun! And when the
Lama came he at first believed I had slain the girl and
stolen the stone. But he is not entirely a fool in all respects, and the *chela* Samding has more brains than a
grown man with a beard down to his belly. It was the
chela who said that if I had in truth stolen the stone I
would certainly have run away with it and not have
stayed in Tilgaun like an eagle hatching eggs. And the
Lama, having listened to a million lies and discovered the
truth like a bird in the mist among them, told me I might
earn much merit by following the trail of Tin Lal to the
southward and recovering the stone. The Lama Tsiang
Samdup said to me, 'Slay not, but obtain the stone from
Tin Lal and I will pay thee more for it than any other
dozen men would pay.' And he named a price—a very
great price, which set me to dreaming of the girls in Spiti,

and of a valley where I am minded someday to build a house.

"So I, having furthermore a grudge of my own against Tin Lal, agreed, and I followed the rat Tin Lal to Delhi, where, as I have told you, I saw him, through the shop-window where the snake is, sell the stone to Chutter Chand, the jeweler.

"But the Lama and Samding had come to Delhi likewise, and to them I told what I had seen, having lost sight of Tin Lal in the crowd. And now give me back the knife, Ommon*ee*, that I may hunt for Tin Lal. I have an extra grudge against him. Has he not robbed me of the price the Lama would have paid me for the stone? *Ohe* —my honor and my anger and his end are one! Give me the knife, Ommon*ee*."

The Hillman smiled winningly, as one who has talked his way into a hard man's heart. He held his hand out, leaning forward as he squatted on the mat.

"Tin Lal is in the jail," said Ommony.

"Oh, is that so? That makes it easy. I will wait outside the jail. They will not keep him in there for ever."

"What is that house, where you tried to kill me this afternoon?" Ommony asked.

"A place kept by Tibetans, where the Lama stays when in Delhi. That is where the actor people come to see him."

"Why did you attack me?"

"Why not? You had said, the Lama shall have the stone. Therefore it was clear to me that *you* must have it. Therefore, if I should take it from you I could sell it to the Lama. I am no fool!"

Ommony, with something like contentment in his eye, began to translate for the benefit of the others as much as he could remember of Dawa Tsering's tale, tossing occasional questions to the Hillman to get him to repeat some detail. It was the company the Lama kept that seemed to interest him most.

"If you like," said McGregor, when the tale was finished, "I'll have those Tibetans searched."

Ommony was about to refuse that offer, but his words were cut short by an uproar on the porch. Diana—on guard and therefore unable to be tempted from her post —was barking like a battery of six-pounders. He strode into the hall and listened—heard retreating footsteps— some one in no hurry pap-pad-padding firmly on soft-soled shoes toward the garden gate.

He opened the door. Diana glanced angrily at a long, narrow, white envelope that lay on the porch floor under the electric light, and resumed her furious salvoes at the gate.

"So-ho, old lady—some one you knew brought a letter, eh? You weren't indignant till he threw it down and retreated. You never said a word while he was coming up the path." He wetted his finger and tested the hot night air. "Uh-huh—wind's toward you—recognized his smell—that's clear enough. All right—good dog—on guard again."

He picked up the envelope and walked into the house.

"Did you tell the Lama where you were coming to-night?" he asked, standing over Dawa Tsering, looking down at him.

"Aye. I did. Why not? How should I know, Om-mon*ee*, that this was not a trap—and I with no knife to hack my way out of it! Suppose that you had thrown me in the jail—who should then have helped me unless the Lama knew? I am no fool."

"Did you tell him I said he shall have the green stone?"

"Nay! How often must I say I am no fool! *Would* he buy the stone from *me*, after I had told him *you* said he shall have it?"

"The letter! The letter!" exclaimed Mrs. Cornock-Campbell. "Are you made of iron, Cottswold? How can you hold a mysterious letter in your hand without dying to know what is in it? Give it to me! Let me open it, if you won't!"

Ommony passed it to her. John McGregor lit another cigarette.

It is the teaching of financiers and statesmen, and of them who make laws, and of most religionists, that of all things a man should first seek safety—for his own skin— for his own money—for his own soul. Yet I find this teaching strange; because of all the dangers in the universe, the greatest lies in self-preferment.

FROM THE BOOK OF THE SAYINGS OF TSIANG SAMDUP.

CHAPTER VII

THE letter was written on the same long, ivory-colored paper as that which had reached McGregor's office in the silver tube, but this time it was not European hand writing, although the words were English. Some one more used to a brush, such as the Chinese use, and who regarded every pen-stroke as a work of art in true relation to the whole, had taken a quill pen and almost painted what he had to say, in terse strong sentences.

"To Cottswold Ommony, Esquire,
   "At the house of his friend.

"May Destiny mete you full measure of mercy. The piece of jade is neither yours nor mine. By deeds in the valley of indecision a soul ascends or descends. You are one to whom reward is no inducement; to whom honor is no more than wealth a pleasing substitute for right doing. There is nothing done in this life that is not balanced by justice in the lives to come and the ultimate is peace. So do. And not by another's hand are deeds done; nor is the end accomplished without doing all that lies at the beginning. Thus the beginning is the end, and the end the beginning, as a circle having no beginning and no end, from which is no escape but by the Middle Way, which lies not yonder but at the feet of him who searches. Take the stone to Tilgaun, which is one stage of the journey to the place whence it came. From Tilgaun onward let those be responsible on whom the burden falls. There is danger in another's duty. Peace be with you. Peace give you peace that you may multiply it.
                              "Tsiang Samdup."

78

Mrs. Cornock-Campbell read the letter aloud. Not
smiling, she passed it to Ommony and watched his face.
He read it twice, frowning, and gave it to McGregor, who
emitted his staccato, fox-bark laugh, which Diana heard
and answered with one deep musical bay from the porch.

"That links him technically—tight," said McGregor,
folding the letter with decisive finger-strokes and stowing
it into his pocket. "Where did he learn to write such
English?"

"Oxford," said Ommony. "He took D. D. and LL. D.
Degrees, or so Marmaduke told me. We're not the only
section of humanity that runs to Secret Service, Mac. We
look for one thing, they for another. There isn't much they
don't know about us, along the line that interests them."

Mrs. Cornock-Campbell looked incredulous.

"A Ringding Gelong Lama—an English Doctor of Divinity? Wonders don't cease, do they! What could he
gain by taking *that* degree? Amusement? Are they as
subtle as all that?"

"Subtle, yes. Amusement, no," said Ommony, frowning darkly. "How spike the guns of the persistent missionary, unless they know how the guns are loaded?
That's the gist of one of his letters to me. But damn the
man! Why couldn't he meet me by appointment instead
of writing this stuff? I've suspected him for some time
of—"

Mrs. Cornock-Campbell laughed. "He evidently knows
you, Cottswold, better than you know him."

"Know him? I've never met him!" Ommony retorted.
"I saw him to-day for the first time, from behind a brass
Buddha in Chutter Chand's shop. There've been lots of
times when he ought to have met me, to talk over details
in connection with the trusteeship, but it all had to be
done by correspondence. He has set his signature to every
paper I drew up, and he has agreed to every proposal I
have made. Confound him! Why is he afraid of me?
Why couldn't he come in, instead of leaving that fool letter on the door-step?"

"*Wise* letter!" (Mrs. Cornock-Campbell went back to the piano. None but Rimsky-Korsakof could describe her sensations.) "He evidently knows how to manage you. Do you ever bet, John? I will bet you five *rupees* I know what's next!"

John McGregor drew a five-*rupee* note from his pocket and laid it on the piano. Mrs. Cornock-Campbell began playing. Dawa Tsering, his head to one side like a bird's, watched her fingers, listening intently.

"There are devils inside the machine," he said after a while. "Give me my knife, Ommonee, and let me go."

But Ommony, pacing the floor, both hands behind him, frowning, took no notice of any one. He was away off in a realm of conjecture of his own

"Remember: I stand to lose five dibs!" McGregor remarked at the end of five minutes. "Suppose you put me out of agony. I'm Scots, you know!"

"Damn!" Ommony exclaimed. "Why can't he take me into his confidence? I hate to suspect a man. Pen and ink anywhere?"

"I lose," said Mrs. Cornock-Campbell, nodding toward a gilt-and-ivory writing desk against the wall. "Take back your five *rupees*, John. You'll find a five of mine being used as a book-mark in one of those volumes of Walter Pater on the shelf. Put something in its place."

McGregor paid himself. Ommony at the desk tore up sheet after sheet of paper, chuckled at last, and wrote a final draft. "There, that should do. That's obscure enough. That hoists him with his own petard. Why don't women ever have clean blotting-paper?"

He showed what he had written to McGregor, who read it aloud, Mrs. Cornock-Campbell playing very softly while she listened.

"To the holy Lama Tsiang Samdup,
    in the place where he has chosen to secrete himself.
"I will take the Middle Way if I can find it, and I hope neither of us may get lost. I wish you all success.
                    "Cottswold Ommony."

"Sarcasm?" said Mrs. Cornock-Campbell. " I wonder if that ever pays."

"We'll see!"

Ommony sealed up the envelope, on which he had written simply "Tsiang Samdup," and stood over Dawa Tsering.

"Take this letter to the Lama. Come back here with proof you have delivered it, and you shall have your knife."

"Send him in my dog-cart," McGregor advised. "My *sais** is one of those rare birds who do as they're told. He doesn't talk or ask questions."

So Dawa Tsering was seen on to the back seat of the dog-cart, with a horse-blanket under him to keep grease off the cushion, and the conference was resumed. McGregor questioned Ommony narrowly concerning the events of the afternoon, and particularly as to the exact location of the courtyard where the attack had taken place.

"It doesn't look to me as if they meant to kill you," he said at last. "It seems to me they were hell-bent on merely driving you away. Um-tiddley-um-tum-tum— we've made a mess of this—we *should* have had that building watched. Katherine, I will bet these ten rupees that our friend from Spiti draws blank."

"Men are unintuitive creatures," Mrs. Cornock-Campbell answered. "No, John, I won't bet. The obvious thing was to take the Lama at his word and go straight to Tilgaun. I supposed Cottswold would see that, but he didn't—did you? What is the objection?"

"This," said Ommony, pausing, looking obstinate, "he is either my friend, or he isn't. He has every reason to be frank with me. He has chosen the other line. All right."

"All wrong!" she answered, chuckling. "In that letter, in his own way, he invited you to trust him."

"I don't!" remarked Ommony, shutting his jaws with a snap that could be heard across the room.

---

*Coachman.

He refused to explain himself. He was not quite sure
he could have done that, but had no inclination to try.
If he had opened his lips it would have been to invite Mc-
Gregor to throw a plain-clothes cordon around that house
at the end of the courtyard, search the place and expose
its secrets.

Habitual self-control alone prevented that. Twenty
years of living courteously in a conquered country, making full allowance for the feelings of those who must look
to him for justice, had bred a restraint that ill-temper
could not overthrow. But he did not dare to let himself
speak just then. He preferred to be rude—took up a book
and began reading.

Mrs. Cornock-Campbell went on playing. John Mc-
Gregor smoked in silence, pulling out the Lama's letter,
reading it over and over, trying to discover hidden meanings. So more than an hour went by with hardly a word
spoken, and it was long after midnight when the wheels
of McGregor's returning dog-cart skidded on the loose
gravel of the drive at the rear of the house and Diana
awoke on the porch to tell the moon about it.

Dawa Tsering was admitted through the back door and
shepherded in by the butler, who held his nose, but who
was not otherwise so lacking in appreciation as to shut
the door tight when he left the room. Ommony strode to
the door, opened it wide, looked into the frightened eyes
of the Goanese and watched him until he disappeared
through a swinging door at the end of the passage.

"Now," he said, shutting the door tight behind him.

"The Lama is gone!" Dawa Tsering announced dra-
matically. "If I had had my knife I would have slain
the impudent devil who gave me the news! Tripe out of
the belly of a pig is his countenance! Eggs are his eyes!
He is a *ragyaba!** The son of evil pretended not to know

---

*Ragyabas are the lowest dregs of Tibetan society, who live on
the outskirts of towns and dispose of the dead. When used, as in
this case, as an adjective, the word has significance too horrible to
be translated. The man was, of course, *not* a ragyaba.

me! When I offered him the letter for the Lama he growled that Tsiang Samdup and his *chela* had gone elsewhere. When I bade him let me in, that I might see for myself, he answered ignorantly.''

"Ignorantly? How do you mean?"

"He struck me with a bucket, of which the contents were garbage unsuitable to a man of my distinction. So I crowned him with the bucket—thus—not gently—and his head went through the bottom of the thing, so that, as it were, he wore a helmet full of smells and could no longer see. So then I smote him in the belly with my fist —thus—and with my foot—thus—as he fell. And then I came away. And there is the letter. Smell it. Behold the *dirt* on it, in proof I lie not. Now give me my knife, Ommon*ee*.''

Ommony went into the hall and produced the "knife" from behind the hat-rack. Dawa Tsering thumbed the edge of the blade lovingly before thrusting the weapon into its leather scabbard inside his shirt.

"Now I am a man again," he said devoutly. "They would better avoid me with their buckets full of filth!"

Ommony studied him in silence for a moment. "Did you ever have a bath?" he asked curiously.

"Aye. Tsiang Samdup and his *chela* made me take one whenever they happened to think fit. That is how I know they are not especially holy. There is something heretical about them that I do not understand.''

"I am worse than they," said Ommony.

"No doubt. They have their good points.''

"I have none! You must wash yourself as often as I tell you, and I shall give the order oftener than they did! From now on, you are my servant.''

"But who says so?"

"I do.''

"You desire me?"

"No, because I already have you. I can dispose of you as I see fit," said Ommony. "I can send you to the jail for killings and for train-robberies, and for trying to murder me this afternoon. Or I can bid you work out the score in other ways.''

"That is true, more or less. Yes, there is something in what you say, Ommon*ee*."

"It is not more or less true. It is quite true.''

"How so! Have I not my knife! Would you like to fight me! I can slay that she-dog of thine as easily as I can lay thy bowels on the floor.''

"No,'' said Ommony, "no honorable man could do that to his master. Are you not an honorable man!''

"None more so!''

"And I am your master, so that settles it.''

Dawa Tsering looked puzzled; there was something in the reasoning that escaped him. But it is what men do not understand that binds them to others' chariot wheels.

"Well—I do not wish to return to Spiti—yet,'' he said reflectively. "But about the bath—how often! Besides, it is contrary to my religion, now I come to think of it.''

"Change your religion, then. Now no more argument. Which way has the Lama gone!''

"Oh, as to that—I suppose I could discover that. How much will you pay me!''

"Thirty *rupees* a month, clean clothing, two blankets and your food.''

"That is almost no pay at all,'' said Dawa Tsering. "To make a profit at that rate, I should have to eat so much that my belly would be at risk of bursting. There is discomfort in so much eating.''

"They would give you enough to eat and no more, without money, in the jail,'' said Ommony, "and you would have to obey a *babu,* and be shaved by a contractor, and make mats without reward. And if you were very well behaved, they would let you rake the head-*jemadar's* garden. Moreover, Tin Lal, who is also in the jail, would mock you at no risk to himself, since you would have no knife; and because he is clever and malignant he would constantly get you into trouble, laughing when you were punished. And since he is only in the jail for a short time, and you

would be in for a long time, there would be no remedy.
However, suit yourself.''

"You are a hard man, Ommon*ee!*"

"I am. I have warned you."

"Oh, well: I suppose it is better so. A soft knife is
quickly dulled, and men are the same way. Yielding men
are not dependable. Pay me a month's wages in advance,
and to-morrow we will buy the blankets.''

But beginnings are beginnings. A foundation not well
laid destroys the whole edifice.

"From now on until I set you free, *your* desires are
nothing,'' Ommony said sternly. "You consider *my*
needs and *my* convenience. When I have time to consider
yours, it will remain to be seen whether I forget or not.
Go and wait on the porch. Try to make friends with the
dog; she can teach you a lot you must learn in one way or
another. If the dog permits you leisure for thought, try
to imagine which way the Lama may have gone.''

Dawa Tsering went out through the hall, too impressed
by the novelty of the situation even to mutter to himself.
Ommony went to the window and said two or three words
to Diana, whose long tail beat responsively on the teak
boards. Presently came the sound of Dawa Tsering's
voice:

"O thou: my time has not come to be eaten.* Have
wisdom!''

A low rumbling growl announced that Diana was considering the situation, keeping Ommony's command in
mind.

"I have no doubt thou art a very evil devil!''

Again the growl, followed by a thump and the shuffling
sound of Dawa Tsering squatting himself on the porch.

"So—thus. We will see whether Ommon*ee* knows what
he is doing. Attack me, and die, thou mother of fangs and
thunder! Then I will know it is not my *karma* to obey
this Ommon*ee*. Lie still, thou earthquake, and I will—''

---

*Referring of course, to the Tibetan custom of throwing out the
dead to be devoured by dogs.

His voice dropped to a murmur and died away. Thoughts too obscure for expression seemed to have riveted his whole attention. Ommony, peering through the shutter slats, could see him sitting almost within arm's reach of the dog, staring straight in front of him at the stars on the north horizon. He turned to Mrs. Cornock-Campbell:

"And now I'll go away and let you sleep. When we come to your house, Mac and I invariably forget manners and stay into the wee small hours—"

But at a sign from her he sat down again. She closed the piano and locked it. "Cottswold," she said, "tell me what you have in mind. You have said too much or too little."

"I have told all I know—that is that I care to tell, even to you," Ommony answered. "I suppose, as a matter of fact, I'm a bit piqued. That Lama has had scores of opportunities to realize that I wouldn't betray confidences. I am told I'm notorious for refusing to tell the government what I know about individuals; and the Lama is perfectly aware of that. I've risked my job fifty times by insisting on holding my tongue. Am I right, Mac?"

"You are!" McGregor answered with a dry smile. "I remember, I once considered it my duty to advise threatening you with drastic penalties. I would have ordered you tortured, but for the cir-r-cumstance that that means of inducement is out of date. And besides, I had ma doots of its efficacy in your instance."

Ommony grinned. He preferred that praise to all the orders in the almanac. "So, damn the Lama!" he went on fervently. "He has kept aloof for twenty years. I'm satisfied there's something he's deliberately keeping from me. I've no notion what it is, but that piece of jade is probably connected with it. I'm going to track him— tempt him—force his hand."

"Are you sure you've no notion what he's keeping from you?" Mrs. Cornock-Campbell asked; and Ommony stared hard at her, while McGregor blew smoke at the ceiling.

"Perhaps I have a sort of notion—yes," he answered slowly. "Sometimes I suspect he knows what took Fred Terry and my sister to the Ahbor country."

"And?"

Mrs. Cornock-Campbell studied him with dark blue eyes that seemed to search for something lacking in his mental make-up.

"He may know what became of them."

Mrs. Cornock-Campbell smiled and sighed. "Well—we three will meet again before you go, I suppose?"

"No," said Ommony. "I expect to be gone before daybreak. I'll write when I get the chance. If we don't meet again this side of Yama's* Bar—"

"This is India—it might happen," she answered. "Your friendship has been one of five things that have made my life in India worth while."

"Oh, nonsense," he said gruffly. The least trace of sentiment frightened him.

"I'm glad I've helped," she went on. "It's a privilege to have friends like you and John McGregor, who don't imagine they're in love when you share their confidences! Good night. I don't believe you're going to your doom. I think I'd know it if you were."

"Doom? There isn't any! There's only a reshuffling of the cards," said Ommony. "Good night."

---

*Yama (pronounced yum) is the name of the god, in the Hindu pantheon, who judges the souls of the dead.

We live in the eternal Now, and it is Now that we create our destiny. It follows, that to grieve over the past is useless and to make plans for the future is a waste of time. There is only one ambition that is good, and that is: so to live Now that none may weary of life's emptiness and none may have to do the task we leave undone.

FROM THE BOOK OF THE SAYINGS OF TSIANG SAMDUP.

CHAPTER VIII

THE MIDDLE WAY

No MAN can learn any more of India in twenty years,
or in any length of time, than he can learn about himself;
and that is a mystery, but it is the door to understanding.
And that is why men like Ommony and John McGregor,
who have given to India the whole of their active lives,
will say in good faith that they know very little about the
country. It is also why they are guarded in their praise
of viceroys, and candidly suspicious of all politicians;
why they listen to the missionary with emotion not entirely disconnected from cold anger; and why, when they
return to England in late life, ripened by experience, they
do not become leaders of men. Knowing how easily and
how often they have deceived others and themselves have
been deceived, they do not dare to pose as prophets.

However, there are naturally some things that they do
know, guide-books, government reports and "experts"
notwithstanding.

They know (some of them) that news travels up and
down India without the aid of wire, semaphore or radio,
and faster than any mechanical means yet invented can
imitate. It seems to travel almost with the speed of
thought, but although it gets noised abroad none will ever
tell which individual released it.*

They also know that there are routes of travel, uncon-
nected with the railway lines or trunk roads, not marked
by recognizable signposts, and obscure to all who have not
the key to them. Some of these routes are suspected to

---

*There is the notorious instance of the news of Lord Roberts'
relief of Kandahar reaching Bombay long before the government in
Simla knew the facts. See *Forty Years in India,* by Lord Roberts.

89

be religious in their origin and purpose; some are political, (and those are better understood). Some, they say, are survivals of forgotten periods of history when conquered people had to devise means of communication that could be kept absolutely secret from the conqueror.

At any rate, the routes are there, and are innumerable, crossing one another like lines on the palm of a man's hand. A man with the proper credentials (and whatever those are, they are neither written nor carried on the person) can travel from end to end of India, not often at high speed, but always secretly; and the strange part is, that he may cross a hundred other routes as unknown to himself as the one he travels by is secret from other people.

The routes are opened, closed and changed mysteriously. The men who use them seldom seem to know their exact detail in advance, and the fact that a man has traveled once by one of them (or even a dozen times) is no proof that he can return the same way. The underground route by which runaway slaves were smuggled from South to North before the Civil War in the United States is a crude and merely suggestive illustration of how the system works; and one thing is certain: these so-to-speak "underground" communications have nothing whatever to do with the ordinary pilgrim routes, although they may cross them at a thousand points. Like eternity, they seem to have neither beginning, end, nor relation to time; midnight is as high noon, and you cut into them at any time or point you please—provided that you know how.

"Hotel, I suppose?" said McGregor, tooling the dog-cart along at a slow trot through the deserted streets. (They were deserted, that is, of apparent life, but there are always scores of eyes alert in India.)

"No. Set me down in the Chandni Chowk. I'll tell you where to stop."

"Man alive, you can't go scouting in a dinner jacket!"

"Why not?" Ommony asked obstinately.

McGregor did not answer.

Ommony spoke his mind in jerky sentences.

"To-morrow morning—*this* morning, I mean, be a good chap—pack my things at the hotel—forward them all to Tilgaun. Send some one you can trust. Let him leave them with Miss Sanburn—bring back a receipt to you."

"Money?" asked McGregor, nodding.

"Plenty. If I need more I'll cash drafts on Chutter Chand."

"What name will you sign on them? I'd better warn him, hadn't I?"

"No need. I'll make a mark on the drafts that he'll recognize."

"Going to take the dog with you?"

"Of course."

McGregor smiled to himself. Ommony noticed it.

"By the way, Mac, don't try to keep track of me."

"Um-m-m!" remarked McGregor.

Ommony's jaw came forward.

"I *might* not know but *they* would, Mac. You can't keep a thing like that from them. They'd close the Middle Way against me."

McGregor whistled softly. The Middle Way to Nirvana* is no particular secret; any one may read of it in any of a thousand books, and he may tread that Path who dares to declare war on desire. But that is esoteric, and no concern of the Secret Service. Exoterically speaking, "The Middle Way" is a trail that for more than a century the Secret Service has desired to learn with all its inquisitive heart.

---

*Nirvana. The ultimate object of attainment for the Buddhist. The word has been translated "nothingness," and the non-Buddhist missionaries are responsible for the commonly accepted and totally false belief that it means "extinction." The truth is that by "Nirvana" the Buddhist means a condition which it is utterly impossible for the human mind to comprehend, but which can be attained, after thousands of reincarnations, by strict adherence to the Golden Rule—that is, by deeds and abstaining from deeds not by words and self-indulgence. It is said that the understanding of what is meant by "Nirvana" will dawn gradually on the mind of him who is tolerant and strives unselfishly.

"I mean it, Mac. All bets are off unless you promise."

"You needn't betray confidences," said McGregor. "You're not responsible, if I keep tabs on you."

"That's a naked lie, and you know it, Mac! I can get through, if I burn all bridges. I haven't learned what little I do know by letting you know what I was doing. You know that."

"Um-m-m! If you're killed—or *disappear?*"

"That's my look-out."

"As a friend, you're all right. As an assistant, you're a disappointing, independent devil!" said McGregor. "You're as useful as a bellyache to open a can of corned beef with! All right. Dammit. Have your own way. Remember, I shall take you at your word. If you're ditched, there's no ambulance."

"Splendid! Then here's where I vanish—pull up by that lamp-post, won't you? Well—so long, old chap. Nothing personal—eh, Mac?"

"No, damn you! Nothing personal. I wish I were coming with you. Good luck. Good-by, old chap."

They did not shake hands, for that might have implied that there was a dwindling friendship, to be bridged or denied recognition. Diana sprang down from behind and Dawa Tsering followed her. McGregor drove away, not looking back, and the *sais*—the sole occupant now of the back seat—sat with folded arms, staring straight along the middle of the street. But Ommony took no chances with the *sais;* he watched until the dog-cart turned a corner before he made a move of any kind.

Then he walked straight to a door between two shop-fronts and pounded on it. He had to wait about three minutes before the door was opened—gingerly, at first, then after a moment's inspection, suddenly and wide.

A very sleepy-looking Jew confronted him—a Jew of the long-nosed type, with the earlock that betokened orthodoxy. He had a straggly beard, which he stroked with not exactly nervous but exceedingly alert long fingers.

"Ommony! This time of night?" he said in perfectly

good English; but there was nothing that even resembled
English about his make-up. He wore a turban of embroidered silk and a Kashmir shawl thrown over a cotton
shirt and baggy pantaloons. His bare feet showed through
the straps of sandals.

"Let me in, Benjamin."

The Jew nodded and, holding a lantern high, led the
way down a passage beside a staircase into a big room at
the rear, that was piled with heaps of clothing—costumes
of every kind and color, some new, some second-hand, some
worthy to be reckoned antiques. There were shelves stacked
with cosmetics and aromatic scents. There were saddles,
saddle-cloths and blankets; tents and camp-equipment;
yak-hair shirts from over the Pamirs; prayer-mats
from Samarkhand; second-hand dress suits from London;
silk-hats, "bowlers," turbans; ancient swords and pistols;
match-locks, adorned with brass and turquoise and notched
in the butt suggestively. And there was a smell of all
the ends of Asia, that Diana sniffed and deciphered as
a Sanskrit scholar reads old manuscripts.

"I will have tea brought," said Benjamin, setting down
the lantern and shuffling away in the dark toward the
stairs. The impression was that he wanted time to think
before indulging in any conversation.

Ommony sat down on a heap of blankets and beckoned
Dawa Tsering to come closer to the light.

"Now you know where to find me," he said abruptly.
"When the Jew returns he shall let you out by the back
door. Find your way to that house in the courtyard.
Tell those Tibetans that unless that letter—you still have
it?—is delivered to the Lama, *he shall never get that for
which he came to Delhi.* Do you understand?"

"Do you take me for a fool, Ommon*ee?* You mean
if he receives this letter he shall have the green stone?
But that is the talk of a crazy man. Tell him he must *buy*
the stone, and then let me do the bargaining!"

Ommony betrayed no more impatience than he used to
when he was teaching the puppy Diana the rudiments of

her education. "I see I have no use for you after all," he
said, looking bored.

"Huh! A blind man could see better than that. It
is as clear as this lantern-light that you and I are destined
to be useful to each other. Nay, Ommon*ee*, I will not go
away!—What is that? I am not worth paying? Is *that*
so! Very well, I will stay and serve for nothing!—Do you
hear me, Ommon*ee*? Huh! Those are the words of a
great one—of a bold one—but it is nothing to me that you
will not have me thrown into prison if I get hence.—I say
I will *not* go away!—You will not answer, eh?—Very well
I will go with the letter and that message. *Then* we will
see! One of these days you will tell me I was right.
Where is that Jew *bunnia?*"*

Benjamin came shuffling back along the passage, looking like an elongated specter as he stood in the door with
the dark behind him. Dawa Tsering swaggered up to him
demanding to be let out, and from behind the Hillman's
back Ommony made a signal indicating the back door.
Benjamin, very wide awake now and taking in everything
with glittering black eyes, picked up the lantern and, leaving Ommony in the dark, led the way into another large
room at the rear, out of which a door opened into an
alley.

"That one not only has a stink, he has a devil! Beware
of him, Ommony!" he said, returning and sitting down on
the blanket pile, making no bones about it, not waiting for
an invitation. He and Ommony were evidently old friends.
"My daughter will bring for us tea in a minute. Hey-hey!
We have all grown older since you hid us in that forest of
yours—where the ghosts are, Ommony, and the wolves
and the tigers! Gr-r-r-agh! What a time that was! Our
own people lifting hands against us! None but you believing us innocent! Tch-tch-tch! That cave was a place
of terrors, but your heart was good. I left my middle-age
in that cave, Ommony. Since fifteen years ago I am an
old man!"

*Merchant.

The daughter came, carrying another lantern and a brass Benares tray,—a large-eyed woman with black hair, plump and the wrong side of forty, dressed in the Hindu fashion, her big breasts bulging under a yellow silk shawl. She made as much fuss over Ommony as if he were a long-lost husband but embarrassed him hardly at all, because she did not use English and the eastern words sounded less absurd than flattery does in any western tongue.

"The son-in-law? Aha!" said Benjamin, "Mordecai does well. He is in Bokhara just now; but that is a secret. He buys Bokhara pieces from the Jews who became poor on account of the Bolshevism. *Tay-yay!* It is a long way to Bokhara, and no protection nowadays. We win or lose a fortune, Ommony!"

The daughter poured tea into China cups that had once been a rajah's and the three drank together as if it were a sacred rite, touching cups and murmuring words that are not in any dictionary. Then the daughter went away and Ommony, leaning back against the wall, with Diana's great head on his lap, discussed things with Benjamin that would have made McGregor's ears burn if he had had an inkling of them.

"Yes, Ommony, yes. I know which way the Lama travels. How do I know—eh? How was it you knew that a she-bear had a young one with her. Because she ground her teeth—wasn't that so? Well, I didn't know that, but I know a little about the Lama. Let me think. There is danger, Ommony, but—but—" (Benjamin's eyes shone, and his fingers worked nervously, as if they were kneading something concrete out of unseen ingredients) "—you love danger as I love my daughter!—You remember the time when you secured the costume business for me in the Panch Mahal in Pegu—when the rajah married and spent a fortune in a week?"

Ommony nodded. Together he and Benjamin had done things that are not included in the lives of routine loving mortals—things that are forbidden—things that the orthodox authorities declare are not so. And there is mirth in memories of that kind, more than in all the comedies at which one pays legitimately to look on. Benjamin cackled and stroked his beard reminiscently.

"Did the rajah ever learn that you and I were actors in that play? Heh-heh-heh! Did the priests ever discover it? Teh-teh-teh-heh-heh! Oh, my people! Eh-heh! You remember how the nautch-girls were inquisitive? Ommony, you had the key to the temple crypts in your hand that minute! What actresses they were! What incomparable artists! And what children! The half of them were in love with you, and the other half were so devoured by curiosity—*akh*, how they wriggled with it!—they would have betrayed the chief priest at a nod from you! And didn't they dislike me! I haven't your gift, Ommony, for getting into the hearts; I can only see behind the brains. And what I see—but never mind. What times! What times! Did you never follow that up? Did you penetrate the crypt? Did you now?"

"No time. Had to get back to work."

"Ah, well—you wouldn't tell me, I suppose. But why not once more be an actor? Ommony, you know *all* the Hindu plays. I have seen you act Pururavas and—well—believe me—I sat and pinched myself—I am telling you the truth!—and even so—but listen: the Lama Tsiang Samdup is planning to take a company of actors North for certain reasons!"

It would have been hard for any one who did not know him intimately to believe that Ommony, as he sat there against the wall in an ultra-conservative English dinner jacket, could act any part except that of an unimaginative Englishman. There was not one trace of Oriental character about him, nor a hint of artistry. The only suggestion that he might be capable of more than met the eye was Benjamin's manifest affection—admiration—half-familiar, half-obsequious respect.

"I'm ready for anything," he said in a matter-of-fact voice. "The question is—"

"Do you dare! That is the question. Hah! You have

the courage of a Jew! Dare you act *all* parts, Ommony?
Oh—oh, but the risk is—Listen! There is a troupe of
actors—''

Benjamin's long fingers began to knead the air excited-
ly, but Ommony sat still, staring straight before him,
frowning a little—aware that Benjamin was itching to
divulge a confidence.

"Their director, Ommony, is a man named Maitraya—
His best male actor died—He will have to act the leading
rôles himself unless—''

"I don't see the advantage," Ommony objected. But
he did—he saw it instantly.

"Listen, Ommony! No bargain is a good one unless all
concerned in it are gainers! Maitraya owes me money.
He can not pay. He is honest. He would pay me if he
could. I hold his *hundis**. I could ruin him. He *must*
do as I say! Now listen! Listen!—there would be a
solution of his difficulties, and—I might even be willing
to advance just a little more money for his needs. He
would not need much—just a little. And he must do as
I say—you understand? He must take you if I say so.
The Lama commissioned *me* to engage the actors—''

"But won't he want to know all about the actors?"
Ommony asked guardedly. He knew better than to turn
down Benjamin's proposals point-blank.

Benjamin grew suddenly calm, shot one keen glance at
Ommony and changed his weapon, so to speak, into the
other hand. It began to be clear enough that Benjamin
had irons of his own to heat.

"Of course, if you ask *me*, Ommony—if you were to
ask *my* advice—as a man to a man of business—I would
ask you, why not go straight to Tilgaun, and there wait
for the Lama? He is searching you say for a piece of
jade, which is in your possession. Will he not follow you
to Tilgaun, if you go straight there? How much trouble
you would save! How much risk you would avoid!''

*Promissory notes.

"And how much information I might lose!"

"Show me the jade, Ommony."

"Can't. I've sent it to Tilgaun. The Lama doesn't know that. He thinks I've got it with me."

"Well? Then if you go to Tilgaun, won't he follow you?"

"Undoubtedly. But I prefer to follow *him*. It's this way: you and I, Benjamin, have been friends for fifteen years, haven't we? If you have anything you want to keep from me—I don't doubt there are lots of things— you tell me point-blank, and I'm careful to shut my eyes and ears. If I stumble on anything by accident, I dismiss it from mind; I forget it. If you tell me a secret in confidence, I keep it a secret—take no advantage of you. I know you treat me in the same way. But the Lama is supposed to have been my friend for twenty years, although I've never met him to speak to—never saw him until yesterday. He has always managed *not* to meet me, without ever giving any reason for it; and he has conveyed the impression that he is keeping some great secret from me, without having the courtesy to ask me to restrain natural curiosity. Now comes this piece of jade, with all sorts of mysterious side-issues. He traces it into my hands. Instead of asking me for it, and asking me, as one friend to another, not to follow up the mystery, he spies on me—deliberately counts on my honesty and courtesy—and keeps out of sight. He plans to meet me at Tilgaun, where his arm might be lots longer than mine. I used to consider him a wise old Saint, but lately he has made me suspect him of deep mischief. His spying on me is an open invitation to me to spy on *him*. I propose to find out all I can about him. If he has been using me as a stalking-horse all these years—"

"You could begin at Tilgaun, Ommony, just as easily as here," said Benjamin, stroking his beard. His eyes were glittering eagerly, but friendship apparently imposed the obligation to find fault with a plan if possible before helping to carry it out.

"No. He wants me to go straight to Tilgaun. I don't propose to play into his hands. The place to begin to unravel a mystery is at one or the other end of it."

"He may have traced you to my place, Ommony. If you should go with Maitraya, the Lama will know it. If he thinks you have the stone in your possession, he will—"

"Probably try to steal the stone. I'm hoping he will exhaust his ingenuity. I can create a mystery on my own account; he'll be puzzled. He won't dare to have me murdered until he knows for certain where the stone is. For fear of losing track of it altogether, he'll have to do everything possible to preserve my life and to save me from exposure."

"If he is clever, *he* will go straight to Tilgaun!" said Benjamin. "That is what I would do in his place. Then *you* would have to follow *him*."

"If he does that, well and good. But if my guess is right, he has a whole network of intrigue to attend to. He proposed to have me cool my heels in Tilgaun while he attended to business on the way."

Benjamin began to pace the floor between the heaps of assorted clothing. He seemed to be torn between personal interest and desire to give Ommony the soundest possible advice. He muttered to himself. His arms moved as if he were arguing. Once he stood still with his back toward Ommony and bit his nails. Then he walked the floor again three or four times, almost stopping each time as he passed Ommony. At last he stood still in front of him.

"If I tell you—things that I should not tell—what will you think of me?" he asked.

Ommony laughed abruptly. "Suppose I tell you first what I think you have in mind!" he said. "You old simpleton! Why do you suppose I came straight to you at this hour of the night?" (He glanced up at the wall behind him.) "You didn't get that devil-mask in Delhi! It's hanging there to inform some sort of Tibetans that they've come to the right place. I've known for more than nine years that you're the business agent for a mon-

astery in the Ahbor country. However, it's your secret—
you don't have to tell me a thing you don't want to.''

Benjamin stared at him—a rather scandalized, a rather
astonished, a rather sly old Benjamin, with his turban a
little to one side and his lower lip drooping. There was
a hint of terror in his eyes.

"How much else do you know? You? Ommony!"
he demanded.

"Nothing. That is—no more than a blind man who
knew you intimately couldn't help knowing. Shut up,
if you want to. I don't pry into my friends' affairs, and
you're not like the Lama. You've kept nothing from me
I was entitled to know.''

"Not—not like the Lama! Ommony—if *you* knew!"

Benjamin began mumbling to himself in Spanish, but
there were Hebrew words interspersed with it. Ommony,
knowing no Hebrew or Spanish, let him mumble on,
frowning as if busy with his own thoughts. There was
still an hour before dawn, when the stirring of a thousand
other thoughts would inevitably break the chain of this
one—plenty of time for Benjamin to outpour confidences
—nothing to be gained by urging him.

"Tsiang Samdup the Lama is good—he is better than
both of us!" Benjamin said at last emphatically. He
seemed to be trying to convince himself. "God forbid
that I should play a trick on him! But—but—"

Not a word from Ommony. To all appearance he was
brown-studying over something else, twisting Diana's ear,
staring into the shadows beyond the lantern, so intent on
his own thoughts that he did not move when a rat scurried
over his feet. Benjamin burst into speech suddenly:

"Fifteen—nearly sixteen years, Ommony, I have been
agent for the Lama Tsiang Samdup! You would never
believe the things he buys! Not ordinary things! And he
pays with bullion—gold bars! Wait—I show you!"

He unlocked a safe in the corner of the store and produced three small bars of solid gold, giving them to Ommony to weigh in the palm of his hand. But there was

no mark upon them; nothing to identify their place of origin.

"I have had dozens like those from him—dozens!"

But Ommony could not be tempted to ask questions; he knew Benjamin too well—suspected that Benjamin was too shrewd an old philosopher to engage in nefarious trade; also that he was itching to divulge a confidence. If you scratch a man who itches, impulse ceases. Besides, he was perfectly sincere in not wanting to pry into Benjamin's private affairs. To listen to them was another matter. Benjamin came and sat down on the pile of blankets—laid a hand on Ommony's shoulder—thrust his chin forward, and screwed his eyes up.

"If he should know I told—"

"He'll never learn from me."

"Girls! Nice—little—young ones!"

Ommony looked startled—stung. There was the glare in his eyes of a man who has been scurvily insulted.

"Little European girls! Little orphans! Seven! Eh, Ommony? Now what do you think? And all the supplies for them—constantly—books—little garments. Ah! But they grow, those young ones! Stockings! Shoes! Now, what do you think of that?"

"Are you lying?" Ommony asked in a flat voice.

"*Would* I lie to you! *Would* I tell it to any other man. First to get the girls—and such a business! Healthy they must be, and well born—that is, nicely born. And the first was a little Jewess, eight years old at that time, from parents who were killed in Stamboul. That was not so very difficult; a Jew and his wife whom I knew intimately brought her as their own child to Bombay; and after that it was easy to dress her as a Hindu child, and to pretend she was a little young widow, and to smuggle her northward stage by stage. And once she reached Delhi there was the Middle Way, Ommony, the Middle Way! Hah! It was not so difficult. And the profit was very good."

"I'm waiting for you to hedge," said Ommony. "So far, I simply don't believe you."

"Well: the next was eleven years old, and she made trouble. She was the child of a sea-captain who was hanged for shooting drunken sailors. Some missionaries took care of her; but they said things about her father, and she ran away—from Poona—the mission was in Poona. So, of course, there was a search, and much in the newspapers. We had to hide her carefully. The missionaries offered a reward, but she did not want to go back to the missionaries. In many ways her character was such as Tsiang Samdup wished. And in the end we conveyed her by bullock-*gharri* all the way from Bombay to Ahmedabad, where we kept her several months in the home of a Hindu midwife. Then the Middle Way. The Middle Way is easy, when you know it.

"The third was from Bangalore—and she was only nine months old—no trouble at all—the daughter of a very pretty lady who was engaged to be married—but the man died. She gave the baby to my wife's sister. That child went North in the arms of a Tibetan woman from Darjiling.

"And the fourth was from London—a Russian musician's daughter. And the fifth was from Glasgow. And the sixth from Sweden, or so it was said. Those three were all about the same age—six, or seven, or thereabouts.

"The seventh—she was nine years old, and the best of them all—was from New York—born in New York—or at sea, I forget which. Her father, an Irishman, died and the mother, who was English, went to visit her people in England. But the people had died too. So she went back to America, and there was some difficulty in connection with the immigration laws. She was not allowed to land. She had to return to England, where there was destitution and I know not what followed after that, though it is easy to imagine things. The mother was dying, and I was told she wished above all things to save the child from being put in an institution. Some people who are well known to me offered to care for the child. It happened I was in London, Ommony. I went and saw the

mother; and, since she was dying, I took a chance and
told her certain things; and perhaps because she was
dying, and therefore could understand and see around the
corner, as it were, she agreed. We had conversed, as you
might say, heart to heart. It was I who brought that child
to India. I had to adopt her legally, and—oh, Ommony,
if I could have kept her! She was like my little own
daughter to me! But what was there that *I* could do for
her—an old Jew, here in Delhi? Money, yes; but nothing
else, and money is nothing. It broke my heart. She went
northward by the Middle Way—you know what I mean
by the Middle Way?"

Ommony's expression was stone-cold; he was speech-
less. He eyed Benjamin with a hard stare that had
reached the rock-bottom of revelation and disgust. He
did not dare to speak. Having pledged his word in advance not to betray Benjamin's secrets, his word was
good; there was no hesitation on that score. A deliberate
promise, in his estimation, stood above all obligations, whatever the consequences to himself. But he felt that sickening sensation of having trusted a man who turned out to
be rotten after all.

He did not dare to say a word that might give Benjamin an inkling of his real feelings. He must use the
man as an ally. In a way he was indebted to him—for
information as to the Lama's real activities. No wonder
the Lama had kept so carefully aloof! Ommony forced
himself to smile—battling with the horror of the thought
of being co-trustee with a Tibetan, who with his right
hand helped to run a philanthropic mission and with his
left imported European girls, for the Powers of Evil only
knew what purpose. There are other purposes, as well
as crude vice, for which children may be stolen. His own
sister—

"You say Tsiang Samdup is better than both of us?"
he remarked at last, surprised at the evenness of his own
voice.

"*Much* better!" said Benjamin. "Ah, Ommony—I see

your face. Old I am. Blind I am not. But listen: have
you seen what happens to the children whose parents die
or desert them? Not the children of the poor; the little
girls who are well born, who feel things that other children do not feel. I am a Jew—I know what feeling is!
Hah! I have seen animals in cages who were happier!
And what is happiness? Provision of necessities? Bah!
They provide necessities for men in jail—and will you
search in the jails to find happiness? I will show you
thousands who have all they want, and nothing that they
need! You understand me? Tsiang Samdup—"

"Never mind," said Ommony, "I'll find out for myself." He did not want to talk; he was afraid of what
he might hear—still more of what he might say. There
are some men, who present an impassive face toward the
world, who can face death grinning and are not afraid of
"the terror that moveth by night" or "the pestilence that
stalketh at noonday," who would rather be crucified than
reveal the horror they have for a certain sort of traffic.
Their emotion, too sacred, or too profane to be discussed,
is nameless—indescribable—only to be borne with set
teeth.

"Ah! I know!" said Benjamin. "I know you, Ommony! What I have said is secret; therefore you don't
wish to hear any more, because you are too much a man
to violate what is told in confidence. And you have made
no promise to the Lama. Am I right?"

Ommony nodded—grimly. That was the one bright
point of light.

"I could tell—I could tell much," Benjamin went on.
"But I saw you shut your mind against me. As well
pour oil on fire to put it out as talk to a man who mis-
trusts! Very well. We have been friends, you and I.
Remember that, Ommony. And now this: you believe in
a devil—some kind of a devil—all Englishmen do. You
believe I am a devil—Benjamin, your friend, whom you
hid in a cave in your forest—me and my wife and my
daughter. We are devils. Very well. A promise that

is made to the devil has not to be kept, Ommony! Go and
see for yourself. I will help you. When you have seen,
you shall judge. Then, after that, if you say I am a devil,
you shall break your faith with me. You shall denounce
me. I will let you be the judge.''

"Have you ever been into the Ahbor country?'' Ommony asked. His voice was sullen now. There was a
leaden note in it.

"No,'' Benjamin answered.

"And those—those children went to the Ahbor country?''

"Yes.''

"Then what proof have you of what the Lama has done
with them?''

"Ommony—as God is my witness—I have none! I
think—I—I am almost positively sure—but—''

He paced the floor twice, and then flung himself down
on the blankets beside Ommony, looking up into his face.
He was afraid at that moment, if ever man was.

"That is why I have told you! I swore never to tell!
Find out, Ommony! Tell the truth to *me* before I die.
I am an old man, Ommony. If I have been a devil, I will
eat—eat—eat the shame to the last crumb! Ommony, I
swear—by my fathers I swear, I believe—I am almost
positively sure—''

He buried his face in his hands, and there was silence,
in which Ommony could hear Diana's quiet breathing and
his own heart-beats and the ticking of the watch in his
vest-pocket.

When the actor, having thrown aside the costume and the wig, departs—is he a villain? Shall we take stones and murder him because for our amusement he enacted villainy?

If he should act death in the play because decency demands that, do we therefore burn him afterward and curse his memory? And is his wife a widow?

And is life not like the play? The gods who watch the drama know that somebody must play the villain's part, and somebody the pauper's. They reward men for the acting. He who acts a poor part well receives for his reward a more important part when his turn shall come to be born again into the world.

He, therefore, who is wise plays pauper, king or villain with the gods in mind.

FROM THE BOOK OF THE SAYINGS OF TSIANG SAMDUP.

CHAPTER IX

"GUPTA RAO"

Dawn came and no Dawa Tsering. Pale light through cobwebbed windows drove the dark into corners and consumed it, until the devil-mask on the wall over Ommony's head grinned like a living thing and the street noises began, announcing that Delhi was awake. Diana stirred and sniffed, mistrusting her surroundings, but patient so long as Ommony was satisfied to be there. Benjamin shuffled away to the stairs. The daughter came, fussily, fatly hospitable, with *chota hazri** on the brass Benares tray—fruit, tea, biscuits, and a smile that would have won the confidence of Pharaoh, Ruler of the Nile.

But Ommony's heart had turned harder than Pharaoh's ever did. He could hardly force himself to be civil. He drank the tea and ate the fruit because he needed it, unconscious now of any ritual of friendship in the act, answering polite inquiries with blunt monosyllables, his mind and memory working furiously, independently of any efforts at conversation. His face was a mask, and a dull one at that, with no smile on it. The iron in him had absolute charge.

He was not by any means the sort of man who flatters himself.

"You damned, deluded fool!" he muttered pitilessly, and Diana opened one eye wide, awaiting action.

He blamed himself, as mercilessly as he always had been merciful to others, for having acted as the Lama Tsiang Samdup's foil for twenty years. Above all things he despised a smug fool, and he called himself just that. He

---

*Early breakfast.

107

should have suspected the Lama long ago. He should have
seen through Benjamin. He had believed his trusteeship
of the Tilgaun Mission was a clean and selfless contribu-
tion to the world's need. Why hadn't he resigned then
from his government job long ago to devote his whole career to the trust he had undertaken? If he had done that,
he knew no Lama could have hoodwinked him. No little
girls would have been smuggled then into the unknown
by way of Tilgaun.

The self-accusation case-hardened him. He set his teeth,
and almost physically reached out for the weapons of
alertness, patience, persistence, cunning, with which he
might redeem the situation. For redeem it he surely
would, or else perish in the attempt. Exposure too soon
would do no good. He needed full proof. And he cared
less to punish the offenders than to rescue the children who
had been carried off, and to make anything of the sort
impossible in future, wondering, as he considered that,
what any one would be able to do for girls in their predicament. The early years are the most impressionable;
their characters would have been undermined. And then
a worse thought: was Benjamin the only agent? There
might be a regular market for European girls in that unknown corner of the earth, with secret agents supplying
it from a dozen sources. If so, he felt and accepted his
full share of responsibility. Who else could share it with
him? Only Hannah Sanburn. She, too, had shielded the
Lama and, if ignorant of what was going on, might at
least have suspected.

And thoughts of Hannah Sanburn did not give comfort.
He remembered now a dozen incidents that should have
made him suspect *her* years ago. That look in her eyes,
for instance, and her nervousness whenever he had urged
her to bring about a meeting between the Lama and himself. He recalled now how carefully she had always shepherded him through the mission, under pretext of observing the proprieties; she had never given him a chance to
talk alone with any of the mission girls, and like a fool he

had believed she did that to prevent the very suggestion of scandal from finding an excuse. He had admired her for it. But there was that room (or was it two rooms) near her own quarters that she had always kept locked, and that he had not cared to ask to inspect, because she said she kept her personal belongings in there.

And now this story, told by Mrs. Cornock-Campbell, a witness as trustworthy as daybreak, of a white girl named Elsa, who spoke English and Tibetan, who had been to Lhassa, and who could draw—for he had seen the drawings—as masterfully as Michael Angelo. And Hannah Sanburn's plea for secrecy. And the fact that McGregor had had suspicions.

Marmaduke might not have been the father of this strange girl, but that did not preclude the possibility of Hannah Sanburn being the mother. It seemed likely— more than likely—that the Lama possessed knowledge which enabled him to blackmail Hannah Sanburn; it was easy enough to understand how that well-bred New England woman would fight to preserve her good name, and how, if the Lama had once tempted her into one false position, she could be terrified from bad to worse. There is more deliberate blackmail in the world than most of its indirect victims suspect.

Nevertheless, Ommony wondered that Hannah Sanburn should not have confided in himself. She might have known he would have shielded her and helped her to redeem the situation. She had had dozens of proofs of his friendship. He smiled rather grimly as he thought to what lengths he would have gone to shield and befriend Hannah Sanburn—and yet more grimly—cynically—as it dawned on him to what lengths he might now have to go. Friendship is friendship—unto death if need be.

Benjamin returned; and an hour's thought had had its effect on him too. His assistants came, and he chased them out on hurriedly invented errands, barring the shop door behind them.

"I have sent for Maitraya," he announced, stroking his

beard, watching Ommony sidewise. He seemed to be not
quite sure that Ommony might not have changed his mind
with daylight.

"All right. Hunt me out a costume."

Ommony stepped off the pile of blankets and began to
strip himself. Benjamin's swift fingers sought and
plucked along the shelves, selecting this and that until a
little heap of clothing lay ready on a table, Ommony saying nothing but observing almost savagely, like a caged
man watching his meal prepared.

"There, that is perfect," said Benjamin at last. "A
dude—a dandy, such as actors are—aping the high caste—
too educated to submit to inferiority—a little of this, a
little of that—fashionable—tolerated—half-philosopher,
half-mountebank—"

Stark-naked, Ommony confronted him, and Benjamin
betrayed the naked fear that has nothing to do with physical consequences. Ommony looked straight into his eyes
and analyzed it, as he had done fifteen years ago when he
protected Benjamin against accusers.

"All right, Benjamin. I'll trust you this once more.
But no flinching. See it through."

He dressed himself, Benjamin watching alertly for the
least mistake, but that was an art in which no man in the
world could give Ommony instruction; he knew costumes
as some enthusiasts know postage stamps, and he bound
on the cream-colored silk turban without a glance in the
mirror that Benjamin held for him.

"I'll need an old trunk now, and three or four
changes," he said abruptly. "No, cow-hide won't do—
no, there's glue in that imported thing—observe caste
prejudices, even if I'm supposed to have none—basket-
work's the stuff. That's it. Throw me in a trousseau."

He began to pace the floor, adjusting himself to the
costume, finding it not difficult; his natural, sturdy gait
learned in forest lanes with a gun under his arm, suggested independence and alertness without a hint of drill,
which is the secret of self-assurance; add good manners

to that and an intimate knowledge; there is not much
acting needed.

He looked stout and a bit important in the flowing cotton clothes. The short beard gave him dignity. His skin,
weathered by twenty years of outdoor life, needed no
darkening. Even his legs, and his bare feet thrust into
red morocco slippers had the ivory color that belongs to
most of the higher castes; and an actor must be of Brahman or Kshattryia origin if he hopes to be admitted anywhere within the pale from which the lower castes are
utterly excluded. His profession makes him technically
unclean, but that is rather an advantage than a handicap.

"And the name? The honored name?" asked Benjamin
admiringly.

"Gupta Rao. I'm a Bhat-Brahman of Rajputana."

Benjamin sat down and laughed with his head to one
side, nursing a knee.

"Oh, you Ommony! A Jew you should have been!
Hey-yey-clever! Now who would have thought of that but
you! *Yah-tchah!* Bhat-Brahman—of whom even rajahs are
afraid! Gossiping tongue! The privilege to slander!
Yah-keh-keh-keh! You are a clever one! Not even a
Brahman will challenge you, for fear you will make him
a laughing-stock! *Keh-hah-hah-hey-hey-hey*! Ah, but wait,
wait! We forgot the *pan.* You must have a pouch to
carry betel-nut. And the caste-mark—keep still while I
paint the caste-mark."

And then at last came Dawa Tsering, not pleased with
himself but trying to appear pleased, adjusting his eyes
to the dimness as Benjamin let him in by the back door.

"Where is Ommonee?"

He stared about him, brushed past Ommony contemptuously, and at last saw the cast-off dinner jacket and
white shirt. He broke into the jargon-Hindustani that
serves for lingua franca in that land of a hundred tongues,
chattering as he hurried along the passage past the stairs
and back again:

"Where is he? Is he hiding? Has he gone?" Then,

shouting at last in something near panic: "Oh—Ommon*ee!*"

He stared at Diana, but she gave him no information.
She lay curled up on the floor, apparently asleep. Benjamin looked non-committal—busy considering something
else.

"Where is he—thou?" the Hillman demanded, coming
to a stand in front of Ommony and fingering the handle
of his knife. The light was dim just there where the saddles were piled in a ten-foot heap.

"Would you know his voice?" asked Ommony.

"Aye, in a crowd!"

"Would you know his walk?"

"None better! Seen from behind, when he is. thinking,
he rolls thus, like a bear. But who art thou? Where is
he?"

Ommony turned his back, walked to the heap of blankets by the wall, and sat down.

"Would you know him sitting?" he asked casually; and
suddenly it occurred to Dawa Tsering that he was being
questioned in his own tongue.

"Thou!" he exclaimed. "Well, may the devils destroy
the place! Art thou then a magician?" He sniffed three
times. "Not even the smell is the same! Was it the Jew
who worked the magic? Art thou truly Ommon*ee?*"

"No, I'm changed. I'm Gupta Rao. If you ever call
me Ommony again without my permission, I will bring
to pass a change in your affairs that you will remember!
Do you understand?"

"Gupta Rao—huh? A change—eh! Hmn! And that
is not a bad idea. Change *me*, thou! There are many garments in this place—buy me some of them. That Lama
played a dirty trick on me. He has vanished. I found
his *chela* Samding, and I told him the Lama owes me two
months' pay; and I said 'Where is the Lama?' But
Samding, standing by a covered bullock-cart (but the
cart was empty, for I looked) laughed at me and said
nothing. I would have killed him if I had not thought of

that letter, which you said the Lama *must* receive. So I
slapped Samding's face with the letter, and threw it on
the ground in front of him, and bade him pick it up and
find the Lama or take the consequences. And *he* said,
with that mild voice of his, that I had become very reckless all at once, so I hustled him a time or two, hoping to
make him strike me, that I might with justice strike him
back. But he has no fight in him. He picked up the letter,
holding it thus, because there was dirt on it and he hates
to soil his hands. And he said to me, 'The Lama has no
further use for you!' Do you hear that, thou—what is
thy new name?—Gupta Rao? Did you ever hear the like
of it for impudence? You wonder, I suppose, why I
didn't smite Samding there and then, so that the Lama
would have no further use for *him*. Trust me, I would
have done; but two great devils of Tibetans came out of
a doorway and seized me from behind. Lo, before I could
draw my knife they had hurled me into a party of Sikh
soldiers who were passing, so that I broke up their formation, they blaming *me* for it, which is just like Sikhs. And it
isn't wise to argue with too many Sikhs, so I ran. Now
—what is thy name again? Gupta Rao? Well—it would
now be fitting to disguise me, so that I may come on that
Lama and his *chela* and the whole brood of them unawares. Then let us see what one man can do to half-a-
dozen!''

Ommony got up and began to pace the floor again. It
would be difficult to disguise Dawa Tsering, even if that
were advisable, for the man had a swagger that was as
much a part of him as his huge frame, and a simplicity
that underlay and would inevitably shine through all cunning. Yet the man would be useful, since he knew more
than a little about the Lama's goings and comings; and,
once in the Hills, where a man without an armed friend
has a short life and a sad one as a rule, he would be almost indispensable.

He had not made up his mind what to do when one of
Benjamin's assistants hammered on the shop door and

announced Maitraya. Dawa Tsering sat down beside
Diana, who seemed to have decided he was tolerable, and
Maitraya entered stagily, as if he thought he were a god,
or wished other people to believe him one. He was not a
very big man, but he had a trick of filling up the doorway
and pausing there before he strode into the room to seize
by instinct the most conspicuous position and command
all eyes.

His face was rather wrinkled, but he was richly clothed
in new Tussore silk, with a gorgeous golden *cummerbund*,*
and his gallant bearing tried to give the lie to fifty years.
There were marks on his handsome face that suggested
debauch, but might have been due to former hardship;
his manner on the whole was one of dignity and conscious
worthiness. One could tell at a glance what were his
views on the actor's art and on the position that actors
should hold in the community; in another land he would
have pestered the politicians for a knighthood. A pair of
gorgeous black eyes, that he knew how to use with effect,
glowed under a heavy lock of black hair that he had
carefully arranged to fall in apparent carelessness beneath
his turban.

"You wished to see me, Benjamin?"

His voice was tragic, his language Urdu, his diction re-
fined to the verge of pedantry. Benjamin signed to him
to be seated on a heap of blankets, but he declined the
invitation like Cæsar refusing a throne (except that Cæsar
could not have done it with such super-modesty).

"May all the glorious gods, and above all friendly,
fortunate Ganesha, have worked on you and made you
change your mind, O stubborn Benjamin! Father of
money-bags! Provider of finery for entertaining fools!
Patient, but too cautious Benjamin! May all the gods
melt butter on you for your former trust in me, Maitraya,
—and may they also melt your heart! I need you, Benjamin. I have a bargain with that Lama struck and bound.

---

*Sash.

The man is crazy, and a traitor to all his gods, but he knows a little. God knows they will tear him between wild asses for debauching his religion, when he gets back to Tibet! Believe me or not, Benjamin—although I *hope* my word rings unsuspicious in your ears—he leans toward modern views! Can you imagine that—in a Ringding Lama from Tibet? He proposes just what I have always preached—to modernize the ancient plays, retaining their charm and morality, but making them comprehensible! The man is mad—mad as an American—but genuinely gifted with imagination. It will make me famous, Benjamin.''

"Does he offer to pay you?" Benjamin asked dryly.

"Richly! Princely! Like a maharajah—with the difference—aha!—that he will settle regularly, instead of forcing me to borrow from his special money-lenders (as the rajahs do) while I await his slow convenience. I tell you, Benjamin, the Lord Ganesha surely smiled on me in the hour of this Lama's birth!"

"Did you ask for money in advance?" asked Benjamin.

"Not I, Benjamin. What do you mistake me for—a parasite? A beggar? A man without dignity? A hanger-on of some courtesan? Nay, nay! I remembered my blessed friend Benjamin, who likes to do business at a reasonable profit, and who will be glad to advance me a little more, in order that I may pay what I already owe. Are we not *good* friends, Benjamin? Have I ever defrauded you or told you a word of untruth?"

"A man's word and his deed should be one," Benjamin answered. "I hold your *hundis** that you have not paid. There is interest due on them."

"True, Benjamin, true. I have been unfortunate. Who could have foretold smallpox, the death of three actors, and the burning of a theater? But another might have repudiated, Benjamin. Another might have told you to hunt for your money where the smallpox and the fire are

---

*Promissory notes.

born! *Kali** can care for her own! Did I repudiate?
Did I not come and tell you I will pay in time?''

"The worst is, you are not the only one," said Benjamin. "I have another here, who is heavily in my debt,
although a famous actor, more famous than you, and a
much finer artist. This is Gupta Rao sahib, of Bikanir.''

"I never heard of him," said Maitraya, looking slightly scandalized although prepared to condescend.

"He is a very great actor," said Benjamin. Whereat
Ommony bowed with becoming gravity, and Maitraya
took his measure, up and down.

"Does he act in that beard?" he inquired.

"I have lately been acting the part of an Englishman,"
said Ommony; and his Urdu was as perfect and pedantic
as Maitraya's.

"An Englishman? There are few who can do that with
conviction." Maitraya stepped back a pace. "You don't
look like an Englishman. No wonder you grew a beard.
That is the only way you could have carried off the part
at all without looking foolish. It takes a man of my proportions to play an Englishman properly. I have been
told that I excel at it. I played once before the officers
of a cavalry regiment at Poona, and they assured me they
believed I was an English gentleman until I stepped down
off the stage. Watch this."

Maitraya inserted an imaginary monocle and gave an
outrageous caricature of a stock Englishman as portrayed
in comic papers on the European continent.

"God-dam fine weather, eh? Not bad, eh? What?"

"I see you are a genius," said Ommony. "I could not
do it nearly so well as that."

"No, I dare say not. The actor's is an art that calls
for technique. However, I dare say you are good in conventional parts," said Maitraya, mollified.

" I have seen him and I am a good judge of such matters," said Benjamin. "What I have to say to you, Mai-

---

*Goddess, among other horrors, of the smallpox.

traya, is that I am anxious about the money which you and Gupta Rao owe me.''

Benjamin put on his extra-calculating air, that Jews use to make their customers believe there is something as yet undecided—an alternative course, less profitable to the customer. It is the oldest trick in the world—much older than Moses. Maitraya showed furtive alarm.

''My son-in-law is away on a long journey. It is costing too much. I need the money,'' Benjamin went on. ''I will not advance you more—no, not a *rupee* more—''

''Unless?'' said Maitraya. He was watching the old Jew's face, flattering himself that he could read behind the mask and swallowing the bait as simply as a hungry fish.

''Unless you take Gupta Rao with you—''

''I could give him small parts,'' said Maitraya, cautiously yet with a gorgeous magnanimity.

''As leading actor,'' Benjamin went on, ''on a leading actor's salary, so that he may have a chance to pay me what he owes.''

''But I must first see him act,'' Maitraya objected. ''I promised the Lama a company of actors second to none, and—''

''And on this new *hundi* both your names must go,'' said Benjamin, ''so that you are both responsible, and I can take a lien on Gupta Rao's salary if I so wish.''

That stipulation started a long-winded argument, in which Ommony joined sufficiently to add confusion to it and support Benjamin by pretending to support Maitraya. Benjamin's investment in costumes, theatrical properties and cash might be considerable, and there was no reason why the shrewd old merchant should not protect himself. At the end of an hour of expostulation, imprecation, gesticulation and general pandemonium Benjamin had his way, vowing he had never made a more unprofitable bargain in his life, and Maitraya was convinced that Gupta Rao had at least a rich vocabulary. Moreover, as fellow victims of necessity, with their names on a joint promissory note, they had an excuse for friendship, of which Ommony took full advantage.

"Being of Brahman origin, of course I have access to inner circles, and enjoy privileges that are denied to you; and if I were an ordinary Brahman I would not *join* forces with you. But we Bhats consider ourselves above caste, and when we find an outcaste of merit and distinction, such as you evidently are, we believe it no dishonor to befriend him. You will find it a great advantage to have me in your company, and for many reasons."

Maitraya was readily convinced of that. A Bhat enjoys more privileges than any scald did in the Viking days, for there is none who dares to call him in question and nowadays, at least in Northern India, there is no authority that can discipline him. An orthodox Brahman is very easily kept within bounds, and it is next to impossible for a man of lower caste to pose as a Brahman successfully because at the first suggestion of suspicion he would be questioned narrowly and be required to give substantial proofs; if the proofs were not forthcoming the Brahmans would simply close their ranks against him. But who shall challenge the College of Heralds on points of etiquette?

The very Pundits themselves, who are the fountainheads of orthodoxy, are at the mercy of the Bhats. A Pundit who should challenge a Bhat's veracity or privilege would lay himself open to such scurrilous attack, in song and jest and innuendo, as he could never stand against. He would be in the position of a public man in Europe or America who should dare to defy the newspapers. The only limits to a Bhat's audacity are imposed by his own intelligence and his own gift of invective. He may act, sing, dance in public and be undefiled; he may accept gifts whose very shadow no orthodox Brahman would dare to let fall on his door-step; and that source of strength is the secret of his weakness at the same time, since, like the Press that accepts paid advertising, he has to be careful whose corns he crushes.

Maitraya, finding himself linked with this Gupta Rao
by a contract, which Benjamin would certainly enforce,
began at once to take good care to establish cordial rela-
tions. He was even deferent in his remarks about the
beard.

"Beautiful it is, and manly—good to see, Gupta Rao,
but—for certain parts and certain purposes—will it not
be inconvenient?"

Ommony conceded that point. He withdrew to a little
dark room and removed the beard by candle-light, using
a razor belonging to one of Benjamin's assistants and,
since the skin was paler where the hair had been, rubbing
on a little dark stain afterward. While that was going
on, Maitraya was regaled by Benjamin with accounts of
Gupta Rao's audacity and influence.

"Then why is he not rich?" Maitraya asked. "These
Bhats are notorious for luxury. Everybody gives them
presents, to keep their tongues from wagging."

"That is just it," Benjamin explained. "Too much
luxury! Too many gifts! It spoils them. This one is a
gambler and a patron of the courtesans, who favor him exceedingly. *Tshay-yay-yay!* What a weakness is the love
of women! But he is on his good behavior at present because, says he, a Bikaniri broke his heart. But the truth
is, she only emptied his pockets."

"And that great dog?" Maitraya asked. "To whom
does that belong?"

Benjamin stroked his beard and hesitated. But Ommony had heard every word of the conversation through
the thin partition.

"And that great savage beside the dog—that Northern-
er—who is he?" asked Maitraya.

Ommony emerged, having reached a conclusion at last
as to what should be done with Dawa Tsering and Diana.

"I must count on your honor's sympathy and good
will," he said, smiling at Maitraya rather sheepishly.
"That hound is the agent of *Hanuman**. The man from

---

*The monkey—god—patron of love-affairs.

Spiti is a simpleton, whose service is to keep the hound in good health and to assist with occasional amorous errands. Our friend Benjamin has not told all the truth. Whose heart is broken while he can communicate with his beloved?"

Maitraya smiled. He had acted in too many plays, in which the plot consisted of intrigue between man and woman, not to accept that sort of story at face-value. Life, to him, was either drama or else mere drudgery. Ommony excused himself, to go and talk with Dawa Tsering.

"Now this dog is used to a dog-boy," he said sternly. "Moreover, she will do as I say, and if you are kind to her, she will be tolerant of you."

Diana smelt Ommony over inquisitively. The strange clothes puzzled her but, having nosed them thoroughly, she lay down again and waited.

"She is an incarnation of a devil," said Dawa Tsering. "I am sure of it."

"Quite right. But she is a very friendly devil to her friends. I am going to tell her to look after you; and she will do it. And I order you to look after her. Keep the fleas off her. Attend to it that she is clean and comfortable."

"What then?"

"The Jew shall provide you with new clothing, after you have cleaned yourself. When I go presently, with that man Maitraya, you are to remain here, and you will see that the dog will remain with you willingly. At the proper time you are to come and find me."

"But how, Ommon*ee*? How shall I find you?"

"Don't call me Ommony! Remember that. My name is Gupta Rao."

"That makes you even more difficult to find!"

"You are going to learn what the dog can do. When I send a messenger, the dog will follow him, but you are to remain here, do you understand? You are not to move away on any condition. When it suits my convenience the

dog will return to this place alone and will bring you to
wherever I may happen to be. Do you understand?"

"No, I don't understand, but I will wait and see," said
Dawa Tsering. "I think you would make a good thief on
the te-rains, Om—I mean, Gupta Rao!"

Men agree that prostitution is an evil, and they who know more than I do have assured me this opinion is right. But there are many forms of prostitution, and it may be that among the least of them is that of women, bad though that is. I have seen men sell their souls more inexcusably than women sell their bodies—and with more disastrous consequences—to themselves and to the buyer.

FROM THE BOOK OF THE SAYINGS OF TSIANG SAMDUP.

CHAPTER X

VASANTASENA

IT took five minutes to convince Diana that she was henceforth responsible for Dawa Tsering, but once *that* fact had been absorbed she accepted the duty without complaint. There was no whimper from the hound when Ommony accepted Maitraya's invitation to go in search of the Lama. He and Maitraya, side-by-side in a *tikka-gharri** drove through the crowded streets, now and then passing Englishmen whom Ommony knew well. Members of the mercantile community, Moslems as well as Hindus, bowed to Maitraya from open shop-windows or from the thronged sidewalk as if he were a royal personage. Men who would not have let his clothing touch them, because of the resulting caste-defilement, were eager to have it known that they were on familiar terms with him; for a popular actor is idolized not only in the West.

"You see, they know me!" said Maitraya proudly. "Men whose names I can't remember pay me homage! Actors are respected more than kings and priests—and justly so. *They* rule badly and teach nonsense. It is *we* who interpret—we who hold example up to them!"

The man's vanity delivered him tied and bound to Ommony's chariot wheels. There was nothing to do but flatter him, and he would tell all he knew, accepting the flatterer as guide, philosopher and friend appointed for his comfort by the glorious gods.

"I am surprised that a man of your attainments should condescend to employment by this Lama person," said Ommony. "Of course, if you are willing, so am I, but how did it come about?"

*A one-horse open cab.

123

"You would never believe. He is a very strange Lama
—more unusual than rain in hot weather or the sun at
midnight; but I have a gift for attracting unusual people.
By Jinendra, Gupta Rao, I have never seen the like of
him—even in these days, when everything is upside down!
He has a *chela* by the name of Samding, who has more
genius in his little finger than any dozen statesmen have
in their whole bodies. Not that it would do to tell him
so—I don't believe in flattering beginners—they can't
stand it. And he lacks experience. That Lama must be
a very expert teacher. The first time I met him, he was
one of a crowd who watched me act 'Charudatta' in *The
Toy Cart*—a part that I excel in. Afterward, he invited
me to witness a performance in private by his *chela*, and I
went with him to a mysterious place kept by some Tibetans
at the end of a stone courtyard—the sort of place where
you would expect to be murdered for your shoe-leather—a
place that smelt of rancid butter and incense and donkey-
stables. Whoof! I shudder now, to think of it! But the
chela was marvelous. Calm—you never saw such equi-
poise—such balance of all the faculties! And a voice as
if a god were speaking! The middle note, true as a bell,
like a gong to begin with every time, rising and lowering
from that with utter certainty—half-tones—quarter-tones
—passion, pathos, scorn, command, exhilaration—laughter
like a peal of bells—wait until you have heard it, Gupta
Rao! You will be as thrilled as I was. You will say I did
not exaggerate. Perfect! If only success doesn't turn the
boy's head!"

"What language?" asked Ommony.

"Prepare to be amazed! Ancient Sanskrit—modern
Urdu—with equal fluency and equal grace! Distinct
enunciation—and a command of gesture that expresses
everything, so that you know what he will say before he
speaks! But that is not all. I tell you he is marvelous!
He has the modern touch. He understands how to play
an ancient part so that it means something to the uniniti-
ated. I am already jealous of him! I tell you, when that

boy has had the advantage of my instruction for a while, he will be great—the greatest actor in the world!"

"What proposal did the Lama make?" asked Ommony.

"A crazy one. I told you the man is mad. He proposes to give *free* entertainments—on tour—at places selected by himself—for an indefinite period. I am to provide a troupe of excellent actors, for whom I am to be responsible. There are to be three women among them, but the dancers will be provided by the Lama, as also the music, and Samding the *chela* is to play the leading female parts."

"I'm surprised he takes any women at all," said Ommony. "There's a prejudice against actresses. They're always a nuisance. Properly trained boys are better. If a man plays leading woman, the women will only make him look absurd by contrast."

"Well, that is *his* affair. I suggested that, but the Lama insisted. And mad though he undoubtedly is, he knows his own mind, and is shrewd in some respects. I lied to Benjamin when I said I had not asked for money in advance. I did my best to hold out for that—naturally. But I suspect the Lama knows a lot about me, and he certainly knows Benjamin; he told me to go to Benjamin and to get what credit I may need from him. Do you see the idea? If he and Benjamin have a private understanding, that gives him an extra hold over me—it makes me practically powerless to oppose him in anything, however ridiculous his demands may turn out to be. You see, I have to pay Benjamin's bill. However—here we are."

And where they were was not the least surprising feature of the mystery. The *tikka-gharri* drew up at an arched gate in a high wall, over which trees leaned in well cared for profusion. There were cut flowers tucked into the carving on the arch, and blossoms strewn on the sidewalk. A dozen carriages, most of them with thoroughbred horses, waited in line near the gate, and the dazzling sun projected on the white wall shadows of thirty or forty men in turbans of every imaginable color, who seemed to

have nothing to do but to lounge near the entrance. Some
of them nodded at Maitraya; several salaamed to him; one
or two were at pains to stare insolently.

In the gateway was a fat *chuprassi* with a lemon-colored
silk scarf, and the whitest clothes that ever any man wore
—whiter than the wall, and starched stiff. He stood
guard over about fifty pairs of slippers, most of which
were expensive, and nearly all of which looked new.
There was no question as to what kind of a house it was—
or rather, palace; and there was music tinkling in a courtyard, which confirmed the general impression.

"Vasantasena's birthday," said Maitraya. "They began to celebrate at dawn. But what does that matter?
We are not rich fools who have to race to do the fashionable thing. Our presence honors her, however late we
come. Have you a present ready? Lend me a piece of
gold, will you?"

"Where should I get gold?" asked Ommony—instantly
aware that he was teetering on the edge of his first mistake. Maitraya cocked a wondering eye at him; it was
quite clear that he knew all about a Bhat's resources, even
if the Bhat himself, for unimaginable reasons, should
choose to have forgotten them.

"I will improvise a poem in her honor," Ommony explained. "Women enjoy poems, and I am good at them.
Give me a glimpse of her, and then see."

"Ah, but they like the poem gilded! Women are practical! Moreover, I am no poet," said Maitraya. "Now
one gold piece from each of us—"

Ommony smiled. Without the beard he looked as obstinate as ever, but humorous lines were revealed at the
corners of his mouth which the beard had hidden. He
decided to put his disguise to a severe test now, while the
consequences of detection might not be too disastrous.

"All right," he said, kicking off his slippers under the
archway and accepting the *chuprassi's* salaam with a
patronizing nod, as if the fellow were dirt beneath his
sacred feet, "I will attend to it."

Beyond the arch there was a small paved courtyard, around the walls of which were flowers growing in painted wooden troughs. There were several tradesmen squatting there with trays of jewelry in front of them, silver and even golden images of gods, and all sorts of valuable gifts that a visitor might buy to lavish on the lady who kept house within. The tradesmen were noisy, and sarcastic when not patronized. Maitraya bridled, his vanity not proof against insinuations that he probably had squandered all his fortune long ago on much less lovely women. But one hard stare from Ommony and the banter ceased.

"I will sing a song to Vasantasena about the jackals at her gate!" he said sternly; whereat one of them offered him money, and another tried to thrust a silver image of a god into his hands. But he brushed all those offers aside.

"Shall a Bhat-Brahman take gifts from such as you?" he demanded.

"*Pranam! Pranam! Paunlagi!*" they murmured, raising both hands to their foreheads; whereat he blessed them, as a Brahman is obliged to, with a curt phrase that means "Victory be unto you," and he and Maitraya passed on, through another arch, into a courtyard fifty feet square. There was a fountain in the midst, around which about a dozen well dressed Hindus were gossiping.

"*I* would have taken the fool's money," said Maitraya. "Are you not entitled to it?"

Ommony glanced at him contemptuously. "A tiger, if he wishes, may eat mice!" he answered. "A bear may eat frogs—if he likes them! A pig eats all things!"

Maitraya looked chastened.

There came across the courtyard, swaggering toward them, an heir to an ancient throne, in rose-pink turban and silken breeches, with silver spurs nearly six inches long, and a little black mustache on his lazy face that looked as if it had been stuck on there with glue. He whacked his long boots with a rhino-hide riding whip and rolled a little in his gait, as if it were almost too much trouble to support his vice-exhausted frame. He was for passing without notice, but Ommony stood by the fountain and mocked him. He knew that youngster—knew him well.

"Do they still wean young princes on camel's milk and whisky in Telingana?" he asked tartly. "I have heard tales of changelings. Return, O treasure of a midwife, and hear me sing a song; I know a good one!"

The gossipers around the fountain pricked their ears. The prince seemed to come out of a day-dream. "Ah! Oh! I kiss feet!" he exclaimed, and made as if to pass on. But Ommony was determined to try his hand to a conclusion.

"Those boots are not respectful. They offend me!" he sneered. "Are they cow-skin? They look like it!"

"Oh, damn!" remarked the prince in English. "Here, take this and confer a blessing," he went on in Urdu, diving into his pocket.

"Gold!" warned Ommony. "I declare you gave gold to the woman in there. All fees are payable in gold!"

"Gold? I have none. You must take this," said the prince and passed a handful of crumpled paper money. *"Pranam."*

"Victory be unto you," said Ommony, accepting it, and the prince made his escape, muttering under his breath at the insolence of Brahmans, and of Bhats in particular.

"But paper money is no good," Maitraya objected. "*I* have paper money," he added, lying for vanity's sake.

But Ommony was creeping into the Bhat-Brahman part.

"Why didn't you say so? Go and buy *mohurs** then from the *sonar*† at the gate," he retorted.

"Nay, Gupta Rao, you said *you* would provide the presents. It is only fair. You owe me a consideration. And besides, now I come to think of it, I left most of my money at home."

---

*A gold coin, value about one pound sterling.
†A goldsmith.

Ommony thrust the paper money contemptuously into Maitraya's hands, smiling in a way that spared the actor no embarrassment.

"Go and buy *mohurs* at the gate," he said. "I wait here."

Maitraya returned presently with four gold coins and offered two of them.

"The *sonar* cheated me—he cheated like a dog!" he grumbled, but Ommony shrugged his shoulders and waved the coins aside.

"Give them all to the woman. I have another way to make her smile," he said, looking important.

Maitraya approached humility as closely as professional pride would permit.

"It occurs to me I did not ask a blessing when we first met. I crave forgiveness. Your honor was so unusually free from false pride that I overlooked the fact you are a Brahman. *Pranam.*"

Ommony murmured the conventional curt blessing, and dismissed the apology as if it were beneath notice. They passed into another courtyard on which awninged windows opened from three sides. In a corner a dozen musicians were raising Bedlam on stringed instruments, their tune suggestive of western jazz but tainted, too, like Hawaiian music, with a nauseating missionary lilt. Fashionable India, in the shape of thirty or forty younger sons of over-rich Hindus and a sprinkling of middle-aged roués, was amusing itself in a bower of roses and strong-smelling jasmine, while in a corner of the courtyard opposite the music three girls were dancing more modestly than the scene would have led a censor of morals to expect.

It was a gorgeous scene, for the sun beat down on a blaze of turbans and the awnings cast purple shadows that made it all seem unreal, like a vision of ancient history. Maitraya was greeted noisily by a dozen men; he bowed to them right and left, as if accepting applause as he entered a stage from the wings. The girls danced more vigorously, under the eyes of an expert now, whose approval might be of more than momentary value. Professional zeal took hold of the musicians; the tune grew louder and less careless.

"Beware! Vasantasena is in a Begum's fury!" some one shouted. "None can satisfy her. Prince Govinda of Telingana gave her a quart of gold *mohurs,* and she sent him away because he had dared to call on her in riding boots! I advise you to try her with two quarts of gold, and to crawl on your belly!"

A stone stair gave on to the courtyard, through a doorway guarded by two tall serving-men—immaculate, proud images of stern propriety, turbaned and sashed with blazing silk. They looked incapable of smiling, or of anything except the jobs they held, but as gilt, as it were, on the surface of sin they were unsurpassable. Ommony's disguise and manner aroused no suspicion, although swift suspicion was what they drew wages for, and they would have thrown him out into the street if as much as a suggestion had crossed their minds that he might be a European. They scrutinized Maitraya and Ommony and passed them as autocratically as if they were Masters of Ceremony passing judgment on attendants at a royal levee.

But royal levees are easier for outsiders to attend than that one was, and royalty, even in India, is shabby nowadays because its power is at most a shadow of the past and its forms mean nothing more than a cheap desire by unimportant folk to strut in a reflected pseudo-glory. Kings and conquerors go down, but whoever thinks that the power of the Pompadours has waned knows very little of the world or human nature. Vasantasena wielded more influence, and could pull more hidden wires than any dozen maharajahs, and the court she kept, if rather less splendid than a royal one, was alive with the mysterious magnetism of actual personal power. It was almost tangible, and much more visible than if she had been surrounded by men in armor.

Up-stairs there was no attempt at glittering display, but art and Old-World luxury in every considered detail.

A hall, paneled in carved teak and hung with Rawalia woven curtains and a silver lamp on heavy silver chains, conveyed no suggestion of wickedness; a Christian bishop could have trodden the soft Persian rug (had he dared) and have imagined himself in the midst of sanctity. But as Ommony and Maitraya reached the stair-head the curtains facing them across the hall were parted, and a girl peeped through whom hardly a Wahabi ascetic would associate with thoughts of Paradise. She was much too paganly aware that life is laughter, and that men are amusing creatures, to be criticized by standard formula; and she looked like a mother o' pearl Undine faintly veiled in mist—one of those fabled spirits who may receive a human soul, perhaps, someday, by marriage with a mortal —when she slipped out through the curtains and stood more or less revealed. She was clothed, and from head to foot, but not in obscurity.

She greeted Maitraya with a smile of recognition that suggested no familiarity. She was friendly, but perfectly sure of herself, and as sure of his unimportance. Then she glanced at Ommony, observed the caste-mark on his forehead, and made him a little mock-salaam, covering her eyes with both hands and murmuring *"Pranam."*

"This is Gupta Rao sahib. The Joy of Asia will be pleased to see us both," said Maitraya, assuming his courtliest air; whereat the girl laughed at him.

"She is not so easily pleased," she answered, glancing at Maitraya's hand. There was not much that her dark eyes missed. He gave her one of the gold *mohurs*, and then she stared straight at Ommony. Maitraya nudged him, trying to slip a *mohur* into his hand; but if you are to act the part of a Bhat-Brahman it is as well not to begin by bribing any one who can be overawed.

"I have a song to sing!" said Ommony. "Shall I include you in it? Shall I add a verse concerning—"

Swiftly she drew the curtain back and, laughing impudently over-shoulder at him, signed to him rather than to Maitraya to follow her down a short wide corridor to

a door at the end that stood slightly ajar and through
which came a murmur of voices. Through that she led
without ceremony into a square room in which half a
dozen men were seated on a long cushioned divan beneath
a window at the farther end. They were wealthy, im-
portant-looking men, one or two of middle age. Girls,
dressed as unobscurely as the one who had acted guide,
were passing to and fro with cigarettes and sitting down
between whiles on heaped cushions near the men's feet.
In the center of the room a white-robed Hindu was making
two costumed monkeys perform tricks, solemnly watched
by the men in the window, who took scant notice of Ommony and Maitraya.

Vasantasena was not there. Her richly draped divan
under a peacock-colored canopy at the end of the room
facing the window was vacant, although two girls with
jeweled fans lounged on cushions, one on either side of it,
as if she were expected to come presently. The sharp
cries of the man with the monkeys and the occasional
giggle of a girl punctuated an underhum of murmured
conversation from the men by the window. The atmosphere was loaded with dim incense and cigarette smoke,
blown into spirals of bluish mist by a punkah that swung
lazily, pulled by a cord through a hole in the wall. Ommony sat down cross-legged on a cushioned couch against
the wall midway between the window and Vasantasena's
divan, and Maitraya followed suit. Two girls, possessed
of patronizing smiles, brought cigarettes and a little gold-
en lamp to light them by.

It was sixty seconds before Ommony grew aware of the
essential fact. He lit a cigarette and blew smoke through
his nose before he dared to look a second time, for fear of
betraying interest. Having satisfied himself that Maitraya was studying the girls with an air of professional
judgment assumed for the perfectly evident purpose of
disguising a middle-aged thrill; and that after one glance
none of the men in the window was in the least interested
in himself, Ommony let his eyes wander again toward the

darkest corner of the room beyond Vasantasena's divan. There, on a mat on the floor, sat no other than the Ringding Gelong Lama, Tsiang Samdup, with his *chela* Samding beside him.

They sat still, like graven images. The Lama's face was such a mass of unmoving wrinkles that it looked like a carved pine-knot with the grain exposed. He was dressed in the same snuff-colored robe that he wore when Ommony first saw him in Chutter Chand's back room, and if he was not day-dreaming, oblivious to all surroundings, he gave a marvelous imitation of it.

The *chela* was equally motionless, but less in shadow and his eyes were missing no detail of the scene; they were keen and bright, expressing alert intelligence, and each time Ommony looked away he was aware that they were watching him with a curiosity no less intense than his own. But they refused to meet his. Whenever he looked straight at the *chela*, although he could not detect movement, he was sure the eyes were looking elsewhere.

He was also very nearly sure that Samding whispered to the Lama; the calm lips parted a trifle showing beautifully even white teeth, but the Lama made no acknowledgment.

"What is the Lama doing in this place?" he asked.

"I don't know," said Maitraya, "but he told me to meet him here. Many important plans are laid in this place. Ah! Here she comes!"

Maitraya was nervous, suffering from something akin to stage-fright, which consumes the oldest actors on occasion. It was clear enough that, though he had been in the place before it was rather as an entertainer than a guest, and he was not quite sure now how to behave himself. He tried to shelter himself behind Ommony—to push him forward as every one rose to his feet (every one, that is, except the Lama and Samding, who appeared to be glued to the mat).

But Ommony was no man's fool, to rush in where Maitraya feared to tread. He wanted time for observa-

tion. He laughed aloud and swung Maitraya forward by
the elbow, arousing a ripple of merriment from the women,
as a door opened behind where the Lama was sitting
and Vasantasena entered to a chorus of flattering comment from every one.

She was worth running risks to see; as gracious, modest
to the eye and royal-looking as her attendant women were
the opposite. Her dress was not diaphanous, and not extravagant; she wore no jewelry except a heavy gold chain
reaching from her shoulders to her waist, long earrings of
aquamarine, plain gold bangles on her wrists, and one
heavy jeweled bracelet on her right ankle. From head to
knees she was draped in a pale blue silk shawl that glittered with sequins.

By far her most remarkable feature was her eyes, that
were as intelligent as Samding's, or almost; but her whole
face was lit up with intelligence, though as for good looks
in the commonplace acceptance of the term, there was
none. She was too dynamic to be pretty; too imperious to
arouse impertinent emotions. She was of the type that
could have ruled a principality of Rajasthan, in the days
before those hotbeds of feudalism went under in a cycle of
decay.

She took her seat under the canopy, settled herself
on one elbow among the cushions, with one small henna-
stained foot projecting over the edge of the divan, noticed
Maitraya and suddenly smiled. That explained her. Her
smile was the miracle of Asia—the expression of the spirit
of the East that so few casual observers catch—a willingness to laugh—a knowledge that the whole pageant of life
is only *maya** after all and not to be taken too seriously—
satisfaction that the sins of this life may be wiped out in
the next, and the next, and that all inequalities adjust
themselves ultimately. The true philosophy is sterner
stuff than that; but it was impossible to see that smile
of hers and not understand why men of the world paid
her homage and tribute; she could see through any make-

---

*Delusion.

believe, and pardon any crime but impudence. One could
see how she wielded more power than a thousand priests,
and would very likely work less evil in the end, although
fools were likely to go to swifter ruin in her company than
elsewhere. She had force of character, and that is very
bad for fools.

Maitraya bowed and stepped forward (for Ommony
shoved him). The birthday tribute she had levied already
that morning lay in a silver bowl on a little table to her
right; Maitraya advanced to add his mite to it, bowed to
her profoundly as he passed, and dropped his coins on
top of the yellow heap, murmuring platitudes.

"Three mohurs!" exclaimed one of the fan-girls, and
the men near the window laughed.

"Liar!" Maitraya cried indignantly. "I threw in five!"

"Three!" the girl repeated, laughing scornfully, whereat every other woman in the room except Vasantasena,
who ignored the whole transaction, mocked him and he
went and sat down on the floor near the Lama with his
back against the wall, scowling as if poison and daggers
were his only joy.

That left Ommony on his feet, wondering whether the
Powers, that had treated him exceedingly well in all emergencies until that moment, would still stand by. It would
not be correct to say his heart was in his mouth; it was
pumping like a big ship's engines, humming in his ears,
and if it had not suddenly occurred to him that this
woman was possibly one of the Lama's agents for the
traffic in white children he might have surrendered to
nervousness. He forgot that she was too young to have
had any hand in the incidents that Benjamin had told
about—remembered only that the Lama was there in her
house, and that a Bhat-Brahman's tongue should be read-
ier than nitroglycerine to go off and shake the pillars of
any society.

"O Brighter than the stars!—O Shadow of Parvarti!
—O Dew upon the Jasmine blossoms!" he began. "I
bring a greater gift than gold."

He was surprised by the ringing arrogance of his own voice. Vasantasena smiled. No man that day had dared to come empty-handed, yet with his mouth so full of brave words. The company had bored her. Here was a man who held out promise of amusement.

"What is greater than gold?" she inquired in tones that came rolling from her throat like organ-music. And on the instant he challenged her.

"Reputation!" he answered. "Shall I sing thine? For thou and I are both from Rajasthan, O Moon of men's desire!"

She frowned and did not answer for a moment. It is quite in order to sing poems to a lady on her birthday, but it is not bad policy sometimes to know the words of the poem before giving a Bhat-Brahman leave to sing; what scandal they don't know they are almost always willing to invent.

"What is thy name?" she inquired, smiling again.

"Gupta Rao."

Her brows grew reminiscent, as if the name suggested vague connection with the past. She seemed not quite able to place it, but the men in the window scented a delicious piece of scandal and began calling for the song, and that naturally settled it; she was not going to be made foolish before a crowd.

"Did you not come with Maitraya?" she asked quietly. "Is your business not with Tsiang Samdup?"

"Subject to the Mirror of Heaven's smile," said Ommony, making an obeisance that verged on the brink of mockery.

She raised her voice, not very loud, but so that it vibrated with power:

"The noblemen who have honored me will find good entertainment in the inner courtyard. I will send down word as soon as I crave to rejoice in your lordships' smiles again!"

Without a murmur the guests got to their feet and bowed themselves out; if she had been an empress they could not have been more complacently obedient. They went with side-glances at Ommony and nods to one another, implying that a great deal went on at times in that room that they would give their ears to know, but on the whole they more resembled overgrown children turned out to play than middle-aged, bearded courtiers given temporary leave of absence.

The most important thing is Silence. In the Silence Wisdom speaks, and they whose hearts are open understand her. The brave man is at the mercy of cowards, and the honest man at the mercy of thieves, unless he keep silence. But if he keep silence he is safe, because they will fail to understand him; and then he may do them good without their knowing it, which is a source of true humor and contentment.

FROM THE BOOK OF THE SAYINGS OF TSIANG SAMDUP.

CHAPTER XI

THE girls took the seat in the window the men had vacated, and sprawled there like sirens on a rock. Even the fan-girls joined them. It was quite clear there was a secret in the air; the ostentatious way in which the girls kept up a low-voiced chatter to show they were not listening was proof enough of that. Vasantasena lay on the wide divan with a cushion beneath her breast and her chin on both hands, considering Ommony for several minutes before she spoke, presumably curious to know why he had come with Maitraya; possibly she thought the silence and the stare would break him down and make him offer an explanation, but he met her eyes with challenging indifference. Silence is the only safe answer to Silence.

"Tsiang Samdup," she said at last, "let the girls put your mat here in front of me."

But the Lama would not move. He shook his head. And Samding spoke:

"The holy Lama knows where it is best to sit. He is not to be moved for convenience."

The voice was no more astonishing than is anything else that sets a key-note. It was like the rhythm of a tuning-fork. It changed the key—the very atmosphere, asserting fundamental fact, to which everything else must adjust itself or be out of harmony. Vasantasena raised her eyebrows, but yielded and changed her position so as to face the Lama, signing to Ommony to squat down on a cushion beside Maitraya; which was disappointing, because it prevented him from watching the Lama's face. He could see Samding's profile beyond Maitraya's only through

139

the corner of his eye, but he marveled at that; it was as
beautiful as a figure of the Buddha done in porcelain.

— "If I am to let my piece of jade go," Vasantasena asked
at last, "what reward have I?"

"None," said the Lama; and that was another fundamental statement, issuing in a voice like the gong that
starts the engines. It left nothing whatever to argue about.

"Then why should I do it?" Vasantasena asked.

"Because you wish to do it, and the wish is wise," the
Lama answered, as if he were replying to the question of a
little child.

"How do you know I wish to do it?"

"How do you know you are alive?" the Lama retorted.

Vasantasena laughed. "I believe you know where you
can sell it!" she said, in an obvious effort to lower the conversation to a plane on which she might have the advantage.

"I know you do not believe that," said the Lama.

Vasantasena sighed. "How do you learn *such* knowledge?" she asked. "You seem to know everything. I
am not ignorant. A hundred men come here, and none
of them can make a fool of me, but—"

"Perhaps you are not a fool," the Lama interrupted.

"No, I am not a fool. I can whisper a word here and a
word there, and some of the evil that would have been
done dies still-born—and some of the good that might
never have been born has birth. And as for me, what does
it matter? And yet—sometimes I think it does matter
about me. And sometimes I think I will give all my money
to the poor—"

"And rob them," said the Lama.

"Rob them of what?" She stared at him blankly.

"Of the moment. It is not wise to deprive them of the
moment. At the moment of our utmost need, we learn."

"Yours is a heartless creed," she retorted, glancing at
the money in the bowl beside her. "That money would
feed a thousand people."

"Nothing is heartless," said the Lama. "It is better
to eat consequences now than to put off the day of retri-

bution. Better the sting of an insect now than a serpent's
bite a year hence. Better an experience in this life than
a thousand-fold the bitterness in lives to come.''

"What says the Bhat to that?" she asked suddenly,
glancing at Ommony, and Samding came out of his immobility to give one swift searching glance sidewise.

Privilege has its disadvantages. It is one of the obligations of a Bhat that when appealed to he must say
something; and the quicker he says it, the better for his
reputation.

"I am not your priest. You would like to quote me
against him, but I am only interested in learning why I
was brought here," Ommony answered.

Vasantasena sneered. "Just like a Bhat! You think
of nothing but your own convenience. Well, I am glad
there is none of your money in my birthday bowl. Rather
I will give you some of it. Here—help yourself.''

"It is unclean money," said Ommony, falling back on
the caste-rules that a Bhat may observe if he chooses, even
if the other Brahmans refuse him recognition.

"Is that true?" she asked the Lama. "This is not all.
I am rich. I have lakhs and lakhs.''

"It is yours," the Lama answered. "It is your responsibility.''

"Well," she said, "as I told you before, if you will
take it all, you may have it. I am about to become *San-
yasin**. I think the piece of jade will help me more than
all my money. I will keep the jade.''

"I will not take your money," said the Lama. "Nor
can you escape responsibility. There is a Middle Way,
and the middle of it lies before you.''

Vasantasena frowned, her chin on both hands, studying
the Lama's face. His bright old eyes looked straight back

---

*In a sense this means "taking the veil," although the process
is almost exactly the opposite. Just as men so often do in India,
women sometimes renounce all worldly possessions and become
wandering hermits, living in caves and practising inhumanly severe
austerities. Such women, whatever their previous occupation may
have been, are deeply venerated.

at her out of a mass of wrinkles, but he did not move; if he smiled, there were too many wrinkles for any one to be quite sure of it.

"Well—I will call the girls," she said at last. "I will test you. You must tell me from which of them I received the piece of jade."

She clapped her hands and the girls came hurrying from the far end of the room, standing in a line self-consciously. They were used to being admired, and it was quite in keeping with the probabilities that every one of them had been bought and sold at some early stage of her career, but there was novelty in this ordeal, and they did not seem to know what to make of it.

"That one," said Vasantasena, nodding at the nearest, "is much the most popular."

"She has no other merit," said the Lama, and the girl looked bewildered—piqued.

"And that one at the other end is the cleverest. She has the quickest wit of all of them. She might have stolen it."

"If so she would have kept it," said the Lama, watching the girls' faces. "The fourth from this end. She is the one. Let the others go."

At a nod from Vasantasena eight girls returned to the window-seat and one stood still. She was the same who had admitted Maitraya and Ommony, only now all her self-possession had departed; she seemed to fear the Lama as a cornered dove fears a snake. She was trembling.

"Why are you afraid?" the Lama asked, as gently as if he were talking to a woman he would woo; but the girl made a gesture to her mistress for protection from him.

"She is afraid because you have read rightly," said Vasantasena. "I, too, am afraid. Are you in league with gods or devils?"

"That is not well," said the Lama. "Whom have *I* harmed?"

"You are too wise," said Vasantasena.

"Macauley the Eurasian had the stone," the Lama went

on in a booming voice. "A certain person gave it to him in a package yesterday, to take it to Simla and thence to Tilgaun. That would have been well. But Macauley the Eurasian was weak and dallied with a woman—"

"No Eurasian has *ever* been in my house!" Vasantasena interrupted, flaring.

"And the woman had a husband; and the husband was a Sudra* who was seeking education from a Brahman, so he gave the piece of jade to *him.* And the Brahman came hither, and boasted—and took opium—"

"He brought the drug with him. I *never* gave any man opium!" Vasantasena interrupted.

"And *she* took the stone from him and brought it to *you.* All this in the space of one night," said the Lama.

"But how do you *know?*"

"I do know."

"How do you know it was this girl?"

"She is the only one who would have given it to you. Any of the others would have kept it."

Ommony managed to master his emotions somehow, but it was not easy, for here was proof of a system of spying that out-spied the Secret Service. How had the Lama learned that the stone had been entrusted to McGregor, to be given in turn to Macauley, to be taken to Tilgaun? Given that much information in the first place it might have been comparatively easy to trace the stone afterward, but—McGregor had surely not talked. Macauley and McGregor's *sais* were the only possibilities.

Vasantasena groped under the cushions and brought out the piece of jade—the same piece that had been in Ommony's possession; there was no mistaking its peculiar shape, or the deep-sea green translucence. The expression of Samding's face changed for a moment; he actually blinked and smiled, and the smile was as attractive as the marvel of the stone. Vasantasena noticed it.

---

*Some Brahmans consent to teach the Sudra castes because of the enormous "gifts" they receive for doing so, but the practise is frowned on by the pundits and the guilty Brahmans are considered degraded, although not outcasts.

"Give me your *chela* in exchange!" she said suddenly.
"I could endure that *chela!* He is almost fit to be a god.
He needs only passion to awaken him. I can not understand this stone, which makes me dizzy to look into it, and
dark with fear of myself. The *chela* makes me feel there
is a future. I can look into his eyes and know that all
wisdom is attainable. I will teach him passion, and he
shall teach me pure desire."

The Lama chuckled engagingly. His wrinkles multiplied and his smile was as full of amusement as a Chinese
fisherman's. "Ask *him*," he said.

Vasantasena smiled at Samding—that same smile that
had explained the secret of her influence. It promised
unrestraint, indulgence without limit, and thereafter forgiveness. She held up the stone in her right hand, ready
to exchange.

"A bargain?" she asked eagerly.

"No"—one monosyllable, abrupt and clear—F natural
exactly in the middle of the note. A golden gong could
not have answered more finally or with less regard for
consequences.

Vasantasena started as if stung. Her eyes flashed and
her mood changed into savagery like a stirred snake's.
The girl who was still standing before her shrank and
half-smothered a scream. Maitraya ducked instantly with
his face behind his hands. Vasantasena flung the stone
at Samding straight and hard. It struck him in the breast,
but if it hurt, he gave no sign. He covered the stone with
both hands for a moment, as if caressing it, wiped it carefully on a corner of his robe, and passed it to the Lama,
who secreted it in his bosom as matter-of-factly as if the
entire proceeding were exactly what he had expected.

"Go!" Vasantasena ordered hoarsely. "Begone from
here! Never darken my door again! Go, all of you—you,
and you—what is a dog of an actor doing here? A Bhat!
A Bhat—a casteless Brahman! You defile my house! A
gang of devil-worshipers! Girls—call the men-servants and
throw them out!"

But the Lama was quite unhurried. He got up from the mat and blessed Vasantasena sonorously in Tibetan, which she did not understand; it might have been a curse for all she knew. Samding rolled up the mat. Maitraya got behind the Lama for protection; and the girls hesitated to obey the order to use violence on any one as sacred as a Lama, or as dangerous as a Bhat. The Lama led the way out of the room with his skirts swinging majestically, and Ommony brought up the rear, aware that the danger was by no means over. He paused in the door and met Vasantasena's furious stare.

"Shall *I* summon the guests from below?" he inquired; for that was the one risk he wanted to avoid. If he proposed it, she might forbid. "They would like to hear me sing a song of this!" he added.

"Go!" she screamed. "I will have you stabbed! I will have you—"

"Shall I sing to them in the courtyard?" he asked; and as she choked, trying to force new threats out of her throat, he shut the door behind him and hurried to follow the Lama, dreading what mood might overtake her during the minute or two before they could reach the street.

But the Lama would not make haste, although Maitraya urged him in sibilant undertones. In the courtyard he chose to think the greetings called out to Maitraya were intended for himself and bowed, bestowing blessings right and left. Then solemnly and very slowly, as if walking were as mathematically exact a process as the precession of the equinox, he led the way into the outer courtyard, where he stood for a moment and studied the fountain as if it contained the answer to the riddle of the universe. The sound of running footsteps did not break his meditation, or upset the equanimity of Samding, but Maitraya, glancing over-shoulder, started for the gate, and Ommony, muttering "Oh, my God!" had to steel himself not to follow. The two enormous sashed and turbaned janitors who kept the stairway to Vasantasena's upper room came shouting from the inner court—shouting to the man on guard at the outer gate; and Ommony's blood ran cold.

But they stopped shouting when they caught sight of the Lama—stopped running—stopped gesticulating. Very humbly they approached him, offering a present from Vasantasena—gold in a silken bag, and a smaller bag of gold for Gupta Rao the Bhat, with a request that he should remember the donor kindly. They pressed the presents— followed to the gate, imploring, swearing their mistress would take deep offense and think it an ill-omen if the gold were not accepted. When the Lama and Ommony persisted in refusing they tried to force both presents on Samding, and even followed to the street, where they snatched the flowers that were tucked into the carving of the arch and thrust them into the Lama's hands. Not until a strange, old-fashioned one-horse carriage with shuttered sides drew up at the gate and the Lama and Samding stepped into it, signing to Ommony and Maitraya to follow, was it possible to escape from the clamorous importunity; and even when the carriage drove away the voices followed after.

The man who knows he is ignorant is at no disadvantage if he permits a wise man to do the thinking; because the wise man knows that neither advantage to one or disadvantage to another comes at all within the scope of wisdom, and he will govern himself accordingly. But he who seeks to outwit wisdom adds to ignorance presumption; and that is a combination that the gods do not love.

FROM THE BOOK OF THE SAYINGS OF TSIANG SAMDUP.

CHAPTER XII

THE heat inside the carriage was stifling. No breeze came through the slats that formed the sides, but they had the advantage that one could see out, and sufficient light streamed through to show the Lama's face distinctly at close quarters. The Lama sat perched on the rear seat with Samding beside him, both of them cross-legged like Buddhas, but the front seat was as narrow as a knife-board, and in the space between there was hardly room for Ommony's and Maitraya's legs. Faces were so close that the utmost exercise of polite manners could hardly have prevented staring, and Ommony took full advantage of it.

But the Lama seemed unconscious of being looked at, making no effort to avoid Ommony's eyes, although Samding kept his face averted and stared between the slats at the crowd on the sidewalks. The Lama's eyes were motionless, fixed on vacancy somewhere through Ommony's head and beyond it; they were blue eyes, not brown as might have been expected—blue aging into gray—the color of the northern sky on windy afternoons.

The horse clop-clopped along the paved street leisurely, the clink of a loose shoe adding a tantalizing punctuation to the rhythm, and a huge blow-fly buzzed disgustingly until it settled at last on the Lama's nose.

"That is not the right place," he remarked then in excellent English, and with a surprisingly deft motion of his right hand slapped the fly out through the slats. He smiled at Ommony, who pretended not to understand him; for the most important thing at the moment seemed

148

to be to discover whether or not the Lama had guessed
his identity and, if not, to preserve the secret as long as
possible. From a pouch at his waist that Benjamin had
thoughtfully provided he produced *pan** and began to
chew it—an offensive habit that he hated, but one that
every Brahman practises. The Lama spoke again, this
time in Urdu:

"Flies," he said, in a voice as if he were teaching
school, "are like evil thoughts that seem to come from nowhere. Kill them, and others come. They must be kept
out, and their source looked for and destroyed."

"It is news to me," said Ommony, in his best Bhat-
Brahman tone of voice, "that people from Tibet know the
laws of sanitation. Now *I* have studied them, for I lean
to the modern view of things. Flies breed in dunghills
and rotten meat, from larvæ that devour the solids therein
contained."

"Even as sin breeds in a man's mind from curiosity that
devours virtue," said the Lama. He did not smile, but
there was an inflection in his voice that suggested he had
thought of smiling. Ommony improvised a perfectly good
Brahman answer:

"Without curiosity progress would cease," he asserted,
well knowing that was untrue but bent on proving he was
some one he was not. The Lama knew Cottswold Ommony
for a thoughtful man (for twenty years' correspondence
must have demonstrated that) and, if not profound, at
least acquainted with profundity; and it is men's expres-
sions of opinion more often than mechanical mistakes that
betray disguises, so he didactically urged an opinion that
he did not entertain.

"Without curiosity, nine-tenths of sin would cease. The
other tenth would be destroyed by knowledge," the Lama
replied. Whereat he took snuff in huge quantities from
a wonderful old silver box.

"Where are we going?" asked Ommony suddenly.

---

*A preparation of betel-nut.

"I have disposed of curiosity." The Lama dismissed
the question with one firm horizontal movement of his
right hand.

"I have a servant, to whom I must send a message,"
Ommony objected.

"The *chela* may take it."

Ommony glanced at Samding and the calm eyes met his
without wavering; yet he did not have the Lama's trick
of seeming to look through a person. Perhaps youth had
something to do with that. His gaze betrayed interest in
an object, whereas the Lama's looked behind, beyond, as
if he could see causes.

Ommony sat still, grateful for the silence, thinking furiously. He had witnessed proof that the Lama commanded
a spy-system perfectly capable of discovering even the
secret moves of McGregor. The odds were therefore ten
to one that he knew exactly who was sitting in the carriage
facing him. Samding had read the name Ommony on
Diana's collar in Chutter Chand's shop. The letter from
the Lama had been delivered to Mrs. Cornock-Campbell's
house. Benjamin was the Lama's secret agent, as well as
more or less openly his man of business. Viewed in all
its bearings, it would be almost a miracle if the Lama did
not at least suspect the real identity of the Bhat-Brahman
who sat chewing betel-nut in front of him.

And the Lama now had the piece of jade for which os-
tensibly he had come all the way to Delhi. Moreover, he
had known where it was, at least for several hours. Then
why did he continue to submit to being spied on? Why
had he not, for instance, stepped into the carriage and
driven away, leaving Ommony on the sidewalk outside
Vasantasena's? That would have been perfectly easy. Or
he could have denounced Ommony in Vasantasena's presence, with consequences at the hands of the assembled
guests that would have been at least drastic, and perhaps
deadly. If the Lama really did know who was sitting in
the carriage with him, the mystery was increased rather
than clarified.

And now there was the problem of Dawa Tsering and
the dog. Ommony wished for the moment he had made
some other arrangement—until he realized the futility of
making any effort to conceal what the Lama almost certainly already knew. He might have left the dog with
McGregor, and have had Dawa Tsering confined in jail,
but he would have lost two important allies by doing it.
A man with a "knife" and a dog with a terrific set of
teeth might turn out to be as good as guardian angels.

On the other hand, the Lama might be planning to disappear along the mysterious "Middle Way" that baffles
all detection. If so, the dog and Dawa Tsering might be
exceedingly useful in tracing him. If the offer to send
Samding with a message were not a trick, it would at
least acquaint the dog with Samding's smell; and it might
be that the Lama was ignorant about a trained dog's hunting ability.

Finally, as the carriage dawdled through the sun-baked,
thronging streets, Ommony reached the conclusion that he
had been guided by intuition when he gave orders to Dawa
Tsering. A man who has lived in a forest for the greater
part of twenty years, and has studied native life and
nature in the raw as methodically as Ommony had done,
achieves a faith in intuition that persists in the face of
much that is called evidence. He decided to carry on, at
least one step farther, trusting again to intuition that assured him he was not in serious danger and wondering
whether the Lama was not quite as puzzled as himself. He
glanced at the Lama's face, hoping to detect a trace of
worry.

But the Lama was asleep. He was sleeping as serenely
as a child, with his head drooped forward and his shoulders leaning back into the corner. Samding made a signal not to waken him.

The carriage dawdled on. The Lama stirred, glanced
through the slats to find out where they were, and dozed
away again. The streets grew narrower, and then broad-
ened into unpaved roads that wandered between high

walls and shuttered windows, in a part of Delhi that Ommony only knew by hearsay and from books. It was shabbily exclusive—drab—with plaster peeling from old-fashioned houses and an air of detachment from excitement in all forms. Here and there a Moslem minaret uprose above surrounding flat roofs, and trees peeped over the wall of a crowded cemetery. They were going northward, toward where the ruins of really ancient Delhi shelter thieves and jackals in impenetrable scrub and mounds of debris; a district where anything might happen and no official be a word the wiser.

Suddenly the carriage checked and turned between high walls into an alley with a gate at the farther end. The driver cried aloud with a voice like a prophet of despair announcing the end of all things; the double gate swung wide, not more than a yard in advance of the horse's nose; paved stones rang underfoot; the gates slammed shut; and the Lama came to life, opening first one eye, then the other.

"All things end—even carriage-rides," he said in English, looking hard at Ommony. But Ommony was still of the opinion it was better to pretend he did not understand that language.

Somebody opened the carriage door from outside—a Tibetan, all smiles and benedictions, robed like a medieval monk—who chattered so fast in a northern. dialect that Ommony could not make head or tail of it. Samding cut short the flow of speech by pushing past him, followed by Maitraya. Ommony got out next, his eyes blinded for the moment by sunlight off the white stone walls of a courtyard; and before he could take in the scene the carriage containing the Lama moved on again and disappeared through a gate under an arch in a barrack-like building: the gate was pulled shut after it by some one on the inside.

It was a four-square courtyard, dazzling white, paved with ancient stones, surrounded on three sides by a cloister supported on wooden posts, on to which tall narrow doors opened at unequal intervals. There was no attempt at ornament, but the place had a sort of stern dignity and looked as if it might originally have been a khan for northern travelers. The windows on the walls above the cloister roof were all shuttered with slatted blinds, and there were no human beings in evidence except Samding, Maitraya and the Tibetan who had opened the carriage door; but there were sounds of many voices coming from the shuttered window of a room that opened on the cloister.

Samding stood still, facing Ommony, silent, presumably waiting for the message he was to take. Ommony spoke to him in Urdu:

"Is this our destination? Or do we go elsewhere from here?"

"Here—until to-morrow or the next day," said the quiet voice.

"Do you know your way about Delhi? Can you find your way to Benjamin, the Jew's, in the Chandni Chowk? Will you take this handkerchief of mine and go to Benjamin's, where you will find a very big dog. Show the handkerchief to the dog, and let her smell it. She will follow you to this place."

Samding smiled engagingly, but incomprehensibly; the smile seemed to portend something.

"Speak louder," he suggested, as if he were deaf and had not heard the message.

Ommony raised his voice almost to a shout; he was irritated by the enigmatic smile. His words, as he repeated what he had said, echoed under the cloister—and were answered by a deep-throated bay he could have recognized from among the chorus of a dog-pound. A door in the cloister that stood ajar flew wide, and Diana came bounding out like a crazy thing, yelping and squealing delight to see her master, almost knocking him down and smelling him all over from head to foot to make sure it was really he inside the unaccustomed garments. And a moment later Dawa Tsering strode out through the same door, knife and all, blinking at the sunlight, looking half-ashamed.

Ommony quieted Diana, stared sharply at Dawa Tsering, and turned to question Samding. The *chela* was gone. He just caught sight of his back as he vanished through a door under the cloister, twenty feet away. He questioned the Tibetan, using Prakrit, but the man appeared not to understand him. Dawa Tsering strolled closer, grinning, trying to appear self-confident.

"O Gupta Rao," he began. But Ommony turned his back.

"Do you know where we are?" he asked Maitraya.

"Certainly. This is where my troupe was to assemble. Let us hope they are all here and that the Jew has delivered the costumes."

"O you, Gupta Rao," Dawa Tsering insisted, laying a heavy hand on Ommony's shoulder from behind to call attention to himself, "listen to me: that dog of yours is certainly a devil, and the Jew is a worse devil, and that man there—" (he pointed at the Tibetan) "—is the father of them both! You had not left the Jew's store longer than a man would need to scratch himself, when that fellow entered and talked with the Jew. I also talked with the Jew; I bade him supply me with garments according to your command, and two pairs of blankets and a good, heavy yak-hair cloak; and there were certain other things I saw that I became aware I needed. But the Jew said that this fellow had brought word that you had changed your mind regarding me, and that I was to go elsewhere with *him*. I gave him the lie. I told him who was father of them both, and what their end would be, and they said many things. So I helped myself to a yak-hair cloak, a good one, and lo, I have it with me; and I also picked out one pair of blankets of a sort such as are not to be had in Spiti; and with those and the cloak and some trifles I encumbered myself, so that neither hand was free.

"And while I was looking to see what else was important to a man of your standing and my needs, lo, the Jew took the socks you had left behind and gave them to this rascal; and the son of unforgiveable offenses showed them

to the dog, who forthwith followed him, notwithstanding
that I called her many names. He led her out of the shop,
and I after him with both arms full, and the Jew after
me because of the blankets and what not else. And lo,
there was a cart outside having four wheels and sides like
the shutters of a te-rain only not made to slide up and
down. And the door was at the rear. And thereinto he
led the dog, she following the socks, and I after both of
them to bring the dog back. And lo, no sooner was I
within the cart—not more than my head and shoulders
were within it—than two men like this one, only bigger,
seized me and wrapped me in my own blankets and bound
me fast, taking my knife.

"So they brought me to this place, where they dragged
me into that room yonder and released me, returning my
knife to me and saying such was *your* order. And if they
had not returned my knife I would have fought them;
but as they did return it, and said it was your order, and
as the dog appeared satisfied, because they threw the socks
to her to guard, it seemed to me there might be something
in it after all. Did you give such an order? Or shall I
slay these men?"

"Have you been here before?" asked Ommony.

"Oh, yes, two or three times. This is not a bad place,
and there is lots to eat, well buttered, with plenty of
onions. This is a place where they think the Lama Tsiang
Samdup is of more importance than a bellyfull. But they
eat notwithstanding—thrice daily—and much. But tell
me: did you give such an order—to have me brought here?"

Ommony had a flash of inspiration. "The man mistook
the order," he answered. (Maitraya was listening; he
did not want to take Maitraya into confidence.) "I will
tell you later what I intend to do about it. Meanwhile,
keep silence, keep close to the dog, and keep an eye on
me."

But Maitraya was growing more than curious, although
he did not understand the Prakrit dialect that Dawa
Tsering used.

"What is a Bhat-Brahman doing with such a servant?"
he asked, stroking his chin, cocking his head to one side
like a parrot that sees sugar.

Ommony fell back on the excuse that Benjamin invented:

"You were told. He attends to my little affairs of the
heart. Isn't the real puzzle, what is *he* doing with such
a master? Why are we standing here? The sun over-
powers me."

Maitraya led the way toward the room whence the
voices emerged and the Tibetan, seeing they knew where
to go, took himself off in the opposite direction. Excepting Dawa Tsering, there were no armed men in evidence;
the double gate that opened on the alley was barred, but
there was no padlock on the bars, and no guard; it looked
as if escape, if once determined on, would be simple
enough. If the place was a prison, its system for de-
taining prisoners was extremely artfully concealed; there
did not appear to be even the sort of passive vigilance employed in monasteries.

Maitraya crossed the cloister, opened a door near the
window whence the voices came, kicked it so that it swung
inward with a bang against the wall, and made an effec-
tive stage-entry into a dim enormous room. There was a
long row of slippers on the threshold, and he kicked those
aside to make room for his own with a leg-gesture that
was quite good histrionics.

Six men, three women and two boys, who had been sitting with their backs against a wall, stood up to greet him.
They were a rather sorry-looking group, dowdy and travel-
worn, without an expensive garment or a really clean turban among them; but that was another form of histrionics; there were bundles on the floor containing finery they
did not choose to show yet, lest the sight of it might prevent their paymaster, for his own pride's sake, from fitting
them out with new, clean clothing. Maitraya looked disgusted. He knew that ancient method of extortion and
assessed it for what it was worth.

"Such a rabble! Such a band of mendicants!" he exclaimed. "I am ashamed to present you to his honor the learned Brahman Gupta Rao, who will play leading parts in our company! He will think it is a company of street-sweepers!"

They bowed to Ommony, murmuring "*Pranam*," and he blessed them perfunctorily. It was more important at the moment to examine the room carefully than to make friends with outcaste actors, who pretend to themselves that they despise a Brahman, but actually fear one like the devil if he takes, and keeps, the upper hand.

The room was about thirty-five feet broad by ninety feet long, extremely high and beamed and cross-beamed with adze-trimmed timbers as heavy as the deck-beams of a sailing ship. There was a faint suggestion of a smell of grain and gunny-bags. Along one end, to the right of the door, was a platform, not more than four feet high nor eight feet deep, with a door in the wall at the end of it farthest from the courtyard; on the platform was a clean Tibetan prayer mat.

The walls were bare, of stone reenforced by heavy timbers, and the only furniture or ornaments consisted of heavy brass chandeliers suspended on brass chains from the ceiling and brass sconces fastened to the timbers of the walls. The place was fairly clean, except for wasp's nests and grease on the floor and walls where the illuminating medium had dripped. There were no prayer-wheels, images of gods, or anything to suggest a religious atmosphere, which nevertheless prevailed, perhaps because of the austerity.

Ommony decided to try the platform; as a Bhat-Brahman he had perfect authority for being impudent, and as a man of ordinary good sense he was justified in taking Dawa Tsering with him, to keep that individual out of mischief; so he beckoned to the dog and Dawa Tsering, climbed to the platform by means of some pegs stuck there for the purpose, and checked an exclamation of surprise.

The trunk full of clothes that he had ordered from Benjamin stood unopened in the far dark corner of the platform, where almost no light penetrated. It was strapped, locked, sealed with a leaden disk, and the key hung down from the handle.

He determined then and there to waste no further effort on conjecture. The Lama knew who he was. Benjamin was the informer. Probably on one of the occasions when Benjamin went shuffling along the passage by the staircase in front of his store he had sent a message to the Lama. Luck must favor him now or not, as the Powers who measure out the luck should see fit. He sat down cross-legged in deep shadow on top of the trunk, which creaked under his weight, signed to Dawa Tsering to be seated upon the floor, watched Diana curl herself in patient boredom in the shadow beside him, leaned into the corner, listened to the chattering of the actors and to Maitraya's pompous scolding, and presently fell asleep. Not having slept at all the previous night, he judged it was ridiculous to stay awake and worry. Opportunity is meant for wise men's seizing.

THE MAGIC INCANTATION OF SAN-FUN-HO

Lords of evolving night and day!
Ye spirits of the spaceless dreams!
O Souls of the reflected hills
Embosomed in pellucid streams!
Magicians of the morning haze
Who weave anew the virgin veil
That dews the blush of waking days
With innocence! Ye Rishis*, hail!
I charge that whosoe'er may view
This talisman, shall greet the dawn
Degreed, arrayed and ranked anew
As he may wish to have been born!
Prevail desire! A day and night
Prevail ambition! Till they see
They can not set the world aright
By being what they crave to be!
Be time and space, and all save Karma† stilled!
Grant that each secret wish may be fulfilled!

---

*The guardians of the esoteric Law, whose ordinances are regarded as infallible and binding, and from whom the Brahmans are supposed to be descended.

†The Law of Cause and Effect, governing the consequences of every thought and deed.

CHAPTER XIII

SAN-FUN-HO

How long Ommony slept he did not know, but probably for at least an hour. At first his doze was broken by the sound of the actors' voices, but after a while they may have slept too for lack of better entertainment; the buzz of conversation ceased and he was left to the pursuit of unquiet dreams, in which the Lama plotted and disputed with Vasantasena for possession of Samding in a place in which there was a fountain brim-full of golden *mohurs*.

He awoke quietly after a while, that being habit, and noticed that Diana's tail was thumping a friendly salute on the platform floor. The next thing he saw was the Lama sitting notionless on the prayer mat, with Samding as usual beside him. Below them, on the floor of the room, stood Maitraya looking upward. The gabble of angry argument that he caught between sleeping and waking made no clear impression on his brain. The first words he heard distinctly were the Lama's, speaking Urdu:

"My son, you are convinced of a delusion. That is not good. You believe you are answerable for results, whereas you are not even connected with the cause. You have but to obey. It is I who am burdened with the tribulation of deciding how this matter shall be managed, since I conceived it. From you there is required good will and whatever talent you possess for your profession."

The voice was kind, but it did not allay Maitraya's wrath. He scolded back.

"I am famous! I am known wherever we will go. Men will mock me! Am I to be a common mountebank? Vishnu! Vishnu! Why engage me, if you won't listen when I tell you the proper way to do a thing, and what the public will accept and what it will not accept?"

160

The Lama listened patiently, not changing his expression, which was bland and gently whimsical.

"All ways are proper in their proper place. Men will usually take what they receive for nothing," he answered after a pause. "As for *your* dissatisfaction, you may go, my son. You may go to Benjamin, and he shall pay you one week's money."

"I have a contract!" Maitraya retorted, posturing like Ajax defying lightning.

"That is true," said the Lama gently. "There would be merit in observing the terms of it."

Maitraya smote his breast, disheveled his turban desperately and turned to throw an appealing gesture to the troupe. But they were a hungry-looking lot, more interested in being fed and paid than in Maitraya's artistic anxieties. The Lama looked kind and spoke gently. In silence, with eye-movements, they took the Lama's side of the dispute.

"Prostitutes!" exclaimed Maitraya in a frenzy. "You will make apes of yourselves for the sake of two months' wage! Oh, very well. I will out-ape you! I will be a worse ape than the one who ate the fruit out of the Buddha's begging bowl! Behold me—Maitraya, the prostitute! I will be infamous, to fill your miserable bellies!" Then, facing the Lama again with a gesture of heartbroken anguish: "But this that you ask is impossible! It is not done—never! My genius might overcome a difficulty, but how can these fools do what they have never learned?"

"How does the wolf-cub know where to look for milk?" the Lama answered, and all laughed, except Maitraya, who tried to rearrange his turban. A woman finished the business for him, grinning in his face as boldly as if there were the slats of a zenana window in between.

"Do you observe that woman?" Dawa Tsering whispered to Ommony. "Now if she were in Spiti there would be knife-work within the day. She lacks awareness of what might be!"

Aware that he, too, lacked that most desirable of assets

at the moment, Ommony frowned for silence. There was just a chance that he might pick up a clue to a part of the mystery if he should attract no attention to himself. Maitraya—supposing he knew anything—was in a frame of mind to explode a secret at any moment. He was blowing up again.

"Krishna! By the many eyes of Krishna, I swear to you that some of them can not read!" he shouted, strutting to and fro and pausing to throw both arms upward in a gesture of despair.

"Krishna is a comprehensive Power to swear by," said the Lama mildly. "How many can not read?"

Two women confessed to disability; the third boasted her attainment proudly.

"Not so insuperable!" said the Lama. "That one woman shall read for the three. Thus the two will learn. Give their parts to them. They have almost nothing to say in the first act."

Samding picked up a dozen wooden cylinders with paper scrolls wrapped around them and bundled the lot into Maitraya's hands.

"We must cast them," said Maitraya. "The cast is all-important. Who shall play which part? It is essential to decide that to begin with."

"No," said the Lama, "the essential thing is that every one shall understand the play. Give the women's parts to that woman. Distribute the others at random."

Maitraya, with a shrug, chose the biggest scroll for himself and distributed the others. Samding beckoned to Dawa Tsering, who got up leisurely as if in doubt whether obedience was not infra dig. now that he had changed masters. Samding gave him a scroll, which he carried to Ommony, but neither Samding nor the Lama gave a glance in Ommony's direction.

The scroll was written in Urdu in a fine and beautifully even hand, heavily corrected here and there by some one who had used a quill pen. It looked as if Samding might have written and the Lama, perhaps, revised. There was

no title at the head, but the part was marked "The
Saddhu," and the cues were carefully included. To get
light enough to read by Ommony sat at the edge of the
platform with his face toward the Lama, and presently
began to chuckle. There were lines he liked, loaded with
irony.

There followed a long silence while Maitraya glanced
over his own fat part and consulted stage directions in
the margin; it was he who first broke silence:

"O ye critical and all-observing gods!" he exclaimed.
"This is modernism, is it! Who will listen to a play that
only has one king in it, and no queen, and no courtiers—
but a shoe-maker, and a goat-herd, and a seller of sweetmeats, and three low-caste-women with water-jars, and
only one soldier—he not a general but a sepoy, if you
please!—and a wandering *saddhu**, and no vizier to support the king, but a tax-gatherer and a camel-driver, and
a village headman, and two farmers—and for heroine—
what kind of a heroine is this? A Chinese woman? And
what a name! San-fun-ho! Bah! Who will listen to
the end of such a play?"

"I will be the first to listen," said the Lama dryly.
"Let us begin reading."

"And not even a marriage at the end!" Maitraya
growled disgustedly. "None marries the king—not even
the Chinese woman and her pigtail! No gods—one goddess! Not even a Brahman! How do you like *that*, Gupta
Rao? Not as much as one Brahman to give the play dignity! What part have you? The *saddhu's?* Let us hope
it is a better part than mine. Listen to this: I am a king.
I enter right, one sepoy following. (O Vishnu! Thy sharp
beams burn! A king, and one sepoy for escort!) The
sweetmeat seller enters left. Back of the stage the Chinese
woman is beside a well under a peepul-tree, talking with
three women who carry water-jars—and may the gods explain how a Chinese woman comes to be there! I address
the sweetmeat seller. Listen:

---

*Holy man.

" 'Thou, who sellest evanescent joy—and possibly enduring bellyache—to little ones, what hast thou to offer to me, who am in need of many things?'—What do you think of *that* for a speech for a king to make his entry with?"

"To which, what says the sweetmeat seller?" asked the Lama. "Who has the sweetmeat seller's part? Read on."

They sat down in a semicircle on the floor, Maitraya standing in the midst of them, and one of the men read matter-of-factly:

" 'Mightiest of kings, thy servant is a poor man, needing money to pay the municipal tax. May all the gods instruct me how to answer! Who am I that I should offer anything to the owner of all these leagues of forest and flowing stream and royal cities? An alms, O image of the sun?' "

"If he were a real king, and this a real play," Maitraya exclaimed, consulting the directions, "he would order that sweetmeat seller into jail for impudence! But what does he do? He looks sad, gives the fellow an alms, and turns to face the women at the well. How can he do that? I tell you, he *must* face the audience. Are they interested in his back? And this is what he says:

" 'Bearers of refreshment! Ye who walk so straight beneath the water-jars! Ye who laugh and tell a city's gossip! Ye who bring new men into the world! What have *ye* to offer me, whose heart is heavy? Lo, I bring forth sorrow amid many midwives. Wherewith shall I suckle it?'—It is just at this point that the audience begins to walk out!" said Maitraya.

"A woman speaks. What says the woman?" boomed the Lama; and the woman who could read held her scroll to the light, speaking sidewise, jerking her head at the Lama, as if *he* were the king:

" 'O Maharajah, thy servants are but women, who must toil the day long; and the water-jars are heavy! If we bring no man into the world, we are unfortunate; but if we do, we must suckle him, and cook, and keep a house clean, and go to the well thrice daily notwithstanding. Lo, the young one robs us of our strength and increases our labor. We are women. Who are we to offer comfort to a king?' ''

"Enter the *saddhu*," read Maitraya. "He leans on a staff and salutes the king with quiet dignity—''

"The *saddhu* shall have a dog with him," the Lama interrupted. "Samding," (he glanced sidewise at the *chela*) "there is merit in the dog. Consider well what part the dog may play."

The *chela* nodded. He and the Lama seemed to take it quite for granted that the dog and her master were obedient members of the troupe.

"Whoever heard of a dog in a play?" Maitraya grumbled. "Krishna! But the very gods will laugh at us! Read, Gupta Rao. What says the *saddhu*?"

" 'O King, thou art truly to be pitied more than all of these. Mine—the path I take—is the only way from misery to happiness. Alone of all these, I can give advice. Forswear the pomp and glory of a kingdom—' ''

"Pomp—and one sepoy!" Maitraya exploded.

"Silence!" commanded the Lama, in a voice that astonished everybody. His face was as mild as ever. Ommony continued:

" '—Discard the scepter. Let the reins of despotism fall, and follow me. I mortify the flesh. I eat no more than keeps the body servant to the soul. No house, no revenues are mine, no other goods than this chance-given staff to lean on and a ragged robe. None robs me; I have no wealth to steal. None troubles me, for who could gain by it? I sleep under the skies, or crawl into a cave and share it with the beasts; for they and I, even as thou and I, O King, are brothers.' ''

"Now the king speaks," said Maitraya. "Listen to this!—'Brothers? Yes; but some one has to beat the ox. And who shall rule the kingdom, if the ass and the jackal and the pigeon and the kite are reckoned equals with the king? Answer me that, O *Saddhu*.' ''

" 'Rule!' " read Ommony. " 'Are the gods not equal to the task! What is this world but a passage to the next —a place wherein to let the storms of *Karma* pass and store up holiness? Beware, O King!' "

"The *saddhu* passes on, turns and stands meditating," Maitraya read, consulting his scroll. "A shoemaker approaches. What says the shoemaker?"

"He salutes the king," said the Lama, "and walks up to the soldier. Now, let the shoemaker speak."

A voice piped up from the floor: " 'Thou with the long sword, pay me or kill me!' "

"He turns to the king," the Lama interrupted, "read on."

" '—O mighty king, O heaven-born companion of the gods! This sepoy owes me for a pair of shoes. Nor will he pay. Nor have I any remedy, since all fear him and none will give evidence against him. I am poor, O prince of valor. May the gods answer if there is any justice in the world! As I am an honest laborer, there is none!' "

"To which the king answers," said Maitraya, " 'True. And if you were king, what would you do about it?' "

The shoemaker: " 'Ah! If I were king!' "

"Now," said the Lama, "a crowd collects. They enter left and right, the tax-gatherer, the goatherd, the farmers, the camel-driver and the village headman. They all make complaints to the king."

"A crowd of seven people!" sneered Maitraya.

"There are dancing women also," said the Lama. "They are not wanted to dance until later; therefore they may take part in the crowd in various disguises. They have nothing to say. Read on."

Maitraya read: " 'The crowd salutes the king, and the *saddhu* watches scornfully; the *saddhu* speaks.' Read on, Gupta Rao."

" 'So many men and women, so many fools! Waves crying to an empty boat to guide them! O ye men and women, children of delusion and blind slaves of appetite, how long will ye store up wrath against the hour of reckoning?' "

"Now the shoemaker," said the Lama.

" 'Tell us how to collect our debts, thou *Saddhu!* Tell us how to feed our young ones! To that we will listen!' "

"Now the tax-collector.

" 'Tell me how to get the tax-money from men who declare they have nothing! Tell me how to conduct a government without a revenue! Tell me what will happen if I fail, O mouther of *mantras!** ' "

"The king," said the Lama, and Maitraya spoke with the scroll behind him, to prove how swiftly he could memorize.

" 'Peace, all of you! Ye little know how fortunate ye are to have a king whose only will is that the realm shall ooze contenting justice. Day and night my meditation is to spread contentment through the land. Is this your gratitude?' "

The *Saddhu*: " 'To whom? For what?' " Ommony's voice charged the line with sarcasm that made the Lama glance at him.

"A farmer," said Maitraya.

" 'The locusts spread through the land, and there is no ooze of dew, nor any rain. The crops have failed; and nevertheless, the tax-gatherer! He fails not with his visits! Meditate a little on the tax-gatherer, O King.' "

The *Saddhu*: " 'Aye, meditate!' "

"A camel-driver," said Maitraya.

" 'O King, they wait beside the mother-camel for the unborn calf. They take from us in taxes at the frontier more than the freight is worth. We fetch and carry, but the profit of the labor goeth to the rich. Our very tents are worn until the women can no longer patch them.' "

The *Saddhu*: " 'Live in caves, O brother of the wind!' "

"The shoemaker," said Maitraya.

" 'And the owner of goats charges twice as much as formerly for goatskins!' "

"The goatherd,'

_____
*A verse from the Vedas, any spoken charm or religious formula.

" 'Maybe. But he pays me less than half of what is right for herding them!' "

"The soldier."

" 'Listen, all of you! Behold your king—a great king and a good one! Know ye not the nature of a king? Lo, ye should rally to him and support him! A realm is ruled by force of discipline, wherein is strength; and to the strong all things are possible! Rally to your king and bid him lead you to a war on foreigners, who nibble at our wealth like rats and give us no return.' "

"A woman," said the Lama.

" 'Tell us first, whose sons shall fight this war!' "

"Another woman."

" 'And who shall console the widows!' "

The *Saddhu:* " 'The widows of the conquered nation will console them. *They* will naturally see the justice of the war!' "

"The soldier," said Maitraya. "He shakes his sword at the *Saddhu.*"

" 'Peace, idiot! They will invade us, unless we first attack *them.* Then in which cave will you hide? If I had my way, I would send you in the front rank to the war to show us whether your sanctity isn't really cowardice after all!' "

"All laugh at the *saddhu,*" said the Lama. "Now the king." And Maitraya postured splendidly.

" 'Ye men and women, know ye not that I have neither will nor power to make war unless ye brew the war within you as a snake brews venom in its mouth?' "

The *Saddhu:* " 'Yet a snake slays vermin!' "

Maitraya read on: " 'Peace, *Saddhu!* There is merit everywhere. Am I not king? And how shall I please all, who so unfairly disagree? Ye see these lines that mark my worried brow; ye see this head that bends beneath the burden of your care; and ye upbraid me with more tribulations? What if I should wreak impatience on you all? Am I alone in travail? Is none among you, man or woman, who can offer me a counsel of perfection?' "

"I!" It was Samding's voice, resonant and splendid yet peculiarly unassertive. It was as if the tone included listeners in its embrace. All eyes turned to Samding instantly, but he sat motionless.

"The crowd divides down the midst," said the Lama. "San-fun-ho steps forward from beside the well beneath the peepul-tree. She speaks."

" 'O King!' " The *chela's* voice was not unlike a woman's, although its strength suggested it might ripen soon into a royal baritone. " 'I come from a far land where wisdom dwells and all the problems that can vex were worked to a solution in the birth of time. Well said, O King, that there is merit everywhere! Well said, ye men and women, that ye have no words nor wealth to offer to your king. Nor could he understand, nor could he listen, since the ears of kings are deaf to common murmurings, even as *your* ears are deaf to royal overtones. But lo! I bring a talisman—a stone enchanted by the all-wise gods—whose virtue is to change from dawn to dawn the rank, condition, raiment and degree of all who look on it! Avert thine eyes, O King! I would not change *thy* rank, not even while a day and night shall pass. Look, *Saddhu*—soldier—goatherd—women—all of you!' "

"She holds up the stone," said the Lama, "and they stare at it in superstitious awe. They show astonishment and reverence. Then San-fun-ho intones a *mantra*."

The *chela* began to chant in a voice that filled the huge room with golden sound, as solemn, lonely and as drenched with music as a requiem to a cathedral roof. Without an effort Ommony imagined stained-glass windows and an organ-loft. Maitraya bowed his head, and even the other actors, outcaste and irreverent, held their breath. It sounded like magic. All India believes implicitly in magic. The words were Sanskrit, and probably only Ommony, Samding and the Lama understood them; but the ancient, sacred, unintelligible language only added to the mystery and made the spell more real.

None, not even Maitraya, moved or breathed until the

chanting ceased. The Lama glanced at Ommony, who was
so thrilled by the *chela's* voice as to have forgotten for
the moment that he held the *saddhu's* scroll. He looked
at it and read aloud in solemn tones:

"'I did not look! I turned mine eyes away!'"

The King: "'I looked!'" Maitraya put a world of
meaning into that line.

"And that," said the Lama, "ends the first act."

"Too short! Much too short!" exclaimed Maitraya.

"Too long," said the Lama. "I may have to cut one
of your speeches. Now there would be merit in the learning of your parts until the gong sounds for dinner. After
dinner we will take the second act. Peace dwell with you.
Samding!"

The *chela* helped him to his feet, rolled up the mat, and
followed him out through the door at the end of the platform, where neither of them paused; some one on the far
side of the door opened it as they drew near, pulled back
a curtain, admitted them, slammed the door after them,
and locked it noisily.

For a moment after that there was no sound. All stared
at one another. Ommony felt snubbed. He had intended
to force an interview with the Lama at the end of the rehearsal, but the calm old prelate seemed to have foreseen
that move!

"What do you think of it, Gupta Rao?" asked Maitraya.

"Crafty!" answered Ommony, still thinking of the
Lama. "I mean, full of craft—I mean, it is a good play;
it will succeed."

"Perhaps—if he neglects to charge admission!" said
Maitraya. (But he seemed tempted to share Ommony's
opinion.) "If he would let me give him the benefit of my
experience, it *might* be made into a real play," he added.
"And the *chela?* What do you think of the *chela?*"

"I *know!*" said Ommony. "He will make all the rest
of us, except the dog, look and sound like wooden dum-
mies!"

"There again!" said Maitraya. "The dog! Before

you know it he will order the *chela* to write a part for that knife-swinging savage of yours from Spiti!''

''I wouldn't be surprised. By Vishnu's brow, I wouldn't be surprised at anything!'' said Ommony, and cut off further conversation by returning to the trunk and squatting on it with his back to the light, to study the scroll of the *saddhu*—or rather, to pretend to study it. He was too full of thoughts of the Lama and the *chela*, and of his own good fortune in having stumbled into their company, to study anything else.

''The Lama knows I'm Cottswold Ommony. He knows I know who he is. Is *he* using his own method of showing me what he knows I want to see? Or is he keeping an eye on me while he attends to his own secrets? Or am I trapped? Or being tested?''

He had heard of the extraordinary tests to which Lamas put disciples before entrusting them with knowledge.

''But I have never offered to be his disciple!'' he reflected. And then he remembered that Lamas always choose their disciples, and that thought made him chuckle. It is notorious they do not choose them for what would pass for erudition according to most standards.

''I'd better see how stupid I can be,'' he decided. ''I chose Diana without asking her leave,'' he remembered. ''*She* likes it all right. Maybe—''

But the thought of becoming an ascetic Lamaist was too much like burlesque to entertain, and he dismissed it—puzzled more than ever.

The ways of the gods are natural, the ways of men un-natural, and there is nothing supernatural, except this: that if a man does a useless thing, none reproves him; if he does a harmful thing, few seek to restrain him; but if he seeks to imitate the gods and to encourage others, all those in authority accuse him of corruption. So it is more dangerous to teach truth than to enter a powder magazine with a lighted torch.

FROM THE BOOK OF THE SAYINGS OF TSIANG SAMDUP.

CHAPTER XIV

THE SECOND ACT

ALTHOUGH the first act was no more than a prologue, the second was long, constituting almost the entire play, followed by a short third act which was not much more than epilogue. For more than half an hour Ommony studied his part in silence, and the more he studied it the more its grim irony appealed to him. The *saddhu* typified intolerant self-righteousness and the beautifully written lines were jeremiads of abortive sanctity. Whatever else the Lama, or whoever wrote the play, might be, he was witty and aware of all the arguments of the accusers of mankind.

It appeared that, having refused to look at the magic jade while the *mantra* was being chanted, the *saddhu* alone went through the second act unchanged. The king, who had looked although warned not to look, became turned for a day and a night into an incredibly wise man (which was just what he wanted to be) but surrounded by the sweetmeat seller, shoemaker and so on, transformed into members of his court, whose ignorance exasperated him to the verge of insanity. The soldier had become a general, who prated about patriotic duty. The camel-driver was a minister of commerce, who believed that the poor were getting their exact deserts and would be ruined by paternalism. The village headman was a nobleman with vast estates, who rack-rented his tenants and insisted that he did it by divine right. The farmers had become a minister of finance and his assistant, who conspired to bring about a better state of things by wringing the last realizable *rupee* from the merchant classes. The goatherd, strange to say, became a courtier pure and simple, who had no ambition but to make love to every

woman who came within his range. The sweetmeat seller
was a chancellor whose duty was to invent laws, and the
shoemaker was a judge who had to apply them.

San-fun-ho, it seemed, had also looked into the magic
jade, and had become a goddess, with her name unchanged,
who came and went, heaping Puck-like irony on every one,
king included, and engaging in acid exchanges of wit with
the *saddhu,* who had much the worst of it.

The women with the water-jars had all become court
favorites, who lolled on divans and complained of their
tedious, unprofitable fate, inclining rather to the *saddhu's*
view of things but unwilling to give up sinecures for
austerity (which they declared had gone out of fashion
long ago) and cynically skeptical of the morals of the
dancing women, who entered early in the second act to
entertain the court. The long and the short of it was, that
nobody was any happier for being changed, and least of
all the king, who had only implored the Powers to make
him fabulously wise, and who found his wisdom sterile
because foolish people could not understand it.

The second act was supposed to take place at night, after
a long day's experience of the results of the sudden change
of character, and at the close they all departed to the
well, to greet the dawn and welcome a return to their
former condition.

The third act found them at the well-side, changed
again, and San-fun-ho, once more a Chinese woman, took
them to task for having failed to see the future seeded in
themselves, depending for fruition solely on their own use
of each passing moment. Because the *saddhu* had to interject remarks, the whole of San-fun-ho's last speech was
written on Ommony's scroll, and as he read he chuckled
at the *saddhu's* vanquishment. He loved to see cant and
pseudo-righteousness exploded. He could imagine the
saddhu, typifying all he most loathed, slinking off-stage,
brow-beaten, ashamed—and just as bent as ever on attain-
ing Heaven by the exercise of tyranny, self-torture and
contempt of fun.

Then San-fun-ho's last lines—a *mantra*—sung to Man-jusri, Lord and Teacher, "free from the two-fold mental gloom," as redolent and ringing with immortal hope as sunshine through the rain.

He was reading that when the gong sounded—a re-verberating, clanging thing of brass whose din drowned thought and drove the wasps in squadrons through the window-slats. And that brought another problem that invited very serious attention. As a Brahman—even a Bhat-Brahman, who is not supposed to be above commit-ting scores of acts the orthodox would reckon unclean—he might not eat in company with actors, nor even in the Lama's company, nor in any room in which non-Brahmans were. He began to exercise his wits to find a way out of the difficulty—only to find that the Lama had foreseen it and had provided the solution.

Long-robed servants entered from the courtyard bearing bowls of hot food for the actors, but none for Ommony or Dawa Tsering or the dog. Instead, a tall Tibetan came, announcing that a meal cooked by a Brahman would be served in a ritually clean room, if his honor would conde-scend to be shown the way to it.

The room turned out to be a small one at the far corner of the cloister, and no more ritually clean than eggs are square, nor had the meal been cooked by a Brahman; but the actors were none the wiser. Dawa Tsering's food was heaped in a bowl on a mat outside the door, and he, having no caste prejudices, squatted down to gorge himself, with a wary eye on Diana. Ommony relieved his mind:

"She eats only at night. She won't touch food unless I give permission."

Dawa Tsering promptly tried to tempt the dog, but she turned up her nose at the offer, and the Hillman grinned.

"I think you have more than one devil in you, Gupta Rao! However, maybe they are not bad devils!" He nodded to himself; down in the recesses of his mind there was an evolution going on, that was best left to take its own course.

Ommony left him and the dog outside and shut himself
into the small square room. There was only one door;
one window. He was safe from observation. There was a
plain but well-cooked meal of rice and vegetables laid out
on a low wooden bench with a stool beside it, and a pitcher
of milk that smelt as fresh as if it had come from a model
dairy; also a mattress in a corner, on which to rest when
the meal was finished—good monastic fare and greater
ease than is to be had in many an expensive hostelry.

He finished the meal and sprawled on the mattress, con-
fessing to himself that in spite of the Lama's having
avoided him for twenty years, in spite of the evidence of
an astonishingly perfect spy-system that had enabled the
Lama so infallibly to trace and recover the jade, and even
in spite of Benjamin's confession, it was next to impossible to believe the old Lama was a miscreant. Because
of the story of traffic in white children, reason argued
that the Lama was a fiend. Intuition, which ignores deduction, told him otherwise; and memory began to reas-
sert itself.

There was, for instance, twenty years of correspondence
from the Lama, mostly in English, with reference to the
business of the Tilgaun Mission; not one word of it was
less than altruistic, practical and sane; there had never
been a hint of compromise with even those conventional
lapses from stern principle that most institutions find
themselves compelled to make. In fact, he admitted to
himself that the Lama's letters, more than anything else
during his life in India, had helped him to see straight and
to govern himself uprightly.

And now this play. And Samding. Could a man who
made victims of children so educate a *chela* as that
one evidently had been educated? Youth takes on the
taint of its surroundings. Samding had the calm self-
possession of one who knew the inherent barrenness of evil
and therefore could not be tempted by it.

And *would* a man, who permitted himself to outrage
humanity by hypnotizing children, write such a play as

this one, or approve of it, or stage it at his own expense?
The play was not only ingeniously moral, it was radically
sound and aimed equally at mockery of wrong ideals and
the presentation of a manly view of life. A saint might
have written it, and a reckless "angel" might finance it,
but a criminal or a man with personal ambitions, hardly.

Then again, there was the mystery of the Lama's treatment of himself. How much had Benjamin told? The
old Jew had sent the trunk, so there had been plenty of
chance to send a message with it. Benjamin might have
brought the trunk in person. Anyhow, the Lama now
unquestionably knew who the Bhat-Brahman was; and he
was evidently willing for the present not only to submit
to espionage but to protect the spy!

It might be, of course, that the Lama had views of his
own as to what constitutes crime. He had radical views,
and was not averse to voicing them before strangers. But
if his conception of morality included smuggling children
into the unknown Hill country, how was it that he was
so careful for the Tilgaun Mission and so insistent on
safeguards against mental contamination?

Above all, why was he so careful to avoid an interview?
What did he propose to gain by pretending not to see
through the Brahman disguise? True, he had spoken
English once or twice, but he had made no comment when
the Bhat-Brahman pretended not to understand him. Was
he simply amusing himself? If so, two could play at that
game! For the present Ommony had to let the problem
go unsolved, but he dismissed the very notion of not solv-
ing it and he determined to get at least as much amusement out of the process as ever the Lama should enjoy.

He had about reached that conclusion, and was con-
templating a siesta, when the same attendant who had
brought him to the room came to announce that "the
holy Lama Tsiang Samdup" was expecting him in the
great hall. When he reached the hall rehearsal of the
second act was already under way; Maitraya was getting
off a speech he had already memorized, strutting, de-

claiming, trying to impress the Lama and the troupe with
his eloquent stage personality. The Lama took no notice
as Ommony entered with the dog and Dawa Tsering, but
told Maitraya to repeat the lines. Maitraya, rather net-
tled, gave a different rendering, more pompous, louder and
accompanied by gestures more emphatic than the first.
The troupe applauded, since Maitraya plainly expected it,
but the Lama broke into a smile that disturbed his wrinkles as if they had been stirred with a spoon.
"My son," he said quietly, "the whistle does not pull
the train." Maitraya's jaw dropped. "Samding, show
him how I like to have those lines read."

Samding spoke the lines from memory, not moving his
body at all, and the amazing thing was that while he spoke
one forgot he was a *chela* and almost actually saw a king
standing where he was sitting—a king who was bored to
distraction and trying to explain kindly to stupid people
why their arguments were all wrong. One felt immensely
sorry for the king, and saw the hopelessness of his attempt. But all that was between the lines, and in the
wonderful inflection of the voice.

"And now, my son, try once more," said the Lama.
"Imagine the audience is on the stage, and speak to them
as you would like a king to speak to you; not as you yourself would speak if you were king, but as a king *should*
speak to unwise people."

Maitraya swallowed pride, tried again, and so surprised
himself with his second effort that he tried a third time
without invitation; and the third rendering was almost
good. The man had imitative talent.

The whole of the afternoon was given up to the reading
and re-reading of the second act, and Dawa Tsering slept
—and snored—throughout the entire performance. Several times the Lama obliged Ommony to repeat his lines,
without once calling him by name, and once he made
Samding repeat them for him, the *chela* doing so from
memory, apparently knowing the whole play by heart.
The Lama was as exacting with Ommony as with Maitraya and the rest. Once he said:

"My son, you *know* the *saddhu* is a false philosopher.
You *like* to see him ridiculed by San-fun-ho. And that
shows wisdom. There is merit in appreciation. But it is
not good to forget that *you* are the *saddhu.* Those who
listen must not be aware that you expect to be worsted in
argument. Now speak the lines again."

Ommony complied, and did his best, for he was enjoying the game hugely; and that put Maitraya in a somewhat similar frame of mind; Maitraya imitated anything,
including mental attitudes, and the rest of the troupe took
example from him. When the East sets forth to play a
part in earnest, it becomes audience as well as actor, and
accepts the drama for reality. Even the Lama was pleased.
He praised them after a fashion of his own.

"Because you are doing well, it would not be good to
believe you can not do better. Even the sun and stars are
constantly improving. Let vanity not slay humility, which
is the spirit reaching upward."

Then, as if that perhaps were too great praise, which
might deceive them, he picked out an actor here and there
for comforting rebuke:

"You must remember that to play the part of a stupid
character requires intelligence. You will grow more intelligent as you endeavor. Now let us begin again at the
beginning, trying to forget how stupid we have consented
to be hitherto. Let us consent to be intelligent."

He did not once betray impatience. When he needed
an example he commanded Samding, and the *chela* spoke
at once from memory, occasionally descending to the floor
to act as well as speak the lines. Once the *chela* acted the
same part in the same way twice in succession, and then
he came in for reprimand:

"Samding, no two atoms in all nature are alike. No
day is twice repeated. No second breath is like the first.
Do that a third time. Do it differently."

Tyrant, however, was no right name for the Lama.
There was no sense of oppression, even at the end of a long
afternoon, when every faculty, Samding's apparently in-

cluded, ached from exercise. Samding worked harder
than them all together, because all through the second act,
in the rôle of a goddess, he had to come and go and speak
the all-important lines on which the action hinged. But
when darkness came, and tall monk-like Tibetans, armed
with tapers, lit the hanging lights and set candles in the
wall-sconces, the *chela* was as self-possessed and full of
life as ever, which he hardly would have been if he had
felt imposed on.

At last the Lama dismissed the troupe to the far end of
the hall, where they sprawled wearily on the floor and
awaited supper. Not moving from the mat, he beckoned
Ommony and Dawa Tsering to come and squat on the
floor in front of him, not on the platform. They had to
look up.

"Now for the show-down! Good!" thought Ommony,
stroking Diana's head as she crouched on the floor beside
him. But the Lama spoke to Dawa Tsering, using the
northern dialect:

"Why did you say to Samding that I owe you two
months' pay?" he asked, not offended, curious.

"Oh, I had to say something. I had to have an excuse
for seeing you. I had a letter to deliver."

The Lama nodded, but his voice became a half-note
sterner: "Why did you use violence to Samding?"

"I am a violent man, and the *chela* offended me."

"What offense did the *chela* commit?"

"Oh, he looked too satisfied. He was a fool to stir the
devil in me. Also I was disgusted."

"Why?"

"Because he did not look afraid. And I knew he was
afraid—of me! Therefore he was a liar. Therefore I
smote him with the letter, and hustled him a time or two.
He was afraid to hit back. Let him hit me now, if he is
not afraid to!"

The Lama meditated for a moment—seemed to fall
asleep—and then to come out of a dream as if emerging
from another universe.

"There is a certain merit in you," he said quietly. "Are you now the servant of this Brahman?"

"I am keeper of the dog. I pick the fleas from her. She is a very wise and unusual devil."

Dawa Tsering glanced at Ommony, who rather hoped he would say something to the Lama about the Bhat-disguise and thus bring that subject to a head; but he was disappointed. Nothing was farther from Dawa Tsering's intention; he was thoroughly enjoying what he thought was a perfect imposition on the Lama.

"This Gupta Rao," he went on, "is a devil even greater than the dog. I like him. He and I are friends."

"Well," said the Lama, "that seems to be excellent, because friends must stand together. There is a devil needed in this play of mine, and you shall act the devil. You will like that. But remember: there must be no offense to Samding, or to any one. You and Gupta Rao are together, being, as you say, friends. If I should need to dismiss you, because of wrong-doing, I will dismiss him also. Therefore his safety—do you hear me?—his *safety* will depend on you, and you must behave accordingly."

The word safety was plainly intended for Ommony's ears and the *chela* glanced at him, but the Lama's eyes did not move. After a slight pause he continued:

"You and the dog will both receive instruction." Then at last he looked at Ommony: "Will the dog open her mouth when she is told?" he asked.

Ommony ordered Diana to sit upright. He did not need to speak. At a sign from him she opened her mouth wide and yawned.

"That is good," said the Lama. "That will do. Peace dwell with you, my son. Samding!"

The *chela* helped him to his feet, rolled up the mat, and followed him to the door exactly as on the first occasion, leaving Ommony and Dawa Tsering looking at each other until the Hillman threw his shoulders back and laughed.

"*Now* you see why I have served him all these months! I, who have a devil in me! I, who mean to slay a man in

Spiti! I, who hate a long-faced monk as an ape hates the
river!'' Then another thought occurred to him. ''You
must pay me more money, Gupta Rao, else I will offend
the old Bag of Wisdom and he will discharge the two of
us!''

But instead of answering Ommony got up and found
his way to the little room reserved for him. Through the
slats of the window he could hear Dawa Tsering, squatting
beside Diana, taking her into confidence:

''It would be amusing, thou, to betray this Ommon*ee*
and see what happens. But I am afraid that what would
happen might be serious. I think I had better say nothing, because what may happen then will probably be
amusing. Thou, I think a person who can teach thee such
obedience might be a bad enemy and a good friend!''

Tibetans brought the evening meal, with a huge bowl
of rice and a bone for Diana, but Diana refused to touch
the food although the man set the bowl down in front of
her and Dawa Tsering urged. It was not until Ommony
gave her permission that she fell to greedily.

''Thou, Gupta Rao, put no such spell upon *me!*'' Dawa
Tsering urged solemnly. ''I am used to eating when my
belly yearns for it!''

Ommony finished his meal and decided to find out
whether or not he was under any personal restraint. He
crossed the courtyard and approached the double gate
through which the carriage had entered that morning.
There was a Tibetan standing near, who bowed, saw his
intention, and opened the gate civilly to let him through!
Diana followed, but he sent her back, making her jump
the gate, which she managed at the third attempt, and he
could hear the Tibetan on the far side laughing good-
humoredly. He knocked on the gate from outside and
the Tibetan opened it. Plainly there was no restriction
on his movements; so he whistled Diana and started stroll-
ing down the alley, considering Benjamin and wondering
whether the old Jew had lied about the smuggled children
—and if so, why? What did Benjamin stand to gain by

telling such a tale if it were not true? "The more you know of India the less you know!" he muttered.

It was Diana who transferred his thoughts to another angle of the problem. She had paused at the end of the alley and was signaling in the way she used to in jungle lanes when she detected a human who had no ostensible right to be there.

Ommony stood still, which obliged her to glance around at him for orders. He signed to her to come to heel and then walked very quietly to the end of the alley, where the corner of a high wall intensified the gathering darkness. No lamps were yet lighted, although there was one fixed on an iron upright at the angle of the masonry above him; it was almost pitch-dark where he sat down, with his back against the wall, giving no orders to Diana, simply watching her.

The hair on the scruff of her neck began to rise; she could hear voices, and so could he presently. He pulled her closer against the wall where she crouched obediently, trembling because she added his alertness to her own. She was quite invisible in the depth of the shadow; Ommony was between her and the road into which the alley opened; but he knew his own figure could be seen, something like a wayside idol, by any one with sharp eyes who should pass close to the corner.

There were two men approaching very slowly, deep in conversation. One wore spurs. Unexplainably (without delving into such science as Chutter Chand expounds in his room behind the jewelry store) Ommony received an impression that they had been pacing to and fro for a considerable time. They came to a halt around the corner within three steps of where he sat, and when he held his breath he could hear their words distinctly:

"You see, Chalmers, if we raid the place without being sure of our ground, all we'll do is make trouble for ourselves and serve them notice to cover their tracks. We must have evidence that'll make conviction certain, or they'll hold us up as another horrid example of official tyranny."

"I tell you, sir, I *know* the women are in here."

"But do you know they are *the* women? We can't interfere with religion. We'd be in a fine mess if we haled a bevy of legitimate nautch-girls into court. We've got to have *proof*."

"Pardon *me*, sir. Lamaism doesn't run to nautch-girls. These people are Tibetans. They've no proper business in Delhi, and absolutely no excuse for lugging unexplainable women around the country. The Lama was *seen* to enter Vasantasena's place, and I myself saw him come out and drive off with his *chela* and two other people. I had him followed, and I *know* he drove in here. He hasn't come out since. You know what kind of a place Vasantasena keeps."

"Yes, but we also know every member of her household. And she's another individual it's deadly dangerous to monkey with unless we're certain of our facts."

"We've got circumstantial evidence enough to hang a rajah, sir."

"Circumstantial won't do, Chalmers. I spoke with McGregor about it to-day; he assured me there isn't a thing on the Lama in the Secret archives. He admits there's slavery on the Assam border*, and that slaves are sold into Nepaul and Tibet. But that doesn't justify us in raiding this place, warrant or no warrant. We'd be inviting a riot. The way things are at the moment, Moslems and Hindus 'ud get together and make common cause even with *Christians* if they thought they could jump on us by doing it—and slit one another's throats afterward! They'd call it another Amritsar. I'll tell you what you may do if you like: surround this place and shadow every one who leaves it. That way we may get evidence."

There was silence while some one suppressed ill-temper. Then a voice:

"Very well, sir."

A piece of mortar from the top of the wall fell to the

---

*See United States daily papers, 1923; also official Indian Government reports.

ground beside Ommony. He glanced up. It was growing
very dark, but he thought he saw the shadow of a man's
head, vague against the colored gloom of an overhanging
tree. The men who were talking moved on, toward the
alley-mouth—passed it—turned, and started back again.

"Hullo!" said one of them, the taller, he with the
spurs. "Do you notice the audience? Wait! Don't go
down there—that's a nasty, damned dark alley—might
be an accident.—*Good evening!*" he said, coming to a
stand six feet away from Ommony. "*I hope we haven't
disturbed your meditations.*"

Ommony's hand closed on Diana's muzzle. She crowded
herself closer against the wall.

"*I say, I hope we haven't disturbed your meditations!*"
Ommony did not move.

"Maybe he doesn't know English, sir."

"Dammit, I can't see his caste-mark. He looks like a
Hindu. Haven't a flash-light, have you?"

The younger of the two men struck a match; its yellow
glare showed Ommony in high relief, but darkened the
shadow behind him.

"By gad, sir, that's the Brahman who came out of Vasantasena's with the Lama!"

The last thing Ommony wanted was police recognition;
with the best will in the world the police may bungle any
intricate investigation, through over-zeal, and because
they must depend on underqualified subordinates. He was
satisfied to learn that McGregor had kept his promise not
to unleash the Secret Service on the trail; disturbed to
learn the police on the other hand were busy. During thirty
seconds, until the match went out, he cultivated the insolent
stare to which Brahmans treat "unclean" intruders.

"Brahman and a Lama keeping company? That's
strange."

"I'd call it suspicious, if you asked me, sir! What's he
doing here? He's not even sitting on a mat. That corner's ritually unclean—fouled by dogs and God knows
what else."

"I'll try him in the vernacular. —*I'm curious to know why you are sitting here,*" said the man with spurs. "*Is there anything wrong? Are you ill? Can I help you in any way?*"

"Leave me to my meditation!" Ommony answered in a surly tone of voice.

"*Why meditate just here, O twice-born? This is a bad place—dangerous—thieves, you know. Don't you think you'd better move on?*"

Ommony was in doubt whether or not to answer, but he was afraid Diana might betray her presence unless he could get rid of the inquisitors. He made up an answer on the spur of the moment and growled it indignantly:

"A year ago my son died on this very spot, slain by a bullet from a soldier's rifle. Therefore I choose this place to meditate. I abase myself in dirt before the gods who visited that evil on me."

"Damned unlikely story, sir, if you asked me!"

"Everything in this damned country *is* unlikely! Have him watched. You'd better stand at that corner, and if he moves off, have one of the men follow him. I'll go back and send you twenty or thirty men to surround the place.—*Good night, O twice-born! Meditate in peace!*"

Ommony listened until their footsteps died away in the near distance. Then, taking very great care that Diana should understand she was still stalking danger, not defying it, he crept on tiptoe to the gate at the other end of the alley and drummed on it with his knuckles.

There was no answer. He tried the gate, but it was fastened on the inside. So he made Diana jump it, and in less than a minute after that Dawa Tsering came and undid the bars.

"O thou, Gupta Rao, there are happenings!" he said, showing white teeth that gleamed in the dark.

To him who truly seeks the Middle Way, the Middle Way will open. One step forward is enough.

FROM THE BOOK OF THE SAYINGS OF TSIANG SAMDUP.

CHAPTER XV

WITHIN the courtyard there was not confusion but a silent flitting to and fro as purposeful and devoid of collision as the evening flight of bats. Tall, specter-like figures, on the run, were carrying out loads and arranging them in a long row under the cloister. There was no sign of the Lama, nor of Maitraya, and only one dim light was burning—a guttering candle set in a sconce under one of the arches.

"They go!" said Dawa Tsering. "They go!" He was excited—thrilled by the atmosphere of mystery. "There was a fellow on the wall, along there at the corner of the garden, where the tree is. He came running; and another summoned the Lama; and there was an order given. May devils eat me if they weren't quick! They are like ants when the hill is damaged!"

Ommony approached the cloister where the candle-light threw dancing shadow, and the first thing he recognized was his own trunk, with the bags and bundles of the other actors laid alongside it, in a line with scores of other loads all roped in worn canvas covers. There was every indication of orderly but swift and sudden flight; and only one reasonable deduction possible. Dawa Tsering voiced it:

"Women—trouble! Trouble—women! It is the same thing! They bring a man to ruin in the end!"

Ommony sat down on the trunk, and suddenly jumped up again. A woman's voice cried out of darkness from an upper story.

"Did you hear that?"

"So screams a woman when the knife goes in!" said

Dawa Tsering pleasantly. He was having an entirely
satisfying time. "Look to thyself! There is room to
hide dead men in this place, and none the wiser!"

But Ommony was not quite sure the woman's cry did
not hold a suggestion of laughter.

A Tibetan unlocked the door of the great hall in which the
rehearsals had taken place, and Maitraya emerged in a
tantrum.

"Krishna! This is too much!" he snorted. "Is that
you, Gupta Rao? What do *you* think of it? To lock us
in like criminals! To take our luggage—by the Many-
armed Immaculate—what is happening?"

The other actors trailed out after him, the women last,
peering over the shoulders of the men in front. One of
them was half-hysterical and, seeing nothing else to be
afraid of, screamed at the dog. Ommony retreated into
darkness. Dawa Tsering followed him, immensely free as
to the shoulders, like an old-time mercenary fighting-man
who foresaw trouble of the sort that was his meat and
drink.

"Have you a weapon, Gupta Rao? If you asked me,
I should say you would need one presently!"

Ommony dragged the Hillman down beside him and the
three—he, Dawa Tsering and the dog—sat with their backs
against the wall in impenetrable shadow, out of which
they could watch what was passing in the ghosty candle-
light.

"How many women has the Lama with him?" asked
Ommony.

"Oh, lots! I never counted. There were one or two I
had my eye on, but the crafty old Ringding looks after
them more carefully than an Afghan watches a harem.
He and the *chela* are the only ones who can get within
talking distance. Never mind. We will have our opportunity now, unless I am much mistaken."

"Why didn't you tell me about these women before?"
asked Ommony.

"Oh, I thought you knew everything. Besides, you are

probably a gay fellow yourself. I don't like interference. If you and I should love the same one—''

The Lama stepped into the circle of candle-light, entirely unexcited, and as usual Samding was with him. Samding counted all the loads twice over.

"Wait until I get my yak-hair cloak and the other things," said Dawa Tsering, and disappeared.

The Lama said one word and Samding promptly commenced a roll-call, from memory, in a clear commanding voice, beginning with a string of northern names, following with Maitraya and all his actors, Ommony's almost last. It was as thrilling as a roll-call on a battle-field.

"Gupta Rao?"

"Here."

"Dawa Tsering?"

"Coming!"

"And the dog?"

Ommony whispered to Diana and she bayed once. Everybody laughed, including the Lama, who stood so upright that he could have passed for a young man until Samding came and stood beside him, when the contrast exposed the trickery of darkness.

The Lama spoke in low tones to a Tibetan, who repeated the order to others, and in a moment all the loads were on men's heads. There was a prodigious number of them; men had arrived like ghosts, apparently from nowhere, and the discipline was perfect. Not a man spoke. There was no sound except for a grunt now and then and the rutching of heavily loaded bare feet on the paving stones; and not a woman yet in evidence except Maitraya's actresses, who seemed too frightened to make a fuss, or too interested to be frightened; it was hard to tell which.

If there was another order given Ommony did not hear it. The procession started across the courtyard, in through the stable-door into which the Lama's carriage had vanished when they first drove in that morning; some one opened the door from inside. The Lama stood in the courtyard watching, Samding beside him counting, and

they two entered last, a dozen paces behind Ommony; and
the moment they entered the echoing arch the door
slammed shut at their backs.

One candle on an iron bracket showed the shadowy outlines of three carriages on the right, and three horses in
stalls beyond that. The place seemed clean, with plenty
of fresh air, and the stable-smell was not overpowering.

"Have you been here before?" asked Ommony.

"Not I," said Dawa Tsering. "Maybe it is here he
keeps the women! This is one of those places the police
dare not look into lest men accuse them of committing
sacrilege. In my next incarnation I will study to be a
priest, because then I can laugh at the police instead of
being inconvenienced by them."

Diana trotted right and left into the shadows, sniffing,
interested but not suspicious. It was she, three or four
yards ahead who presently gave warning of danger in the
form of steps descending into absolute obscurity. The
candle-light did not penetrate to that point and it was
impossible to see whether there was a door to conceal the
steps when not in use. The voices of three women added
to Maitraya's complaining of darkness and danger, answered by cavernous rumbling as some one reassured them,
proved that the steps did not go very deep, but there was
nothing else to judge by, until, twenty paces beyond the
foot of the steps, the tunnel turned and another solitary
candle burning at a corner in the distance showed the
long procession shuffling toward it.

There were no rats, no dirt, and it was not particularly
damp. The tunnel, which was floored and lined with
heavy masonry, was roofed in places by the natural rock,
but there were spaces beamed with heavy timber and other
spaces filled with what looked like fairly modern concrete.
The floor and walls seemed very ancient, but the roof had
undoubtedly been repaired more than once within the
century. The level could not have been more than thirty
or forty feet underground, and there was a distinct
draught of cool air passing through.

It was not until he came within a dozen paces of the candle that Ommony's ears, growing accustomed to the echoing shuffle of about two hundred feet, detected that not all that noise came from in front. He looked back, and saw shadowy, black-draped figures behind the Lama and Samding. It was impossible to guess how many, since he looked with the light behind him, into darkness, and when he passed the candle the tunnel turned again rather sharply to the right. He stood still at the corner, looking backward, but the Lama boomed to him to go on—boomed so cheerfully and confidently that it would have been churlish to refuse.

"Do you suppose those are women behind us?" he asked.

"I know they are," said Dawa Tsering. "For a jest, O Gupta Rao, send thy she-dog to them. There will be a happening!"

There was more in that notion than its propounder guessed. Ommony snapped his fingers for attention, and spoke to Diana as loud as he could without letting the Lama hear:

"Friends! Go and make friends!"

He waved his hand toward the rear. Diana turned and darted past the Lama, who tried to intercept her; failing, he made a curt exclamation whose meaning Ommony could not catch.

"What did he say?" he asked.

"It means to be silent because they are not afraid," said Dawa Tsering.

And whoever they were, they were not afraid, which was sufficient cause in itself for much hard thinking. Diana was as high at the shoulder as a Great Dane; as shaggy and lean and active as a monster from the folk-lore legends. As an apparition suddenly emerging out of darkness with her eyes aglare in candle-light she was enough to have thrown old hunters into panic. But instead there was nothing but laughter, much snapping of fingers and enticing noises made between the lips; and the laughter was as merry and appealing as the sudden

view-hallo of children when a circus-clown kisses a pig.
The Lama had to boom a second time for silence, although
why he called for silence after that ringing revelation was
not exactly clear; surely there was no risk, down there in
the tunnel, of the noise being heard by the police. And
another thing: his voice was not alarmed, not even anxious
or offended; it more resembled that of an engineer who
orders steam turned off, or of a clerk convening court—
quite matter-of-fact, with hardly the suggestion of command in it.

Ommony let Diana stay behind there making friends. He
chuckled to himself. There were few but he who knew
the possibilities of that dog. Having once established in
her mind that certain individuals were friends, he would
have no particular difficulty in using her to penetrate any
screen the Lama might contrive. There was no further
need to risk an issue with the Lama by appearing over-
curious; he could wait for opportunity and let Diana open
up communications.

Meanwhile, it would not have helped him in the least
to be inquisitive just then. The tunnel turned again and
grew pitch-dark—became a stream of echoing noise in
which a man could only feel his way by touching the man
next to him or elbowing the wall, letting himself flow forward as it were in the general movement, which some forgotten sense reported to the brain.

Then dim light, far ahead, and at last a glimpse of sky,
framing half a dozen stars, that made the tunnel seem even
darker and a backward glimpse impossible. Diana came
sniffing for Ommony and shoved her nose into his hand.
Then she suddenly bayed at the sight of the sky in front
and raced away to investigate.

Ommony did his best to memorize the details of the
tunnel opening, but failed. There were steps, but not
many of them. Then he found himself in a courtyard
about thirty yards square, with stars overhead and the
shadowy columned entrance of a place that looked in the
dark like a temple behind him. He was aware that a stone

floor had come sliding forward to conceal the flight of steps; a man had shouted to him to hurry lest he be caught in the gap, and he had seen that the sliding stone was two feet thick. There was no sign of the Lama, or of Samding, or the women.

There were camels in the courtyard; he knew that by the smell before he saw them kneeling in two uneven rows. Diana, who hated camels, came to heel, growling to herself in undertones, and Dawa Tsering laughed aloud.

"I smell travel and the road that runs north!" he said triumphantly. "The devil may have these hot plains! Wait while I pick us two good camels—wait here!"

He disappeared and within the minute there were sounds of hot dispute—three voices. A camel rose like an apparition from another world, and snarled as if this world were not satisfying. A heavy thump—a louder oath —and Dawa Tsering limped back.

"In the belly! Kicked me in the belly!" he gasped, unable to stand upright but with enough wind left in him for agonied speech. "I would have hamstrung the brute, but—those Tibetan—devils—eh, but it hurts!—they pushed me toward his hoof again and—yow! let me sit so —stand beside me—yah-h, I have a bellyache!"

The courtyard was alive with movement, but there was hardly a spoken word. The camels moaned and gurgled, as they always do when loads are being heaped on them, and now and then some one called out for an extra package to balance an animal's burden; but on the whole there was even less noise than when Bedouins strike tents and vanish. After a while, as his eyes grew accustomed to the gloom, Ommony could make out men who certainly were not Tibetans; they wore turbans and were more like Bikaniri camel-men. Then, huge and shadowy against the sky, there loomed seven elephants with curtained howdahs, making no noise, effortless, coming through an open gate like phantoms in a dream.

Next there came from behind Ommony, a man in a turban and long cloak, followed by a younger man whose

stride seemed familiar, who wore a scimitar at his waist
and the dress of a chieftain. Diana knew them instantly
and wagged her tail. They were the Lama and Samding,
changed almost out of recognition! Ommony followed
them wondering at the Lama's strength of gait that he
seemed to have acquired along with the change of costume; but they were presently surrounded by Tibetans,
who seemed to be receiving whispered instructions. Unable to get close enough to hear what was being said, Ommony turned his attention to the elephants, and noticed
that they bore the trappings of a rajah, although he did
not know which rajah. He asked one of the mahouts, who
told him gruffly to mind his own business.

He walked up close to one of the camel-men, but it was
too dark just there under the wall to see his features.

"Whose man are you?" he asked.

"Mine own man!" the fellow answered in a plucked,
flat harp-string tone of voice. "Have a care! This camel
bites!"

Ommony jumped in the nick of time to avoid the vicious
teeth. Diana flew at the camel; the heavily loaded brute
struggled to its feet, tried to kick four ways at once, and
bolted. Ommony grabbed Diana. Nine or ten men chased
the camel into a corner, managed it amazingly with forked
sticks and compelled it to kneel. It was plainly enough a
desert outfit, used to meeting all emergencies without fuss.

Then the shadowy elephants moved in single file across
the yard and halted, swaying, at a door beside the one
that Ommony had come through; he could see the top of
a ladder laid against the first one from the far side, but
could not see who mounted it. A moment later, however,
he caught sight of the Lama and Samding, the Lama walking like a warrior, skirted, pantalooned, seeming to have
thrown off thirty years; they climbed on to the last of the
elephants, and moved off first, the others following.

After that there was confusion for about a minute; several more elephants came through the gate, colliding with
the loaded ones, and for reasons that were doubtless logical

to them, the camels all got up at once and stampeded into
the jam. But a little, low-muttered swearing, some sharp
cries and a lot of stick-work straightened that out. The
camels were herded out into the open behind the elephants; the second lot of elephants came in, and a Tibetan
seized Ommony's arm.

Not a word. No explanation. Two other men seized
Dawa Tsering, taking no chances with him, pouncing on
him from behind and shoving him along toward the same
elephant to which the first man led Ommony. Maitraya's
voice was raised in protest somewhere in the dark and a
woman cried out hysterically, but none answered either of
them. The whole party of actors was hauled into curtained howdahs like so much baggage. Diana jumped—
Ommony caught her by the scruff of the neck, hauled her
in after him, and found himself in a howdah with Dawa
Tsering and one Tibetan, who leaned forward, touched
Dawa Tsering on the shoulder and shook a finger at him
meaningly. For answer the Hillman made a gesture
toward his knife.

But they were off, swaying like insects on an earthquake, before that argument could ripen into happenings,
and in less than two minutes the Hillman was seasick,
hanging on and moaning that he could smell death.

"That camel kicked my belly into ruins! Peace! I will
get down! I have had enough of this!"

But the Tibetan leaned forward and lashed him very
neatly to the howdah with a rope.

"Cut me loose, Gupta Rao—or I call thee Ommon*ee!*"

"Nay," lied Ommony, "it was my order."

"Thou! Oh, very well! OMMON*EE!*" he yelled.
Then again between spasms of vomiting, "OMMON*EE!*
OMMON*EE!*"

It did not seem to matter. The Tibetan took no notice
of it. Such a cry by night, smothered by howdah curtains, was not likely to mean much to chance passers-by.
Perhaps Maitraya could hear it on the elephant ahead,
but he would not know what it meant. Ommony let his

name be yelled until the Hillman wore himself out, hoping
the Tibetan would be too disturbed by it to notice anything else. He had his finger through a small hole in the
curtain and was tearing it for a better view.

He did contrive to snatch one hurried glimpse before
the Tibetan saw what he was doing; but it was dark, there
was no moon, and all he saw was a broken wall with trees
beside it—nothing that would help him identify the route.
The Tibetan touched him on the arm and shook a warning
finger, then climbed over to Ommony's side of the howdah
and tied up the hole carefully with thread torn from a
piece of sacking. He did not seem in the least afraid of
the dog, nor did she object to him. On the principle that
good dogs know what their masters think subconsciously
about a stranger, Ommony decided the Tibetan was quite
friendly.

And the process of self-adjustment to mysterious conditions consists rather in keeping adventitious friends
than in losing them. It seemed much more important to
disarm suspicion and to create a friendly atmosphere than
to find out which direction they were taking.

As a matter of fact, Ommony did not much care where
he was going. He guessed he was on the "Middle Way,"
and that, if true, was the all-important fact. Details of
the route, he knew, might change from hour to hour; the
key to it was probably a string of individuals extended
all across the country, bound together by a secret interest
in common. He decided not to try to memorize the route,
but to look out for and identify those men.

However, he made one casual attempt to draw the Tibetan, in the hope of further disarming suspicion by appearing naturally, frankly curious.

"Where are we going?" he asked in Prakrit.

"Wherever the holy Lama Tsiang Samdup wishes,"
the man answered, almost to himself, as if he were repeating prayers. After which there was long, swaying, hot
silence, broken only by the groans of Dawa Tsering and
the soft, exactly regular footfalls of the elephant.

Treason, as between men, is considered worse than theft; for even thieves despise it. He who betrays his country is considered fit for death. But I tell you: he who betrays his own soul has no longer any link with honesty, and there is nothing sure concerning him, except that he will go from bad to worse. And evil grows little by little; he who is faithless in small things will ultimately lose all honor. Therefore, strive eternally to keep faith, not telling secrets nor inquiring uninvited into those of others; for the Great Offense is grounded on an infinite variety of little ones—exactly as Great Merit is the total of innumerable acts of self-control.

FROM THE BOOK OF THE SAYINGS OF TSIANG SAMDUP

CHAPTER XVI

"WHERE ARE WE?"

EACH to his own heaven. Some men prefer golf. To
Ommony, the seventh heaven of delight—the apex of a
heterodox career was reached that hour in a curtained
howdah, lurching into unknown night. And the best of it
was that he knew the future must hold even more thrilling
mysteries. There was going to be no anticlimax.

He was uncomfortable, sweating so that his dripping
cotton garments clung to him, breathing the smell of elephant and dog and Dawa Tsering (which is no boudoir
mixture), possibly in deadly danger. And he was utterly
contented, having no regret, no backward yearning.

The curtains that cut off the view could not limit imagination. He enjoyed a mental picture of the string of
camels leading and the elephants mysteriously padding
in the wake, beneath colored stars and a blue-black sky,
between broken walls and shadowy trees, toward an obscure horizon. The dusty footfalls were as music. The
mahout's occasional expletives were an open sesame to
mystery beyond the reach of ordinary men—and that, perhaps, explained nine-tenths of the delight. It is doing
what the other fellows can not do, that satisfies; and so,
through vanity, the gods make use of us. No millions, nor
fame, nor offers of a sterilized and safety-infested Heaven
could have tempted Ommony to forego that journey in
the howdah, although there were not wanting opportunities to steal away.

Now and then there were halts, when muffled voices of
unseen men on foot, who turned up out of the night, delivered terse commands that were barely audible and quite
incomprehensible through the howdah curtains. Time and

199

again he could have tumbled out of the howdah and lowered himself to the earth by the elephant's tail. But he
preferred to act Jonah in a whale's belly, especially since
the whale was willing.

He knew that with the dog's help he could have tracked
the caravan to its destination and so have learned the details of the course it took. But he also guessed that none
who saw it pass would answer questions; and at the other
end there was the risk that he might find a blank wall,
silence, and perhaps a knife's edge for inquisitive intruders. To play for safety—to look for it—to expect it,
would be ridiculous. He must run all risks without a
gesture of self-protection. He was glad he had not even
a revolver with him, for a hidden weapon might betray
him into rashness of the wrong kind. He made up his
mind, if he were threatened, to rely solely on whatever
wits the gods of emergency might sharpen for him at the
moment.

Meanwhile, he felt reasonably sure of one thing: that
the elephants were a rajah's property. The camels might
possibly belong to some one else, but it was more likely
they were also the same rajah's. There might be a rajah
who would not ask questions, but who was linked in some
chain of more or less esoteric brotherhood, akin perhaps to
Masonry. If so, the procession would arouse no comment
on the countryside, for it is no man's business and to no
man's profit to inquire too closely into a rajah's private
doings; he who does so may count with almost absolute
precision on what the jury will subsequently call an accident. "I don't know, I didn't see" and "I forget" are
difficult, exasperating pegs on which to hang a chain of
evidence.

At the end of two hours' swaying Dawa Tsering's
stomach, void of embarrassing content, began to recover.
His sunny disposition followed suit.

"Loose me, Gupta Rao. I am sorry I bawled out thy
other name. I will slay this fool who heard me. Then
none will be the wiser, and thou and I are friends again."

"Do you hope ever to see Spiti?" Ommony inquired.

"By the wind that blows there, and the women who laugh there, surely! I have a treasure tucked away in Spiti—earned on the te-rains. Loose me, Gupta Rao, or I call thee by thy other name again! I can shout louder, now my belly aches less."

"Shout, and let us see what happens," Ommony suggested.

The small boy's mind that had its kingdom in the Hillman's bulk considered that a moment.

"Nay," he said presently, "I think that an evil might happen. The luck is not good lately. Who would have thought a camel would kick me? The devils who live in the hills around Spiti owe me for many a good turn I did them. The devils of these parts seem very mischievous. I had better behave myself."

"How about a promise?" Ommony suggested.

"You mean, a promise between me and you? But I would have to keep it. That might be inconvenient."

"I would promise for my part to assist you to return to Spiti at the proper time."

"Oh, very well. Only I shall judge the proper time by when the devils have turned friendly. Loose me. I *will* behave myself."

Ommony undid the rope and the Tibetan, far from objecting, stuck a stump of candle on the bare wood of the howdah frame, lighted it, produced a pack of cards, and challenged Dawa Tsering to a game. They played interminably, both men cheating, both appealing to Ommony to settle constant arguments, although there was no money involved.

"My honor is at stake," Dawa Tsering grumbled after about a dozen furious disputes. "This ignorant Tibetan says I am a liar."

"So you are," said Ommony.

"That may be. But he has no right to give himself airs. He is the greater one. Look! He has five cards tucked under his knee, whereas I had but two!"

He shoved the Tibetan so that his knee moved and uncovered the missing cards, two of which slipped down between the howdah and the elephant's flank, thus putting
an end to the game.

"But I have dice!" said Dawa Tsering; and from then
until dawn they murdered time and peace with those
things, while Diana, her tongue hanging out with the heat,
panted and shifted restlessly, but Ommony snatched scraps
of sleep, dimly aware that Dawa Tsering was losing more
often than he won, growing more and more indignant with
devils who refused to bring him luck.

"I will obey thee, Gupta Rao, until the luck changes,"
he said at last. "My dice are loaded, yet even so I can
not win! Luck is funny stuff."

It was about ten minutes after dawn, the choicest hour
in India, alive with cock-crow and the color-drenched
solemnity of waking day, when the tired elephant came to
a final halt in some sort of enclosure, and shuffled a slow
measure to call the mahout's attention to sore feet. At
a sharp word of command the beast lay down, like a hill-
side falling. Diana sprang out through the curtains and
Ommony followed, yawning and sitting down on the elephant's forefoot to pretend to watch the mahout's ingeni-
ous ministrations to a corn, while he surveyed the scene
from under lowered eyelids.

The other elephants, already offloaded, had shuffled
away to a roofed enclosure at the far end of a compound,
where great heaps of food awaited them and equally huge
vats of water. The camels, still burdened, were lying down
in picturesque confusion, carrying on a camel conversation, which consists in snarling at the world in general.
Along one side of the compound was a row of mules, tied
by the heel with their rumps toward the wall, squealing
for breakfast, which was being brought by naked boys,
and by a *bhisti*, who poured water into buckets from a
goatskin bag. The opposite side of the compound was
formed by a low two-storied building with a double-decked
veranda supported on square wooden posts running the

entire length. There were flies, much litter and a most
amazing smell.

Over the roof of the building, where a long line of crows
formed a mischievously interested audience, there appeared a jumble of other roofs that made no pretense to
architecture. Small-town noises, such as a smithy bellows
and the hammer-ring on iron, the patter of goats' feet and
the heavier tread of cattle being driven forth to graze,
arose on all sides. There was one minaret in sight, and
one Hindu temple-roof ornate with carvings of deific passion. The compound gate was locked and there was a
guard of two men standing by, not evidently armed, but
obviously sullen and alert. There was no sign of the
Lama, nor of any women.

After a minute or two Maitraya looked out from a door
midway under the long balcony and greeted Ommony with
the familiarity of boon companionship established by
journeying together. It only needs one night of shared
discomfort on the road to produce that feeling, or else its
opposite. One either hates or likes one's fellow traveler;
there is no middle ground on the dawn of the second day
out.

"Do you know where we are?" Maitraya asked cheerfully.

Ommony did not know, but he was no such fool as to
admit it. In his capacity of wiseacre he gave the mahout
good advice regarding elephants' corns, about which he
knew nothing; in his rôle of privileged extortioner he demanded arrack from a man who seemed to be the master
of the stables, and established friendship with the elephant
by giving the grateful beast two-thirds of a bottle-full of
the atrocious stuff.

Meanwhile, Diana was exploring on her own account,
alarming many mules, offending camels, and reducing
elephants to a state of old-maidish nervousness, at which
their mahouts yelled in chorus, offering to throw sticks,
dung and missiles of all sorts, but daring no more than
the threat. Diana, solemnly indifferent to abuse, and con-

temptuous of elephants since she had ridden on the back of one, snooted around in corners until she reached the end door under the balcony; and finding that open, she entered. There was an instant chorus of women's voices. Maitraya grinned.

"Gupta Rao," he said, "I have seen a many curiosities in my day, but those dancing girls surpass all! If they are Tibetans, Krishna! I will risk my life and go to Tibet! *I* saw them descend from the elephants, and Vishnu! Vishnu! I assure you my heart thumps! Such beauty! Such chastity redeemed by mirth! Such modesty of manner uncontaminated by humility! I foresee adventures, Gupta Rao! That divinity of yours who broke your pocketbook in Bikanir will have a dozen strong competitors! Krishna! I am impassioned! I am enflamed with love! If I can find a shrine of Hanuman, I will make gifts and a sacrifice this morning!"

Diana emerged, led out through the door by Samding, who held her collar; seeing Ommony, the *chela* signaled to him with a smile to call the dog.

"I hate that *chela!*" said Maitraya, grinning. "Did I not tell you I had an intuition to be jealous of him! Is it possible those twice-born creatures are the *chela's* wives?"

"Whom are you calling twice-born?" Ommony demanded, instantly assertive of a Brahman's rights.

"*Pranam!*" said Maitraya. "But wait until you have seen them!"

Impelled by a feeling that perhaps the luck might favor him, and partly in order to live up to his Bhat reputation, Ommony strolled toward the door whence Samding and the laughter had emerged. It was slightly ajar. But he had scarcely reached it when the Tibetan who had been fellow traveler during the night touched him on the shoulder, led him back to a door at the extreme opposite end, and almost violently shoved him into a room furnished with a clean wooden table and a bench. Food was on the table—loads of it—fruit, milk, chupatties, honey, butter, boiled rice, and flowers enough to have graced a wedding feast. The Tibetan slammed the door, and Ommony heard him turn a key on the outside.

However, there were two doors to the room, and the window was not fastened. He went first to the window and made sure that Diana was within hail; she was watching Dawa Tsering gorge his breakfast from a bowl in the shade of the compound wall not fifteen feet away. Having satisfied himself on that score, he discovered that the inner door was not locked, so he attacked the food, that being an important consideration when you don't know what the next five minutes may bring forth. The locked outer door, and the guard on the compound gate were not exactly reassuring.

The Lama came in through the inner door just as Ommony finished eating. He was alone, no longer dressed in the warrior-like garb of the night before, and looking old again—immensely old, because the morning light streamed through the slats of the window and showed all his wrinkles. The snuff-brown color of his robe was streaked with old-gold by the sunlight. In that moment one could believe he was a rather world-weary, very wise old saint; it was next to impossible not to believe it.

Yet there was humor in his eyes and a gaze unconquerable—blue-gray—very wide awake. His frame for the moment seemed shrunken, yet his height, though he stooped from shoulders that seemed almost too weary to support his head, was considerably more than Ommony's.

"Peace perfect you in all her ways!"

The blessing was solemn but the voice rang with assurance, as if he knew that his will to bless was infinitely overpowering.

"And to you, my father, peace," said Ommony. He had stood up when the Lama entered.

"And the food was enough? And good enough?" the Lama asked. "The journey not distressing?"

"Where are we?" Ommony retorted bluntly. But the Lama merely smiled until his wrinkles were all in movement, and the fearless old eyes shone with kindly humor:

"My son, he who knows *where* he is knows more than all the gods. He who knows *what* he is knows all things. Is it not enough that each moment we are where we should be? Is not the whole universe a mystery? How shall the part be more comprehensible than the whole, since it must partake of the quality of the whole?"

But Ommony did not propose to be put off by wise conundrums. His jaw came forward obstinately.

"I was locked in here," he said. "I have a right to know why."

"To keep out those whose ignorance might cause them to intrude," the Lama answered, exactly as if he were teaching school. "It is not good to place temptation in the path of the inquisitive."

Feeling as if stilts had been kicked from under him, Ommony tried again, more bluntly:

"You *know* who I am," he began, speaking English; but the Lama interrupted in Urdu:

"My son, if I knew that, I should be wiser than all those whose duty is to rule the stars! You have answered to the name of Gupta Rao."

"For God's sake," said Ommony, again in English, "why not tell me outright what your business is? I'll *begin* by being frank. I'm spying on you! I would like to believe you are above suspicion. I'm in doubt."

"My son," said the Lama, answering in Urdu, "no man is above suspicion. The sun and the moon cast their shadows, and therein the destroyers lurk. Doubt is the forerunner of decision. Shadows move. All revelation comes to him who waits."

That sounded like a promise. Ommony jumped at it.

"We have one interest in common—Tilgaun. Why treat me as an enemy? Why not clear the air now by telling me the truth about yourself?"

"My son," said the Lama, in Urdu again, "no man can ever be told the truth, which either is in him, or it is not in him. If it is, he will *see* the truth. If it is not,

he will see delusion and will confuse himself with surmise. He who looks for negation beholds it. He who looks
for truth beholds negation also, but perceives the truth
beyond. Wherein have I shown you enmity?"

For a moment there was silence. Ommony tried to think
of another way of getting past the Lama's guard, but the
old man's impersonal dignity was like armor.

"There are things you may see, but you must put your
own interpretation on them," said the Lama. "One by
one we attain to understanding. The wise ponder in
silence, but the fools are noisy, and the noise precedes
them to their doom."

That sounded like a threat, but his face was as kindly
as ever, rippled again with quivering wrinkles, as a smile
broke and vanished into the recesses of brown-ivory skin.

"Come!" he said; but instead of opening the door behind him he strode first to the window, threw the shutters
back, glanced out and made a clucking noise. Diana
jumped in, and Ommony wondered; she was trained to
be wary of strangers, and was not given to obeying even
her master's friends unless carefully charged with that
duty by Ommony himself. She thrust her nose into the
Lama's hand before she came and fussed over Ommony.

The Lama led the way into a narrow passage on to which
many doors opened to right and left; it extended from end
to end of the long building, its walls forming a double
support for the heavy beams of the floor above. Two-
thirds of the way along it he opened a door on the right
and a chorus of women's voices burst through the opening. But there were no women to be seen yet, because the
door opened on to a gallery; there was a lower story
on that side of the building, and the gallery ran around
two sides of a large room, screened from it by a
breast-high balustrade. The Lama led the way to the
farther end, where the gallery was twenty feet wide and
Samding waited, standing beside a spread Tibetan prayer
mat, marvelously dressed in ivory white and looking like
a young god. However, god or no god, he had to alter the

position of the mat by an inch or two before the Lama would sit down, after which he motioned to Ommony to be seated on the floor in the farther corner, where he could see through a slit in the wooden panel and look down on the floor below.

It was a surprising room to discover close to mule- and elephant-stables, but not so surprising as its occupants. The walls were hung with painted curtains, and the floor was strewn with cushions on which Indian women, many of them high-caste ladies, sat chattering with girls who resembled no caste or tribe that Ommony had ever seen anywhere. They were lively, full of laughter, young, but no more beautiful, as far as actual features went, than any gathering of normally good-looking women anywhere. Six or seven of them, if not Tibetans, were at any rate of part-Mongolian origin; but Ommony counted fourteen who fitted into no mental pigeon-hole of races he had seen and studied.

In more than one way those fourteen and the Tibetans were all alike. They were dressed in the same loose, almost Greek, white cotton robes; they all wore stockings, which the native Indian women in the room did not wear; and they used more or less the same gestures, were alert with the same vivacity. But there the resemblance ended.

The fourteen were fair-complexioned; one had golden hair that hung in long plaits—she would have looked like a German Gretchen, if it had not been for the dress and something else—something quite indefinable.

The whole proceedings, the whole scene was like a weird figment of imagination. There was nothing natural about it, simply because it was too natural. It was not India. There were Moslem as well as Hindu ladies in the room, betraying no self-consciousness and no objection to one another's presence; and there were actually low-caste women—*sudras**—chatting with the rest apparently on

---

*Sudra: the lowest of the four great Hindu castes, which in fact. although not always in theory, includes many of the merchants and artizen classes, and some agriculturists.

equal footing. True, there was no food being passed around, but every other caste rule seemed to be forgotten or deliberately flouted; yet there was no sign of self-consciousness or strain.

They were talking Urdu, a few of them with difficulty, but it was next to impossible to catch the conversation from the gallery because there was so much of it—so many chattering and laughing all at once.

The fourteen girls in white kept glancing up at the gallery apparently expecting some sort of signal, so Ommony had plenty of opportunity to scan their features. He did not doubt they were the smuggled children Benjamin had spoken of, only there were fourteen instead of seven. There were therefore other agents besides Benjamin. But the fact in no way simplified the mystery; rather it increased it. Their ages ranged at a guess from seventeen to twenty-three or twenty-four which, allowing for the years elapsed, tallied with Benjamin's description near enough; and they had grown to wholesome-looking womanhood. Not a trace of shyness. No awkwardness. No vulgarity. Not one symptom of forced manners or repression. The whole thing was incredible; yet there they were. And who had educated them? The Lama? That seemed more impossible than for a river to flow up-hill; he might have made priggish nuns of them, or downright Tibetans, but not that. It began to be evident that there was something worth investigating in the Ahbor country, or wherever else the Lama kept his secrets!

It was the Lama who at last cut short the flow of talk. Sitting still on the mat, where his head was not visible from below, he boomed a word in Tibetan, as commanding as the gong that brings sea-engines to a halt, and there was instant silence as in an aviary when the chattering birds are frightened. Whatever he might be, the old man knew what drama meant—and discipline. He whispered to Samding, and the *chela*, opening a swinging door in the front of the gallery, walked down a carpeted flight of steps to the floor below.

He was received in silence. He took from his breast the
broken piece of jade that Ommony had lost and that the
Lama had recovered from the courtesan, and holding it in
both hands on a level with his shoulders passed among them,
pausing to let each woman in turn devour it with her
eyes. Some of them appeared to fall into a state of superstitious rapture; others were curious; all were respectful
almost to the point of worship. And the Lama watched
them through a slit in the swinging gate as if all destiny
depended on the outcome, every tendon in him rigid; the
neck tendon stood out like a bow-string. Then suddenly,
as if to calm himself, he took snuff and rubbed his nose
violently with his thumb.

The *chela* said nothing, but the women were allowed to
touch him and appeared to think the touch conferred a
priceless boon. They laid a finger of the right hand on his
shoulder as he passed, and one woman, a Moslem, who laid
both hands on him and clung almost passionately, was
quietly reproved for it by two of the girls in white.

"The game begins to look political," thought Ommony,
watching the Lama clean a snuff-filled nostril with a meditative forefinger. "Vasantasena—umm! Now these
women—I've always wondered why some genius didn't try
to conquer India by winning the women first! They rule
the country anyhow."

The Lama just then looked as calculating as a medieval
cardinal, but despite that air of playing a deep game for
tremendous stakes, there was now something almost Puck-
like in his attitude. Ommony noticed for the first time
that his ears did not lie close to his head, were large and
slightly pointed at the top. Seen sidewise in the rather
dim light there was a faint suggestion about him of one of
those gargoyles that survey the street from a cathedral
roof. He was even more interesting to watch than the
proceedings on the floor below.

Suddenly the Lama spoke again. When he did that his
leathery throat moved like a pelican's swallowing a big
fish, and the noise that came out was hardly human—

startling—so abrupt that it completely broke the sequence
of all other sounds. It monopolized attention. In the
ensuing silence he sat back, took snuff again, and seemed
to lose all interest in the proceedings.

But to Ommony the interest increased. The girls in
white threw black cloaks over their shoulders. The Hindu
and Moslem women smothered themselves in the impenetrable veils without which it is pollution to face men-folk
out-of-doors; and all of them, in groups of three or four,
each little group in charge of one of the Lama's female
family, who shielded their faces in masked hoods that
formed part of the black cloaks, departed toward the
street.

There was no doubt that they did go to the street; a
door opened on to a vestibule, and sunlight shone through
a street door at its farther end.

Samding returned up the steps and gave the piece of
jade to the Lama, who stowed it somewhere in his bosom
without glancing at it. Ommony watched the *chela* narrowly. Was he a European boy? There was something in
the clean strong outline of his face and in the lithe athletic figure that might suggest that. But he was too ab-
stract-looking—altogether too impersonal and (the word
was as vague as the impression Ommony was trying to fix
in his mind) too fascinating. No European youngster
could have looked as he did without stirring resentment
in whoever watched. Samding aroused in the beholder
only admiration and an itching curiosity.

THE LAMA'S LAW

O ye who look to enter in through Discipline to Bliss,
Ye shall not stray from out the way, if ye remember this:
Ye shall not waste a weary hour, nor hope for Hope in
    vain,
If ye persist with will until self-righteousness is slain.
If through the mist of mortal eyes, deluded, ye discern
That ye are holier than these, ye have the whole to learn!
If ye are tied with tangled pride because ye learn the Law,
Know then, your purest thoughts deny the Truth ye never
    saw!
If ye resent in discontent the searchlight of reproof,
Preferring praise, ye waste your days at sin's not Soul's
    behoof!
Each gain for self denies the Self that knows the self is
    vain.
Who crowns accomplishment with pride must build the
    whole again!
But if, at each ascending step, more clearly ye perceive
That he must kill the lower will, who would the world
    relieve
And they are last who would be first, their effort thrown
    away;
Be patient then and persevere. Ye tread the Middle
    Way!

CHAPTER XVII

DIANA REHEARSES A PART

THE moment the last woman had vanished from the room the Lama let Samding help him to his feet and clucked, snapping his fingers to Diana. She glanced at Ommony, he nodded, immensely curious, and promptly she trotted to the Lama's side as matter-of-factly as if she had known him all her life.

The Lama and the *chela* went down to the room below, taking Diana with them. The *chela* spread out the mat, rearranged it in accordance with the Lama's instructions, and the two sat down on it facing the balcony, conversing in low tones, evidently waiting for something preordained to happen. Diana sniffed around the room, inspecting cushions curiously, but they took no apparent notice of her. After a minute or two she sat down and looked bored. Instantly the Lama called to Ommony:

"Can you cause the dog to open her mouth, from where you are, without speaking?"

Ommony stood up, his head and shoulders visible above the rail, and seeing him Diana pricked an ear. The trick was simple enough; ever since she was a puppy she had always dropped her jaw when he held up a finger at her; by education, for his own amusement, he had simply encouraged and fixed a habit. Her mouth opened, closed and opened wide again.

Samding laughed delightedly, but the Lama very seriously beckoned to Diana to come nearer and she obeyed at a nod from Ommony. She wanted to sit on the mat, but the Lama would not allow that; he pushed her away and she squatted down facing the balcony, watching Ommony, awaiting orders.

213

"Now again!" said the Lama.

Ommony raised his finger. The ear went up, the mouth opened and stayed open until the finger was lowered.

The Lama was as pleased as a child with a toy. Diana would have been satisfied to go through all her tricks, but a Tibetan entered through the door the women had used. The Lama froze into immobility and Samding followed suit.

There entered a man whom Ommony knew from his photographs—Prabhu Singh—the almost middle-aged but younger son of a reigning rajah. He knew him well by reputation—had admired him in the abstract because he was notorious for independence and for fair, intelligent, outspoken and constructive criticism of foreign rule. He was said to be an intimate of Gandhi and was, in consequence, about as much appreciated by the ruling powers as a hornet at a tea-party.

He was tall, lean, lithe, big-eyed under a plain silk turban and extremely simply dressed in tussore stuff that showed every line of his athletic figure—not very dark-skinned—clean-shaven except for a black mustache. He wore no jewelry, strode barefooted with manly dignity to a point midway between the Lama and the door, bowed low, and stood still. Diana went up and sniffed him. He showed surprise, but laid his hand on the dog's head and rubbed her ear.

"Peace be with you. Peace perfect you in all her ways," the Lama boomed.

"And to you, my father, peace," he answered. "Was it well done? Was anything lacking for your comfort? Have my servants failed in anything? Were there enough elephants?"

"It is all good," said the Lama.

"And the mission succeeded?"

"The first part."

The Lama's hand went into his bosom and produced the piece of jade. Prabhu Singh approached to the edge of the mat, received the jade into his hands, and stepped back to examine it, holding it to the light from a window. He did not appear to have any superstitious reverence for it, but handled it as if it were a work of art, rare and valuable.

"I am glad," he said simply after about two minutes, handing it back to the Lama, who returned it to his bosom. The *chela's* eyes were missing nothing.

"San-fun-ho!" said the Lama suddenly; and the *chela* stood up on the mat. Was the stage-name his real one? The mystery increased.

Prabhu Singh's attitude underwent an instant change. He became embarrassed. He bowed three times with much more reverence than he had shown the Lama, and when the *chela* smiled the lineal descendant of a hundred kings was as nervous as a small boy being introduced to a bishop. Samding said something to him that Ommony could not catch, and the murmured answer seemed to be no more than a conventional formula of politeness. The *chela* was as perfectly at ease as if he had been receiving the homage of princes all his life.

Prabhu Singh bowed again three times and retreated backward, stumbling against Diana and recovering his balance awkwardly. He appeared almost physically frightened; yet he was famous on polo fields from end to end of India, and was notorious for speaking his mind bluntly to viceroys at real risk of personal liberty. His back to the door at last, he made his escape with better grace, recovering presence of mind and remembering to salute the Lama.

The moment the door shut the Lama turned on Samding and rebuked him in Tibetan; Ommony could only catch occasional sentences; but it seemed that the Lama was angry because Samding had not put the visitor at ease.

"That is only vanity—self-approval. Worshipers are mockers . . . turned your head . . . I would rather see you pelted with stones . . . better for you and for them . . . break the shell of the egg before the chicken hatches . . . *schlappkapp!* (whatever that meant). . .

dirt under your feet will some day cover your grave . . .
all these years and yet you know so little . . . if you
are going to fail you had better not begin . . . presumption . . . ''

It was a wonder of a discourse. Samding listened,
standing for a while, then sat down cross-legged—off the
mat—facing the Lama—head bowed humbly—not once
moving until Diana came and sniffed his neck to find out
what the matter was.

That stopped the Lama's flow of speech. He glanced
up at the gallery and called to Ommony in an absolutely
normal tone of voice, as if he had entirely forgotten the
whole incident of Prabhu Singh's visit and the rebuke
and all connected with it.

''Now again, my son. Make the dog do the acting
again.''

Samding resumed his position on the mat at the Lama's
right hand; he, too, seemed to dismiss the lecture as if it
had never taken place; and Ommony, directing from the
gallery, made Diana open and shut her mouth. The Lama
insisted on her doing it again and again and at last he
and Samding chuckled together over it as if it were the
greatest joke that ever happened.

Still chuckling, they got up and left the room by the
door leading to the street, taking the mat with them and
locking the door as they went out. No explanation; not
a word to Ommony as to what was expected of him; not
even a backward glance at the gallery to suggest that they
had him in mind. Ommony sat still for a while; then,
whistling Diana, he made his way to the gallery door,
found that open, and proceeded to explore; but he found
all the other doors along the passage locked, except the one
at the end that opened into the room assigned to himself.

He looked through the window into the compound,
where there were all kinds of noise and confusion. Four
men were trying to throw a mule and several other mules
had broken loose; an elephant was lying on its back near
a water-butt while two mahouts scrubbed its belly; and

two bull camels were fighting with everything except their tails while twenty onlookers heaped humorous advice on rather bored-looking experts who were watching for a chance to rope the brutes by the leg and separate them.

And in the midst of all that riot, with the sun pouring down on them and crows and sparrows hopping about among them, Maitraya and his troupe sat on boxes, repeating their lines to one another.

It appeared that the devil's part already had been written. Maitraya held a small scroll in addition to his own, and was trying to teach the lines to Dawa Tsering, who was disposed to believe he could play the devil better if left to his own resources.

"I tell you, a devil is devilish!" he shouted. "A devil is like one of those bull camels—you never know what he'll do next! Or like a mule—you have to look out for his teeth and heels! This devil of yours is like a pretty gentleman. Here, let me show you how to act the devil!"

But Maitraya stuck to it, patiently correcting the Hillman's mispronunciation of the Urdu words. Catching sight of Ommony through the window, he called to him to come out and take part in the rehearsal; but the door was still locked, and though he could have climbed through the window easily enough Ommony hardly liked to confess that he was locked in, not knowing what effect that news might have on Maitraya. After a moment's hesitation he excused himself on religious grounds:

"I must recite the *mantras*."

Even Maitraya, possessed by the almost absolute of religious cynicism, respected that Brahman's privilege, so Ommony was left to his own meditations, which were mixed, amused and mystified in turn.

His thoughts were interrupted by a knock on the door behind him. The *chela* came in. He had changed his clothes again and was in the same snuff-colored robe in which Ommony first saw him in Chutter Chand's back room. His face was an enigma—a mask with a marvelous smile on it; but the eyes, to Ommony, suggested excitement; or, it might have been, extremely keen amusement; at any rate, some strong emotion was shining through the self-controlled exterior. The remarkable thing was, that the youngster's calm did not suggest fanatical asceticism or conceit. He seemed human, curious and not unfriendly.

Diana's tail thumped on the floor. Flies buzzed in and out through the window. There was nothing in the situation to cause nervousness, and yet Ommony confessed to himself that he felt an inclination to shudder; the sort of inclination that forewarns a man of something that his eyes can not see. He spoke first, purposely in English, hoping to catch the *chela* off-guard:

"Maitraya has suggested that those young women who are with the party are your wives. That seems improbable. Tell me the truth about it."

If eyes mean anything, the *chela* understood; he was laughing. No muscle of his face moved. He pretended to assume that the words were some form of greeting, and answered in kind, in Tibetan, then broke into Urdu:

"Tsiang Samdup sends a blessing. He is unwilling that you should speak of what occurred this morning."

"You mean, of the performance of the dog?" asked Ommony.

But the *chela* appeared to be an expert in dealing with stupidity. "Of *anything* that occurred." Ommony chose another angle of assault:

"Whatever the holy Lama wishes. Kindly tell him so. *As long as I am his guest,* I will be silent. Wait!"

The *chela* had started to go, but Ommony stepped between him and the door and stood with his back to it.

"Don't be alarmed."

But the *chela* had only retreated a pace or two. Excepting that, he seemed hardly more than curious to know what would happen next. It was Ommony who felt uncomfortable. "I want you to tell me," he said, "whether it was Tsiang Samdup or some one else who educated you and those young women."

The *chela*, still standing erect, did not answer.

"Come on, tell me. There must be some one else besides the Lama."

"Is that why you stand between me and the door?" the *chela* asked. The voice was ironic—amused. Ommony tried emphasis:

"I won't let you go until you answer a few questions. Tell me—"

But the *chela* had already gone. He had crossed the room in three strides, laid a hand on the window-ledge, and vaulted through, tucking his legs up neatly under his chin and landing almost noiselessly on the veranda. He contrived the whole swift maneuver without a moment's loss of dignity, and walked away unruffled, not glancing behind him.

Ommony strode to the window feeling cheap, wishing he had gone about things differently; he supposed it would take an interminable time now to establish himself in the *chela's* confidence; he had possibly totally ruined his chance of doing that. The *chela* was sure to go straight to the Lama and tell him.

But there stood the Lama, in the midst of the group of actors, with Samding already beside him; and apparently Samding was talking about the play to Maitraya; the Lama seemed to be encouraging Dawa Tsering to rehearse his lines. They did not glance in Ommony's direction. But a minute or two later a Tibetan came and unlocked the door, and when Ommony stepped out under the veranda the Lama turned and beckoned to him.

However, the Lama had nothing to say. He led the entire troupe at once toward the elephant stalls, down a gangway between two of the big beasts, whom he saluted in passing as if they were human beings, and through a gate at the rear into an alley fifty yards long. The alley seemed to have been used as a sheep-corral the preceding night; there were some loose boards that probably served to enclose it. Across its end ran a street, in which a dozen or more nondescript humans lounged in front of back doors. It was a back street; all the houses faced the other way, their rears were an irregular jumble of yards and walls, with empty kerosene cans, rubbish heaps and faded cotton *purdahs** much in evidence.

The Lama led straight across the street into a doorway, and down a long passage that admitted to the wings of a fair-sized theater, almost modern in some of its details.

Some one had been busy, for the stage was set. A hideous back-drop had been almost concealed by branches up-ended, that gave a very good suggestion of a clump of trees; and in front of those, in mid-stage, was a wickerwork affair covered with cotton cloth that had been painted to look like the stone-work of an old well; a beam with a rope thrown over it, supported on two uprights completed the illusion well enough. The flies had been very simply painted to resemble house corners at the end of a street, and the whole scene suggested the extreme fringe of a village, with the audience looking out through it toward the open country.

For a wonder, there was electric light, although none too much, and the switchboard was a mystery, painted red and labeled in English "Keep away!"

At the rear of the theater and along both sides was a balcony for women, screened off with narrow wooden slats that left openings about four inches square. The orchestra "pit" was a platform, three feet lower than the stage, in full view of the audience. The musicians were already squatting there—Tibetans to a man; four were armed with _radongs_†; four more had tomtoms; the remaining dozen were provided with stringed instruments. The _radongs_ blew a fog-horn blare to greet the Lama as he stepped on to the stage.

In the opposite wing, no longer in white or in stockings, protected by three stalwart Tibetans, who lounged in the flies, were the women of mystery. They were in costume,

---

*Curtain, veil; any kind of screen. Women who keep out of sight of men are known as *purdah-nashin.*

†A sort of trumpet, very long, with the bell-shaped end set at an angle to the tube.

which so orientalized them that Ommony almost doubted
recognition. Memory plays strange tricks; his took
him back to the day when he and Benjamin had played
a part at Chota Pegu and the nautch girls had been wild
with inquisitive mischief—ready to betray the chief-priest
at a nod. These girls now, in gauzy draperies, less naked,
but as subtle in their motions, so resembled those nautch-
girls at first glance that he was not sure they were the
same he had seen in the room among the Hindu ladies
until he noticed that they laughed and chattered on a
comparatively low note instead of a high-pitched dis-
sonance.

The Lama clapped his hands and sat down inside the
well, where he could see out through holes in the painted
cloth. Then he told Ommony to make Diana sit down almost exactly in front of the well, and the rehearsal began
at once, as if preordained from the beginning of time, the
girls in their Indian costume mingling with the stage
crowd, and so well versed in their part that they pushed
the other actors into place, needing no direction by the
Lama.

Ommony had plenty of chance to observe some of them
closely, for three had been told to engage the *saddhu* in
mock-conversation during parts of the first act. One—
the Gretchen-girl—put an offering into his begging-bowl.
But though he missed his cue twice through trying to engage her in real whispered conversation, he failed; she
was as evasive as abstract thought—as apparently engaging and as actually distant as a day-dream. She turned
every advance he made into an excuse of by-play for the
imaginary audience's benefit, and all Ommony accomplished was to draw the Lama's irony from behind the
well:

"Some *saddhus* hide lascivious hearts under robes of
sanctity, but you are *supposed* to be one who has truly
forsaken the pursuit of women, Gupta Rao!"

When the laugh that followed that rebuke had died
down Ommony was still not sure of the Gretchen-girl's

real nationality. He had tried her with English, French, German and two or three Indian languages, watching her face, but detecting no expression that suggested she had understood him. As for the others, one might be a Jewess; but there are many well-bred women, for instance in Rajputana, and in Persia, who are fair-skinned and who resemble Jewesses in profile. Even fair hair was no proof of their origin; most eastern women, but by no means all, have dark hair.

The only really convincing evidence that they were Europeans was their behavior, and even that was offset by the fact that some of them were certainly Tibetans, whose manner was equally unembarrassed in the presence of men, yet equally free from familiarity. The difference from their behavior and that of Maitraya's actresses grew more and more noticeable as the professionals became aware of an atmosphere to which they were utter strangers. They tried at first to imitate it; then grew resentful and sneered; resorting at last to low jests in loud whispers and attempts to scandalize by bold advances to the men—until at last the Lama stood up in the well like a priest in a pulpit and beckoned those three women to come and stand in front of him.

"I could show you your secret hearts," he said, in a kind voice that was much more withering than scorn, "and ye would die in horror at the sight. It is not good to slay, not even with the rays of truth. So I show you instead what ye *may* become." Mildly, patiently, a little wearily, as if he had done the same thing very often, he included all his own mysterious family in a gesture that conveyed diffidence and hesitation. "Life after life ye shall struggle with yourselves before ye shall come as these. And these are nothing—nothing to what ye *may* become. The road is long, and there are difficulties; but ye *must* face it. Take advantage of the moment, for it is easier to imitate than to find the way alone. Ye can not undo the past, nor can all the gods, nor He who rules the gods, undo it. But now, this moment, and the next one, and the next, for ever, ye yourselves by thought and act create the very hair's-breadths of your destiny.—Now let us begin again, from the beginning."

They began again so meekened and subdued that for a while the first act suffered. But that was overcome by Diana, who produced such peals of laughter that the Lama had difficulty in restoring order and had to reprimand the musicians for thrusting their heads above the level of the stage to watch. At a signal from Ommony standing near the wings, Diana's mouth opened and the Lama from inside the well croaked words that sounded, even on the stage, as if the dog were speaking them.

When the shoemaker said "Ah, if I were king!" Diana's mouth opened wide and the retort came from behind her:

"It *might* be better to be a dog like me and not worry so much!"

The illusion was perfect because everybody on the stage looked at the dog as if expecting her to speak; and the best of it was that Diana cocked an ear, put her head to one side, and was immensely interested.

In answer to the *saddhu's*, "How long will ye store up wrath against the day of reckoning?" there was put into Diana's mouth:

"For myself I bury bones, but jackals come in the night and make away with them!"

When the king asked, "Is this your gratitude?" and the *saddhu* replied, "To whom? For what?" Diana's retort was:

"The *saddhu* is like the vermin on my back; he helps himself but isn't grateful. And when he is scratched he just goes to another place!"

Diana was easy to manage, and Ommony's signals, made with his right hand, were invisible from the front of the theater on his left. But Dawa Tsering was a hard problem; he was supposed to be one of those wandering clown-fakirs who amuse and terrify village gatherings by alternately acting like idiots and pretending they are in communication with the underworld of demons and lost souls. He could neither remember his lines nor keep his head, but blundered in at the wrong cues and then laughed self-consciously. Ommony advised the Lama to dispense with him altogether.

"Nay," said the Lama. "All things are good in the proper place. There is a part he *can* play."

Whereat he ordered the stage set for the second act, which was a simple business. The flies reversed suggested a palace interior. Curtains at the rear concealed the greenery. The well was replaced by a carpeted dais with a large throne on top of it, inside which the Lama could conceal himself quite easily. A few heaps of cushions and settees were carried on the stage and while the change was being made the orchestra rehearsed amazing music.

Tomtoms, *radongs* and stringed instruments thundered, howled and jingled like a storm in the Himalayas with the voices of a thousand disembodied spirits carrying on an argument in the teeth of wind and rain. It was stunning —weird—a sort of cataclysmic din foreboding marvelous events, but music, nevertheless, in every quarter-note of its disturbing harmonies.

He who would reform the world must first reform himself; and that, if he do it honestly, will keep him so employed that he will have no time to criticize his neighbor. Nevertheless, his neighbor will be benefited—even as a man without a candle, who at last discerns another's light.

FROM THE BOOK OF THE SAYINGS OF TSIANG SAMDUP.

CHAPTER XVIII

WORK. Ommony had been a worker all his days, but had never known the real meaning of the word until that afternoon. The Lama, as placid as a temple idol, as exacting as fate, as tireless as time itself, kept everybody occupied. There was no return to the place across the street where the beasts of burden rested; the only pause between rehearsals was at noon, when food was brought in baskets and all except Ommony munched greasy chupatties in the wings; for him there was special food provided, brought by an ostensible Brahman and served behind a screen.

A Tibetan make-up man, a master craftsman, spread the tools of his trade on the stage behind the well and took every one in hand in turn under the Lama's critical supervision. Even Diana had to be touched up; daubs of paint were smeared around her eyes to make them look huge and supernatural, and her ordinary gauntness was enhanced by dark streaks that made her ribs appear to stand out prominently.

Trunks full of costumes were dumped in the wings by methodical, matter-of-fact Tibetans, who seemed to have gone through the same performance scores of times and to know exactly what to do, and when, and how. They dressed the protesting actors more or less by main force, ignoring Maitraya's protests, pulling, adjusting, stitching, until every costume hung exactly as the Lama said it should. They provided Dawa Tsering with a devil-mask and a suit of dragon-scales—then showed him himself in a mirror, which entirely solved that problem; he liked himself so well in the disguise that he could have acted

226

Hamlet in it. But all he was required to do was to laugh
like a fiend at intervals, and to dance on and off stage
whenever the Lama signaled from behind the well. He
was supposed to be the spirit of the underworld who
mocked men's efforts.

There was no supper; nobody remembered it. Rehearsals continued until they had to lower the curtain because the audience began to straggle in and squat on the
matted floor in groups, munching betel-nut. The orchestra
tuned up at once. Three quarters of an hour before the
curtain was supposed to rise the house was crowded to
suffocation. Stunned by the music, which crashed and
blared arresting heraldry of doom or something like it
(and nothing fascinates as much as doom foretrumpeted)
the audience forgot to talk. When the curtain went up
slowly as if raised by the last resounding boom of the
radongs there was utter silence, in which the thrill behind
the women's gallery grating could almost be felt in the
wings.

And at the very last minute, before the king walked on,
the Lama, from behind the well, signaled to Dawa Tsering
to laugh like a ghoul and dance across the stage. It was
inspiration. In a country that believes implicitly in devils,
that following the cataclysmic music produced the perfect
state of mind in which to watch the play; when Maitraya
walked on he was heard with almost agonied attention.
There was not a gasp from the audience until it was
Diana's turn to speak, when the Lama croaked her line
so comically that even the actors laughed; and, presumably because the gods who guard coincidence approved,
she put her head to one side and cocked an ear at the
audience.

It brought the house down. It was so exactly timed to
break suspense, the marvel that a dog should speak was
so astonishing, that an earthquake after that could hardly
have called the crowd's attention to itself. Every spoken
word and every move was watched as if earth's destiny
depended on the actors' lips, and Diana's three short

speeches were received as if some god in the form of an
animal were on the stage. When she had spoken about
vermin the Lama tickled her with a straw and she
scratched herself; and shrill laughter from behind the
women's grille gave evidence that not a gesture of her
left hind-foot was missed. When the curtain came down
at the end of the prologue the applause out-thundered the
orchestra.

"It succeeds!" announced Maitraya, strutting across
the stage in the way of the scene-shifters. "I told you
so! I said it would! Trust me to know. Acting—good
acting—technique can accomplish anything!"

The Lama recognized familiar symptoms and was
prompt. He gathered all the actors close around him in
the wings and what he said was aimed straight at Maitraya, although he appeared to be watching Dawa Tsering
through the corner of his eye:

"That which is not excellent is not good. There shall
be no second act, unless I can be sure of more attention
to my signals. I am disappointed. If we can do no better
before such an audience as this, what could we hope to do
in the large cities?"

Dawa Tsering nearly burst the devil-mask with indignation.

"Thou!" he exploded. "Go back to thy monastery! *I*
will entertain these princes and princesses! Hah! This
is the greatest success there ever was!"

"You will not be needed," said the Lama, and at a
sign from him, as if they had known from the first what
to expect, three Tibetans seized Dawa Tsering and led
him away to a small room at the rear where his roars of
protest were inaudible.

That was all that was needed. Even the vainglorious
Maitraya forced himself into a careful frame of mind,
and the second act began as the first had done, with everybody striving to deliver each line as the Lama wished it.

Quite early in the second act the girls came on to dance
and entertain the king's court. They were preceded by

mysterious music, quiet and rhythmic, pulsing with a
tomtom under-throb that made the audience breathe in
time to it and sway unconsciously.

They floated on to the stage, barefooted, swinging so
perfectly in unison that each seemed to reflect the other.
Lowered lights produced a filmy, other-world effect.
What little sound they made was swallowed by the pulsing
subdued music, until one *radong* boomed an arresting note
and they began to sing, never changing the dance step,
weaving in and out and around and around as reflections
mirrored in the water weave interminably. Song, step and
dimness were all in harmony. There was one mysterious,
monotonous refrain that held a hint of laughter, and yet
such sadness as is felt when the wild-fowl cry across treeless wastes under a rainy sky.

And there was no more than just enough of it to make
the audience feel that it had not had enough—no encore,
although the stifling theater became a pandemonium of
acclamation and the king's next speech had to be twice
repeated from the throne (the Lama, underneath the
throne, insisted on it, lest the audience should miss one
word of the thought-laden lines).

Diana had only one line in the second act. When the
king, worried and perplexed by the ignorant disputing of
his courtiers, exclaimed, "Oh, who is wise enough to tell
these idiots what to do?" Diana walked up to the throne,
turned at a signal from Ommony to face the audience, and
from under the throne the Lama croaked:

"A wise *dog* chooses its own master and obeys him. It
saves lots of trouble!"

Then she walked off, swaying her long tail contentedly
as if she had solved the riddle of the Sphinx. Because of
the heat, that made the grease-paint on the actors' faces
run, her tongue lolled out and she seemed to be grinning
in response to the applause as she vanished into the wings.

About midway through the second act Dawa Tsering
was set free from durance vile and allowed to resume his
ghoulishness, now somewhat chastened by conviction that

after all he was not indispensable. There was nothing pre-
arranged about his entrances, whenever a line fell flat or
the action seemed to drag a little the Lama signaled for
the devil to dance on and arouse laughter. He was particularly useful when Maitraya remembered he was an
actor instead of acting the part of a king; the devil was
immediately summoned then to take the conceit out of him
by burlesque antics.

There was nothing in the play an audience could mis-
interpret, for it mirrored their own melancholy to them
and their own confusion, while Samding in the Chinese
robes of San-fun-ho laughed at it triumphantly, his gold-
en voice repeating lines that suggested, hinted, vaguely
alluded to a way out of all the difficulties that *he* knew
all about, even if nobody else did. All through the second
act Samding's lines were mockingly destructive, as one
actor after another, from king to *saddhu,* tortured imagination with his own ideas of how to make the world con-
venient to live in. Between them they proposed almost
every solution that has ever passed current in the realm
of politics, and the *saddhu* seasoned the stew with pep-
pery religious nostrums; but when, before the curtain fell,
they all decided they were better off as shoemakers and
goatherds Samding still mocked them. Nevertheless, there
was a hint in his last line of a solution if they chose to
look for it:

"Ye mortals, there is no success in jealousy. There is
no comfort in complaint. Ye win no excellence by finding fault."

The applause made the curtain swing and sway but it
did not drown the orchestra for quite so long as after the
first act. It changed into a buzz of conversation, syn-
copated, rising from a low note to a higher one in choppy
sound-waves of expectancy; and when the curtain rose on
the scene by the well at dawn there was silence in which
the mouse-note creaking of a door moved by a draught of
hot air sounded like whipcracks.

The rising sun would hardly have passed muster with a

western audience. It was a thing of gilded wood, on which the strongest electric light available was focused from the wings, but to the eastern mind, long versed in symbolism, it was intelligible, and the fact that mystic signs were painted on its face enhanced its effect. There was no need to tell any one that San-fun-ho had used the magic jade at dawn to restore every one to his original condition. There they all were, grouped before the well, with the dancing girls costumed as members of a village crowd and some Tibetans in the background helping to swell the number.

The whole of that last act belonged to San-fun-ho, who stood before the well with the magic jade in his right hand and, with the rising sun behind him, revealed the mystery of hope and courage. The jade gleamed like a living thing whose light came from within. His voice was like a peal of magic bells rung by the gods who keep the secrets of the dawn. His face was lit with reassuring laughter. His manner was as one who had experienced all emotions and had conquered fear.

It was a long speech; its delivery required ten minutes, but the audience received it as the East receives a benediction always, straining breathlessly to catch the subtleties of meaning, preferring allegories and a proverb now and then to meat and drink.

" . . . Does dawn die? Nay, it passes on. It lives for ever. Dawn *is* dawn, and never changes. Discontent *is* discontent; its fruits are of the elements of discontent —all bitter—none can sweeten them. Who wallows in the mire of jealousy, and blames another for the want he feels, may load his bins aburst with golden goods, but he shall know *more* smarting jealousy and ache with gnawing wants he never guessed.

"But hope—is hope not sweet? And is the fruit of sweetness bitter? Nay. I tell you, Hope is a creative force whose limitless dimensions lie within the boundary of each existing minute. Irresistible, Hope's magic is accomplished *now*. It comprehends no lapse of time. Nay!

Instant are its dawn, its noon and its accomplishment!
Hope, if it is true hope, fills the mind, affording malice
and deceitful dread no room. Hope lives in action. *All*
the elements of hope are deeds done now!

"Deeds—the very echoes are the fruit of deeds! One
stone laid on another in Hope's name is greater service to
the gods than all the pomp of conquest and the noise of
prayer! A deed—who measures it? Who knows the
limits of a mended wheel or reckons up the leagues it shall
lay underfoot?—what burdens it shall bear?—whose destiny it shall await and serve? A new-born Krishna may
descend into the world and ride on it to glories such as
earth has never known!

"O people, ye have overpraised calamity! Too much
ye have considered night; and not enough have ye observed the dawn! Your hope has died because ye starved
it like a pot-bound plant within the shell of envy, in the
drought of greed! Too truly ye have longed to gain and
to possess; too little ye have hoped to add one gift to each
gift-laden moment as it comes!

"Lay one stone on another, and give thanks! Add one
deed to another and sing praises to the lords of tide and
time who measure the ant's labors and record kings' idle-
ness! Sing! Your very song shall vibrate in the universe
when ye return to earth a thousand lives from now!"

The orchestra stole its way into his last half-dozen sentences and, as he finished, burst into the splendid opening
bars of a hymn that was already ancient when the Hills
were young. Conquering, it sounded, rising, overturning,
splendid with the bloom of life and Hope that knows it is
immortal.

And how those girls, and the trained Tibetan chorus
massed behind them, sang! They swept the audience
along with them into a surging spate of sound whose mel-
ody was like the rolling wonder of long rivers.

The curtain came down amid such deafening applause
that not even the *radongs* could blare above the thunder
of it and the Lama had to shout like a mountaineer to

make himself heard behind the scenes. Ommony had seen no messenger arrive, no consultation held, but the word the Lama shouted rang with a strange note of anxiety, and though the audience was yelling for more song, and to see the dog again, the stage and the wings took on the aspect of a stricken camp—all haste, all running to and fro, but strangely no confusion.

Ommony was seized and stripped of his *saddhu's* costume—left to dress himself in Brahman clothes as best he might, while Maitraya fought against a similar indignity with as much effect as if he were a scarecrow struggling with a Himalayan wind. The other actors threw their costumes off before the wardrobe men could get to them; and before they could pull on their ordinary clothes the framework of the well and every detail of stage furniture had vanished. The girls had disappeared almost before the echo of the Lama's warning cry had ceased, and within five minutes from the time the curtain came down Ommony found himself alone in the wings with Diana and Dawa Tsering, who wanted to stay there and brag of his performance.

"I have made up my mind I will be an actor, Gupta Rao! I am good at it! Did you hear how they laughed when I showed myself? That play would have failed but for me! Ha-hah! The Lama knew it, too! He had to tell his lousy Tibetans to let me out of that room back there, so that I might come and save the day!"

Ommony did not waste time to disillusion him, but even so they were nearly caught by a tide of men who tried to surge in through the stage door, sweating, laughing, shouting questions, wanting to know when the next performance would take place, wanting to see the dog and to hear her talk again, demanding to be shown the Chinese actor and to know whether he was really Chinese—above all, when would the next performance be?

Ommony had to shove his way through the midst of them, holding Diana by the collar and hustling Dawa Tsering, who wanted to stop and wallow in flattery. Not

even loud commands to keep their unclean fingers off a
"twice-born" served to keep the crowd from getting in
the way; and they would have followed across the street
to the elephant stable if Ommony had not thought of telling them that the dog must be fed before she could possibly go to the temple of Siva and speak a couple of *mantras* from the street near the temple porch. (It was quite
safe to mention the temple of Siva; there is always one
where there are Hindus.) They stampeded toward the
temple to take up good positions, and only a few small
boys saw Ommony, Dawa Tsering and the dog go into
the elephant compound by way of the alley, which was
full of sheep through which they had to thread their way.

The pitch-dark compound was in quiet confusion. There
were camels being loaded, and the elephants were all in
line beside the balcony, from whose upper deck the girls,
already masked in black, were stepping down like goblins
into the curtained howdahs. Ommony found the Lama,
Samding beside him, standing near the last elephant of
the line; and as he drew near, some one whose outline
suggested Prabhu Singh returned thanks for the Lama's
blessing and disappeared into the darkness.

"Why the hurry?" Ommony demanded. "They came
crowding to the door to insist on another performance.
Why not stay and give it?"

"My son," the Lama answered, with the slightest trace
of tartness in his voice, "no course is good unless there are
seven reasons for it, even as no week is whole that has not
seven days. You may ride on that elephant—that third
one. May peace ride with you."

He who is wise is careful not to seem too virtuous, lest they who dislike virtue should exert unceasing energy to demonstrate that he is viler than themselves. True virtue suffers from advertisement.

FROM THE BOOK OF THE SAYINGS OF TSIANG SAMDUP.

CHAPTER XIX

A TUMULT in the street announced that Ommony's ruse had only gained a moment's respite. The night was alive with curiosity; a voice that bellowed like a fog-horn asked who the actors were—when they would perform again—whether San-fun-ho was a Mahatma—if so, which of all the pantheon he favored. Another voice shouted for San-fun-ho to come out and speak.

However, it appeared the Lama had foreseen all that. The bleating sheep gave notice that the barrier was down and the crowd swarmed into the alley. But a string of elephants to all appearance loaded filed down the alley from the compound and the crowd had to retreat; those elephants paraded through the town streets, drawing the crowd after them, and there were no spectators when the gate at the opposite end of the compound opened and the Lama's long procession—camels, elephants and this time mules as well—swayed toward open country.

The same Tibetan shared a howdah with Ommony, Dawa Tsering and Diana, and was just as uncommunicative as before. They crossed a railway line; an engine whistled and they had to cling to the howdah when the elephant climbed an embankment and descended on the far side; and once there was hollow thunder underfoot as the procession crossed a long bridge. The pace was much more leisurely than on the first night, and there were fewer interruptions; but twice out of the darkness, once in the gloom of overhanging trees, and once where the crimson glow of a bonfire shone through the howdah curtains, muttered orders came from men on foot and the direction changed.

236

About two hours before dawn a halt was called in what appeared to be some kind of royal park; there was a wall all around it and there were peculiar walled subdivisions, but nothing to show who the owner might be. The elephants, camels and mules returned by the way they had come, leaving the baggage heaped in a clearing between trees. Somebody shouted a long series of incomprehensible commands, repeating it all three times, and Ommony was hurried away to a tent in a triangular space with a stone wall on either hand and trees in front. There was a good bed in the tent, and a generous meal all ready on a linen-covered table.

When Ommony had finished eating Samding emerged out of the darkness like a ghost and stood framed in the tent opening, looking like a cameo against the sky.

"Tsiang Samdup sends a blessing," he said calmly. "He requests that you will not leave this enclosure. Kindly do not go beyond the trees."

He disappeared again. It was not until he had gone that it occurred to Ommony the language he had used was English. Speaking, thinking in two languages concurrently, occasionally listening to a third, one does not identify them without an effort. For a minute or two Ommony sat still, trying to recall the *chela's* voice, intonation and accent; it seemed to him that if the words had not been perfectly pronounced he would have noticed instantly that the *chela* was talking English, not Urdu. He recalled the exact words one by one. "Blessing," "enclosure" and "the" were key-words that would inevitably have betrayed a foreign accent had there been one; as far as he could remember all three words had been stressed exactly as a well educated Englishman would use them; he was sure there had been no accent on the vowel in "the"—a shibboleth that everlastingly betrays the Asian born.

"I'll swear that youngster is European," he muttered —and then laughed at himself. No European—certainly no English youth ever had it in him to seem so saintly and

at the same time to be so inoffensive. There would have
been an almost irresistible impulse to kick any western
youth who dared to look as virtuous as that. One did not
want to kick Samding.

Ommony turned Diana loose to roam wherever she
pleased; no inhibition had been laid on her. He hoped
natural canine curiosity might lead her to make new acquaintances who in some way would help to throw light
on the mystery; for as he threw himself on the bed to
sleep the whole thing seemed a deeper mystery than ever.
Was it propaganda intended to foist Samding on the
country as a new mahatma? A political mahatma, who
should bring on revolution? If so, why the sudden flight?
What could be the advantage of creating intense enthusiasm and then running away from it?

He was awakened late in the morning by a man who
removed the dishes and spread a fresh meal on the linen-
covered table. The man was some one he had not seen before, as silent as an oiled automaton. Diana was coiled
up asleep on her sacking. Dawa Tsering, smelling hot
food, awoke with a start to devour it, and it was he who
first noticed the silence.

"Gupta Rao, we are—"

He left his bowl of food and ran to the trees that
screened the end of the enclosure, peered between them,
and came hurrying back with a grin on his face.

"It is true. They have gone and left us!"

Ommony's obstinate jaw came forward with a jerk. An
insult from the Lama's lips could not have produced a
tenth of the effect.

"Damn him after all!" he muttered. "I admitted I
was spying. If he'd simply asked me to clear out, I'd have
gone and waited for him at Tilgaun. I'll be blowed,
though, if I'll let up now. I'll trace him if I have to—"

He sat down on the bed, glancing in the dog's direction,
wondering how much she had seen in the night and wishing she could really talk. She was curled up fast asleep,
but his eye detected something on her collar. He called

her, and removed a piece of paper that had been wired
to the brass ring; it was twisted and soiled, but the writing on the inside was perfectly legible, English, and done
in heavy quill pen strokes that he believed were the Lama's,
although there was no signature.

"There is a time for silence and a time for speech; a
time for seeing and a time for covering the eyes. This is
the time for silence and not seeing. Obey him who will
attend you."

But the man in attendance had vanished. The only
living creatures in sight outside the tent were crows on
the top of the near-by wall and kites wheeling lazily overhead. There was almost perfect silence—no roofs—no
smoke—nothing to suggest that there were human beings
within ten miles.

"I will explore," said Dawa Tsering. "That old Lama
is a great one at writing letters that mean nothing. Maybe I shall find that fellow who brought the breakfast. If
I beat him he may interest me with some news."

Ommony sat still and read the note again. The Lama
might be simply inducing him to waste time instead of
starting in pursuit; but there were several other possibilities, not the least that the Lama's route might be leading
somewhere where it would be dangerous for a foreigner to
go disguised. There are individuals, in India as elsewhere,
who would dare to ask the devil or even a Bhat-Brahman
for his identification papers.

Another not unreasonable theory was that the Lama
might be willing to be spied on at just such times as his
actions were not mischievous, but would prefer to keep the
spy at a distance when events of true importance were
under way.

At any rate, the wording of the note might be held to
imply a diplomatic threat that disobedience would termi-
nate all communication. And on the other hand, he supposed the Lama—a remarkably good judge of human
nature—knew that he, Ommony, would not permit himself to be dropped into the discard quite so easily as that.

If it was a trick, there would be more to it than merely leaving him behind; the best course was to sit still and await developments.

He awaited them for fifteen minutes, and then Dawa Tsering came, but not as a free agent. He was being led by the ear, although his huge "knife" was in his right hand and there seemed to be nothing to prevent plunging it into his custodian's stomach. Diana growled a challenge and ran forward to sniff quarrelsomely at the legs of the stranger, who ignored her as if she were not there; after a few sniffs she seemed to recognize him and returned to the tent, where she lay down close to Ommony and watched. She had ceased growling. The hair on her neck was no longer on end.

The stranger appeared to be a Sikh, but was possibly a Rajput. He was more than six feet tall, wore his black beard parted and brushed upward, looked extremely handsome in a gray silk turban whose end fell down over his shoulder, and was dressed in almost military looking khaki—jacket and trousers, with a gray silk cummerbund around his waist. He strode with consummate dignity that appeared to be natural, not assumed.

He let go Dawa Tsering's ear when he came within three strides of the tent, and took no further notice whatever of the Hillman, who stood a couple of paces away and thumbed the edge of his weapon, making grimaces that were nearly as inhuman as the grin on the devil-mask he had worn on the stage. There was nothing to show there had been a struggle; both men's clothes were in order; neither man was breathing hard. The stranger's dark-brown eyes looked steadily into the gloom within the tent and he presently saluted after a fashion of his own, quite unmilitary, something like the ancient Roman, raising his right hand, palm outward.

"Mr. Ommony？" he asked, in English.

"No!" roared Dawa Tsering. "Gupta Rao, thou ignorant idiot! A Bhat-Brahman from Bikanir—a man who has a devil in him, who can teach thee manners!"

"Yes, I'm Ommony."

There was something in the voice and in the eyes that warned Ommony there was nothing to be gained by evasion. He stood up and returned the salute, also in his own way, adding to the gesture of his right hand an almost unnoticeable finger movement. The other man smiled.

"I am Sirdar Sirohe Singh, of Tilgaun."

Ommony laughed sharply, the way a deep-sea captain coughs sarcastic comment when a pilot has missed the tide. Here was the Secret Service after all! It was Sirdar Sirohe Singh who had sent the written report of the missing piece of jade to McGregor.

"Come in," he said abruptly, and made room on the bed for the *sirdar* to sit down. He did not try to pretend to be glad to see him, but the *sirdar's* next words altered the whole aspect of affairs.

"I do hope my letter to Number One did no harm," he began, stretching out long legs in front of him and speaking at the tent wall. His English was almost perfect, but guttural and a trifle aspirated. "I was in a difficult position. As a member of the Secret Service I was obliged to report. As the Lama's friend I felt—naturally—other obligations. It was not until I learned that you were assigned to investigate that I ceased to worry."

"Who told you?" asked Ommony.

"Oh, I heard it. News travels, you know. No, I have not been in Delhi." (He had answered Ommony's thought; the question was unspoken.) "I arrived last night from the north. The Lama asked me to submit myself to your disposal."

"Does this place belong to you?" asked Ommony, examining the calm strong profile against the light. He had heard that the *sirdar* was a wealthy landowner.

"No. The Lama has the temporary use of it."

"It was kind of you to—how did you express it?—submit yourself to my disposal. What I most need is information," said Ommony.

"Ah. That is elusive stuff."

"Not if you keep after it. Tell me what you know about the Lama."

The *sirdar* turned his head quickly and looked straight at Ommony.

"Did you receive a note from him?" he asked. "It was tied to the dog's collar."

Ommony looked into the baffling dark eyes and could read nothing there except that the *sirdar knew much more* than he proposed to tell. He was also conscious of dislike, and knew that it was mutual.

"Just to what extent are you at my disposal?" he asked bluntly.

"I am to convey you to another place. Of course, that is, at the proper time and if you wish to go; not otherwise."

"Will the Lama be there?"

"Possibly."

"Tell me what you know of Samding."

"Did you read the note?" asked the *sirdar*, again meeting Ommony's stare. "I have a message for you from Miss Sanburn at the Tilgaun Mission. She entertained me the night I left Tilgaun. I admitted to her it was possible I might meet you somewhere. She asked me to convey affectionate regards and to say that she would appreciate notice of exactly when she may expect you."

Ommony turned that over in his mind for half a minute. He could imagine no legitimate reason why Hannah Sanburn should ask for notice in advance. As a trustee it was his duty to pay surprise visits. Mrs. Cornock-Campbell's story of a girl named Elsa of whose very existence he had never previously heard, was a perfectly good reason for paying his next visit unannounced.

"When will you be seeing Miss Sanburn again?" he asked.

"Oh, quite soon."

"Will it be necessary to admit to her that you have seen me?"

"Just as you like."

"Please don't admit it then."

The *sirdar* nodded; he seemed to regard the message as quite unimportant. Ommony followed the train of thought, however, and tried to catch him off guard with a question asked casually, as if he were merely making conversation:

"Have you seen Miss Sanburn's friend Elsa lately?"

But the *sirdar* was not to be caught. It was impossible to tell whether or not he knew any girl of that name.

"Elsa?" he said.

"I see you don't know her," said Ommony, unconvinced but judging it would be useless to pursue the subject. He did not see how a man who lived on the outskirts of such a small place as Tilgaun could very well be ignorant of the existence of Hannah Sanburn's remarkable protégée, more especially since he was a trained and trusted member of the Secret Service, whose duty it would be to report any unusual circumstance. He did not doubt that the *sirdar* had been retained in the Secret Service roster as much to keep an eye on the Mission as for any other reason.

"When are we to leave this place?" he asked.

"To-night. The Lama asked me to suggest to you the wisdom of not leaving the tent until I come for you—after the evening meal."

"Very well," said Ommony, standing up to cut short the interview. There was no sense in talking to a man who was determined to say nothing. "I'll be here when you come."

The *sirdar* bowed with dignity and strode away. The moment he was out of earshot Ommony called Dawa Tsering into the tent.

"Is my trunk in sight?" he demanded.

"Nay, everything is gone. My yak-hair cloak is gone, and my good blankets. Those Tibetans—"

That looked as if the Lama intended to await them somewhere. Ommony interrupted with another question:

"How did that *sirdar* manage you so easily?"

Dawa Tsering looked sulky. "I will lay him belly-up-ward one of these days!"

"How did you come to let him lead you by the ear then?"

"Huh! He lives at Tilgaun."

"What of it?"

"He is the friend of Missish-Anbun at the Mission."

"What of that?"

"He is also the friend of the Rajah of Tilgaun; and of the monks in the hills around Tilgaun; and of all the rascals who make Tilgaun a byword all the way from Lhassa to Darjiling. He has a servant with him, who would have seen, and would have told tales, if I had done more than draw my knife; and I tell you, Ommon*ee,* that dog of a *sirdar's* influence reaches all the way to Spiti. I don't want too many enemies; I have enough of them in Spiti as it is."

"Why did you draw your knife?"

"Because I saw him, and he saw me, and I said to him, 'Thou! We are not in Tilgaun. Have a care; the kites in this part are just as hungry as those that live farther to the north!'

"And to that he said, 'Maybe. But the kites must say prayers to Garudi*, it is not I who must feed them.' And at that he took me by the ear and led me hither. He is altogether too despotic."

"I'm afraid you'll be a poor friend to rely on in a tight place," said Ommony, smiling.

"I? I am a terror in a tight place! That is just what I am good at. But I like first to be sure it *is* a tight place, and that the luck is reasonable. Lately I have had bad luck. But wait and see!"

He sat down to sharpen his knife with a small imported hone that he had stolen somewhere, humming to himself a song about the feuds of Spiti, where

---

*The God of the birds.

"A white mist rolls into a valley and sleeps,
     O-ayee-O-ayee-O-ah!
There's a knife in the mist, and a young widow weeps,
     O-ayee-O-ayee-O-ah!"

Ommony lay on the bed in the tent and forced himself
to accept the situation calmly. There was no use in racking his brains; the mystery now had become still more
involved by the fact that Sirdar Sirohe Singh was a member of the Secret Service, who considered himself obli-
gated to report unusual incidents to McGregor and yet
did not hesitate to lend a hand in obscuring the very trail
he had requested McGregor to investigate; who instantly
returned the secret identification signal, and yet refused
to give information; who had been ordered by McGregor
to remain in Tilgaun and observe events, and yet did
not mind showing himself within two days' march of
Delhi (nearly a thousand miles from Tilgaun) to a fellow
member of the Secret Service, who he had no reason to
suppose would not report him!

The mystery increased again when night fell. The same
dumb, nondescript servant who had brought breakfast
came with supper and hovered twenty yards away, signaling with a white cloth when Ommony had finished eating. Promptly in answer to the signal the *sirdar* stepped
out from the trees with a lantern and called for Gupta
Rao in a loud voice, retreating as Ommony advanced
toward him until, on the far side of the belt of trees, Ommony was aware of shadowy forms of men—horses, at
least a dozen of them in a long line, with gaps between—
great shadowy carriages that filled the gaps as he drew
nearer—and at last, smiling as placidly as if the new
moon that shone like a sliver of pure gold over his shoulder were a halo he had just discarded, the Lama himself.

Samding was in attendance, moving about among the
horses, patting them; Ommony noticed him ease a bearing
rein. The Lama nodded to Ommony, stepped into the
foremost carriage followed by Samding, and drove away

at a gallop, the carriage swaying like a big gun going into action. Sirdar Sirohe Singh pushed Ommony into the next carriage (which had only four horses, whereas the Lama's had six) allowed Diana just sufficient time to jump in behind him, and slammed the door, almost shutting it on the dog's tail. A whip cracked instantly and the carriage started rocking and bumping in the Lama's wake. A moment later a third and a fourth carriage followed.

Within was almost total darkness. There were two windows made of slats, forming part of the doors; Ommony tried them both, but the slides were nailed in position. He opened a door and swung himself out on the footboard to get a view of the following carriages, which he could just discern through the gloom and the cloud of dust, their drivers swaying on the high box-seats and shouting as they plied the whip. There was no way of guessing whether Dawa Tsering had been left behind or not. He climbed back into the carriage, holding the door open, but could not see much except dust, darkness and occasional shadowy tree-trunks.

The pace was furious. The flight was evidently pre-arranged, and managed perfectly. Horses were changed every ten miles or so, but whenever that happened men came to either side of Ommony's carriage and held the doors shut, riding on the footboards afterward until the place where the change was made was out of sight. The route, except at intervals, did not lie along macadamed roads; once they lurched into a dry stream-bed and followed that for a mile or two, the wheels sinking in sand. But that, too, had been foreseen; men were waiting there, who ran alongside and seized the wheels whenever they sunk too deep, toiling as silently and smartly as a gun crew.

It was almost dawn when they rumbled over the paved streets of a fair-sized town, but there was nothing to show what town it was. At last squared stones rang underfoot, a great gate slammed, and a Tibetan opened the carriage door. Ommony found himself in a courtyard in front of

what looked like a temple door, only there seemed to be
no temple at the back of it—nothing but a wall and a
dense thicket of trees on ground that sloped up-hill for
more than a mile.

The Tibetan, taking him by the elbow, led him up steps
through the entrance and down again into a cavern that
was lighted with little imported kerosene lamps set in
niches in the hewn rock walls. There was a maze of passages to right and left, and one wide tunnel that wound
snake-wise until it opened into a vault, part natural and
part very ancient masonry, that would have held five
thousand people.

The Tibetan led him across that great crypt, down a
passage at the far end, through a short tunnel into a shaft
about fifty feet square at the base. Its sides sloped inward so as to be utterly unclimbable and seventy or eighty
feet overhead was a patch of sky not more than twenty
feet across.

In the midst, exactly under the square patch of daylight was a tank, brim-full of clean water. On every side
of the enclosure there were square openings half-concealed
by curtains made of matting. Ommony was led through
one of those into a cave about twenty feet long, very
plainly but quite comfortably furnished, and there the
Tibetan left him without a word.

There was no restraint placed on him; he went and sat
down in the opening, watching the dawn gradually fill
the place with light until the clouds shone clearly reflected
in the shallow tank.

After a while the Lama entered, followed by Samding
and several Tibetans, or men who looked like Tibetans;
they crossed to the far side and disappeared through one
of the curtained openings. Not long after that great
quantities of food—enough for twenty or thirty people—
were brought in earthenware bowls; enough for two men
was set down beside Ommony and the remainder was carried through the opening through which the Lama had
disappeared.

Ommony was left entirely to himself. After a while he sent Diana to explore, but though she disappeared through the Lama's entrance and stayed within for more than half an hour, nothing came of it; she returned and lay down beside him with her head on her paws, as if she had no information to convey.

So he proceeded to explore on his own account, commencing by merely walking around the tank. Nothing happened, so he peered into one opening that had no mat in front of it, walked in and found a cave almost exactly like his own, leading nowhere. He stayed in there a minute or two examining a very ancient carving on the wall, that bore no resemblance to any monument he had ever seen and yet was vaguely familiar; he could not guess its significance; it was extremely simple, almost formless, and yet suggestive of an infinite variety of forms; he tried to memorize it, for future reference, and then remembered that the glyph, with which the letter to McGregor in a woman's handwriting had been signed, was almost if not quite the same shape.

He was on his way out when Samding met him in the door, his brown turban and cloak outlined in gold by the daylight at his back. More than ever the *chela* seemed like some one from another world, and as usual he spoke without preliminary, in a voice no man could quarrel with:

"Tsiang Samdup desires you should not ask questions." The words were English, beautifully spoken. "If anything is lacking for your comfort you are to command *me.*"

Ommony laughed. "All right. I command you. Explain what all this means!"

Samding's face became lit with sudden laughter—not aggravating—friendly—wise—humorous

"Tsiang Samdup says, knowledge comes from within, not from without," he answered. "As a man thinks, so are his surroundings. Tsiang Samdup says, the eyes of curiosity see only what is not so, and it is not only a man's lips that ask questions; the eyes and the taste and the touch are all inquisitive, seeking to learn from without what shall deny the truth within. He who would see the dawn must wait for it; and even so, if he is blind, it will be darkness to him.''

"Where did you learn English?'' Ommony demanded.

"From within,'' said the *chela*. "All knowledge comes from within.''

Ommony laughed back at him. "All right. Tell me from within where Dawa Tsering is.''

"He shall tell you himself,'' said the *chela*.

He stepped back and pointed to Ommony's cave. There sat Dawa Tsering in the doorway, scratching his back against the rock. The *chela* walked away, stroking Diana's head, who followed him as far as the entrance to the Lama's cave.

"Where have *you* been?'' asked Ommony, going over and standing in front of the Hillman.

"Nowhere. I rode in the carriage behind you, with a lot of Tibetans. They are fools, and I won their money playing dice. Thinking to follow the luck, when I reached this place I discovered where those girls are—all in a big cave together—may it fall in and destroy them! They were too many, and they made a mock of me. But wait until I get them one at a time! I am not one to be mocked by women, Gupta Rao!''

This much I know: that it is easy to cause offense and easy to give pleasure, but difficult to ignore all considerations except justice, and much more difficult to judge rightly whoever, ignoring both offense and pleasure, leaves the outcome of his actions to the Higher Law. Therefore, judge yourself alone, for that is difficult enough; and, depend on it, the Higher Law will judge you also.

FROM THE BOOK OF THE SAYINGS OF TSIANG SAMDUP.

CHAPTER XX

DAWA TSERING would say no more about his adventure among the women, but it was plain enough that he had been made ridiculous. He was fortunate not to have been caught and manhandled; he realized it.

"If it had not been for some Tibetans," he grumbled, and then lapsed into moody silence, sharpening his knife on the edge of the entrance to Ommony's cave.

They were left entirely alone, watching birds that moved like specks on the infinite blue through the opening overhead, until night fell and the gloom within the shaft grew solid. Sound died with the light, and one lantern that a man set over the entrance to the Lama's cave made hardly any difference.

They brought food again, with some bones for the dog, and a candle to stick on the floor of the cave; but nothing else happened until the Lama's sonorous voice called through the darkness and Ommony followed him down the tunnel into the vast cavern he had crossed that morning. It was already thronged with people seated on mats or on the bare floor, who filled the place with whispers; a shuffling of feet like the sound of wind and running water came from the entrance, where hundreds more were coming down the long tunnel.

Such light as there was, came from little smoky lamps set on ledges in the rock walls. A bell rang when the Lama appeared and the orchestra, almost invisible in shadow, burst into tune such as Stravinsky never dreamed of, filling the cavern with din that made the hair rise— restless yearning noise, accentuated by the hoarse *radongs*.

Across one end of the cavern a strong stage had been

251

erected and a very rough curtain. The Lama led the way
behind it, where the stage was already set and the make-
up man was busy with the last of the actors. Tibetans
pounced on Ommony and dressed him for his part by
candlelight, but in the improvised wings, where the girls
waited, whispering and laughing, there were batteries of
acetylene lights all ready to be turned on, in charge of a
man who looked like a Parsee. Where the footlights should
have been there were mirrors arranged to throw the light
back in the actors' faces. Everything was make-shift; yet
everything appeared to have been done by men who knew
precisely what was wanted and who had worked without
confusion to provide it.

Just before the play began the Lama went before the
curtain and the music ceased. There was no light where
he stood; to the audience he must have resembled a shadow dimly outlined on the dark cloth.

He told a story interspersed with proverbs, and the
only sound from the enormous audience was in the pauses,
when they caught their breath. The moment his make-up
was complete Ommony stood at the edge of the curtain,
where he could hear and look out at the thousands of eyes,
on which the faint light from the lamps shone like starlight on still water.

" . . . So they spoke to the god who had come among
them. And the god said, 'Ye have a government; what
more do ye want?' Whereto they answered. 'But the government is bad, nor is it of our choosing.' And the god
said, 'Is the weather of your choosing?' And they said,
'Nay.' Whereat the god laughed pleasantly, for he was
one who knew the cause and the effect of things. 'As for
the weather,' he said, 'ye make the most of that. When
it is hot ye wear lighter garments; and when it is cold
ye light fires. When it rains ye stay indoors, and when it
is dry ye sally forth. If a man complains about the
weather, ye say he is a malcontent who should know that
all sorts of weather are of benefit to some folk, and that
all communities in turn receive their share of heat and

cold and drought and moisture. Is that not so?' the god asked; and they answered, 'Yea.'

"So the god asked them another question. 'If ye so adapt yourselves to what ye say is not of your contriving, how is it that ye say the government can not be borne? Can ye say that the rain and the snow and the heat are good, but the government is not good?' And the god laughed loud at them saying, 'Out of mischief and destruction no improvement comes. Like comes from like. Improvement is the product of improvement, not of violence. Ye have the government ye earn, exactly as the earth receives the weather it deserves. For the weather, which comes and goes, came and went before your time. Indeed, and also there were governments before your time. The weather has altered the hills and the plains. The governments altered your fathers and will alter you, and your sons after you.'

"Thus said the god. And they answered, 'Aye. But what if we alter the government?' And the god said, 'Ye can change the name by which ye call it, and ye can slay those in authority, putting worse fools in their place, but change its nature ye can not, ye being men, who are only midway between one life and another. But as the hills are changed, some giving birth to forests, some being worn down by the wind and rain, the weather becomes modified accordingly. And it is even so with you. As ye, each seeking in his own heart for more understanding, purge and modify yourselves, your government will change as surely as the sun shall rise to-morrow morning—for the better, if ye deserve it—for the worse if ye give way to passion and abuse of one another. For a government,' said the god, 'is nothing but a mirror of your minds— tyrannical for tyrants—hypocritical for hypocrites—corrupt for those who are indifferent—extravagant and wasteful for the selfish—strong and honorable only toward honest men.' And having spoken to them thus, the god departed, some remembering his words and some forgetting them. To those who remembered, life thereafter was

not so difficult, because of hope that brought tolerance so
that they minded each his own business, which is enough
for any man to do. But to those who forgot, there was
trouble and confusion, which each created for himself, but
for which each blamed the government, which therefore
persecuted him. Because a government is only the reflection of men's minds. May peace, which is the fruit of
wisdom, perfect you in all your ways.''

The *radongs* roared, drowning the last echo of the sonorous benediction. The orchestra crashed into the overture.
The Lama stepped behind the curtain with a glance to
right and left to make sure every one was in his place, sat
down behind the well and signaled for the play to begin.

As before, Dawa Tsering danced on first, but in no
other respect was the play quite the same as on the previous night. The Lama's signals, made at unexpected moments, changed things as if he were making music with
the actors for his instrument. *Sotto voce* he prompted,
and no one on the stage dared to slacken his attention for
a moment for fear of missing a changed cue. He seemed
to know how to adapt and modify the play to fit the different environment and, in keeping with the solemn gloom
of the huge cavern, he subtly stressed the mystery. The
acetylene lights threw a weird, cameo-like paleness over
everything; the Lama made the most of that, instead of
struggling to overcome it.

Toward the end of the last act the audience was spell-
bound, for the moment too interested to applaud; and the
Lama took advantage of that, too. He hurried in front of
the curtain and stood with both hands raised, the messenger of climax.

"Peace!" he boomed. "Peace is born within the womb
of silence! Go in silence. Break not the thread of peace!
Ye have conceived it! Bring it forth!''

The orchestra played softly, blending sounds as gentle
as falling rain with the burble of streams and the distant
boom of waterfalls. There were bird notes, and the sighing of wind through trees—half-melancholy, yet majestic

rhythm with an undernote of triumph brought out by the muffled drums.

"And if they would not talk for a day or two, they might perhaps remember!" said the Lama, pausing as he walked past Ommony, who was being stripped of his *saddhu's* costume. "There is virtue in silence."

"Listen, O Captain of Conundrums!" said Ommony, trying to speak with emphasized respect but failing, because a Tibetan was rubbing his face with a towel to remove grease-paint. "I can see I was too hasty to suspect you of wrong-doing. I capitulate. From now on, I'm your friend for all I'm worth." It was the most emotional speech he had made in twenty years, but emotion gripped him; he could not help himself.

The Lama smiled, his wrinkles multiplying the shrewd kindness of the bright old eyes.

"For all you are worth! If you knew, my son, how *much* that is, you might be less extravagant. Jump not from one emotion to another, lest you lose self-mastery!" He passed on, beckoning to Samding.

There was the same swift, exactly detailed rush to pack up and depart; the same apparent flight for no apparent motive—this time in covered bullock-carts that creaked through dimly lighted streets, until they came to a pitched camp on the outskirts of town, where camels and horses waited. Thereafter, cloaked beyond recognition, everybody except the Lama rode horseback, he sitting on a camel at the head of the procession looking like an old enormous vampire, his head drooped forward on his breast.

The girls rode surrounded by hooded men, who let no other men except Samding come near them. Ommony tried to draw abreast to see whether they sat their horses skilfully or not, but two Tibetans rode him off and, saying nothing, held his rein until the girls had a lead of a hundred yards. After that they kept two horses' lengths ahead of him, and even drove Diana back when Ommony sent her forward just to see what would happen.

There was only a thin new moon, and the road ran for

most of the distance between huge peepul trees that rendered the whole caravan invisible. Two hours after midnight they reached a village, where a change was made back to bullock-carts, which conveyed them to a town that they entered shortly after daylight and now, for the first time, no precautions were taken to prevent Ommony from learning where he was. The Lama had taken him at his word.

Ommony laughed as he recognized the inevitable effect of that. He would almost have preferred continued mistrust. He must now regard himself as the Lama's guest. Intensely curious still, immensely interested, as much puzzled as ever, but satisfied that the Lama was, as he expressed it to himself, "a pukka sportsman," he had to make up his mind to learn nothing that he might be called on to explain (for instance to McGregor) later on.

"I hate this business of condemning a man on mere suspicion. The old boy's entitled to the benefit of doubt. From me, from now, he gets it. I'm ashamed of having doubted him. Damn! I hate feeling ashamed!"

Obstinacy has its good side. Having made up his mind that the Lama was entitled to respect, Ommony could no more have helped respecting and protecting him than he would have dreamed of not protecting, for instance, Benjamin in the old days when Benjamin was a fugitive from rank injustice.

He began deliberately to shut his eyes to information. The advice of the Chinese prince-poet, not to watch your neighbor too closely when he is in your melon patch, about defined his attitude. And it is surprising how much a man can avoid seeing, if he is determined not to expose another's secrets.

He laughed at himself. He could not resist the impulse to continue in the Lama's company, although it was likely enough that sooner or later his presence in disguise might endanger the lives of the entire troupe. He was perfectly aware that he had received no definite proof of the Lama's honesty, pretty nearly sure that his own change of attitude was due to the same psychology that had won the applause of the crowd, and finally excused himself (with a laugh at his own speciousness) on the ground that he and Dawa Tsering and the dog were indispensable.

But when he had been shown into a small room at the rear of a temple enclosure, that seemed to have been deserted by its Hindu owners and, by some mysterious means, reserved for the Lama's use, the Lama came to him, accompanied as usual by Samding, and after looking at him for a moment seemed to read his mind, and promptly blew the argument to pieces.

"My son, I do not need you, or the dog or Dawa Tsering. All three are good, but I am not the molder of your destiny. Is there another way you would prefer to take?"

"I'll go with you," said Ommony, "if you'll accept my word that I'm not spying on you."

The Lama looked amused. His wrinkles moved as if he had tucked away a smile in their recesses.

"My son, to spy is one thing; to absorb enlightenment is something else. A man might spy for all eternity and learn nothing but confusion. For what purpose did you spy on me in the beginning?"

Ommony jumped into that opening. Here was frankness at last!

"I think you know without my telling. I began with the sole intention of finding my way into the Ahbor Valley to look for traces of my sister and her husband, who vanished in that direction twenty years ago. The piece of jade fell into my hands, and you know how that led to my meeting you. Then I heard a story about little European girls smuggled into the Ahbor Valley. I have seen these girls you have in your company. Explain them. Clear up the mystery."

The Lama seemed to hesitate. "I could talk to you about the stars," he said presently. "Yet if you should meditate about them, and observe, you would learn more than I could tell you. My son, have you meditated on the subject of your sister?"

"On and off for twenty years," said Ommony.

"And you now pursue the course your meditation has discovered? It appears to me that is the proper thing to do."

"You mean, if I follow you I'll find out?"

"I am no fortune-teller. Electricity, my son, was in the world from the beginning. How many million men observed its effects before one discovered it? Gold was in the world from the beginning. How many men pass where it lies hidden, until one digs and finds it? Wisdom was in the universe from the beginning, but only those whose minds are open to it can deduce the truth from what they see."

"Do you *know* what became of her?" Ommony asked abruptly. The tone of his voice was belligerent, but the Lama ignored that. He answered with a sort of masked look on his face as if he himself were still pondering the outcome:

"If I were to tell you *all I know,* you would inevitably draw a wrong conclusion. There are pitfalls on the way to knowledge. Suspicion and pride are the worst: but a desire to learn too quickly is a grave impediment."

During about three breaths he seemed to be considering whether to say more or not; but he leaned an arm on Samding's shoulder and walked out of the room without speaking again.

Sooner or later we must learn all knowledge. It is there-fore necessary to begin. And for a beginning much may be learned from this: that men in pain and men in anger are diverted from either sensation by a song—and very readily.

FROM THE BOOK OF THE SAYINGS OF TSIANG SAMDUP.

CHAPTER XXI

THE LAY OF ALHA

THEREAFTER life for two months was a dream of many colors, through which the Lama led without explaining any of it. At times Ommony abandoned hope of ever learning what the Lama's purpose was; at other times he dimly discerned it or thought he did, midway between the rocks of politics and the shoals of some new creed. And whether he guessed at the truth, or believed he never would know it, he reveled in the swiftly moving, nigh incredible procession of events.

No day was like another. No two receptions were alike in any town they came to. They put on the play in ramshackle sheds at country fairs with the din of sideshows all around them, in pretentious theaters built of corrugated iron, in temple courtyards, in more than one palace garden,—once in an empty railway godown* from which a greatly daring Eurasian clerk had removed stored merchandise,—in a crypt under a pagoda (and there was a riot that time, because some Brahmans said the place had been rendered unclean by the actors, and Ommony came within a hair's breadth of exposure)—in the open, under trees, where roads led to seven villages and a crowd of at least three thousand people gathered silent in the bonfire light that shone between enormous trees. Once they played in an empty tank, from whose bottom an acre of sticky mud, two inches thick, had to be cleaned out before the crowd could squat there; once in a cave so stuffy that Maitraya's women fainted.

They traveled by elephant, camel, horse, mule, cart, in

---

*Warehouse.

litters, for fifty miles by train, and once, for a day and
a night, in barges along an irrigation ditch, concealed
under hurdles on which vegetables were heaped to look
like full boat-loads.   They went alternately like hunted
animals, and like a circus trying to attract attention.

There were places where the Lama seemed to go in fear
of the police; other places where he ignored them as if
non-existent. He always seemed to know in advance what
to expect, and whether it was wise to move by daylight.
Most of the traveling was done by night, but there were
some places where crowds gave them an ovation as they
passed through streets at noon.

Once, when a man who looked like a rajah's son arrived
breathless on a foaming horse and talked with the Lama
under a wayside baobab, the party separated into four
detachments, and Ommony lay hidden for a whole day
under the blistering iron roof of an abandoned shed.
There was never any explanation given. None of the apparently chance-met providers of food and transportation
asked questions or gave Ommony any information.

Sometimes the Lama himself did not seem to know the
right direction. On those occasions he would call a halt
by the roadside and wait there until some mysterious individual arrived. Sooner or later some one always came.
Once they waited for a whole day within sight of a fenced
village. But they never lacked for food, or for the best
the country could provide in the way of accommodation.

In one large town of the Central Provinces, in which
three thousand people packed an assembly hall, there
were police officers on chairs near the stage, who made
notes ostentatiously. The Lama's speech before the curtain
on that occasion was rather longer than usual and Ommony, watching the policemen, recognized the insanity that
impels men to interfere with what they can not understand. That night he slipped off the stage before San-fun-
ho's last speech was finished, hurried into his Bhat-Brahman clothes, and was standing close to the police officers
when the crowd began to leave the theater. There was one

man with whom he had dined in the club at Delhi, another
who was notorious for drastic enforcement of the "Seditious
Practices" Act, and a third whom he did not know. They
were all three very hot under the collar. Said one:

"A damned nasty seditious play—obviously propaganda
to prevent enlistment. They've chosen this place because
recruiting's going on here for the army. It's anarchistic."

"Oh, decidedly. Part of Gandhi's non-cooperation tactics."

"Financed in America, I'll bet you. That's where all
the propaganda money comes from."

"Anyhow, we've a clear case. Seditious utterances
—uncensored play—no permit. Step lively and bring the
squad, Williams; we'll lock 'em all up for the night and
find out who they are."

But an obstinate Bhat-Brahman stood in Mr. Williams'
way and spoke in English, curtly:

"No, you don't! I'm detailed to this investigation by
McGregor! I won't have police interference! Keep your
constables out of sight!"

"Who are you?" asked the senior officer, pushing himself forward.

"Never you mind."

"Show me your credentials."

"At *your* risk! Come with me to the telegraph office
if you like and watch me get you transferred to the salt
mines! You'll enjoy a patrol up there—you'll get one
newspaper a month!"

"At least tell me your name."

"My number is 903," said Ommony. His number on
the Secret Service roster was not 903; but one does not
squander truth too lavishly on men who will surely repeat
it. He was not anxious that McGregor should have an
inkling of his whereabouts. The mere mention of a number was enough; the policemen walked out, abusive of the
Secret Service, conscious that the "Bhat-Brahman" was
grinning mischievously at their backs.

The Lama saw, but said nothing. That night he di-

rected the departure more leisurely than usual, as if satisfied that Ommony had made him safe from the police;
but from that time on he kept himself more than ever
aloof, and during two whole months of wandering Ommony did not succeed in having two hundred words with
him.

However, the Lama and *chela* reciprocated in due time.
They reached a town in the Central Provinces where not
even certified and pedigreed Bhats would have been welcome, and an uncertified one who traveled in doubtful
company was in danger of his life. A committee of "twice-
born" demanded his presence for investigation in a temple
crypt, and Ommony's retort discourteous, to the effect
that he recognized no superiors, aroused such anger that
the self-appointed judges of sanctity resorted to the oldest
tactics in the world.

Those who hate the Brahmans the most are most amen-
able to skilful irritation by them and most careful to insist after the event that Brahmans had nothing to do with
it; so it is just where the Brahmans are most detested that
they are most difficult to bring to book; and a mob can
gather in India more swiftly than a typhoon at sea.

It was a hot, flat, treeless city, as unlovely as the commercialism, that had swept over it these latter years, was
cruel. The streets ran more nearly at right angles than
is the rule in India, and the temples faced the streets with
an air of having been built by one and the same contractor, he a cheap one. The quarters the Lama's party occupied consisted of a hideously ugly modern theater that
backed on a cellular stack of ill-built living-rooms, the
whole surrounded by four streets, three of which were as
narrow as village lanes.

That night the packed audience was restless, and whenever the *saddhu* spoke his lines there were noisy interruptions, cat-calls, jeers. Some one threw a rotten orange
that missed Ommony but put Diana in a frenzy, and for
minutes at a time it looked as if the curtain would have
to be rung down before the close; but the Lama's quiet

voice from behind the well and from under the throne
kept up a steady flow of reassurance inaudible beyond the
footlights: "Patience! Forbearance! There is strength
in calmness. Proceed! Proceed! You are a king, Maitraya; you are not affected by ungentleness! Proceed!"

But even San-fun-ho's long speech was received with irritation; some one in authority had told the crowd it was
a trick to destroy their sacred religion. The *chela's* voice
rang through the theater and overcame the murmurings,
but the hymn to Manjusri that followed was drowned in
a babeling tumult as half of the audience poured in panic
out of one door while a mob stormed another, breaking
it down and surging in with a roar that shook the theater.

The stage-hands stripped the actors faster than usual
and herded them out through the back door to the living-
rooms. They tried to make Ommony go too, but he fought
them off when they seized him by the arms; he had hard
work to keep Diana from using her teeth to protect him
while he hurried into his Bhat-Brahman clothes, wondering what solution the Lama would discover for this predicament. "I'll bet the old sportsman won't surrender
me to the mob!" he muttered. "If I live through this,
I'll know exactly what to think of him! If he's a—" But
there was no word for what he might be. The crowd was
yelling, "The Bhat! The Bhat! The spy! The impos-
tor. Bring out the unclean ape who poses as a twice-
born!" Two scared-looking "constabeels" who had appeared from somewhere, standing at either corner of the
stage with their backs to the curtain, were valiantly preventing the mob from swarming behind the scenes. The
Lama seemed to have disappeared, and Ommony felt a
sudden, sickening sensation that the old man and his *chela*
were only fair-weather intriguers after all.

But suddenly the mob grew quiet—seemed to hold its
breath. The Lama's voice, not very loud, but unmistak-
able and pitched like a mountaineer's to carry against
wind and through all other sounds, was holding their attention from behind the footlights.

Then Samding passed across the stage and slipped in
front of the curtain; he had changed into that ivory-white
costume in which he had received Prabhu Singh, and was
smiling as if the prospect of a battle royal pleased him.
Ommony went to the edge of the curtain to watch, holding Diana's collar, ready to loose her in defense of the
Lama in case of need.

"Bring out the Bhat!" yelled some one. There was a
chorus of supporting shouts, but that was the last of the
noise. The mob grew still again, spell-bound by curiosity.

Samding took the center of the stage and the Lama
squatted down beside him, eyes half-closed, apparently in
meditation. The *chela* spoke, and his voice held a note of
appeal that aimed straight at the heart of simplicity.

"O people, if ye have been wronged, it is we ourselves
who first should put the matter right. Ye, being pious,
unoffending people, will afford us that privilege. We
ask no trial. That is unnecessary. Which among you
are the individuals who have suffered at our hands? Un-
wittingly, it may be we have done you harm. You will
agree it is the injured one to whom redress is due. Let
the injured stand forth. Let him, who of his own body or
possessions has suffered harm at our hands, step forth
and name his own terms of settlement."

He dared to pause for thirty seconds, while the mob
glared, each expecting some one else to hurl an accusation.
But the original instigators of violence are careful to keep
out of reach when the trouble begins, and there was no
spokesman ready with a definite accusation—nothing but
a disgusting smell of sweat, a sea of eyes, and a hissing of
indrawn breath. The Lama whispered, not moving his
head, and the *chela* continued:

"It is possible the injured are not here. Let some one
bring the men for whose injury we are in any way responsible!"

There was another pause, during which the Lama got
up and walked meditatively toward the edge of the curtain, where he came face to face with Ommony.

"My son, can you act the Bhat as well as you can the *saddhu?*" he inquired. "Otherwise escape while there is opportunity! Be wise. There is no wisdom in attempting what you can not do."

"Yes, I can act the Bhat," said Ommony. His jaws were set. He had been a last-ditch fighter all his life. Of all things in the world, he most loved standing by his friends with all resources and every faculty in an extremity.

The Lama returned to the *chela's* side, whispered and squatted down. The *chela* went on speaking:

"It may be ye have been misguided. There are always unwise men who seek to stir up indignation for their own obscure advantage. Are there any Brahmans in your midst?"

There was only one possible answer to that question. No "twice-born" would risk personal defilement by mingling with such a mob of "untouchables." A laugh with a suggestion of a sneer in it rippled across the sea of upturned faces.

"It would seem then that the Brahmans have sent you to pass judgment on a Bhat who is one of their own fraternity," said the *chela* calmly. "It appears they trust you to conduct the investigation for them. That is a very high compliment from Brahmans, isn't it? If *they* are willing to accept your judgment on such an important point, who are we that we should not abide by it? The Bhat shall give you his own account of himself. Henceforth ye may say to the Brahmans that they are no longer the sole judges of their own cause."

There was a laugh—a laugh of sheer delight that grew into a good-tempered roar. There was doubtless not a member of the mob who had not suffered scores of times from the blight of Brahman insolence. The Brahman's claim to be a caste apart and an unindictable offense for ever soothes his own self-righteousness but does not exactly make him popular.

"I pray you to be seated," said the *chela;* and after a

few moments' hesitation the mob sat down on the floor, first in dozens, then in droves.

There was no more danger, provided Ommony could play his own part; but if he should make one mistake the situation would be worse than ever. He beckoned one of the musicians, who was guarding the door at the rear of the stage, signed to him to bring his instrument, stepped out in front of the curtain and sat down beside the Lama. Hostile silence broke into a sea of grins and chuckles when Diana, still in her grease-paint, followed and squatted on his left hand between him and the musician. The musician was deathly scared, but unfroze and tuned his instrument when the Lama looked at him. Ommony surveyed the crowd with the best imitation of insolence his strained nerves could muster, taking his time, absorbing the feel of the Lama's calmness. He needed it; he sensed that the old man's courage was a dozen times as great as his.

"And now, my son," the Lama whispered, "we are face to face with opportunity."

That was a brave man's view of danger! Ommony laughed, cleared his throat and thrust his lips out impudently:

"People who don't know enough to ask a blessing, may expect to get—what!" he demanded tartly.

"*Pranam*," said two or three voices, and the murmur caught on. It was not unanimous, but it sufficed to put him in countenance. He blessed them with an air of doing it because he had to, not for any other reason.

"Now," he said in the nasal, impromptu. doggerel singsong of the minstrel, "I could sing for you a ballad of your own abominable shortcomings, and it would serve you right; but it would not make your souls white, and it would take all night. It would give me much delight, but it would put you all to flight, and I'm compassionate. Or I could sing you a few measures about the Brahmans of this place, who are a lousy lot, but if I sang of their disgrace, not a one would show his face again among you.

You need the Brahmans to keep you from thinking too
much of yourselves! They're bad, but you're worse;
you're the sinners and they're the curse. Take that thought
home and think about it!—Is there anybody here," he asked
with his head to one side, "who would like me to sing
about him personally? No? You're not anxious? Don't
be backward. Don't think it's too difficult. Stand up
and tell me your name, and I'll tell you all about you and
your father and your uncles and your son, and what mischief you were up to this day fortnight. Nobody curious?
Oh, very well. Then I'll sing you the Lay of Alha."

India will listen to that song hours without end. It is
a saga of Rajput chivalry, and men who know no chivalry
nor ever were in Rajputana love to hear it better than the
chink of money or the bray of the all-conquering gramo-
phone. Since the white man first imposed himself on
India there have not been half a dozen who have learned
that lay by heart from end to end, not three who could
have sung it, none but Ommony who could have skipped
long, tedious parts so artfully and have introduced in
place of them extempore allusions to modern politics and
local news. He outdid any Bhat they had ever heard,
because he did not dare to count, as Bhats do, on the song's
traditional popularity and so to slur through it anyhow.
He had to win the audience. But what obsessed him most
was a desire to win the Lama's praise; the harder he tried,
the more he admired the Lama, sitting as calm as a Buddha beside him.

Regarded as music his effort was not marvelous. As a
feat of wit and memory it was next thing to a miracle.
His voice, not more than fair-to-middling good and partly
trained, survived to the end because he pitched it through
his nose, relieving the strain on his throat, and his manner
grew more and more confident as he realized that memory was not playing tricks and he could recall every line
of the long epic. He sang them into a merry frame of
mind; he sang them thrilled, compassionate, intrigued,
excited, sentimental, bellicose and proud in turn. He had

them humming the refrain with him. He had them swaying in time to the tune as they sat, their laughing, upturned faces glistening with sweat. He had them throwing
money to him before the lay was half sung; and it was
then that the Lama whispered:

"Enough, my son. Forget not to put skill in the conclusion."

Ommony stopped singing, and gagged at the crowd,
with his tongue between his teeth, pretending that his
voice had given out.

"Did any Brahman in this city ever do as much for
you?" he croaked, and they roared applause.

"I am a Bhat, and I can bless or I can curse more ef-
ficaciously than any thousand Brahmans in the province!
Watch!"

He turned to Diana and made her sit up on her
haunches.

"What do *you* think of the Brahmans of this city?"
he demanded, and Diana growled like an earthquake.

"What do you think of these people in front of you?"

She barked and got down on all four feet to wag her
tail at them.

"There! There you are! Even a dog knows you are
well-meaning folk who have been fooled by rascally Brahmans, who mouth *mantras* and do unclean things when
none is looking! Get out of here, all of you, before I curse
you! Go while I am in a good temper—before I put a
blight on you! Hurry!"

They yelled for more song, but it was after midnight
and the Lama had other plans. He hustled Ommony off
the stage, himself remaining at the corner of the curtain
for a minute to make sure of the crowd's mood. Ommony
heard the chink of money as he rewarded the two "constabeels." Then, as placid as Ommony had ever seen him,
but a little stooped and tired, he led the way to the stage
door, saying over his shoulder to Samding:

"Did you study that lesson? Have you learned it?"

Ommony did not catch the *chela's* answer. He felt the

floor jerk underfoot and stepped off a trap-door. It moved, and a hand came through, then the outline of a face that appeared to be listening. He bent down to lift the heavy trap and Dawa Tsering climbed out on hands and knees, sweating profusely and rubbing dust out of his eyes.

"Yow, there are rats in that place, Gupta Rao—big ones, and it is dark! Go down and look if you don't believe me."

"What were you doing down there?" Ommony inquired.

"I? Down there? Oh, I was looking to see if there was a passage by which that mob could reach you from the rear. Yes, I was! Don't laugh at me, or I will call you by your right name! Why didn't you turn me loose with my knife to drive the mob forth, instead of singing to them like a nurse to a lot of children? I could have cleaned the place of that rabble in two minutes. You should have left it to me!"

"Did you kill any rats?" asked Samding, grinning mischievously. He was holding the door open, waiting for them.

"Thou! I will kill thee, at any rate!"

The Hillman rushed at the *chela,* but Ommony tripped him. Samding slipped through the door and let it slam.

"There, did you see that?" Dawa Tsering grumbled, picking himself up. "That *chela* uses the black arts! He threw me to the floor with one wink of his eye. Did you see? He is no good! He is a bad one! Now I am never tempted to slay the Lama, which is why I endure his objectionable righteousness; but that *chela*—I never see him but I want to squeeze his throat with my two thumbs, thus, until his eyes pop out!"

The secret of the charm of the lotus is that none can say wherein its beauty lies; for some say this, and some say that, but all agree that it is beautiful. And so indeed it is with woman. Her influence is mystery; her power is concealment. For that which men have uncovered and explained, whether rightly or wrongly, they despise. But that which they discern, although its underlying essence is concealed from them, they wonder at and worship.

FROM THE BOOK OF THE SAYINGS OF TSIANG SAMDUP.

CHAPTER XXII

DARJILING.

THE standing miracle was the Lama's skill in having his own way and in keeping his own secrets without any discoverable method. His way seemed more alertly excellent, his secrets more obscure, from day to day. For instance: those mysterious young women. Not for one minute during two months and eleven days did Ommony or Dawa Tsering find an opportunity to speak with them alone, not though Diana grew dangerously fat on sticky sweetmeats that they gave her, she construing orders to go and make friends with them into permission to accept food.

The only key that seemed to fit the mystery was that the girls had been too well trained to be tricked into indiscretion. Tyranny could never have accomplished it. Once, Ommony picked up an amethyst earring, dropped in a corridor: he wrapped it in paper on which he scribbled a humorous verse, tucked it into Diana's collar, and sent her nosing around in the girls' quarters. The dog returned after an hour or so with a caricature of himself drawn on the paper in charcoal, extremely clever but not flattering. On another occasion he sent Diana with a note asking for the words of the song that the girls chanted on the stage; he saw the Lama read that note on the stage the same night and, after a quiet glance at him, deliberately tear it up. The following morning he received the words of the song in the Lama's heavy handwriting. He was acutely aware that the girls discussed him with a great deal of amusement, but he could never get them to exchange glances or make any response to his overtures.

Dawa Tsering made a dozen attempts to invade the women's quarters. Several times he was caught by the

272

Tibetans and disposed of cavalierly, usually simply chucked into the nearest heap of garbage. Three times he managed to get into a room in which the girls were, but he would never tell afterward what had happened to him; once he emerged so angry that Ommony really believed for an hour or two that he might murder some one, and took his knife away, but returned it at the Lama's instigation.

"It is not always wise to prohibit," said the Lama. "His imagination needs an outlet. Give him his toy."

It was a baffling conundrum why the Lama should go to such pains to present his play in more than sixty towns and villages, and always escape immediately afterward. It was not always the police; he treated the occasional difficulties they presented pretty much as a circus director regards bad weather. He appeared to be much more afraid of the results of his own success, and to run away from that as from a conflagration. Offers of money, prayers, nothing could persuade him to repeat a performance anywhere. The greater a crowd's importunity, the swifter his flight.

By the time they reached Darjiling Ommony was convinced of two things: that the "Middle Way" is undiscoverable to outsiders, being opened, closed and changed in detail by unknown individuals, obeyed implicitly, who do their own selecting; and that the Lama was himself in receipt of orders from a secret hierarchy.

The latter was almost certainly true. A Ringding Gelong Lama does not rank as high in the Lamaistic scale as a cardinal does in the Roman Catholic Church. Even supposing Tsiang Samdup, as was rumored, was an outlaw who had been turned out of Tibet for schism, that would make it even more unlikely that he could command an extensive spy system and mysterious service along the "Middle Way" without some long established hierarchy to support him.

And if he *were* an outlawed heretic, why was it that in Darjiling he went straight to a Tibetan monastery, that opened its doors to the whole party? They arrived at

dawn, having ridden all night on mule-back up a winding
path that crossed and recrossed the circling railway track,
ascending through clouds that wrapped them in wet
silence, until dawn shone suddenly through pine trees and
the monastery roof glistened a thousand yards ahead of
them.

The roar of *radongs* came down the chilly wind, announcing they were seen. A procession of brown-robed
monks filed out to meet them, each monk spinning a
prayer-wheel and grinning as he mumbled the everlasting
*"Om Mani Padme Hum"** that by repetition bars the door
of the various worlds of delusion and permits pure meditation. It seemed to give no offense that Tsiang Samdup
and his *chela* had no prayer-wheels. Maitraya and his
actors were as welcome as the rest. Ommony was greeted
with child-like grins from oily, slant-eyed Mongolian faces
that betrayed no suggestion of suspicion. The dog was
chuckled at. Maitraya's actresses were greeted no more
and no less cordially than the rest.

But the *chela's* reception was peculiar. The Abbot
blessed him solemnly, then stared at him for a long time.
From the others there was an air of deference; a peculiar
form of treating him as a mere *chela*, with an attitude of
deep respect underlying it and not nearly concealed. They
exchanged glances and nodded, formed a group around
him, regarding him with curiosity, and with something
akin to awe. The *chela* appeared more disposed to be
friendly than distant, but kept a deliberate course midway
between the two extremes, watched all the while intently
by the Lama, who finally leaned on his shoulder and almost hustled him in through the gate.

Once within the monastery wall Ommony was led away
to a cell high up under a gabled roof, where a smiling old
monk brought breakfast, laughing and snapping his fingers at Diana, not in the least afraid of her, but dumb

---

*Om, of the heavenly world; *Ma*, of the world of spirits; *Ni*, of
the human world; *Pad*, of the animal world; *me*, of the world of
ghosts; *hum*, of the spaces of hell.

when asked questions. He knew Ommony was no Brahman—laughed at the caste-mark—touched his own forehead comically—and went out spinning a prayer-wheel that he kept tucked into his girdle whenever both hands were occupied; he seemed anxious to make up for lost time.

The unglazed window provided a far view of Kanchenjunga, twenty-eight thousand feet above sea level—twenty-one thousand feet higher than the monastery roof—a lonely, lordly monarch of the silences upreared above untrodden peaks that circled the whole horizon to the north. Six thousand feet below, the Rungeet River boiled through an unseen valley. For a moment all the boundaries of Sikhim glittered in every imaginable hue of green, and between and beyond colossal snow-clad ranges the eye could scan the barren frontiers of Tibet. Then, as swiftly as eyes could sweep the vast horizon, mist of a million hues of pearly gray, phantom-formed, changing its shapes as if the gods were visioning new universes in the cloud, rolled and descended, stunning imagination with the hugeness that could wrap that scene and hide it as if it never had been.

Then rain—cold dinning rain that drummed on roof and rock, and splashed in cataracts to mingle with the spate of the Rungeet River crowding through a mountain gap toward the rice-green, steamy lushness of Bengal; rain that swallowed all the universe in sound, that beat the wind into subjection and descended straight, as if the Lords of Deluge would whelm the world at last for ever. Rain, and a smell of washed earth. Rain pulsing with the rhythm of a monastery bell, like the cry of a bronze age, drowning.

That bell seemed to clamor an emergency and Ommony hurried along cold stone corridors until he found his way into a gallery from which he could peer down into a dim hall through swimming layers of incense smoke. Silken banners, ancient but unfaded, hung all about him; images of the Gautama Buddha and disciples were carved on shadowy walls; the gloom was rich with color—alive with quiet breathing. He could see the heads of monks in rows, but could distinguish no one for a while because the heads were bowed and most of the light was lost in baffling shadows.

At one end was an altar, gilded and most marvelously carved, backed by an image of Chenresi. All the altar furniture was golden, and the monastery's pride—the book named *Zab-choes-zhi-khro-gongs-pa-rang-groel-las-bar-dohi-thoes-grol-chen-mo**—lay in the midst on a golden plate before Chenresi's image.

Dim music began and a chant, long grown familiar—that hymn to Manjusri that had thrilled so many audiences—and at last through the layering incense Ommony could make out the forms of the Lama and Samding. The *chela* was holding the fragment of jade in both hands and was walking solemnly toward the altar, where the Abbot and the Lama waited to receive him.

The drumming of the rain on roof-tiles ceased. One shaft of sunlight, beaming through a narrow window, shone on the jade as the *chela* laid it on the altar, making it glow with green internal fire. The *radongs* roared. The hymn changed to a chant of triumph, swelling in grand chords that shook the roof-beams. But Ommony hardly heard it. Something else, as the *chela*, almost exactly underneath him, moved into the beam of sunlight, held his whole attention.

"Well, I'll be blowed!" he muttered. He rubbed his eyes, made sure they were not lying to him by glancing at the image of Chenresi and at the rows of monks' heads, then stared again. "May I be damned, if—"

He looked at Diana, crouching in the gallery beside him, her head full of information that lacked only power of speech.

*This has been translated to mean: "The great liberation by hearing on the astral plane from the profound doctrine of the divine thoughts of the peaceful and wrathful deities emancipating the self." Mr. Evans Wentz translates it "The book of the Dead," but this is a very free and decidedly doubtful rendering of the manuscript's shorter title: "Pardo Todol."

"I suppose if you could talk, Di, you'd lose your other gifts," he muttered. Then he whistled softly to himself.

Not for a fortune and a hundred years of life would he let up now! Let the Ahbor country be as savage as the fringe of Dante's hell, as inaccessible as Heaven, and as far away as righteousness, he would go there, if he must die for it!

"Di, old lady, this is the grandest scent you ever laid nose on! Mum's the word. I'll take a feather out of your cap!"

The service no longer interested him. He did not wait to see what they did with the piece of jade—no longer cared a rap about it. He was almost drunk with new excitement and a mystery compared to which the jade was mere mechanics—a mystery half-unraveled that set his brain galloping in wild conjecture, so wild that he kicked himself and laughed.

"Maybe I'm mad. They say India gets us all sooner or later." But he knew he was not mad. He knew he had strength enough and sense enough to hold his tongue and to keep on the trail with every sharpened faculty he had. He was itching now to get to Tilgaun, partly because that was midway to the Ahbor country, but for another reason that made him laugh because he knew he held a secret key that would unlock more secrets.

He returned along draughty corridors to the cell that was full of white mist pouring through the unglazed window, and sat down to consider whether he should keep up the Bhat-Brahman rôle or let his beard grow and resume the garb of an unimaginative Englishman.

He had not made up his mind when a rap came on the door and the Lama blew in on a gust of rising wind, his long robe fluttering clear of the strong brown legs. The *chela* followed him and slammed the door, unrolled a prayer-mat and presently sat down on it beside the Lama. Ommony fought hard to suppress the triumph in his eyes as he stood, and then sat down on the truckle bed in obedience to the Lama's gesture.

"It is cold," said the Lama. "You must have a sheep-skin coat, my son. We mountaineers are too prone to forget that others suffer from what we consider comfort. Samding, see that Gupta Rao is provided."

He did not glance at the *chela*. His eyes were on Ommony's.

"And what have you learned, my son?" he asked presently.

"Very little," said Ommony. "I have learned that all my power of observation isn't much more than a beetle's."

"But that is a great deal to have learned," the Lama answered. Then, without a pause: "And you are not yet satisfied?"

"On the contrary. I hold you to your promise to let me pursue whatever course my meditation opens up."

"My son, I am not the appointed keeper of such permits!"

"You can make things difficult or make them easy for me. Which are you going to do?" asked Ommony; and it seemed to him that the *chela* was smiling behind that marvelously molded face.

"What is it you wish to learn most?" asked the Lama; and Ommony, after one hard look at the *chela*, closed his eyes to think. It would be useless to tell anything but raw truth; he had a feeling that the Lama could detect the slightest taint of falsehood; yet he was determined not to confess to what he now knew, because in all likelihood that would shut all doors against him. "A little knowledge" is usually doubly dangerous, if the other fellow knows you know it.

"I wish to demonstrate that I was really right to decide to trust you," he said at last.

"But you know that," said the Lama. "Your heart tells you you were right. A man's heart does not lie to him; it is the brain that lies, imagining all kinds of vanities."

Ommony took thought again. He sensed that he was on trial, not for his life but for something more important —leave to go ahead and find out for himself the whole solution of the mystery. He had to find an answer that should not be false, that should not betray the knowledge he already had, and that should nevertheless appeal to the Lama's sense of fitness. Superficiality would receive a superficial answer. Deep was asking deep for a disclosure of ultimate motive.

"My job in the forest is gone. I want to find work worth doing," he said at last.

"And do you think I can show you that?" asked the Lama, looking straight at him. One moment he looked very old, the next not more than middle-aged. It was as if he hovered between this world and another, in which were visions that he could bring back with him to earth. Ommony threw evasion to the winds.

"I want to learn your secret!"

"Ah! But to obey? Not me, but to obey your own heart, if I help you to see what none of your race has ever yet seen?"

"I'll do what I believe is right," said Ommony, and the Lama nodded, glancing sharply at Samding, as if to see whether the *chela* confirmed his opinion. The *chela* smiled inscrutably.

"You should go to Tilgaun," said the Lama, "where you might have gone in the beginning. If you wish, you may follow me to Tilgaun, and await what comes of it."

He had a way of ending a discussion as abruptly as he had begun it, his mind almost visibly closing, vaguely suggestive of the way a tortoise draws in its head. One realized it would not be the slightest use to speak another word to him on the subject. The *chela* got up and helped him to his feet, rolled up the mat and followed him out of the room almost mechanically, but turned in the doorway suddenly and looked back. It was dark there, for the door was set in a stone arch six feet deep and there was no window at the end of the draughty corridor. But Ommony could almost have sworn the *chela* laughed silently. There was a momentary glimpse of white teeth and a movement of the head that certainly suggested it.

"It beats the deuce!" he reflected. "That *chela* knows now that I know she's a girl, although I can't imagine *how* she knows it; and that means that the Lama knows I know it—for they haven't a secret apart. And the strangest part is that they don't seem to give a damn—either of 'em!"

If a vain man should value your virtue, beware! For he will steal it in the name of God, and he will sell your reputation in the market-place.

FROM THE BOOK OF THE SAYINGS OF TSIANG SAMDUP.

CHAPTER XXIII

TILGAUN

THERE was no more rain that day, but mist that wrapped Darjiling in a dripping shroud. Beads like perspiration gathered and trickled down interior walls, and there were no fires; the monks led the austere life that includes indifference to such minor afflictions as ague, and through indifference they seemed to have become immune. But Ommony suffered.

A monk brought him a long sheepskin coat, and in that he paraded the corridors to keep his blood circulating. He begged more sheepskins and set Dawa Tsering to work making a coat for Diana, because animals used to the plains die of pneumonia in those altitudes more readily than human beings. He tried to decide whether or not to go into Darjiling and buy European clothes, while he leaned over a parapet to watch strong-legged Sikhim women looming out of the mist loaded like camels with huge piles of cord-wood for the monastery kitchen, until that bored him.

He was feverish with impatience. At noon he made up his mind to go and ask the Lama's advice about disguise, supposing he could find him. But as he left the cell to hunt for the Lama a monk came with the midday meal and stood by to watch him eat—a cheery old monk, who laughed when questioned and talked about everything under the sun except what Ommony wanted to know, spinning his prayer-wheel furiously as if to immunize himself against heretical contagion.

And when the monk had shuffled away with the empty platters and Ommony set forth again to hunt for the Lama, Maitraya met him midway along the first draughty

282

corridor—Maitraya smothered in a sheepskin coat like
Ommony's and blowing great clouds of breath in front of
him.

"I am paid, O Gupta Rao! I have a draft on Benjamin
and money for the railway fares to Delhi—enough for
first-class fares for all of us and liberal provision for the
way. Would that there were more men like Tsiang
Samdup! May the generous gods bless him! No argument, Gupta Rao; no deductions; no delay; a bag of
money, an order on Benjamin, and such courteously
worded thanks as Vishnu never received from a mother
just delivered of a son! I feel as if my whole body had
been drenched in thanks from inside outward! Are you
on your way to your cell?"

"I am on my way to find the Lama. Where is he?"

"Gone! Didn't you know that? He left an hour ago,
he and all the women and Samding, on little Tibetan
ponies. There was no ceremony. They rode away like
ghosts into the mist."

Maitraya took Ommony's arm in rank defiance of caste
decorum.

"Come along, Gupta Rao. I know you are no Brahman.
You are possibly a Kshattriya like me, but what the devil
has caste to do with our profession! Whatever you are,
you have the approval of me, Maitraya! You are a great
actor. You are a man after mine own heart—a little con-
ceited possibly—a trifle grumpy on occasion—but we all
have faults. I know a first-rate actor, when I see him!
I forgive the little insignificances. I respect the strength
of character—the genius! Come, let us go along to your
cell; I have a proposal for you."

Ommony led him to the cell and sat down on the truckle bed. Maitraya would not sit; he threw an attitude and
paced the floor, striving to create an atmosphere of tremendous drama, that somehow refused to materialize between those dripping walls. He shuddered at the cold
when he should have gestured like a Mogul chieftain, and
coughed, which rather spoiled the grandeur of his voice.

"Gupta Rao—let us accept our destiny! If two men, mutually worthy of respect, were ever brought together for immortal purposes, those two are we! Consider! Have we not a task in common? Have we not a great ideal to espouse together? Is it not our duty to inspire the stage of Hind*? Have we not a ripe field waiting for us? Should we not revisit all the scenes of our success and stage such plays as shall uplift the drama of this land of Hind for ever? Think of those audiences, Gupta Rao! Think of the profits! Charge no more than one-half *rupee* admission, and we make our fortunes!"

Ommony cast about for an excuse for refusing, that should not turn a friend into an enemy.

"Who do you propose should write the plays?" he asked.

"We have a play! *Ye Rulers of the Upper Spheres*— a play, I tell you! I have memorized the whole of it! Let the Jew finance us, Gupta Rao! Let us go to Benjamin and use our joint persuasion to wheedle a decent contract out of him. I offer you a one-third interest! Commercialism—pah! The Jew is a commercialist, so we must feed him with *rupees*. The Lama, on the other hand, is ignorant of money's value; he fails to see that it is good for the audience to pay a fair price for its education. As for us, let us take the middle way between two crass extremes. And if in the process we make a fortune, that will be no more than what is due to us. Have you heard that Christian adage, that the laborer is worthy of his hire?"

"I seem to have heard another one about stealing," said Ommony dryly. "The play is the Lama's."

"Bah! It isn't copyright. He should have taken elementary precautions. Besides, he has no right to keep for his own use an idea that has universal application. The play is religious; who can copyright religion?"

"Did you think of obtaining the Lama's permission?" asked Ommony.

---

*India.

"No, I confess, I never thought of that. But it's too late now; he's gone. Let us go to Benjamin. The Jew will see the point of not letting a good profitable play lie idle for the sake of a bit of squeamishness. Come along. Let Benjamin convince you."

Ommony jumped at that solution. He knew Benjamin.

"All right," he said. "You make the proposal to him. If Benjamin agrees, I will then consider it. And don't forget, you'll need a genius to act the part of San-fun-ho!"

"Aha!" exclaimed Maitraya. "Genius! I can act that part much better than the *chela* did! Not that he was bad, mind you—not that he was bad. I will play San-fun-ho, and you the king. Together we will create dramatic history!"

"First create confidence in Benjamin! I'll answer yes or no when you have persuaded *him*," said Ommony.

He got rid of Maitraya with difficulty. No argument availed until it dawned on Maitraya that he could pocket the cost of transportation by leaving Ommony behind; then he permitted himself to be led along the corridor and lost in the maze of passages and stairways.

Ommony went in search of the Abbot, and found a monk at last who did not shake his head and grin when spoken to, but led up an outside stairway to a grimly austere cell just under the roof, where the Abbot sat cross-legged on a stone platform at one end, meditating. He opened his eyes and gazed at Ommony for several minutes before a smile at last spread over his Mongolian face and he passed one lean hand down the length of his scrawny gray beard. He appeared to be well pleased with the result of his inspection.

"The spirit of restlessness is difficult to overcome," he said at last. "It is sometimes wise to yield to it. There are many lives. Not all knowledge can be acquired at once. In what way can I help, my son?"

Ommony thought of asking a dozen questions, but discerned that the gentle courtesy concealed an iron aptitude for silence. He came straight to the point.

"I beg forgiveness for intrusion. I return thanks for
food and lodging. Did the holy Lama Tsiang Samdup
make a statement of his wishes with regard to me?"

The Abbot's face became wreathed in smiles again. He
nodded.

"Where do you wish to go, my son? To Tilgaun?
When?"

"Now!"

The Abbot struck a gong that hung on the wall beside
him; before its overtones had died a young monk appeared
in the doorway and received swiftly spoken singsong
orders in a language Ommony did not understand. The
monk gave guttural assent, and waited in the door for Ommony to go with him, but there was two or three minutes'
delay while the Abbot amused himself by playing with
Diana almost childishly, laughing at her new sheepskin
coat and using his staff to measure her height at the shoulder and her length from the tip of her nose to the end
of her tail. Ommony made Diana sit up and salute him,
whereat he blessed the dog solemnly. Finally he gave
seven turns to a prayer-wheel fixed in an iron bracket
within comfortable reach, nodded to the monk, and smiled
farewell at Ommony, dismissing him with a blessing that
sounded like the first bars of an anthem to eternal peace.

Followed laughter, bustling, friendliness, and no delay.
They speeded the departing guest. A dozen monks made
themselves agreeable; two of them carried out Ommony's
trunk into the courtyard; some led out little sturdy Tibetan ponies and held them while others lashed the loads
in place with the unhurried speed of old campaigners.
There was ample supply of provisions, including grain for
the ponies, and when Ommony suggested paying for it all
they laughed. They seemed amused at the idea that any
guest of theirs should pay for anything.

However, he noticed that two sturdy-looking Tibetans
who were certainly not monks, had been told off to ac-
company him; they were listening to instructions from the
young monk who had received the Abbot's incomprehen-

sible orders; standing at a little distance apart, they kept nodding as the instructions were repeated again and again.

There were in all eight ponies and the party was on the way, filing through the wide gate with one Tibetan leading and the other Tibetan bringing up the rear, within thirty minutes. Dawa Tsering burst into song as he rode under the arch behind Ommony and they were all swallowed in a drifting bank of cloud that even hid the monastery wall as they turned sharp to the right and followed the track that ran beside it. The sturdy little ponies put their best foot forward as they always do when they are headed northward.

The ninety miles to Tilgaun meant four days of strenuous going, for the miles are reckoned as the crow flies, whereas men and their mounts must climb and descend over the shoulders of hills heaped on one another by the gods to keep away intruders. The trail wound down through phantom deodars and dipped into a fleecy white fog that condensed in dew on everything warm that it touched, descending seven thousand feet into the Rungeet Valley before they crossed a long bridge and commenced to climb again.

Most of the time it was like sitting on an earthquake; there was nothing to do but cling tightly and watch the pony's ears in the mist as the nimble legs slid, struggled and recovered. There was no chance for anything but single file among the rocks and rhododendrons; even Diana had to trot behind the pony to escape being trodden on. It was not the surfaced highroad they were taking, but presumably a short-cut, which the Tibetan guide appeared to know as intimately as a mole knows tunnels.

They climbed nine thousand feet and slept in a windy hut above the clouds, where the Tibetans cooked greasy supper and sang plaintive songs in which Dawa Tsering joined. There was no sign of the Lama's party, nor any answer to Ommony's questions as to how far ahead the Lama might be; nor was there any indication that the

Lama's party had crossed that pass ahead of them. But at dawn, when Ommony wanted to make an early start the Tibetans had scores of excuses that ended with blunt refusal. They were not impudent or surly; they smiled as cheerfully as Chinese statues and simply did not load the ponies.

"If I slew them, as they deserve, there would be none to do the work," said Dawa Tsering. "Why not offer them money, thou? Never fear—I will win it back from them at dice!"

Ommony offered money, but the Tibetans only showed their teeth in wider grins than ever. There was nothing to do but wait until they were pleased to move, and they did not do that until the sun was over the highest ridges by a full hour and a wind had blown new banks of mist into the ravines. Then suddenly, as if they had received a message through the ether, they began to pack the ponies and were off in no time without a word of explanation.

The hills lay in parallel waves that must be crossed diagonally, as a boat offers its shoulder to a rising sea. To the northward the huge range of the Himalayas made itself felt but was invisible; there was a sense of impending immensity, increased by the curtain of cloud that drifted between earth and Heaven. Wherever passes gaped between the shoulders of the mountains, dense white clouds flowed down along them, looking like incredibly swift glaciers. Half of the time the rump of the pony ahead was just discernible through the mist, but once in a while some trick of wind would reveal enormous vistas that a man could hardly contemplate and keep his balance.

But the ponies were content to climb hour after interminable hour, and Dawa Tsering sang about the wind-swept hills of Spiti as they rose and descended through every imaginable plane of vegetation, from steamy bottoms where dense jungle stifled them, up through bamboo and rhododendron to where oaks and maples flourished—up beyond those to the fir-line—up again until the firs gave out and raw wind rolled the clouds around them straight from

Kanchenjunga—then down again into the suffocating
tropics, where woodticks fell on them and a man's hands
were kept constantly busy picking leeches off the ponies
and Diana had to be gone over carefully three times within the hour.

They crossed rock-cluttered torrents over bamboo
bridges that swayed and danced under the weight of one
pony at a time, and bivouacked again at midnight in the
clouds, where icy wind shrieked through the chinks of a
deserted herdsman's hut; then descended two hours after
dawn into a steaming cauldron where black water quarreled on its way through aromatic jungle.

Never a sign of the Lama's party, although they passed
stone *chortens** every mile or so, and cairns built by pilgrims, to which every passer by had stuck little prayer-
flags to flutter the eternal formula *"Om mani padme
hum."* There were messages on bits of paper from one
pilgrim to another, weighted down with stones near some
of the *chortens*, but none that the Lama had left.

And there were unaccountable delays. At times the
two Tibetans seemed to think they had come too fast and,
after a whispered consultation, unloaded the ponies
whether they appeared to need a rest or not. The ponies
rolled on sky-hung moss-banks within a dozen feet of the
edge of an abyss, and the Tibetans chewed oily seed by the
handful, offering Ommony some, and pointing out good
places to sit down when he showed impatience. Dawa
Tsering flicked at the edge of his knife with a suggestive
thumb-nail, but they laughed at that, too, showing him a
tough tree, dwarfed by the wind, that he could cut down
if he needed exercise. In their own good time they started
off again without excuse or argument, usually singing
hymns to pacify the spirits of the mountains

As he drew near Tilgaun Ommony's thought dwelt more
on Hannah Sanburn than on the Lama and Samding.
Aware now that for twenty years she had kept a secret

---

*Vase-shaped stone monuments of Buddhist origin.

from him, in spite of mutual respect and confidence that in every other way he could think of had been almost absolute, he wondered how to tackle her about it. He did not care to know even a part of her secret without letting her know that he knew it.

There had been times when he had seriously thought of asking Hannah Sanburn to become his wife; other times, when the thought that he could hardly live at the mission without marrying her had been all that kept him from resigning his forestry job and spending the remainder of his life in active duty as a trustee at Tilgaun. He was too confirmed a bachelor not to flinch from matrimony when he reasoned out all the pros and cons, but in the back of his head there was a conviction that Hannah Sanburn would not refuse, if he should ask her. But he also had known, any time these past ten years, that he never would ask her to marry him unless—he wondered what the reservation was; he had never quite defined it.

Hunted through his mind and pinned at last into a corner, up there thirteen thousand feet above sea-level with a view of Kanchenjunga to adjust mere human problems to their right proportion, he realized that he would marry Hannah Sanburn—gladly enough—at any time— if by doing so he could solve a difficulty from which she could not otherwise escape.

He was almost convinced that there was a page in Hannah Sanburn's life which needed very careful protecting; something which called for limitless generosity. He had no use for generosity that hedged itself within conventional limits. He liked his freedom and the habit of consulting no one's inclinations but his own in private matters, that becomes almost second nature in an independent man of forty-five, but he knew he could forego all that and be a reasonably companionable married man, if his interpretation of the law of friendship should impose that course on him. To Cottswold Ommony friendship was the highest law; no conceivable claims could outweigh it; Hannah Sanburn was his friend; there was nothing to argue about.

But he hoped—without much confidence, but he hoped—
that she was not in the predicament he guessed her to be in;
suspecting that, since she had kept him in the dark for
twenty years, she could quite easily have fooled Mrs. Cornock-Campbell, who notoriously believed the best of every
one.

He rather dreaded meeting her—very much dreaded
the inevitable interview; and although he fretted to overtake the Lama he was much more patient with delay than he
might otherwise have been, leaving untried a good many
methods with which he might have persuaded the Tibetans
to hurry. He salved his conscience by grumbling aloud to
them and *sotto voce* to Dawa Tsering, but there was not
much energy in his complaints.

At last, toward the end of the fourth day out, they
topped a fifteen-thousand-foot rise and looked over a sheer
ravine, where eagles perched, toward Tilgaun that nestled
in a valley with a Lamaist monastery perched on a crag
three thousand feet above it. The mission buildings glowed
warm in the westering sun—one instance where a rich
man's money had been spent on art as well as altruism,
with good manners and respect for other men's historical
associations, such as missionaries commonly dispense with.
The graceful contour of the buildings and the color of the
carved stone matched the panorama. There was no asser-
tiveness, no challenge. The Tibetan roof-lines paid acknowledgment to older art on crag and cliff around them.
Without beauty there is no beatitude. Old Marmaduke,
who tortured thirty million dollars from protesting pigs,
had somehow learned that; so the mission buildings were
a monument to beauty, not to his ambition or his zeal.

Ommony was thrilled by the sight, as always on his rare
visits. All the way down the winding track, that looked
so short and actually was a half-day's journey, he recalled
the days when Marmaduke had hurled Chicago business
methods into battle with obstruction, subtly raised against
him by foes that were easy enough to identify but undiscoverable when it came to issues. Rajahs, all the mission-

aries, all the Indian priesthood, politicians and the press had joined in opposing the project, occasionally praising, always preventing.

Even the banks, that levied toll on Marmaduke's long purse, had invented difficulties. There were strikes of labor-gangs (imported in the teeth of government obstruction) because money for the pay-roll did not arrive punctually. There had been personal attacks on Marmaduke—three bullets, and a dose of ground glass in his food, in addition to assaults on his reputation. Missionaries had declared (and perhaps believed) that he was a satyr who sought to corrupt young innocents. Consignments of supplies, machinery and what-not else had failed to reach the destination, or had arrived so smashed as to be useless. Marmaduke had grinned, continued grinning, and had won, dying with his boots on six months after Hannah Sanburn was installed in charge, hoping, as they laid him on a stretcher, that the pigs he had slain for sausage-meat might have most of the credit; since it was they who made the mission possible

His will, in which he appointed a Tibetan Lama chief trustee, had been a nine days' wonder, partly because of its novelty, but mostly because that masterly provision introduced an international element, which made it next to impossible for politicians to undo the work. Tibet as a military power can not be taken seriously: but it is noteworthy that not even "big business" has succeeded in controlling its government or in penetrating its frontiers. The backing of the Dalai Lama is worth more, in some contingencies, than a billion dollars and a million armed men. (There is a European parallel.)

And the Tashi Lama is to the Dalai Lama as is the differential calculus to the simple rule of three, only if anything rather more so.

My son, the wise are few; for Wisdom very seldom pleases, so that they are few who seek her. Wisdom will compel whoever entertains her to avoid all selfishness and to escape from praise. But Wisdom seeks them who are worthy, discovering some here and there, unstupified and uncorrupted by the slime of cant, with whom thereafter it is a privilege to other men to tread the self-same earth, whether or not they know it.

FROM THE BOOK OF THE SAYINGS OF TSIANG SAMDUP.

CHAPTER XXIV

HANNAH SANBURN

THERE is a narrow bridge, swung high above a noisy stream, that forms the only practicable gate to Tilgaun. On the Tilgaun side is a high mound that resembles a look-out post, with a big prayer-flag on top that might be the defiant emblem of an army. The track leads below that mound, across a hollow, and climbs again toward the mission, more than a mile away.

As Ommony rode across the bridge behind the leading Tibetan he was aware of faces peering from the top of the mound beside the prayer-flag. When he was midway over the bridge the faces disappeared. When he reached the foot of the mound there were six Bhutani mission girls standing in a row on the rim of the hollow.

They wore the Marmaduke Mission costume, which is made from one piece of daffodil-yellow fabric woven on the mission looms. Their hair was decked with flowers, and they were laughing, that being a part of old Marmaduke's legacy, he having had a notion that to laugh with good reason, is two-thirds of an education. The other third is harder to acquire, but comes much easier because of laughter; or so said Marmaduke, who had considered many pigs, that perished.

They were not so poised and self-reliant as the Lama's dancing girls, but they looked marvelously better than the common run of Hill women, and as different from ordinary mission converts as a live trout is from a dead sardine. At a glance it was obvious that nobody had told them they were heathen in their blindness; somebody had shown them how to revel in the sunshine and to wonder at the wine-light of gloaming. It was conceivable that

294

they had studied nature's mirth instead of watching frogs
dissected with a scalpel, and had learned to be amused
with each existing minute rather than to meditate on metaphysical conundrums.

But they had their heritage nevertheless. Their eyes
were on Dawa Tsering. It was just as well that there were
six of them together.

Dawa Tsering, gasconading on pony-back with his feet
within nine inches of the ground, called two of them by
name, inquired about a third who was not there, and
asked whether they had forgotten him.

"I know a good way to remind you who I am!" he
boasted, and got off the pony to act the satyr among
wood-nymphs. Ommony checked him curtly. He pro-
tested:

"I tell you, Ommon*ee*, the gods make free with women
and the devils do the same! It is ridiculous to pretend we
are better than gods and devils. What are women for, do
you suppose?"

It was so that they discovered who Ommony was. In
that Bhat-Brahman costume covered by a sheepskin coat
and without his beard they had not recognized him. All
six looked at him sharply, hesitated, glanced at the sky,
accepted that as an excuse, and ran, gathering up the
yellow robes and showing copper-colored legs, their long
hair streaming in the wind behind them.

"Why are they afraid of *you?*" asked Dawa Tsering.
"Are you such a terror among women as all that?"

"It was the rain," said Ommony. But he knew better.
The girls were giggling.

The sky had clouded over suddenly, and in a moment,
on a blast of icy wind, the rain came down in sheets that
cut off the view of the mission buildings. The ponies
turned their rumps to it and stood, heads down, tails blown
tight under. Diana whimpered and took refuge under the
end of the bridge, where Ommony joined her; there was
no hope of getting the ponies to move until the storm
passed. It turned to hail and swept the bridge like con-

centrated musketry, lightning and terrific, volleying
thunderclaps heightening the illusion.

Twenty minutes later, when the sky cleared as suddenly
as it had clouded and the setting sun shone on drifts of
melting hail, Ommony saw the drenched girls leave the
shelter of a rock and scamper for the mission gate. He
did not doubt for one fraction of a moment that they had
been sent by Hannah Sanburn to the bridge-end to keep
a look-out for him. Discontented—it was aggravating to
be treated as a potential enemy—he rode on prepared to
see the Lama hurrying away ahead of him.

However, Hannah Sanburn met him in the gate and
laughed at his disguise. He judged she was relieved, not
annoyed to see him. There was all the old friendliness
expressed on her New England face. Boston, Massachusetts—Commonwealth Avenue or Tremont Street—stood
out all over her, even after twenty years of Tilgaun. She
was dressed in tailored serge with a camel-hair overcoat
turned up to her ears. A wealth of chestnut hair, beginning to turn gray, showed under a plain deerstalker hat.
She had not lost one trace of her New England manner—
not a vestige of her pride. No weakness, but a firm and
comprehending kindness dwelt on the almost manly forehead, at the corners of her mouth and in the grand gray
eyes.

"All alone?" asked Ommony, dismounting, shaking
hands. He liked her laughter; it was wholesome, even if
she did look quizzically at his jaw and chin that she had
never seen before without the modifying beard.

"Yes, Cottswold. You're a day late. Tsiang Samdup
left this morning."

"Why?" he asked bluntly.

She did not answer but looked straight at Dawa Tsering,
nodded, smiled at his sheepish grin, and walked straight
up to him.

"Give me your knife," she said quietly, and took it
from him almost before he guessed what she intended.
He made no effort to prevent, but sat still on his pony,

looking foolish. "You shall have that back if you behave
yourself, not otherwise. If you look twice at one of the
mission girls I will order the blacksmith to break your
knife in two. You understand me?"

She made friends with Diana next, saying hardly a
word but lifting her by the forelegs to see whether the feet
were injured by the long march. The hound accepted her
authority as promptly as Dawa Tsering did.

Stroking Diana's head with one shapely, rather freckled
hand, ordering the Tibetans to lead the ponies to the
stable, she led the way into the stone-paved courtyard.
Cloistered buildings of worn gray stone formed three sides
of it, and in the midst there was an oval mass of flowers,
damaged by the hail but gorgeous in the last rays of the
setting sun.

There was a room reserved for Ommony's exclusive use,
in a corner facing that front courtyard, and though he
had never used it oftener than once in three years it had
always been kept ready for him. Another room, used less
seldom, was reserved for Tsiang Samdup in the corner
opposite.

"Mr. McGregor sent your clothes by messenger. You'll
find them all unpacked and cared for—lots of hot water—
I'm sorry you can't grow a beard in fifteen minutes!
Come to my room when you're ready. I'll take the dog."

Ommony shut himself into the room to smoke and think.
He dreaded the coming interview more and more, the
longer he postponed it—realized that what he most detested, in a world full of discordances, was to have to account for his actions to any one else. "Marriage might
be all right," he muttered, "if women would govern themselves and concede men the same privilege."

He let an hour slip by before he presented himself in
Hannah Sanburn's private room—a long room over an
archway leading to an inner cloister, bow-windowed on
both sides, paneled in teak, with a blazing fire at one end.
The crimson curtains had been drawn; the shaded oil
lamps cast a warm glow over everything; a square table

had been spread near the fire and Hannah Sanburn was making toast, stepping back and forward cautiously across Diana, who had made herself thoroughly at home on the hearthrug. Old Montagu's portrait, life-size, head and shoulders, smiled at the scene from the end-wall, the flickering firelight making his shrewd, peculiarly boyish features seem almost ready to step out of the frame and talk.

It was more difficult than ever to put her to the question in that atmosphere. She had changed into a semi-evening dress, that aged her a little but added an old-worldly charm. It would be difficult to imagine a hostess whom one would less like to offend, and the arrival of bacon and eggs on a silver tray carried by a seventeen-year-old Bhutani girl provided welcome excuse for delay.

Hannah Sanburn seemed entirely unembarrassed and, if she noticed Ommony's air of having something on his mind, she concealed the fact perfectly, talking about the events of the mission in a matter-of-fact voice, relating difficulties she had overcome, outlining plans for the future, avoiding anything that might lead to personal issues.

"I don't know how much good we're doing—sometimes I think scarcely any," she said at last. "We rear and educate these girls. The best ones, of course, stay on for a while as teachers. But they all get married sooner or later and lapse into the old ways. It will be a century at least before this school begins to make much visible impression."

Ommony stared at the fire. "Thank goodness, we'll be dead then, with something different to fret about," he grumbled, angry with the destiny that he felt compelled him to probe a gentlewoman's secrets. She noticed the tone of his voice—could not very well ignore it.

"What is troubling _you_, Cottswold? I supposed you were the most contented man on earth. Have you lost your interest in your forest?"

"I've resigned from the forestry." He stared at her, and broke the ice suddenly, doing the very thing he was determined not to, blurting a blunt question without tact or even a preliminary warning. "Who is this girl Elsa, who is never at the mission when I'm here, but who has been to Lhassa, talks English and Tibetan, and can draw like Michael Angelo?"

He jerked his jaw forward to conceal the contempt that he felt for himself for having blundered in so clumsily, all the while watching her face but detecting no nervousness. To his surprise and relief she laughed and leaned her head against the high chair-back, looking at him humorously from under lowered eyelids, as she might have listened to a lame excuse from some one in the school.

"Poor Cottswold! How you must have felt uncomfortable!—you're so faithful to your friends. No, Elsa is not my daughter. I have never had *that* experience. If she *were* my daughter I know quite well I would have said so long ago. I can imagine myself being proud of her, even —even in those circumstances."

"I confess I'm mightily relieved," said Ommony, grinning uncomfortably. "Not, of course, that I'd have—"

"No, I know you wouldn't," she interrupted. "You are the last person on earth I would hide that kind of secret from."

"Why any kind of secret, Hannah? Am I not to be trusted?"

"Not in this instance. You're the one man who couldn't be told." Then, after a dramatic pause: "Elsa is your niece."

"Niece?" he said, and shut his teeth with a snap. That one word solved the whole long riddle.

"Her name is Elsa Terry."

He did not speak. He leaned forward, staring at her under knitted brows, his eyes as eloquent as the silence that lasted while the Bhutani girl came in and removed the supper table. Even after the girl had gone, for two or three minutes the only sounds were the solemn ticking of a big clock on the mantelpiece, the cracking of a pine-knot in the fire, and a murmur of song from a building fifty yards away.

"You and almost everybody else have always believed Jack Terry and your sister Elsa vanished twenty years ago without trace," she said at last. "They didn't."

"Didn't they go to the Ahbor country?"

"Yes."

"You mean they're alive and you've known it all these years?"

"They have been dead nearly twenty years. I learned about it soon afterward. You know *now* why they went up there?"

"I've no new information. Jack Terry was as mad as a March hare—"

"I think not," Hannah Sanburn answered, her gray eyes staring at the fire. "Jack Terry was the most unselfish man I ever heard of. He adored your sister. She was a spiritual, other-worldly little woman, and that beast Kananda Pal—"

"I blame Jenkins," said Ommony, grinding his teeth. "Kananda Pal was born into a black-art family and knew no better. Jenkins—"

"Never mind him now. Jack Terry did his best. Your sister Elsa used to have lapses; she would cry for days on end and write letters to Mr. Jenkins begging him to give back the mind he had stolen from her. No, she wasn't mad; it was obsession. I did *my* best, but I hadn't much experience in those days and she was difficult to understand; the phases of the moon seemed to have something to do with it; Jack Terry and I were agreed about that. You've met Sirdar Sirohe Singh of Tilgaun?"

Ommony nodded.

"He has always been a friend. He appears to be a mystic. He knows things that other people don't know, and hardly ever talks of them. Jack Terry learned from him—Jack set his arm, or a collar-bone, I forget which—anyway he told Jack about the Crystal Jade of Ahbor."

Ommony's lips moved in the suggestion of a whistle and Diana opened one eye.

"All the people hereabouts seem to have heard of the

jade," Hannah Sanburn went on, "but the *sirdar* seems to be the only one who really knows anything about it. All *I* know is that I have had a piece of it in my hands in this house. It nearly drove me frantic to look into it, so I locked it away in that cupboard over there. It was stolen by a girl I should never have trusted, and I'm nearly but not quite sure it was the *sirdar* who bribed her to steal it from me. She was murdered, apparently while on the way to the *sirdar's* house a few miles from here. Tsiang Samdup was here last night and showed me the piece of jade; he said he had recovered it in Delhi."

"What else did he say?" asked Ommony, but she ignored the question, continuing to stare into the fire, as if she could see in it pictures of twenty years ago.

"Jack Terry told me," she went on presently, "that he believed the Crystal Jade of Ahbor had magic properties. You know how he believed in magic, and how he always insisted that magic is merely science that hasn't been recognized yet by the schools. He said mineral springs can heal the body, so there was no reason why there shouldn't be a stone somewhere, possessed of properties that can heal the mind in certain conditions. I didn't agree with him. It seemed to me utter nonsense, although —I'm less inclined than I was then to say things can't be simply because we have been taught the contrary. I have held a piece of the Jade of Ahbor in my hands and—well, I don't know, and that's all about it."

She paused again, perfectly still. Ommony got up, heaped wood on the fire, and sat down again. The cracking pine-knots and the ascending sparks broke her reverie.

"It was no use talking to Jack Terry," she continued, "and your sister would have gone to the North Pole with him, or anywhere else, if he had as much as proposed it. The two set off like Launcelot and Elaine into the unknown. You know, the very heart of the Ahbor Valley isn't more than fifty miles from here, although they *say* nobody has ever gone there and returned alive. Jack Terry—you remember how he always laughed at the impossible—said they would probably be gone not more than three or four weeks. They took scarcely any supplies with them—just a tent and bedding—half a dozen ponies— two servants. The servants deserted the third night out and were killed by Bhutani robbers."

"Yes," said Ommony. "That was all I could ever find out, and *that* cost a month's investigation."

"I knew the whole story two or three weeks before you got permission to leave your forest and come to investigate; I wasn't allowed to tell."

"Weren't *allowed*. Who in thunder—"

"Tsiang Samdup came down from the Ahbor Valley and in this room, sitting on that hearthrug where the dog lies now, told me the story. I remember how he began— his exact words:

" 'My daughter, there is danger in another's duty. There is also duty in another's danger. There is merit in considered speech, but strength consists in silence. Truth, that may be told to one, may lead to evil if repeated. I am minded to speak to your ears only.'

"Offhand I told him I would of course respect his confidence, but he sat still for about half an hour before he spoke again. Then he took at least half an hour to commit me to a pledge of secrecy that I could not possibly break without losing my own self-respect. I discovered before he was through that he had been quite right to do that, but I confess there were moments that evening when it looked as if he had trapped me into something against which every moral fiber in me rebelled instinctively. For an hour I hated him. And there have been times—many times since—when it has been extremely difficult to keep the promise. However, I *have* kept it. It was only yesterday that he gave me leave to tell *you* as much as I know."

"He might have confided in me in the first place," said Ommony, but Hannah Sanburn shook her head.

"I did suggest that to him. I urged it. But he made me see that he was quite right not to. It would have placed you in an impossible position. What had happened was this: the Terrys did succeed in entering the Ahbor Valley. They seemed to have undergone frightful hardships, and nobody knows how they found the way, but they did. They were hunted like animals, and when Tsiang Samdup rescued them Jack Terry was dying from wounds, hunger and exposure; he had managed somehow to find enough food for his wife, and he had persuaded her to eat, and to let him go without."

"Are you sure of your information?" Ommony asked. "That doesn't sound like Elsa."

"There was a baby coming."

"Oh, my God!"

"Tsiang Samdup took them to his monastery, which is somewhere in the Ahbor Valley. The only way he was able to protect them from the Ahbors, who have never allowed strangers in the Valley and vow they never will, was by prophesying that the baby shortly to be born would be a reincarnation of an ancient Chinese saint, named San-fun-ho. There was no hope of saving Jack Terry, but Tsiang Samdup hoped to save the mother's life. However, she died giving birth to the child, and Jack Terry followed her the same night."

"Did they leave anything in writing?"

"I have letters I'll show you presently, written and signed by both of them, in which they speak of the Lama Tsiang Samdup as having risked his own life to save theirs. Jack Terry wrote that he was dying of wounds and exposure. The Lama gave me both letters after he had told the story. But I would have believed him without that. I have always believed every word that Tsiang Samdup said, even while I hated him for having pledged me to silence."

"Go ahead. I mistrusted him not long ago—and changed my mind."

"Tsiang Samdup is not to be doubted, Cottswold. He lied to Ahbors, but that was to save life. It was an inspiration—the only way out of it—to tell those savages that the unborn baby was to be a reincarnation of a Chinese saint. I admire him for the lie. Imagine, if you

can, old Tsiang Samdup—for he was old even then—
rearing and weaning that baby in a monastery in the midst
of savages. The Terrys' death seems to have made it easier
in one way: the natives saw them buried, which satisfied
their law against admitting strangers, and Tsiang Samdup
prevented them from digging up the bodies to throw them
in the river, by casting a halo of sainthood over them on
the ground that they had brought a saint into the world.
You know how all this country to the north of us believes
implicitly in reincarnations of saints—the Tashi Lama is
supposed to be the reincarnation of his predecessor; and
so on. Do you see how Tsiang Samdup became more and
more committed?''

There was a long silence. Ommony poked the fire restlessly. A native teacher came in, offered a report for
signature, and went out. Hannah Sanburn went on with
her story:

''He had promised those savages a baby saint. He had
produced the baby. Now he had to educate the saint, and
its being a girl made it all the more difficult. But it
seems there are people to whom Tsiang Samdup can go
for advice. I don't know who they are, or where they
are; he mentions them rarely, and very guardedly; I think
he has referred to them twice, or perhaps three times during all the years I have known him, and then only for the
purpose of suggesting that he isn't exactly a free agent.
The conclusion I drew from his guarded hints was, that
he acts, and is responsible for what he does, but that he
would lose the privilege of conference with these unknown
individuals if he should allow personal considerations to
govern him. At that, I'm only guessing. He said nothing definite.''

''The Masters!'' said Ommony, nodding. ''I'll bet you
he knows some of the Masters!'' But if Hannah Sanburn
knew who *they* were she gave no sign. She went on talking:

''It seems that the Ahbors trust him implicitly within
certain limits. They would kill him and burn his monas-

tery if they caught him practising the least deception; and they watched that baby day and night. The wife of an Ahbor chieftain became the wet-nurse, and the child throve, but it very soon dawned on Tsiang Samdup that however carefully he might educate her—(you knew *he* had an Oxford education?)—she would grow up like a half-breed, unless he could have skilful assistance from some one of her own race. So he consulted these mysterious authorities, and 'they,' whoever *they* are, told him that a way would open up if he should take *me* into confidence.

"As I told you, he first bound me to secrecy. He didn't make me swear, but he gave me a lecture on keeping faith, that was as radical as the Sermon on the Mount, and he tested me every inch of the way to make sure I agreed with him. I have used that sermon over and over again in teaching the teachers of this school.

"When he had me so tied up in my own explanations of what keeping faith really means, that there wasn't any possible way out for me, he told me the story I have just told you, and made me an astonishing proposal. I have sometimes wished I had accepted it."

Hannah Sanburn paused for a long time, staring at the fire.

"He offered," she said at last, "to find some one else for my position here; to smuggle me into the Ahbor Valley; and to teach me more knowledge than Solomon knew —if I would give unqualified consent, and would agree to stay up there and help him educate that baby."

"And—?"

"And I refused," she said quietly. "Won't you put some more wood on the fire?"

And this I know: that when the gods have use for us they blindfold us, because if we should see and comprehend the outcome we should grow so vain that not even the gods could preserve us from destruction.

Vanity, self-righteousness and sin, these three are one, whose complements are meekness, self-will and indifference.

Meekness is not modesty. Meekness is an insult to the Soul. But out of modesty comes wisdom, because in modesty the gods can find expression.

The wise gods do not corrupt modesty with wealth or fame, but its reward is in well-doing and in a satisfying inner vision.

FROM THE BOOK OF THE SAYINGS OF TSIANG SAMDUP.

CHAPTER XXV

THE COMPROMISE

OMMONY stacked up the fire and resumed his seat in the leather armchair that Marmaduke had always used. Diana, belly to the blaze, barked and galloped in her sleep. Hannah Sanburn went on talking:

"Tsiang Samdup said last night that you have been with him two months. Do you know then what I mean when I say one can't argue with him? He just sat there on the hearthrug and—it's difficult to explain—he seemed to be listening for an inside message. It may sound idiotic, but I received the impression of a man waiting for his own soul to talk to him. He was perfectly silent. He hardly breathed. I felt absolutely sure he would find some way out of the difficulty. But the strange thing was, that the solution came from me. I suppose ten minutes passed without a word said, and I felt all the while as if my mind were being freed from weights that I had never known were there. Then suddenly I spoke because I couldn't help it; I saw what to do so clearly that I simply had to tell him.

"It wasn't hypnotism. It was just the contrary. It was as if he had *de*hypnotized me. I saw all the risks and scores of difficulties. And I saw absolutely clearly the necessity of doing just one thing. I told him I would take the child for six months out of every year and treat her as if she were my own. He might have her for the other six months. Every single wrinkle on his dear old face smiled separately when I said that. I had hardly said it when I began to wish I hadn't; but he held me to my word.

"He brought me the baby the following week, and she

307

was here in this building all the while you were ranging
the hills for some word of the Terrys. The hardest work
I ever had to do was to keep silent when you returned here
worn out and miserable about your sister's fate. But, if
you had been let into the secret, you would have interfered
—wouldn't you? Am I right or wrong, Cottswold?"

"Of course. I would never have dreamed of letting my
sister's child go back to the Ahbor Valley."

"Yet, if Tsiang Samdup hadn't taken her every year
for half a year, the Ahbors would have killed him. And
remember: I had bound myself in advance not to tell any
one—and particularly not to tell you. The Lama was only
able to loan her to me for six months of every year by
consenting to the Ahbors watching her all the time she was
with me. Whenever she has been with me Ahbors have
watched day and night. The excuse Tsiang Samdup gave
to them was that unless she should be with me for long
periods she would die and the Ahbors would find their
valley invaded by white armies in consequence. They fear
invasion of their valley more than anything else they can
imagine. On the other hand, they regard the child as a gift
from Heaven and the old Lama as her rightful guardian.

"I don't quite understand the situation up there; the
Ahbors don't accept Tsiang Samdup's teachings, they
have a religion of their own; and he isn't one of them;
he's a Tibetan. But they recognize him as a Lama, protect his monastery, and submit to his authority in certain
ways. Perhaps I'm stupid; he has tried very hard to explain, and so has Elsa. Privately I called her Elsa, after
her mother, of course. Tsiang Samdup gave her the
Chinese name of San-fun-ho. The word is supposed to
signify every possible human virtue."

"Who called her *Samding?*" Ommony asked bluntly.

Hannah Sanburn stared. "You know then? This
isn't news! I remember now: Tsiang Samdup said last
night: 'That of which a man is ignorant may well be kept
from him, but that which he knows should be explained,
lest he confuse it with what he does not know.'"

"I'm putting two and two together," Ommony answered. "I leaned over a monastery gallery in Darjiling. The *chela* was straight underneath me. A beam of sunlight showed a girl's breasts. Am I right? Are San-funho, Samding the *chela* and my sister's child Elsa one and the same person?"

"Yes. I wonder you never recognized your sister's voice—that almost baritone boyish resonance. You didn't?"

"Who are those other girls?"

"Companions for her! Don't rush me. Wait while I explain. Elsa developed into the most marvelous child I have ever known. It was partly Tsiang Samdup's influence; he gave up his whole life to training her; and he's wise—I can never begin to tell you how wise he is. But it was partly due to her heredity. You see, she had your sister's spiritual qualities, and something of Jack Terry's gay indifference to all the usual human pros and cons— the courage of both of them—and something else added, entirely her own. I wish she were my child! Oh, how I wish it! And yet, d'you know, Cottswold, down in my heart I'm glad she isn't, simply because, if she were mine, she would have missed so much!"

Hannah Sanburn stared into the fire again, silent until Ommony grew restless.

"There's so much to tell!" she said at last. "I knew from the first, and Tsiang Samdup soon discovered that the odds would be all against her unless she could have white children of her own age for companions. When he came and spoke of that I tried to persuade him to let me send her to America; but at the very suggestion he looked so old and grieved and disappointed that I felt it would kill him to lose her. I suggested that he should go with her, but he said no, he had a duty to the Ahbors. I thought then he was afraid the Ahbors would torture him to death and burn his monastery if he should let her go; but he read my thoughts and assured me that consideration had no weight. I believed him. I believe he is per-

fectly indifferent to pain and death. He sat still for a
long time, and then said:

"'It is better not to begin, than to begin and not go
through to a conclusion. *Then* we should only have deprived ourselves of opportunitv. *Now* we should rob the
child.'

"He asked me to obtain white children for companions
for her. I refused, of course, at once to have anything to do
with it. We quarreled bitterly—or rather, I did. He sat quite
still, and when I had finished scolding him he went away
in silence. I did not see him again for several months,
and he never told me how he obtained white children. I
can't imagine how he did it without raising a scandal all
over the world. I have been in agonies over it, for fear
this mission would suffer. You know, if word once got
around that we were importing white children into the
Ahbor Valley, no proof of innocence would ever quiet the
suspicion. Just think what a chance the Christian missionaries would have for destroying our good name! Can
you imagine them sparing us?"

Ommony grinned and nodded. As trustees of a Buddhist mission to the Buddhists, he had tasted his share of
that zealotry.

"He obtained the children through the agency of a Jew
named Benjamin," he said. "They were all orphans.
They were saved from God knows what. Go on."

"I have only seen the other children rarely. Now and
then they would come here in twos and threes, and I used
to question them, but they all seemed too happy to remember their past, and they only had the vaguest notions as
to how they ever reached the Ahbor Valley. The general
plan was for me to do my best with Elsa during the six
months of the year she was with me, and for *her* to teach
them. Tsiang Samdup said it would be good for her to
have to teach them—that she would learn more in that
way than any other; and as usual he was entirely right.

"To help the other girls he made *them* pass their teaching on to Tibetan children. But he hasn't had quite the

success with the others that he has had with Elsa; they hadn't her character to begin with. He never punishes. Have you any idea what patience it calls for to educate growing children without ever inflicting punishment of any kind—what patience and skill?"

Ommony glanced at Diana. "It's the only way. I never punish," he said quietly. "Go on."

"My own share in Elsa's education has been very slight indeed," Hannah Sanburn went on. "I had to teach her Western conventions as to table manners and so on, and to explain to her what sort of subjects are taboo in what we call civilized society. I have taught her to wear frocks properly, have corrected her English pronunciation and have given her music lessons. I can't think of anything else. The real education has been all the other way; it is *I* who have learned—oh, simply countless things—by observing *her*. She never argues. You can't persuade her to tell more than a fraction of what she knows. She is afraid of nothing and of nobody. And she is as full of fun as the veriest young pagan that ever lived."

"Is she affectionate?" asked Ommony.

"Intensely. But not demonstrative. I should say she loves enormously, but without the slightest jealousy or passion. She has learned Tsiang Samdup's faculty of divining people's weakness, and of playing up to their strength instead of taking advantage of the weakness or letting it annoy her. The result, of course, is that she is instantly popular wherever she goes."

"How in the world have you kept these mission girls from talking about her?" asked Ommony.

"That was quite easy. They adore her. She is *their* special secret; and they quite understand that if they talk about her outside the mission she will stay away. Besides, the mission girls don't have much opportunity to talk with outsiders, and those to whom they do talk are superstitious people, who speak with bated breath of Sanfun-ho of Ahbor. There have been much harder problems than that."

Hannah Sanburn stared into the fire again. It appeared there were painful memories.

"You see, there have been European visitors at times. Some of them came unannounced, and sometimes Elsa was here when they came. There were times when I could pass her off as a teacher, but sometimes she was discovered in boy's clothes, which made that impossible; and whether she was dressed as a boy or girl she aroused such intense curiosity that questions became pointed and very difficult to answer. I have dozens of letters, Cottswold, from friends in Massachusetts asking whether it is true, as they learn from missionary correspondents, that I have a child. Some ask why I kept my marriage secret. Some insinuate that they are too broad-minded to hold a lapse from virtue against me, as long as I don't come home and make it awkward for them. Others preach me a sermon on hypocrisy. Quite a number of my friends have dropped me altogether. I suppose the strict provisions of the penal code have kept people from libeling me in India, but that has not prevented them from writing scandal to their friends abroad."

"What was the idea of boy's clothes?"

"Education. Tsiang Samdup insists she must know everything he possibly can teach her. She has been to Lhassa, far into China, and down into India. He could not have taken her to some of those places unless she were disguised as his *chela*; a girl *chela* would have aroused all sorts of scandal and difficulties. Then again, he says all human life is drama and the only way to teach is by dramatic presentation; but who, he asks, can present a drama unless able to act all parts in it? He says we can only learn by teaching, and can only teach by learning; and he is right, Cottswold, he is absolutely right."

"Does he propose that she shall preach a crusade or something like that in India?" Ommony asked, frowning.

"He proposes she shall be an absolutely free agent, possessed of all knowledge necessary to freedom. That tour into India was only a part of her education."

"But I saw her as Samding receiving princes of the blood and being almost worshiped," Ommony objected.

"Education. Tsiang Samdup says she will be either flattered or hated wherever she goes. He says the hatred will strengthen her. He wants to be sure no flattery shall turn her head."

"And those other girls?"

"They are to go free also, as and when she goes. Tsiang Samdup is fabulously rich. He pays for everything in gold, although I don't know where he gets it. He has secret agents all over India—sometimes I think they're all over the world. He says wherever Elsa goes, she and the other girls will be provided for and will find friends."

"Where does he propose to send them?" Ommony asked, a wave of rebellion sweeping over him. He was well schooled in self-control, but all the English in him rose against the notion of his sister's child being subject to an Oriental's whim. Education was one thing: heritage another.

Hannah Sanburn laughed. The expression of her face was firm, and yet peculiarly helpless.

"I am not to tell you that."

"Why in thunder not? You have told so much, that—"

"If you were as used as I am, Cottswold, to trusting that grand old Lama, and always discovering afterward that his advice was good, you wouldn't press the point."

"My sister's child—" he began angrily; but she interrupted him.

"Don't forget: Tsiang Samdup saved the mother from death at the hands of savages. It is thanks to him, and to nobody but him, that the baby was born alive."

"Yes, but—"

"Tsiang Samdup told me, and I believe him, that your sister put the new-born baby into his arms and begged him to care for it as if it were his own. She *gave* him the baby with her dying breath."

"What else could she do?" asked Ommony. "Poor girl, she was—"

"Yes. But she did it," said Hannah Sanburn. "Can you name one instance in which Tsiang Samdup has failed to keep trust to the limit of his power?"

There followed a long silence, broken only by the faint murmur of singing in a hall across the rear courtyard, the falling of burned wood on the hearth, and the muttered barking of Diana chasing something in her dreams. It endured until Diana awoke suddenly, sat up and growled. There came a man's voice from the front courtyard. Two or three minutes later there was a knock at the door and a toothless old Sikhimese watchman announced a visitor, mumbling so that Ommony did not catch the name. A moment later Sirdar Sirohe Singh strode into the room, greeted by thundering explosions from Diana, who presently recognized him and lay down again.

The *sirdar* without speaking bowed profoundly, once to Hannah Sanburn, once to Ommony, then crossed the room and sat down cross-legged on the floor, with his back to a corner of the fireplace at Hannah Sanburn's right hand, where his own face was in shadow but he could see both hers and Ommony's. Diana went up and sniffed him but he took no notice of her.

"I have word," he said gruffly, at the end of three or four minutes' silence.

He seemed to expect comment.

"From whom? About what?"

The *sirdar's* amber eyes met Ommony's. "You remember? When we met the first time I said I was at your disposal to escort you to another place."

Ommony nodded.

"But I am not your superior." (The *sirdar* used a word that conveys more the relationship of a *guru* to his *chela* than can be expressed by one word in English; but at that, the significance was vague.) "Do you *wish* to come with me?"

In the West it would have been the part of wisdom to ask when, why, whither? Twenty and odd years of India had given Ommony an insight into arguments not current

in the West, however. He did not even glance at Hannah
Sanburn.

"Yes."

"I am ready."

The *sirdar* stood up. There was magic in the air. Diana
sensed it; she was trembling. Hannah Sanburn rose and
placed herself between the *sirdar* and the fire, so that he
could not pass her easily.

"Do you accept responsibility?" she asked.

The *sirdar* nodded.

"Will he return here?"

"As to that I am ignorant. He will arrive there."

"You will escort him safely to the Lama?"

Again the *sirdar* nodded.

Hannah Sanburn moved and the *sirdar* strode past her
toward the door. Ommony started to follow him, but
turned, walked deliberately up to Hannah Sanburn and
kissed her, hardly knowing why, except that he admired
her and possibly might never see her again. She seemed
to understand.

"Good-by," she said quietly. "If you reach the Ahbor
Valley you'll be safe enough—only do what he tells you."
Then, divining his intention: "No, take the dog. I would
like her, but you may need her. The Lama said so. Good-
by."

It was cold outside. Ommony tied on Diana's sheepskin jacket, which was hanging, cleaned and dried, from
a peg in the hall. Below in the courtyard the *sirdar* turned
and said abruptly:

"To your own room first."

It was like being led out to be shot. In the gloom in
the corner near Ommony's door a brown-robed Tibetan
waited, carrying something on his arm; Ommony seized
Diana's collar to keep her from flying at him. He and
the *sirdar* followed Ommony into the room and waited
while he lit the candles; then the *sirdar* struck a match
and lit the overhead oil lamp.

"Where is Dawa Tsering?" Ommony asked suddenly.

The *sirdar* smiled, showing wonderfully even teeth that suggested not exactly cruelty, but the sort of familiarity with unavoidable unpleasantness that surgeons learn.

"He will come with us part of the way," he said in a dead-level tone of voice.

Ommony bridled at that. It touched his own sense of responsiblity.

"The man is my servant. What do you propose to do to him?"

"I am not his master."

"You said 'part of the way.' What do you mean by that?"

"Wait and see," said the *sirdar*.

"No," Ommony answered. "I will lead no man into a trap. What do you intend?"

The *sirdar* spoke in undertones to the Tibetan, who tossed a bundle of garments on the bed and left the room.

"You might save time," the *sirdar* suggested, pointing to the bundle on the bed. His manner was polite, and more mysterious than commanding; he undid the bundle himself and spread out a Tibetan costume.

"How about you?" asked Ommony, beginning to undress.

"I go as I am."

Ommony put on the warm Tibetan clothes and examined himself in the mirror—laughed—remarked that he looked like a monk whose asceticism consisted in at least three meals a day. But he looked better when he pulled on a cloth cap and threw a dark shawl over it. The *sirdar*, walking around him, viewing him carefully from every angle, appeared satisfied.

Then Dawa Tsering came, unaccompanied by the Tibetan, standing burly and enormous in his yak-hair cloak, almost filling up the doorway.

"Thou!" he said, grinning as his eyes met Ommony's. "Say to Missish-Anbun she should return my knife to me. We go where there *might* be happenings."

"Where do you suppose we are going?" Ommony asked.

"To that old Lama's roost, I take it. Between you and me, Ommon*ee*, I am glad to go anywhere, so be I get away from this place. My wife is in Tilgaun and has sent two of her husbands to catch me and bring me to her!"

The *sirdar* grinned, watching Ommony's face. "They practise polyandry in these hills," he remarked.

That was no news, although there was less of it around Tilgaun since the Marmaduke influence had begun to make itself felt.

"Seven husbands are enough for her," said Dawa Tsering. "I grew weary of planting her corn-fields and being beaten for my trouble. I am for Spiti, where a man can have as many wives as he can manage and *they* fear *him!* Let us be off before that she-wolf's husbands catch the two of us, thou!"

Ommony nodded. The *sirdar* put the lights out and led the way to the outer gate, Dawa Tsering following, complaining bitterly about his knife.

"I am ashamed, Ommon*ee*—I am ashamed to go back to Spiti without my belly-ripper! Where shall I find such another as that? Get it for me! I would pay its weight in gold for it—if I had that much gold," he added *sotto voce.*

Once outside the gate, though, he was much too eager to be going to fret about anything else. The whites of his eyes showed alert in the darkness. There were two ponies; he held Ommony's, urging him to mount in haste, then ran behind, slapping the pony's rump, pursuing the *sirdar's* beast, that cantered with a Tibetan clinging to its tail. Diana circled around and around the party, barking.

"Thou! Command thy she-dog!" Dawa Tsering panted. "We go through the village—she will awake my wife's husbands—command her to be still, or we are lost!"

Oh, I went where the Gods are, and I have seen the Dawn
Where Beauty and the Muses and the Seven Reasons dwell,
And I saw Hope accoutered with a lantern and a horn
Whose clarion and rays reach the inner rings of hell.
Oh, I was in the storehouse of the jewels of the dew
And the laughter of the motion of the wind-blown grass,
The mystery of morning and its music, and the hue
Of the petals of the roses when the rain-clouds pass.
And so I know who Hope is and why she never sleeps,
And seven of the secrets that are jewels on her breast;
I stood within the silence of the Garden that she keeps,
Where flowers fill the footprints that her sandals pressed;
And I know the springs of laughter, for I trod the Middle
*   Way,*
Where sympathies are sign-posts and the merry Gods the
*   Guides;*
I have been where Hope is Ruler and evolving realms
*   obey;*
I know the Secret Nearness where the Ancient Wisdom
*   hides.*
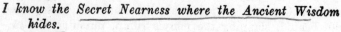

CHAPTER XXVI

AHBOR VALLEY GATE.

THEY cantered down the village street and over an echoing plank-bridge beneath which starlit water growled over a gravel bed. Only a rare light or two shone through the chinks of shuttered windows. Village dogs yelped at Diana's heels, but fled when she turned on them. The *sirdar* never glanced backward but rode like a shadow, bolt-upright, vanishing, vanishing, for ever vanishing into the darkness, yet never more than half a dozen ponies' lengths ahead. The sound of his pony's feet was all that made a human being of him; otherwise he was a specter.

The track rose sharply after they crossed the bridge and the ponies slowed to a walk, the *sirdar* maintaining the lead. Dawa Tsering, utterly winded, sat down on a rock, swaying his body back and forward to ease the stitch in his side. Ommony drew rein to wait for him, peering over a cliff-side into hollow darkness filled with the booming of water among rocks two hundred feet below. The *sirdar* shouted from around a bend a little higher up the trail, and stones fell into the track as if his voice had loosed an avalanche.

A dark figure shrouded in black cloth slid down following the stones and, before Ommony could move, had jumped to his rein. A young woman's face peered up at him, flashing white teeth, but the smile vanished instantly.

"Dawa Tsering," she muttered, and then began talking so fast that Ommony could hardly understand her. Dawa Tsering was in danger; that seemed clear enough. Also, she, her own self, wanted him, desired him desperately. She had a baby wrapped in a shawl slung over her shoulder and had laid another bundle on the ground.

319

Ommony pointed down the track, and as he moved his arm two men leaped out of a shadow and rushed up-hill at Dawa Tsering. Diana flew at them and they backed away. They had weapons, but appeared afraid to use them. Dawa Tsering ran up-hill toward Ommony, feeling for the knife that was not there, and Ommony whistled to Diana. The two men followed her cautiously, advancing step by step as she retreated, snarling. From the opposite direction around the bend, the *sirdar* came cantering back down-hill, sending stones scattering over the cliff-side. The girl flung herself at Dawa Tsering, seizing him around the neck and pouring out a stream of words, half-intelligible, choked with anger, grief, laughter, command, and emotions unknown to those who have not loved and do not still love an adventurer from Spiti.

"Sooner than expected!" the *sirdar* grunted, drawing rein.

The *sirdar* seemed pleased, and to have changed his mind about being in a hurry. He sat bolt-upright on his pony and waited in silence for something to happen; but the Tibetan behind him drew a long knife and showed it to the two men who were standing in the attitude of wrestlers. Dawa Tsering seemed to want to run, but the woman clung to him. Diana growled thunderously but awaited orders.

"Who are these men?" asked Ommony.

"My wife's husbands!" Dawa Tsering shook the girl off and stepped between Ommony and the *sirdar*. It appeared he meant to slip away, but the *sirdar's* pony made a sudden half-turn, and there was nothing left for him but to stand or jump over the cliff. "Protect me, Ommon*ee!* I have been a friend to you. That dog hasn't a flea on her. Moreover, Missish-Anbun has my knife."

"Who is this young woman?" Ommony demanded.

The *sirdar* answered. The two husbands were about to speak, but waited, open-mouthed. The woman was watching the *sirdar* as if destiny hung on the movement of his lips.

"She is his. It is his child. Choose!" he commanded, shoving Dawa Tsering, making him turn to face him. "Go with *her* to Spiti, or go with *them* to Ladak and the wife of many husbands. Which?"

"But how do I know it is my child?" Dawa Tsering grumbled.

The *sirdar's* face was in darkness from the shadow of the overhanging cliff. He did not laugh, but his smile was almost audible. "*She* knows. You may learn from her. Choose quickly!"

"Is it a man child?" Dawa Tsering asked; and the woman burst into excited speech, beginning to unwrap the bundle that swung at her back.

"Well, that is different," said Dawa Tsering. "If it is a man child—there is need of men in Spiti. Very well, I will take the woman."

"To Spiti!" the *sirdar* conmmanded. "Understand: I will write to the Rajah of Spiti. You will stay in Spiti and obey him. If you ever again cross the boundaries of Spiti without a letter from your rajah giving permission and stating the reason for it, you will deal with *me!*"

"Oh, well!" said Dawa Tsering, shrugging his broad shoulders. "Must I go now?"

"Now!" said the *sirdar*.

"Good-by, Ommonee. Now you must pick your own fleas off the dog. I will be sorry for you when I think of you without a servant, but I am too well born to be any man's servant for long, and this woman is a good one. I will sing songs of you in Spiti after you are dead. I think you will die soon. Look out for that *sirdar;* he is a tricky fellow."

He kicked the bundle the woman had dropped, as a signal for her to pick it up and follow him. In another moment he had vanished, clambering by a goat-track up the cliff, humming cheerfully through his nose each time he paused to let the laden woman overtake him.

The *sirdar* faced the discontented husbands, lifting his right hand for silence.

"Go back to that woman in Ladak,* and to her say this from me," he ordered. "That it may be I will come to Ladak. If I come, and when I come, it will be well for her if I have no reason to concern myself about her. Turn neither to the right nor to the left, nor delay on the road to Ladak, but hasten and tell her my message. And when she has beaten you, tell her a second time, and add this: that if again she sends men across the boundaries of Ladak, she shall lose them! Go!"

They went, retreating backward down-hill toward Til-gaun, whence another track led over a seventeen-thousand foot pass toward their polyandrous neighborhood. The Tibetan followed them, presumably to see the order was obeyed. The *sirdar* turned and rode up-hill in silence, keeping the middle of the track so that Ommony had no room to draw alongside. On the left a cliff fell sheer into the darkness; on the right it rose until it seemed to disappear among the stars.

Ommony rode with his woolen clothes wrapped closely against the penetrating wind that moaned from over the ravine on his left-hand. Mystified by the *sirdar's* confidently used authority, that could not possibly have been vested in him by the British or by any other government (for it seemed to extend into several states), his sensations began to be mixed and bewildering.

Suggestions of fear are assertive on a dark night, riding into the unknown, without a weapon; and the *sirdar's* mysterious silence was not reassuring. Hannah Sanburn had said he was "always a friend"; but a woman all alone in charge of a mission, surrounded by potential danger, would be likely to overestimate the friendship of any one who was not openly hostile.

It occurred, and kept on recurring, however hard he tried to dismiss the thought, that, with the exception of Hannah Sanburn, he alone knew the secret about Elsa Terry—

---

*Spiti and Ladak are Hill States separated by huge ranges, and their customs are as different as their climate and geography, although their actual distance apart is not great.

he and probably that *sirdar* just ahead of him; and the *sirdar* might be one of those dark fanatics whom jealousy makes murderers. What if the *sirdar* were leading him now to his death in the unknown?

For what purpose had Elsa been educated? Why had she been taken into India on that weird dramatic venture? Why had she been to Lhassa, the "forbidden city?" Who were the men to whom Hannah Sanburn said the Lama went for advice? Mahatmas? Masters? Or something else? What was *their* purpose? The Lama might easily be a saint and yet their tool—an unworldly old altruist in the hands of men who had designs on India; as pliable in their hands as the girl appeared to be pliable in his. That journey into India might have been a trial venture to discover how far the girl's trained personality could be counted on to turn men's (and women's) heads. Gandhi in jail, all India was ripe and waiting for a new political mahatma.

Why, if not to spy on Ommony, had the Lama tolerated Dawa Tsering in his company? Dawa Tsering's suspiciously prompt obedience to the *sirdar* rather looked as if the whole thing had been prearranged. In fact, it certainly *was* prearranged; the *sirdar* had admitted he expected something of the sort. And Ommony remembered now that back in Delhi Dawa Tsering had been remarkably complaisant about transferring allegiance from the Lama to himself.

Then—the Ahbor Valley. Was it likely that the *sirdar* could be leading him into that forbidden country for any other purpose than to make sure of his death or possibly to keep him prisoner up there? No white man, no government agent, not even one trained Nepalese spy who had penetrated the Ahbor Valley had ever returned alive. The only one who ever did return had floated, dead and mangled, down the Brahmaputra River. Thirty-five miles —not a yard more—from the boundary of Sikhim; perhaps thirty miles from where they were that minute, the Upper Ahbor Valley was as unknown as the mountains of the moon. Why should he suppose that *he* was to be specially favored with permission to go in there and return alive?

But there was no turning back now—nothing, of course, to prevent but nothing further from intention. Afraid, yes. Faint-hearted, no. The two emotions are as the poles apart. Fear acted as a spur to obstinacy, the unknown as a lure that beckoned more compellingly than safety; habitually, since his school-days, personal safety had been Ommony's last, least consideration. He told himself it was the cold wind that made the goose-flesh rise, and all that night, shivering, he forced himself to believe that was the truth, following the *sirdar's* pony along trails like a winding devil's stairway that led alternately toward the sky and down again into a roaring underworld.

It was pitch-dark, but the deepest darkness lay ahead, where the enormous range of the Himalayas was a wall of silence ridged with faint silver where the starlight shone on everlasting snow. Darkness may be a substance for all that anybody knows about it; it lay thick and somber, swallowing the sounds—sudden, crashing sounds, that volleyed and were gone. A tree fell into a watercourse. A rock went cannoning from crag to crag and plunged into an abyss. Silence; and then a howl along the wind as a night-prowler scented the ponies.

Bats—unimaginable thousands of them, black, and less black than the night—until the air was all alive with movement and the squeak and smell. Chasms into which the ponies' hoofs struck stones that seemed to fall for ever, soundless. Dawn at last, touching untrodden peaks with crimson—gleaming gold, and stealing lemon-colored down the pillars of the sky, to awaken ghosts of shadows in the black ravines. Tree-tops, waist-deep in an opal mist, an eagle—seven thousand feet below the track—circling above those like a fleck of blown dirt. A roar ascending full of crashing tumult; and at last a flash of silver on the waves of Brahmaputra, a mile and a half below, plunging toward

Bengal through the rock-staked jaws of Ahbor Valley
Gate.

Downward then, by a trail that seemed to swing between
earth and sky, the ponies sliding half the time with their
rumps against the rock or picking their way cautiously
with six-inch strides along the edge of chasms, over which
the riders peered into fathomless shadow that the sunlight
had not reached. Down to the eagle-level, and the tree-
line, where the wet scent of morning on moss and golden
gravel made the ponies snort and they had to be unsaddled
and allowed to roll.

Not a word from the *sirdar,* although he stroked Diana's
head when she approached him, and laughed at the ponies'
antics. On again downward, and a hut at last, built of
tree-trunks, perched on a ledge of rock above a waterfall,
on the rim of a tree-hung bowl through which the Brahmaputra plunged.

CHANT PAGAN

When that caressing light forgets the hills
That change their hue in its evolving grace;
When, harmony of swaying reeds and rills,
The breeze forgets her music and the face
Of Nature smiles no longer in the pond,
Divinity revealed! When morning peeps
Above earth's rim, and no bird notes respond;
When half a world in mellow moonlight sleeps
And no peace pours along the silver'd air;
When dew brings no wet wonder of delight
On jeweled spider-web and scented lair
Of drone and hue and honey; when the night
No longer shadows the retreating day,
Nor purple dawn pursues the graying dark;
And no child laughs; and no wind bears away
The bursting glory of the meadow-lark;
Then—then it may be—never until then
May death be dreadful or assurance wane
That we shall die a while, to waken when
New morning summons us to earth again.

CHAPTER XXVII

SMOKE came from the hut, through a hole in the roof, giving the sharp air a delicious tang, all mixed with the aroma of fallen leaves and pine trunks. Over beyond the hut spray splashed from the waterfall—rose-colored diamonds against moss-green. The air was full of bird-music, that the ear caught after it was once used to the ponderous roar of water.

A man who was undoubtedly an Ahbor—black hair low down on his forehead, high up on his cheeks—Mongolian cheek-bones—glittering, dark, bold eyes—hairy legs showing beneath a leather-colored smock—waist girdled with a leather belt, from which a *kukri* like a Gurkha's hung in a wooden scabbard—peered from the hut door. He stared at the *sirdar* in silence, curiously, as at some one he must tolerate; it was the half-shy, half-impudent stare of a yokel at a wealthy man from town.

He took the ponies and was very careful of them, unsaddling, leading them to drink, dragging out a sack and spilling grain in the hollow of a rock, feeling their legs and rubbing them down with a piece of bark while they munched contentedly.

The *sirdar* led the way into the hut, but laid a finger on his lips for silence. The reason for silence was not evident; there was nobody else in there. The place was clean, but almost bare of furniture; there was a hearth of rough stones in the midst, a rough table, and a bunk in one corner, littered with blue trade-blankets. There was no bench—no chairs or stools—but there were wooden platters on the table, with big silver spoons beside them, and on the hearth imported cereal was cooking in an earthen

327

vessel set in a brass one containing water. There was honey in a white china bowl, and a big glass pitcher full of milk, which looked as if it had stood there overnight; the layer of cream was more than an inch thick. There were two cups, without handles, made of alabaster.

In silence, as if it were a ritual, the *sirdar* served the meal and they ate it standing. Then he walked out and sat on a rock that overhung the waterfall. He was not cross-legged in the usual Indian attitude of meditation; his long booted and spurred legs were out in front of him, the way a white man sits, and he leaned an elbow on one knee, his chin on his right fist; motionless in that attitude he stared at the bewildering view until he seemed almost physically to become a part of it.

Ommony watched him from the hut door, now and then losing sight of his form in the spray as he wondered what sort of thinking it might be that could so absorb the man, and as he watched, wondering, his own inclination was to take his shoes off; he felt a pagan reverence possess him, as if that dew-wet, emerald and brown immensity, with the thundering river below and the blue sky for a roof, were a temple of Mother Nature, in which it were impertinence to speak, imposture to assert a personality.

Diana was watching fish in a pool above the waterfall; the aborigine from Ahbor was using his *kukri* to fashion a wooden implement with which to comb the ponies' manes and tails; the birds were hopping on tree and rock about their ordinary business, and an eagle circled overhead as if he had been doing the same thing for centuries. But there began to be a sensation of having stepped into another world.

Things assumed strange and strangely beautiful proportions. The whole of the past became a vaguely remembered dream, in which the Lama, Samding and Hannah Sanburn stood out as the only important realities. The present moment was eternity, and wholly satisfying. Every motion of a glistening leaf, each bird-note, every gesture of the nodding grass, each drop of spray was, of and in itself, in every detail perfect. Something breathed—he did not know what, or want to inquire—he was part of what breathed; and a universe, of which he was also a part, responded with infinite rhythm of color, form, sound, movement, ebb and flow, life and death, cause and effect, all one, yet infinitely individual, enwrapped in peace and wrought of magic, of which Beauty was the living, all-conceiving light.

The enchantment ceased as gradually as it had begun. He felt his mind struggling to hold it—knew that he had seen Truth naked—knew that nothing would ever satisfy him until he should regain that vision—and was aware of the *sirdar* walking toward him, normal, matter-of-fact, abrupt, spurs clinking as his heels struck rock.

"Are you ready?" asked the *sirdar*.

Ommony whistled and Diana followed them along a fern-hung ledge. There was opal air beneath them; crags and tree-tops peered out of slow-moving mist that the sun was beginning to tempt upward. Presently, leaping from rock to rock, until they could hear the river laughing and shouting, sending echoes crashing through a forest that had looked like moss from higher up, they descended breathless, downward, and for ever downward, leaping wild water that gushed between worn bowlders, swinging by tree-roots around outleaning cliffs, Diana crouching as she hugged the wall along a six-inch ledge, crossing a yelling cataract by a fallen tree-trunk, whose ax-marks were the only sign that the trail was ever used before. They came at last to a bank with a cliff behind it, still more than a thousand feet above the Brahmaputra, whose thunder volleyed as if a battle were being fought for right of way through a rock- and tree-staked gorge defended by all the underworld.

Ommony threw himself down, panting, his clothes sodden with sweat and his head in a whirl from the violent exertion and the change in altitude. Every sinew in his legs was trembling separately, and his heart thumped like a steam-injector. Diana lay still at his feet. The *sirdar* appeared calm and not particularly out of breath; he sat down on a rock near by with an air of concentrated attention.

Presently Ommony began to feel the chill of damp earth under him. He got to his feet to look for a better place closer to the cliff, and stood for a moment craning upward trying to gauge with his eye the distance they had come from the lip of the ravine that showed at one point sharp as a pencil-line against the sky. He realized he could never find the way back if life depended on it, and guessed there must be another way than that into the Ahbor Valley, or how could men and animals find egress? He turned to speak, leaning one hand against the cliff.

"This way!" said the *sirdar's* voice on his left hand; and before he could turn he felt himself shoved violently.

His head still singing from the strain of the descent, a veitigo still swimming through his brain, he was sure, but only dimly, that he had been pushed, then pulled through a narrow fissure in the shadowy corner of a projecting spur. He had scarcely noticed the opening—had not observed that the lower portion of the spur was split away, like the base of a flying buttress, from the wall itself. Within, the opening turned and turned again, a man's breadth wide each shoulder against the wall, a zigzag passage driven (there were tool marks) into a granite mountain; and when he turned to look, there was nothing to see but the outline of the *sirdar's* head against dim light behind him.

Diana forced her way between his legs and ran ahead to explore; he could hear her hollow barking—"All's well so far—marvelous! mysterious! exciting!"— and then the *sirdar* shoved him forward, saying not one word. He could not see, but felt the whirring of bats, and knew by the sound that he had stepped into a cavern. The *sirdar* groped and found an oil lantern with a bail. Lighting it, and swinging it until the shadows leaped like giant goblins and enormous bats streamed in panic toward the open air, he led the way to a low tunnel at the rear through

which it was just possible to walk by bending nearly
double.

At the end of fifty yards of that uncomfortable going,
there was vastness, black as pitch, and such empty silence
that the ear-drums ached. The lantern light shone into
nothing and was swallowed—ceased, except where it struck
the natural, dark-granite wall and the end of the hewn
tunnel. They were standing on a platform ten feet wide,
from which hewn steps descended for ever and ever for all
the brain could guess. The roof was utterly invisible;
the space beneath it was alive with whirling bats. The air
was breathable but stuffy. Sweat began to stream from
every pore.

"What next?" asked Ommony.

"What next—ot nex—ot nex—ot nex—ot nex!" the
echoes answered, dying away in a grumble at last somewhere in the bowels of the world.

He did not care to speak again. He tried to suppress
thought, lest the echoes should learn that and multiply
and mock it in the solemn hugeness of the underworld.
Diana was afraid now—crouched against his legs and
howled when the *sirdar* started down the smooth stone steps,
that looked dark-green in the lantern light.

The howl let loose the hounds of Pandemonium. A
phantom pack gave tongue in full cry down the valley of
hell—pounced on their quarry leagues away—worried it
—and vanished into silence. The *sirdar* laughed, and the
laugh went after them, until a thousand devils seemed to
mock the ghost the hounds had slain. Diana was seized
with panic and had to be dragged by the collar. Ommony
did not dare to speak to her for fear of the echoes. He
tried whispering once, but only once; it turned into a hiss
that made Diana tremble in abject misery.

The echo of their feet was bad enough. Each downward step was repeated until the darkness became full of
a din like the clapping of unseen hands; the clink of the
sirdar's spurs was multiplied into the jingle and clank
of ghostly squadrons, and the whirring of unseen bat-

wings grew into the snort of the war-horses charging line
on line. It was easy enough to imagine lance and pennon,
and the dead from a thousand battle-fields repeating
history.

Ommony began trying to count the steps, but lost the
reckoning at the sixth or seventh turn; the stairway zig-
zagged to and fro across the face of a wall that seemed
from its smooth, yet irregular feel to have been hewn by
giants from the virgin rock. And when they did at last
reach bottom there appeared by the swinging lantern
light to be a causeway running right and left, gray-white
and firm with a million years' accumulation of the bats'
excreta.

The *sirdar* hesitated—took the right-hand way, and led
with a swinging stride that it took all of Ommony's
strength to follow. There was hardly any echo now, because the bat-dirt underfoot consumed the sound (and
filled the air, too, with acrid dust), but there began to be
a weird, very far-away rumbling, at first not more than
a peculiar, irregular pulsation of the silence, gradually
increasing until it sounded as if all the echoes in the world
were hiding in the cellar of a mountain, crowding one another to find room.

A roof became vaguely visible at last. They were entering a tunnel, whose floor sloped downward. It appeared
to have been originally a natural fissure in the base of a
granite mountain; Titans had hewn and enlarged it, leaving buttresses six feet square of natural rock, that curved
overhead until they met to support the roof. They were
spaced about twenty feet apart, and every gap between
was occupied by an enormous image, hewn out of the wall,
resembling nothing in the world that Ommony had ever
seen. Vaguely, but only vaguely, they suggested temple
images of ancient Egypt. No two were alike. Due to the
moving shadows, they appeared to change position as the
lantern passed them, and the weird sounds that filled the
tunnel suggested conversation in the language of another
world.

The only remark the *sirdar* made of any kind was midway down the tunnel, more than a quarter of a mile from the point where its roof had first become dimly visible. He paused for a moment, seemed to hesitate whether or not to speak, then pointed upward.

"We are under the Brahmaputra."

His voice sounded muffled. The noise of the tremendous river galloping and plunging overhead absorbed all other sounds.

"How thick is the roof?" Ommony asked. But he did not know how to pitch his voice; the words died on his lips; his own ears could not hear them.

In one place there was water; it appeared to be an artificial drain; there was a trickling, sucking sound where it disappeared through a hole in the wall into obscurity. The floor for twenty yards was built of very heavy timber spiked on to transverse beams laid in slots in the rock wall; the slots were very ancient and the timbers not a generation old, marked here and there with the print of ponies' hoofs—which seemed to Ommony to prove one point at any rate: there must be another way out from the Ahbor Valley than that goat-path down the side of the ravine. No pony, laden or unladen, could negotiate the trail by which he and the *sirdar* had come.

Once they had crossed the wooden bridge the track began to rise, but the *sirdar* continued leading at the same speed, neither heat nor stuffiness impeding him. He swung the lantern in his right hand with an air of indifference, as if he had long ago ceased wondering at the titan labors of the men who hewed the tunnel. There was no air of haste about him; his natural speed appeared to be more than four miles an hour, just as his natural mood was silent, and his natural condition fearless, unsurprised, indifferent to circumstance.

The air began to improve at last, as they emerged into a cavern into which one shaft of sunlight shone through an opening so high overhead that its milky-whiteness, spreading and dispersing, formed a layer, below which the gloom grew solid. The sensation was of being in a grotto under water and looking upward through a cave-mouth toward the surface of the sea. One almost expected to see fish swimming across the zone of light.

The *sirdar* allowed Ommony to rest at last. He sat on a rock that resembled an altar, set the lantern on another, and motioned to Ommony to be seated on a third. There were seven stones, exactly similar in shape and size, arranged so as to suggest the constellation of the Pleiades;* the seventh, which might be Merope, was surrounded by a circle of masonry, perhaps to suggest that that one is invisible to the naked eye. About and among the big stones there were hundreds of smaller ones, all of the same shape but of different sizes, arranged in no evident pattern, but nevertheless sunk into place in hollows cut deliberately in the rock floor. It looked as if whoever set them there knew a great deal more about the stars than any naked eye reveals.

As Ommony grew gradually used to the dim light the shapes of enormous carvings revealed themselves on walls so high that imagination reeled in the effort to measure them. The shape of the cavern was that of the inside of a hollow tree-trunk, broad at the base, narrowing toward the top until it vanished in impenetrable gloom somewhere above the shaft of light. The walls were all irregular, almost exactly resembling in rough outline the interior of a hollow tree; and wherever there was space a figure had been carved, half-human, ponderous, as contemplative as the Sphinx.

Wherever the eye rested long enough a figure would develop in the gloom, until the darkness appeared full of awful faces that had been there, pondering immensity, since time began.

---

*The ancient Greek legend of the Pleiades is that they were the daughters of Atlas and Pleione, and that the seventh, Merope, concealed herself out of shame for having loved a mortal. But the legend is doubtless vastly older than the Greeks and has an esoteric, or hidden meaning. A telescope reveals hundreds of stars in the constellation.

As well as Ommony could judge, they were in the core of a hollow granite mountain. He turned to question the *sirdar*, but as he moved a sound like a distant trumpet blast came from above and, glancing upward, he saw a speck that might be a human being, moving on the lip of the opening through which the shaft of light came. Diana howled at the sound, but the howl was lost in the enormous space; there were no echoes.

The *sirdar* made no comment, but got to his feet at once and holding up the lantern examined Ommony's face for a moment intently. His expression was of exercising judgment, but he said nothing, did not even nod. His amber eyes looked hardly human in the dimness, and glowed with a reddish light behind them—leonine, but curiously passionless. Swinging the lantern again, he turned and led the way toward a projection outflung like a buttress from the nearest wall.

There began then an ascent that almost conquered physical endurance. Steps, whose treads, hewn from the rock, were eighteen inches high, followed the outline of the ragged walls and circled the whole huge cavern three times toward the opening through which the light poured in. There were places, but not many of them, where the way ran almost level along a ledge for fifty feet or so, and thigh muscles had a chance to rest from the agony of climbing. The only other resting places were the crowns of smooth gigantic heads that gazed for ever into vastness. There was no rail, no balustrade; the steps were nowhere more than three feet wide, with nothing on their outer edge but darkness and a terrifying certainty of what would happen if a foot slipped or if vertigo prevailed. Diana, thrusting herself between the wall and Ommony, pressed herself against him for the sake of human company, adding to the terror of the long ascents where no huge head projected to afford a sense of something solid between the wall and the abyss.

The *sirdar* seemed tireless. Ommony ached in every sinew of his being. Blood sang in his ears and eyes.

Thirst began to torture him.   A stitch like a knife-jab
gnawed under his ribs.   Repeatedly he had to lie face-
downward on a level place, pressing both hands tightly
on the stone while the whole cavern and all the silent heads
seemed to whirl and whirl around him.   Then Diana licked
the back of his neck, and the *sirdar* waited twenty or thirty yards higher up, swinging the lantern as if its constant
rhythmic movement were in some way necessary.   He
never spoke once, made no sound other than his footsteps
and the clink of spurs, all the way up; but now and then
he stood on the crown of a head overhanging the cavern
and swung the lantern in wider sweeps, as if he were signaling to some one.

The shaft of light faded and almost disappeared before
they reached the opening.   Ommony was in no condition
then to reckon up the hours or to guess at the height he
had climbed.   Not more than barely conscious, he collapsed on a smooth platform that sloped dangerously outward, his fingers trying to grip the rock and his feet continuing to climb.   He felt the *sirdar* (or somebody) seize
him by the arm-pits, heard Diana growl, and the next he
knew he was lying face-upward with cool water on his lips,
a cool breeze on his face, and a star-lit sky overhead.   He
felt Diana nosing at his hair, and knew nothing after that
for several hours.

In this sense we are our brothers' keepers: that if we injure them we are responsible. Therefore, our duty is, so vigilantly to control ourselves that we may injure none; and for this there is no substitute; all other duties take a lower place and are dependent on it.

FROM THE BOOK OF THE SAYINGS OF TSIANG SAMDUP.

CHAPTER XXVIII

THE LAMA'S HOME.

WHEN Ommony recovered consciousness it was some
time before he was sure he was not dreaming. There was
no sense of stability. The universe appeared to sway beneath him, and the sky, when he opened his eyes at last,
swung like a compass-card. He closed his eyes, heard
voices, and presently discovered he was in a stretcher
being borne on men's heads. When he opened his eyes
again the first thing he saw was Diana looking down at
him from a rock. She barked when he moved his hand.

It was a very rough stretcher made of poles and hide.
His feet were loosely tied to it and a rope was passed
over his breast, but he could get his hands under the rope,
and its purpose was explained when the stretcher became
tilted at an acute angle and he rode for a while with his
feet pointed at the sky. On either hand were sloping
limestone cliffs and he was being carried up a dry watercourse between them.

He felt no impulse to ask questions, but was curious
about his own condition. He recalled rather vividly a
time, ten years ago, when he was carried to an operating
room. When the stretcher returned to the horizontal and
he cautiously tested each muscle, he discovered that his
leg-sinews were so stiff that he could hardly bear to move
them. Then he remembered; every step of the climb up
that titanic stairway came back to him like a nightmare.

He craned his neck looking for the *sirdar*, but failed to
discover him. He could not see the stretcher-bearers, but
there were eight Ahbors walking behind, ready to relieve
them—hairy, savage-looking men, possessed of that air of
deliberate indifference that usually hides extreme fanat-

338

icism; their eyes were large, like those of deer, and the
hair came close up to their cheek-bones. They all had
weapons; two were armed with bow and arrows; but no
two weapons were alike, and no two were dressed exactly
alike.

Presently the path began to follow the edge of a cliff
five or six thousand feet above a river—undoubtedly from
its size the Brahmaputra—that galloped and plunged
among rocks in the bed of a valley on the left hand. Incredible, enormous mountains leaned against the sky in
every direction, suggesting barrenness and storms, but
the valley lay golden and green in the sunlight, patched
with the vivid green of corn-fields, dotted with grazing
cattle and with the dark-brown roofs of villages. It
looked like an exceedingly rich valley, and well populated.

After a mile or two of gorgeous vistas the track turned
to the right and passed between miles of tumbled ruins,
whose limestone blocks, weighing tons apiece, had turned
to every imaginable hue of green, gray, brown and yellow.
Blue and red flowers were growing in the crevices, and
trees had forced themselves between tremendous paving
stones that now lay tilted with their edges to the sky. Ommony untied the rope across his breast and sat up to
observe the ruins, laying both hands on his thighs to ease
their aching; and presently he gasped—forgot the
agony.

The track passed between two monolithic columns more
enormous than the grandest ones at Thebes, and emerged
on the rim of a natural amphitheater, whose terraced
sides descended for about two thousand feet to where a
torrent of green and white water rushed from a cave-
mouth and plunged into a fissure in the limestone opposite. The air was full of the noise of water and the
song of birds, intoxicating with the scent of flowers and
vivid with their color.

Every terrace was a wilderness of flowers and shade-
trees, strewn with bowlders that broke up the regularity,
and connected one with another by paths and bridges of

natural limestone where streams gushed from the fern-draped rock and fell in cascades to the torrent in the midst. There was an atmosphere of sunlit peace.

Above the topmost terrace, occupying about a third of the circumference, were buildings in the Chinese style; the roofs were carved with dragons and the rear walls appeared to be built into the cliff, which rose for a thousand feet to a sheer wall of crags, whose jagged edges pierced the sky.

There were no human beings in evidence, but smoke was rising from several of the buildings, which all had an air of being lived in. The track, which was paved now with limestone flags, led under an arch in the midst of the largest building. The arch turned out to be the opening of a tunnel, twenty feet high at lowest and as many wide, that pierced the mountain for more than a hundred yards, making two sharp turns where it crossed caverns and followed natural fissures in the limestone before it emerged on the edge of a sheer ravine, overlooking another valley that appeared to approach the gorge of the Brahmaputra at an angle of nearly forty-five.

Away in the distance, like a roaring curtain, emerald green and diamond white, blown in the wind, the Tsang-po River, half a mile wide, tumbled down a precipice between two outflung spurs that looked like the legs of a seated giant. The falls were leagues away, and yet their roar came down-wind like the thunder of creation. Below them, incalculably far below the summit, the rising spray formed a dazzling rainbow; and where, below the falls, the Tsang-po became the Brahmaputra, there were rock-staked rapids more than two miles wide that threw columns of white water fifty feet in air, so that the rocks looked like leviathans at war.

The path led up the side of the ravine, curved around a projecting shoulder, and entered another tunnel, which emerged at the end of fifty yards into a natural cavern. There the bearers set the stretcher down and two of them offered to help Ommony up a long flight of steps hewn

from the limestone rock. However, he managed to walk
unaided and Diana followed him through a great gap in
the wall into what was evidently the basement of a building.

There he was met by a brown-robed monk—not an
Ahbor, a Tibetan—who smiled but made no remark and
led him up winding stairways between thick masonry
walls to a gallery that overhung the valley from a height
which made the senses reel. It was the upper of two gal-
leries that ran along the face of a building backed against
a cliff; doors and small windows opened all the way along
it, but the Tibetan led around the far corner, where the
wooden planking came to an end at a stone platform and
there was one solitary door admitting to a room about
thirty feet by twenty, that had a window facing the tremendous Tsango-po Falls.

It was in all respects a comfortable room, with a fireplace at one end and a bright fire burning. On either side
of the fireplace there were shelves stacked with European
books in several languages. The stone floor was covered
with a heavy Chinese rug. There was no glass in the window, but there were heavy shutters to exclude wind and
rain, as well as silken Chinese curtains.

The monk went away and returned presently with a
pitcher of milk and some peculiar cakes that tasted as if
made from a mixture of flour and nut-meat, raised with
butter. He signed to Ommony to eat and, when he had
finished, took the pitcher and plate away again.

Ommony warmed his legs at the fire, rubbed them to re-
duce the stiffness, and chose a book at random—Kant's
Critique of Pure Reason; it was well thumbed. He sat
down in a chair before the fire to read, regarding the book
as no more incomprehensible than his own predicament
and likely to keep his mind off profitless conjecture. He
was too tired to think about his own problem—too sore in
every muscle to consider sleep. One fact was clear: he
had been admitted to the Ahbor Valley, and there must
be some reason for it. For the time being, that was enough

—that, and the comforting sense that all motion had ceased and he could sit still within four walls that shut off the stunning hugeness of the scenery. He had no geographical curiosity—was not qualified in any event to make a map that would be of any real value, and was not sure it would be courteous to try to do it. People who don't invade other people's countries have a right to their own privacy. Besides, he was quite sure he could never retrace the way into the valley, and doubtful whether he could find a way out of it, except down that thundering river. He was absolutely at the Lama's mercy, and entirely sure the Lama was a man of superb benevolence, if nothing else.

Finding he could not make head or tail of Kant in the original German (he spent ten minutes trying to find the subject of one verb) he laid the book down and began to wonder whether this was the place in which his sister and Jack Terry had died. Time vanished. Thought took him back to the days when he had sent for his sister Elsa, then seventeen, to come to India and keep house for him. He frowned, blaming himself for having been the cause of all she suffered. They had had so much in common, and he had understood so well her craving for knowledge that is not in any of the text-books, that he had tacitly encouraged her to make acquaintances which his better judgment should have warned him to keep out of her reach. He wondered just to what extent a man is justified in guiding or obstructing a younger sister's explorations into unknown realms of thought—knew that he himself would resent any leading-rein—knew nevertheless, that he felt guilty of having neglected to protect his sister until protection and precaution were too late. He had done his best then, but—

"Dammit, are we or aren't we free agents?" he asked aloud, staring at the fire; and then he heard Diana's tail beating the Chinese rug. It sounded as if the dog were laughing at him! He turned his head sharply—and saw the Lama standing in the doorway.

"We are free—to *become* agents of whatever power we wish," said the Lama, smiling. "Don't get up, my son. I know how thighs ache after a climb up the stairs of the Temple of Stars. The *sirdar* does not know the other entrance to the valley."

"Where is he?" asked Ommony, staring. He was not particularly interested in the *sirdar*. A suggestion as to who and what the Lama might be, had occurred to him suddenly. He was sparring for time to follow up that thought.

"He returned," said the Lama, sitting on a chair before the fire, betraying an inclination to tuck his legs up under him but resisting it. "The Ahbors would have killed him if he passed beyond the opening. They would have killed *you*—if it were not for Diana the dog. My son, you wonder why I left you in Darjiling? There were seven reasons; of which the first is that I have no right to lead you out of your environment; and the second, that you *have* the right to make your own decision. The third reason was that these Ahbors guard their valley very strictly; it is their valley; they also have their rights. The fourth reason was, that an excuse must be presented to the Ahbors for admitting you. The fifth, that I alone could do that. The sixth, that I must make the excuse in advance of your coming, since they would not listen unless given time to consider the matter. And the seventh reason was, that it was fitting you should learn *why* this has been kept from you for twenty years, before you learn as much of the secret as I can show you. Behind each of those seven reasons are seven more beyond your comprehension. You spoke with Miss Sanburn?" Ommony nodded. Suspicion was approaching certainty. He wondered that the thought had not occurred to him long before.

"Where is the *chela*—Samding—Elsa Terry—my niece?" he asked. There is no foretelling which emotion will come uppermost. He felt a bit humiliated. It annoyed him to think he had lived for two months in almost constant association with his sister's child and had never guessed it;

annoyed him more to think that the Lama should not have
trusted him from the beginning; most of all that he had not
guessed the Lama's identity. He felt almost sure that he
had guessed right at last. Nothing but a western dread of
seeming foolish restrained him from guessing aloud.

But the Lama read his thoughts, and answered the
unspoken question first in his own way, his bright old eyes
twinkling amid the wrinkles.

"Those who are trustworthy, my son, eventually prove
it—always, and it is only they to whom secrets should be
told. It is not enough that a man shall say, 'Lo, I am this,
or I am that.' Nor is it enough that other men shall say
the same of him. Some men are trustworthy in some respects, and not in others. He who trusts, and is betrayed,
is answerable to his own soul.—Do you think it would
have been *fair* to trust you with the secret of my *chela?*"
he asked suddenly.

Ommony side-stepped the question by asking another:
"Why do you call her San-fun-ho?"

"It is her name. It was I who gave it to her. She accepted it, when she was old enough to understand its meaning. Do you know Chinese? The word means 'Possessor
of the three qualities,' but its inner meanings are many:
righteousness, virtuous action, purity, benevolence, moral
conduct, ingenuousness, knowledge, endurance, music—
and all the qualities that lie behind those terms."

"You think she has *all* of them?" Ommony asked.
His voice held a hint of sarcasm. He intended that it
should.

"My son, we all have them," said the Lama. "But she
is the first *ordinary* mortal I have known, who could *express them.*"

Ommony pricked his ears at the word "ordinary."

"You *know*—you have *seen* the Masters?" he demanded.

The Lama blinked, but otherwise ignored the question,
exactly as every one Ommony had asked, who was likely to
know, always had avoided it. There is a legend about mys-

terious "Mahatmas,"* whom all the East believes in, but
whom none from the West has ever met (and talked much
about afterward).

"No man ever had such a *chela*," said the Lama, changing the subject and betraying the first hint of personal
emotion Ommony had ever noticed in him.

"*Are you one of the Masters?*" Ommony demanded, sitting bolt upright, studying the old man's face.

But the Lama laughed, his wrinkles dancing with amusement.

"My son, that is a childish question," he said after a
moment. "If a man were to tell you he is one of the
Masters, he would be a liar and a boaster; because it must
be evident to any one who thinks, that the more a man
knows, the more surely he knows there are greater ones
than himself. He is a Master, whose teaching you accept.
But if he should tell you there is none superior to himself, it would be wise to look for another Master!"

But Ommony felt more sure than ever. He knew that
Pythagoras, for instance, and Appolonius, and scores of
others had gone to India for their teaching. For
twenty years he had kept ears and eyes alert for a clue
that might lead him to one of the preservers of the ancient
wisdom, who are said to mingle with the crowd unrecog-
nized and to choose to whom they will impart their secrets.
He had met self-styled Gurus by the dozen—a perfect host
of more or less obvious charlatans—some self-deceived
dabblers in the occult, whose motives might be more or less
respectable—but never a one, unless this man, whose
speech and conduct had appeared to him consistent with
his idea of what a real Mahatma might be.

"Hannah Sanburn told me," he said slowly, "that
there are individuals to whom you go for advice. Did she
tell the truth?"

---

*The legend persists; mocked by the missionaries and denied by
governments, but believed, nevertheless, by multitudes of ignorant
people and by an increasing number of thoughtful investigators.
There is much vague rumor and some corroborated detail, but
whoever really knows the facts is silent.

"She received that truth from my lips," said the Lama, nodding.

"Are *they* the Masters?"

"The Masters are only discoverable to those, who in former lives have earned the right to discover them," the Lama answered. "There is a Higher Law that governs these things. It is the Law of Evolution. We evolve from one state to another, life after life, being born into such surroundings as provide us with the proper opportunity. It was not by accident, my son, that San-fun-ho was brought into the Ahbor Valley to be born."

"Do the Masters live here?"

"No," said the Lama, smiling again.

"Then what is the particular advantage of the Ahbor Valley?"

"My son, I do not rule the Universe! It was not my province to arrange the stars! There is no place, no circumstance that does not have particular advantages. The Ahbor Valley is more suitable to some than to others, but I am not the one who selects those who shall come here."

"Who does?"

"There is a law that governs it, just as there is a law that rules the stars, and a law that obliges one to be born rich and another poor. When did cause begin? And when shall effect cease? Can you answer that?"

"At any rate, *you* were the cause of *my* coming here," said Ommony.

"Nay, my son! No more than I was the cause of your coming into the world. If I should have caused you to come here, I should be responsible for all the consequences; and I do not know what those might be. I have *permitted* you to come here. I have removed some difficulties."

"Why?"

"Because I sought to remove other difficulties from the path of some one else, and it seemed to me possible that you might be the one who can assist. Remember: it was not I who caused you to resign your position under the

Indian Government; not I who appointed you a Trustee
at Tilgaun; nor I who invited you to disguise yourself as
a Bhat-Brahman. Have I ever given you advice on any of
those matters?"

"No," Ommony admitted. "But you have corresponded with me ever since Marmaduke died, and if your
letters weren't educative, what were they?"

"Evocative!" the Lama answered. "Shall I show you
the copies of all the letters I have written to you? I believe you will not find one word in them that might evoke
from you anything except your higher nature, nor one
word that you could twist into inducement to do this, or
to do that. I have taught you nothing. You have tried
to understand my letters, and have found a guiding force
within yourself. I am not your guide."

"Well then—why the interest in me?" Ommony retorted.

"My son, you are immensely interesting. You were
forced on my attention. I have *my* work to do, and I have
nearly finished it."

The old man paused, and suddenly he seemed so old
and tired that all his previous exertions—night-long rides
on camel-back, two months of journeying in the heat of
the Indian plains, patient control of a dramatic company,
and (not least) the return across the mountains to his
home—appeared incredible. For a moment sadness seemed
to overwhelm him. Then he smiled, and as if his will
shone through the cloud and warmed the worn-out flesh,
he threw off fifty years.

"For what purpose are we in the world?" he asked.
"The purpose lies in front of each of us. It is never more
than one step in advance, and whither it leads, who knows?
It is the best that we can do at any moment that is required of us. A tree should grow. Water should run.
A shoemaker should make shoes. A musician should make
music. A teller of tales should tell them. Eyes are to see
with. Ears are for hearing. Each man's own environment is his own universe, and he the master or the victim

of it in exactly the degree by which he governs or is governed by himself. Could you have patience with me, if I should tell a little—just a little of my own experience?"

"Good God!" said Ommony. "I'd rather hear it than find a fortune! Ears are to hear with!" he added, grinning, settling himself back into the chair to listen.

"Some men listen to the wrong sound," said the Lama. "It is good to listen carefully, and to speak only after much thought. I will not tell more than is required to make a certain matter clear. Thereafter, you must use your own judgment, my son."

I have conversed with many priests; and some were honest men, and some were not, but three things none of them could answer: if their God is all-wise, what does it matter if men are foolish? And if they can imagine and define their God, must he not be smaller than their own imaginations? Furthermore, if their God is omnipotent, why does he need priests and ritual?

FROM THE BOOK OF THE SAYINGS OF TSIANG SAMDUP.

CHAPTER XXIX

THE LAMA'S STORY

" I AM a Ringding, of the order of Gelong Lamas. That is neither a high rank nor a low one; but high enough to provide the outer forms of dignity, and low enough to avoid the snares of pride. I have ever found contentment in the Middle Way. I was born in Lhassa," Tsiang Samdup began, and then paused and got down on the rug, where he could sit cross-legged and be comfortable. Diana went and laid her great head on his knee.

"Just a minute," said Ommony. "How old are you?"

But Tsiang Samdup smiled. "My son," he answered, "we live as long as we are useful, and as long as it is good for us to live. Thereafter we die, which is another form of living, even as ice and water and rain and dew are the same thing in different aspects. When the appointed time comes, we return, as the rain returns, to the earth it has left for a season. As I told you, I was born in Lhassa."

He rubbed the dog's head as if he were erasing unnecessary details from the tablets of memory. Then he laid a stick of pine-wood on the fire deliberately, and watched it burn. It was several minutes before he spoke again.

"The Dalai Lama is a person who is mocked by Western thinkers. The few Europeans who have been to Lhassa have hastened to write books about him, in which they declare he is the ignorant head of a grossly superstitious religion. To which I have nothing to say, except this: that it is evident the writers of those books have been unable to expose the Dalai Lama's secrets. An army which invaded Lhassa failed to expose them with its bayonets. I, who took the highest possible degrees at Oxford and have

350

lived in Paris, in Vienna, and in Rome—so that I know at least something of the western culture—regard the Dalai Lama with respect, which is different, my son, from superstitious awe. The Tashi Lama, who does not live in Lhassa, is as high above the Dalai Lama as a principle is higher than a consequence.

"There was a Tashi Lama who selected me, for reasons of his own, for certain duties. I was very young then—conscious of the host of lower impulses and far from the self-knowledge that discriminates between the higher and the lower. To me in those days my desire was law, and I had not yet learned to desire the Middle Way, which leads between the dangers of ambition and inertia."

Tsiang Samdup paused again and stared out of the window at an eagle which soared higher and higher on motionless wings, adjusting its balance accurately to the flukes of wind.

"We learn by experience," he went on after a while. "Few of us remember former lives and those who say they do are for the most part liars, although there are some who are deceived by imagination. But the experience of former lives is in our favor—or against us, as the case may be. Its total is what some call instinct, others intuition; but there is a right name for it, and there are those whose past experience equips them with ability to recognize that stage in others at which the higher nature begins to overwhelm the lower. They are able to assist the process. But such men are exceedingly rare, though there are hosts of fools and rogues who pretend to the gift, which comes not by desire but by experience endured in many lives.

"That Tashi Lama said to me: 'My son, it may amuse you to linger for a few lives on the lower path; for you are strong, and the senses riot in you; and it is not my duty to impose on you one course of conduct, if you prefer another. It is very difficult to rise against the will, but very easy if the will directs.' And I, because I loved him, answered I would do his bidding. But he said: 'Nay.

Each man must, each minute, make his destiny. It is your own will, not mine, that directs you. Shall I fight your will, and force you to attempt the better way? Not so; because in that case you would surely fall, for which I should be responsible. But I perceive that the time has come when you may choose, and that your will is strong enough to make the choice and hold to it. You may be a benefactor or a beneficiary—a man, aware of manhood, or a victim of the lower senses, bound to the wheel of necessity. Which shall it be?'—And because he had discerned, and had chosen the right moment, there was a surging of the spirit in me, and as it were an awakening.

"I said to him: 'I have chosen.' And he asked me: 'Which way?' To which I answered at once: 'The higher.' Whereat he laughed; for I do not doubt that he saw the pride and the ambition that were cloaked within the answer.

"Thereafter he considered me for a long time before he spoke. And when I had waited so long that I supposed he would say no more at all, he said this: 'They who take the higher way in the beginning are consumed with arrogance; they mortify the flesh and magnify the will until there is no balance left; and when, after their period of death, they are born again, it is into a feeble body possessed by a demon will that tortures it; even as they who choose the lower way are reborn into brutal bodies with feeble wills.'

"Whereat I asked him: 'How then shall I choose between the higher and the lower, since both are evil?' And he considered me again, a long time.

"At last he said this: 'There is the Middle Way; but there are few who find it, and yet fewer who persist in it, because pride tempts one way and sloth the other.'

"And I said: 'I have chosen.' And he said: 'Speak.' And I said: 'Let it be the Middle Way.' Whereat he did not laugh, but considered me again for many minutes; and at the end of it, he said: 'My son, you have much strength. If you persist and keep the Middle Way, you have a destiny and you shall not die until you have fulfilled it. But beware of pride; and above all, seek no knowledge for your own sake.'

"At that time he said no more, but I became his *chela*. I washed his feet, and I swept the floor of his chamber, which was less than this one and less comfortably furnished. He taught me many things, but mainly patience, of which I lacked more in those days than a snake lacks legs. I supposed that before his time should come to die he would prefer me to high office. But nay. On a certain day he sent for me and said: 'I shall die on the eleventh day from now, at noon. To-morrow at dawn take the road into India, and go to Delhi, to a certain house in a certain street, and there learn the tongue of the English. Thence, I having made provision for it, journey to England, to a University called Oxford; and there learn all that the University can teach—and particularly all they think they know about philosophy and religion.'

"I said to him: 'Why?' And he said: 'I know not why; but I tell you what I know it is good for you to do. There is a destiny which, if you fail not, you shall fulfill. But beware of the Western knowledge, which is corrupt and strained through the sieve of convenience. I do not know, but it may be that you must learn the Western teachings for another's sake. Who can teach a horse unless he understands the way of horses? Who can make a sword unless he understands the qualities of steel?'

"And I said to him, 'Shall I be a swordsmith?' But he answered: 'Nay. I said you have a destiny to fulfill.' So I asked, 'When?' But he said, 'I know not. However, I know this: if you seek your own advancement, you will fail. And there is a certain condition in you that will inevitably bring you to a death by violence, because of lies that you yourself will tell; but because of your strength that may not come to pass until your work is finished.'

"So I said to him, 'How shall I know what my work is?' And he answered, 'That will appear.' But I said,

'If you, my great and very holy master, are to die, who then shall show me how to fulfill this destiny?' And he answered: 'It is for you to become fit to be the tool of destiny, and to hold yourself at all times ready. There are those from whom, at the proper time, you may receive the right advice.' So I asked: 'How shall I find them?' And he answered: 'They will find you.'

"Thereafter I besought him earnestly that I might remain with him in Lhassa until his death, because I was his *chela*, and that is no commonplace relationship. Its roots lie deeper than the roots of trees. But he answered: 'The first duty of a *chela* is obedience.'"

Tsiang Samdup paused and stared through the open window at the sky for several minutes. Eyes and sky were so exactly the same color that it looked as if the substance of the sky had crept within him and appeared through slits amid the walnut wrinkles of his face.

"It was midwinter," he said after a while, "and no light task to cross the passes. But the route the Tashi Lama gave me was this way, through the Ahbor Valley, and I lay for a month in this monastery, recovering from frost-bite and exhaustion. And as I lay between life and death, one came to me who had a pilgrim's staff, and no outward appearance of greatness, who considered me in silence for a long while; but the silence appeared to me like the voice of the universe, full of music, yet without sound. He went away. But in three days' time, when I was already far recovered (for I was ever strong), he returned and led me to what I will show you to-night and to-morrow. And I saw myself within myself."

He paused again, and again the far-away look in his eyes searched the sky and seemed to blend with it.

"He carried me forth," he said presently, "I lying like a dead man in his arms. His voice in my ear was as a mother's speaking to a child. 'It is well,' said he. 'Now set forth on your journey, and remember. For you know now what you have to overcome, and also what is yours *wherewith* to overcome.'

"So after certain days I set forth, and in due time
I came to Delhi, where I studied English. Thereafter I
went to England."

The wrinkles moved in silent laughter, and the old eyes
twinkled reminiscently as they looked into Ommony's.

"My son, that was no light experience! It was warfare,
and myself the battle-field. Warfare, and loneliness.
Curiosity, contempt,—courtesy, discourtesy, indifference
—all these were shown toward me. And there were very
generous men at Oxford, whose pride was racial, not intellectual, who were as patient in the teaching as the sun
is patient to the growing grass—most worthy and laugh-
ter-loving men, mistaken in much, but as sure of the reward of generosity as there is surely good will in their
hearts. They did not know I was Tibetan; they believed I
was Chinese, because I speak and write that language, and
none knew anything about Tibet.

"I came to understand that the cycles of evolution are
moving westward, and that the West is arrogant with the
strength it feels within itself. I saw, my son, that the
West is deceived by the glitter of results, knowing nothing
of causes, and that the East is in turn deceived by the
wealth and ostentation of the West—for this is Kali
Yuga,* when delusion and a blindness overspreads the
world. I knew—for none had better right to know—that
strength can be guided into the grooves of destiny, and
that knowledge is the key. But I perceived that great
harm can be done by interference. There is danger in
another's duty. Also I saw that *my* voice, however reasonably raised, could accomplish nothing, because of the racial
prejudice. The West is curious about the East, but proud
—contemptuous—and most cruel when it most believes it
is benevolent. The West sends missionaries to the East,
who teach the very culture that is poisoning the life-
springs of the West itself. The strength of the West and
its generous impulse must be guided. Its rapacity must be
restrained. But it was clear to me that I could not ac-

---

*The age of darkness.

complish that, since none would listen to me. The few who
pretended to listen merely sought to use my teaching for
their own enrichment and advantage.

"I met a certain one in London. He appeared to be
English, but that meant nothing. He had the Ancient
Wisdom in his eyes. I had taken my degrees at Oxford
then, and I was sitting in the Stranger's Gallery of the
House of Parliament. I remember I grieved; for I saw
how eager those debaters were to rule the whole world
wisely—yet how ignorant they were of the very rudiments
of what could possibly enable them to do it. I said to
him who was in the corner next to me: 'These men boast
of what is right, and they believe their words; but they
do not know what is right. Who shall save them?' And
he answered, after he had considered me a while in silence:
'If *you* know what is right, you will attend to your own
duty.'

"So I went and lived in Paris for a while, and in Vienna and in Rome, because it was my duty to learn how the
West thinks, and in what way it is self-deceived. And
thereafter I returned to Tibet, wondering. It did not seem
to me that I was one step forward on the path of destiny.
I could see (for I had walked the length of India with
pilgrim's staff and begging bowl) that the West was de-
vouring the East and the East was inert in the grip of
superstition, inclined, if it should move at all, to imitate
the West and to corrupt the Western energy by specious
flattery, hating its conquerors, yet copying those very
methods that made conquest possible.

"An unfathomable sadness overwhelmed me. It appeared to me that all my knowledge was as nothing. I
doubted the stars in the sky; I said 'These, too, are a delusion of the senses. Who shall prove to me that I am
not deceived in all things?'"

Tsiang Samdup paused and thought a while, stroking
Diana's head.

"My son," he said presently, "it was as if the knowledge that was born within me, and all the false Western

doctrine I had studied, were as waters meeting in the basin
of my mind, and in the whirlpool my faith was drowning.
It is ever so when truth meets untruth, but I did not know
that then.

"I went to the Tashi Lama—the successor of my teacher.
He was but a child, and I was ashamed to lay my heart
before him, though I laid my forehead on the mat before
his throne, for the sake of the traditions and my master's
memory. And to me, as I left the throne-room sadly, one
of the regents, drawing me aside said: 'I have heard a
destiny awaits you.' I asked: 'From whom have you
heard that?' But he did not say. To him I laid bare the
affliction that was eating out my heart; and to me he said:
'Good. This is a time of conquest of self by the Self; I
foresee that the higher will win.' Thereafter he spoke of
the folly of stirring molten metal with a wooden spoon.
He bade me let my thoughts alone. And because he saw in
me a pride of knowledge that was at the root of my affliction, he appointed me a temple neophite. He who was
set over me had orders to impose severe tasks. I hewed
wood. I carried water. I laid heavy masonry, toiling
from sunrise until dark. I labored in the monastery
kitchen. I dug gold on the plateau, where for nine months
of every year the earth is frozen so hard that a strong
man can with difficulty dig two baskets-full. By day I
toiled. By night I dreamed dreams—grand dreams full
of quiet understanding—so that to me it seemed that the
night was life, and the day death. I was well contented
to remain there in the gold-fields, because it seemed to me
I had found my destiny; the miners were well pleased
to listen to me in the intervals when we leaned on the tools
and rested, and when the blizzards blew and we were
herded very close together for the warmth, with the animals between us in the tents.

"But when the Tashi Lama, who succeeded him whose
chela I had been, came to man's estate he sent for me. And
after he had talked with me a while on many matters he
promoted me. I became a Lama of the lowest rank, and

yet without the ordinary duties of a Lama. I had time to study and arrange the ancient books; of which, my son, there are more than the West imagines; they are older than the West believes the world to be, and they are written in a language that extremely few can read. But I can read them. And I learned that my dreams were realities —although the dreams ceased in those days.

"Once, that one who had come to me when I lay sick in this place on my journey southward, came to me in Lhassa, where I was pondering the ancient books and rearranging them. And to him I said, 'Lo, I have met my destiny! I see that it is possible to translate some of these into the Western tongues.' But he answered: 'Who would believe? For this is Kali Yuga. Men think that nothing is true unless they can turn it into money and devour what they can purchase with it. If you give too much food to a starving horse, will he thrive? Or will he gorge himself to death?'

"Said I; 'Light travels fast.' Said he; 'It does. But it requires a hundred million years for the light of certain stars to reach the earth. And how long does it take for the formation of coal, that men burn in a minute? Make no haste, or they will burn thee! They have Plato and Pythagoras and Appolonius—Jesus, the Buddha, Mohammed—and others. Would you give them a new creed to go to war about, or a new curiosity to buy and sell for their museums? Which?'

"Thereafter the Tashi Lama sent for me, and I was given no more time to study the ancient books. But I was promoted to the rank of Gelong, and became a Ringding, whose duty was to teach the people as much as they could understand. I discovered it was not much that they could understand. They knew the meaning of desire, and of the bellyache that comes from too much eating. I found that if one man learns more than another, he is soon so filled with pride that he had better have been left in ignorance; and I also found that men will accept any doctrine that flatters their desires or excuses ignorance, but that they seek to vilify and kill whoever teaches them to discipline the senses in order that their higher nature may appear and make them wise. There is no difference in that respect, although men are fond of saying that the West is quite unlike the East. East or West they will murder any one who teaches them to think except in terms of the lower self.

"There was an outcry against me in Lhassa, and there were many Lamas who declared I should be put on trial for heresy. I was stoned in the streets; and the great dogs that devour the dead were incited to attack me. So I said: 'Lo, it may be then I have fulfilled my destiny. For he who was my teacher prophesied that there is that in me which must inevitably bring me to a violent end. Nevertheless, I have told no lies yet, that I know of!'

"But the Dalai Lama sent men—they were soldiers— who, under pretense of throwing me in prison, hid me in a certain place. And escaping thence by night, with one to guide me, I went on a journey of many days, to a village where none knew me, where I dwelt safely; so that I thought that my teacher had prophesied falsely, and for a while again I doubted.

"But there came to me that same one who had come when I lay sick in this place on my journey southward, and he said to me; 'Have you learned yet that the stars and the seasons keep their course and the appointed times, and that no seed grows until the earth is ready?' And I said: 'How shall I know when it is ready? And who shall tell me the appointed time?' For I was full of a great yearning to be useful. But he answered: 'Who rules the stars? Until you can control yourself, how shall you serve others?' But I was burning with desire to serve, and moreover indignant at persecution, for in those days I had very little wisdom. I was a fool who puts his face into a hornets' nest to tell the hornets of the Higher Law. And I said to him: 'I am beginning to doubt all things.' 'Nay,' said he, 'for you began that once before, and made an end of it. You are beginning now to doubt your own impetu-

osity, and that is good, for you will learn that power lies
in patience.   He who will play in the symphony awaits
the exact moment before he strikes his note.   You forget
that the world existed many million years, and that you
lived many scores of lives, before you came to this pass.
Will you sow seed in midwinter because it wearies you to
wait until the spring?'

"And when he had considered me again for a long
while, he went away, saying that he would doubtless speak
with me again, should the necessity arise.   And before
many days there came a message from Lhassa, saying that
one was dead who had charge of this monastery in the
Ahbor Valley, and that the Dalai Lama had appointed me
to take his place.

"So hither I came, and was at peace.   And many years,
my son, I lived here studying the ancient mysteries, considering the stars, and not seldom wondering what service
to the world my destiny might hold in store.   I made
ready.   I held myself ready."

And I have asked this of the priests, but though they answered with a multitude of words, their words were emptiness: If it is true that a priest can pacify and coax God, or by meditation can relieve another from the consequences of his own sin, why should any one be troubled and why do the priests not put an end for ever to all sin and suffering? If they can, and do not, they are criminals. If they can not, but pretend that they can, they are liars. Nevertheless, there is a middle judgment, and it seems to me that SOME of them may be mistaken.

FROM THE BOOK OF THE SAYINGS OF TSIANG SAMDUP.

CHAPTER XXX

THE LAMA'S STORY (*Continued*)

A MONK brought food and set it on a stool between
Tsiang Samdup and Ommony. They ate in silence—the
monk watching—the Lama tossing scraps to Diana, his
wrinkles rippling into a smile each time she caught a piece
of meat in mid-air. Then, when the monk went away
with the remnants, he resumed his story abruptly, before
Ommony could start to question him.

"My son, since the beginning of the world—and your
brain can not imagine how long ago that was—there has
never been one minute when the knowledge that was in
the beginning has been utterly forgotten. There have always been men who possessed and guarded the secrets;
and there always will be such men. There is not a religion in the world that is not based on the tradition that
such secrets do exist; there is not a philosophy that is not
founded on the ancient mysteries; there is not a modern
science, however perverted and material, that is not an
effort to discover and to put to use some aspect of the
ancient knowledge and the Higher Law.

"There is a Law of Evolution. Scientists have touched
the fringe of it, and what do they tell you in consequence?
That man has evolved from the worms! There is a Law
of Cause and Effect, of which one infinitely tiny fraction
has been dimly sensed. To what use do they put it? They
brew poison-gas, with which to murder one another!
There is a Law of Cycles, as the astronomers can tell you,
and as financiers begin vaguely to understand. But those
who think they understand it use the secret to enrich
themselves—by each enrichment of themselves afflicting
others. Men dig in the ruins of Egypt and Babylon, but

buy and sell the trophies and draw the absurd deduction that they know more than all the ancients did—even as worms digging in a carcass may imagine themselves superior to the life that once used that body for a while.

"Do you begin to see, my son, why it would be unwise to reveal the ancient wisdom by more than infinitesimal fragments at a time? I heard, when I was in Delhi, that the men of the West are studying the construction of the atom, and have guessed at the force imprisoned in it. Wait until they have learned how to explode the atom, and then see what they will do to one another.

"But you will notice this, as you grow wiser. There is a fitness in things. There is a balance in the universe and an intelligence that governs it. No man can escape the consequences of his own act, though it take him a million lives to redress the balance. Justice is inevitable. Evil produces evil, and is due to ignorance. But Justice being infinite in all its ways, there is a Middle Way by which we may escape from ignorance. I, who saw the world increasing its downward impetus, while it believes itself to be progressing upward through the invention of new means for exploiting selfishness; I, who saw the ruins of Egypt, and of Babylon; of Rome and Greece; of Jerusalem; of Ceylon; of India; I, who have lived for fifty years within a stone's throw of a city ten times older than Babylon; I *knew* that day follows night, and I waited for the dawn, not knowing the hour. I waited.

"I knew there are those who have won merit in their former lives, whose time comes to be born again. I knew that the key to evolution is in character, not in numbers or material increase—in the character of the soul, my son! I knew that at the right time those would begin to be born, whose character would influence the world as mine could not. And I waited, studying the Jade of Ahbor.

"For the Jade, my son, was set here in the dawn of time by men who understood how to make a mirror for the soul, even as men nowadays make mirrors that reflect stars which no eye can detect. You laugh? That is not wise! Men laughed, remember, at Galileo. They laughed at Newton. I had not thought you were one who mocks what is contrary to common superstition."

"My father," said Ommony, "you are confirming rumors I have heard on and off for twenty years. I was laughing at the men who told me I was a fool to pay any attention to such madness."

"Nor was that wise!" the Lama answered. "It is foolish either to laugh or to grieve over other men's ignorance; the hidden motive of that laughter or grief is pride, which blinds the faculties." He looked at Ommony a very long time in silence, studying him.

"It is also unwise to speak of truths to men who prefer untruths," he said at last. "They proceed to indiscretions, for which the speaker is in part responsible. But I think, my son, you see the error of that way. The Jade of Ahbor is a mirror of the human soul. Whoever looks in it beholds his lower nature first; and there are few who can look long enough to see the first gleam of their higher nature shining through the horrors that the Jade reveals. When I first looked into the Jade, he who led me to behold it carried me forth like a dead man. And I had been the *chela* of the Tashi Lama! I will lead you to the Jade; but will you dare to look?"

He paused, his bright old eyes observing Ommony's with that disturbing stare with which an artist studies the face of one whose portrait he is painting.

"There was a time," he went on, "when those who professed to be teachers were stood before the Jade of Ahbor, that their own characters might be revealed to them. Those who could endure the test (and they were few) might teach; and those who failed, might not. For it is character that must be taught; all else depends on it. That time will come again, but not yet. To-day, if men knew of the Jade of Ahbor they would seize upon it. They would test their rulers by it, as they try their criminals. They would overthrow whoever failed the test—

and all would fail. Thereafter intellectual men would seize power, who would destroy the stone, asserting its magic property was superstition, and *that* one fragment of the ancient knowledge would be lost.

"And now," he paused again, "I read temptation in your mind. You think that I, who have enabled you to reach this valley, will enable you to leave it; and that is true, you shall return to India unharmed. But you think that you, and certain other men, might use that stone discreetly. Imagination tells you that to return to the Ahbor Valley; that to occupy it by force or trickery, and so to obtain access to the stone would be a good thing, which should benefit the human race. Nay, my son, waste no words on denial, for I saw the thought!

"Therefore, I tell you this: the ancient wisdom is more wise than your imagination. They who know cause and effect can foretell consequences. Lest the evils should befall, that must inevitably follow if such an instrument were placed too soon into men's hands, the means to hide the stone, if necessary for another million years, has been placed in the hands of those who guard it. My son, men fight to the death over the Golden Rule. What would they not do with the Jade of Ahbor?

"You have heard that the Tsang-po River holds more water than the Brahmaputra, which is the same river lower down? Part of the Tsang-po pours into caverns, which have an outlet below Bengal to the sea. One man (and there *are* more than one who know the secret) can in one moment admit a mighty river into caverns that are now dry. Then not an army of engineers could find the Jade of Ahbor in a thousand years.—But," he spoke very slowly, "he who had deliberately made that act necessary—having been warned, as *you* are warned—would be responsible. You can not foresee the consequences, but it may be that in a million lives you can not outlive them, because all the harm that, through you, befalls others must inevitably return to you for readjustment. It is well not to deceive yourself that this life is the last."

Ommony had sat still, lest interruption break the thread of the Lama's story. But it appeared to be broken. His own personal relation to it stirred impatience.

"How, where, when did my sister and Jack Terry die?" he asked.

"Bear with me, my son. I have a great deal to tell, and not much time in which to tell it. My hour comes soon. There is a death awaiting me, and I am nearly ready."

The Lama closed his eyes, his right hand patting Diana's head, as if he were eliminating detail and remembering the thread.

"I studied the Jade of Ahbor," he resumed after a long while. "Which is the same as to say that I studied my own failings and my own strength, using the one with which to conquer the other, so that light might flow into my mind. And many times that one came to me, of whom I spoke before—he who first led me to the Jade. Many times I journeyed into India. Many men I spoke with. And there came Marmaduke the American to Darjiling, much wrought up about the future of the world and very angry with the Christian missionaries. And as you know, he founded the Marmaduke Mission at Tilgaun and endowed it. He wished me to be a trustee, but I refused, until that one came to me, of whom I spoke before, and said it was not good to refuse the work that destiny had given me to do. Then I accepted, although it did not appear to me then that my act was wise.

"And you and Hannah Sanburn became the other trustees. And you and I corresponded, from which it became clear to me that you are a determined man, of good faith, having courage, but possessed by indignation against those whose vision of right and wrong is shorter than your own. And in indignation there is not much wisdom; so I avoided meeting you.

"And then came Doctor Terry and your sister to this valley—children!—hand in hand—as innocent as lambs— as brave and simple as two humming-birds—in search of

me, because, forsooth, they had been told I knew the secret of the Jade of Ahbor. She far-gone with child; he
dying of wounds; the Ahbors hunting them—for the
Ahbors guard this valley as cobras guard ancient ruins.''

"How did they get into the valley?" asked Ommony.

"None knows. Not even I, nor the Ahbors. They suffered; they had no memory, except of caverns and of being washed along an ancient conduit underground. I
heard of them, because the Ahbors asked me whether it
were best to crucify them living or to cut them up and
throw them into the Brahmaputra. The Ahbors said they
seemed such unoffending people that it might be the gods
would be angry if they should put them to further pain.
They also said there was a baby to be born, and it is
against the Ahbors' law to slay the mother until one month
after childbirth; nevertheless, it is also against their law
to admit strangers and to let them live.

"Therefore I lied to the Ahbors, inventing an ancient
prophecy that a saint was to be born of strangers in this
valley. Thus I rescued those two innocents, there being—
as that Tashi Lama, whose *chela* I was, said—a condition
in me, due to faults in former lives, that, though I may
fulfill a useful destiny, I must come to a violent death
through lies of my own telling.

"I lied to the Ahbors, and I had to keep on lying to
them. But he who lies does well, my son, who gladly eats
the consequences when he may, and ends them. Better a
little self-surrender now than unknown consequences in
the lives to come! I am answerable to the Ahbors. I
would rather receive their judgment than that of the Unseen! It pays not to postpone the reckoning.

"The baby was born here, in this room, and those two
children who were its parents died, though I did what
might be done for them. I eased their death as well as I
was able, giving them comfort in the knowledge that there
are many lives to come, in which there is recompense for
every thought and deed, as also opportunity to undo all
the evil of the past. They died in peace, and I buried

their bodies yonder; you can see the grave below this window—that mass of rocks, over which the purple flowers trail.

"Before she died, that child who was your sister gave her baby into my hands. It was her last effort. She *gave* the baby to me, not at my request. In the clarity of vision and the peace that precedes death, she *gave* her baby into my hands, smiling, saying: 'I see that this is as it should be. It could not have been otherwise.'"

For five minutes the Lama was silent, remembering, his sky-blue eyes on vacancy, his wrinkles motionless.

"And so I understood my destiny," he went on presently. "I understood that in my hands lay one who was greater than myself—whom I might serve, that she might serve the world, as I can not by reason of my limitations. That little spark of life, if I should do my duty, should be fanned into a flame, whose light should blaze across the world, and bless, and brighten it.

"And I have served, my son. I know of no regrets. Day in, day out, for more than twenty years I have fanned that flame, and nursed and fed it, letting no consideration hinder, omitting no experience that might serve, sparing her no duty, killing out my own pride, and my own weakness, lest it rob her of one element of virtue, inflicting no punishment (for who am I that I should dare to punish?), omitting no reproof (for who am I that I should dare to let the child deceive herself?)

"I obtained a wet-nurse, who was doubtless born into this valley to that very end, the wife of an Ahbor chieftain, whose recent ancestors were healthy, whose mind was modest, unassuming, calm. I made that wet-nurse stand before the Jade of Ahbor, before I trusted the flow from her breasts.

"And I received advice, as he whose *chela* I had been prophesied. He, who had come to me in this place and in Lhassa, came again. From him I learned that Hannah Sanburn might be trusted, and that if I should see fit to trust her no harm would come of it. I think she has told you, my son, what share she had in mothering the child.''

Ommony nodded. "Hannah is a noble woman," he said gruffly. "I imagine she sacrificed more than—"

But the Lama interrupted with a gesture of his hand. "My son, there is no such thing as sacrifice, except in the imagination. There is opportunity to serve, and he who overlooks it robs himself. Would you call the sun's light sacrifice? But you are right when you say Hannah Sanburn is a noble woman. Her nobility is part of her. It works. It overcomes the fear of what the world might say. It conquers pride. It leaves adjustment of all consequences to the Higher Law. It keeps faith. It knows no malice. It is brave. My burden, when I took that child to Tilgaun, was all that I could bear, because I loved her and I feared for her: but Hannah Sanburn's was no less—no atom less—when she returned the child to me.

"My hardest task has been to provide children of her own age, with whom she might play and be happy without besmirchment from their ignorance. For, though she is able now to stand alone, and to burn up trash in the pure flame of her own character, she was then only a little, very clear flame, needing care—my son, I wonder if you guess how much care she has needed. The Tibetan children would have dimmed her light. They might have smothered it; because the lower yearns toward the higher. And though yeast is plunged into the dough and leavens it, the yeast is spent. It is not good to clean corruption with a golden broom, nor is it wise to take sap from the growing tree.

"But I have agents—agents here and there. We, who pursue the Middle Way, are not without resources. There was Benjamin, who is a man of very faithful pertinacity in some respects; and there are certain others, whom I employed. It is easy to find children who need saving from the rapacity of the world's convenience; but it is very difficult to make selection—much more difficult when agents do the choosing—and impossible, my son, to find such another child as San-fun-ho, because there is none like her in the world. I tell you, great ones are not born many at a time.

"I obtained children. I obtained many children, hoping that among the many one or two might excel, as indeed it happened. The others are incapable in this life of much advancement, because of *karma* and the circumstances into which they had been born. It is very difficult to help some individuals, because those who are born into an heredity are so born in order that they may make that experience, and battle with it, and acquire strength for the lives to come. But they have served; they have done royal service. For, as I have educated my *chela,* in turn she has educated them, learning through them how to practise the wisdom, which is nothing unless put to use. And, lest they lose one rightful opportunity, I found Tibetan girls for them to teach. You have seen for yourself that those children have grown into women, who are not without nobility. Some may make good teachers at Tilgaun."

"How many laws did you break in obtaining those children?" asked Ommony, smiling. He felt less critical than curious to know how the Lama would defend himself.

"Many, perhaps. I do not know, my son. There is that which, because of errors in past lives, makes it impossible for me to do good without inflicting evil on myself. But it is better to do good than to fear evil. It is he who breaks the laws who must accept the consequences. It appears to me that I have injured none except myself and, although I must meet in lives to come the consequence of having broken even human laws, I do not doubt that the service I have rendered will provide me strength with which to meet and overcome the *karma.* We can not do *all* the self-cleansing in *one* life. It is enough that we do what we can, and serve others."

"I am sorry I spoke. I beg your pardon."

The Lama looked keenly at Ommony. "My son, it is not within your power to offend me, even if you had the wish to give offense, which I preceive is not so. I would not impose on you an account of my fumblings with duty, if it were not that you are entitled to sufficient facts on which to base your judgment of what *your* duty may be. I endeavor to be brief.

"Life—right living is Art, my son, not artifice, and not an accumulation of possessions, or of power, but a giving forth of inner qualities. San-fun-ho has had encouragement to exercise herself in all the arts; she will not be deceived by the many who will deny the merit of her art—no more than the lamp's flame is deceived by darkness.

"Above all, drama! Drama is the way to teach. All life is drama; and by allegories, parables and illustrations men learn easily what no amount of argument will drive into their understanding. Because of sympathy, compassion and a knowledge of what difficulties and what ignorance the greatest and the least most face, my *chela* can play all parts. She understands. She knows the difference between the higher and the lower, and is not to be deceived by noise, or fear, or any man's opinion.

"Nor can her head be turned by flattery; for I have let men tempt her in the subtlest ways, they not knowing that they tempted. The superstitious worship those whose art excels their own—until the time comes when they meditate murder, and slander, (which is more cruel than murder) because they grow weary of emulation. And worship is the most poisonous of all corruption, to him who is the object of it. When an Ahbor, who was bribed by some ambitious men, broke away and stole a fragment of the Jade of Ahbor, and I learned that there were plans on foot to seduce men into all kinds of superstition with its aid, I seized that opportunity.

"I let word go forth through secret channels into India that she who is the rightful priestess of the Jade will come and find it. For there was never a doubt about that, my son. I knew I could trace the fragment and lay my hand on it. I seized that opportunity. I led my *chela*, clothed as a boy, for she can play all parts, on a journey into India, as you know. And, my son, I have made many errors in my day; I am but an old man seeking, through the cloud of ignorance, to do my duty, knowing what the duty is, but often misled by my own unwisdom. There were times, while my *chela* was growing, when I dreamed of triumphs for her among India's millions. In those deluded moods it had appeared to me—although none had better right than I to know the contrary—that if she should seize on the imagination of the East, which might very easily be done, the East would rise out of its ignorance and teach the West. I did not see, in those deluded hours, that the East would become filled with a self-righteousness that would be even worse, if that were possible, than what consumes the West and, seeking to throw off its conquerors, would plunge the whole world into war. You have heard of Gandhi? That is a man of singleness and merit, seeking, as it were, to hasten the precession of the equinox.

"Even as Gandhi has made mistakes, I made them, though with less excuse. During the lonely months when San-fun-ho was with Hannah Sanburn at Tilgaun I used to journey into India with staff and begging-bowl, making my preparations for the day when San-fun-ho should teach an awakening multitude. Unwise—and the unwisdom multiplied by zeal! I raised too many expectations.

"He, who had come to me before, came once again rebuking me. I told him of this and that which I had done, expecting praise. He said to me: 'Blood will flow. It will be you to whom the dead may look for recompense. How soon can you repay them all?' And I said: 'But I have promised. If I fail, will they not look to me for the fulfilment?' But *he* said: 'Which is better? To fail to do evil, and to eat the fruit of disappointment; or to do great evil, and to interfere with destiny, and then to eat the fruit of that? I tell you, San-fun-ho will light a flame too fierce for India; but in the West she may do some good; and the East may imitate the West, but the West will not imitate the East for many a year to come, being too proud and too full of energy.'

"And then I asked him: 'Who shall shield her in the West? Lo, I have made these friends for her in India.

that she may have a foundation to begin with when the time comes.' To which he answered: 'Is a dollar without friends? And is she less than a dollar? Moreover, there will come to you a man of her own race, who can serve her better than you when his turn comes. He will know less, but he will have the qualities she needs. Be on the watch for him, and when you think you have found him, put him to many tests.'

"So, as I told you, I took my *chela* into India, recovering the piece of jade, and making use of my mistakes for the testing of San-fun-ho, since even a man's mistakes are useful, if he has the will to conquer false pride. And you have seen, my son, that my *chela's* head was not turned, even though we traveled with great evidence of secret influence, which is a very subtle agent of corruption. You have seen how women broke the rules of caste to approach her; how men of high position trembled in her presence; how the crowd shouted to see more of her; how her voice stilled anger and turned violence into peace. Yet she was always my patient and obedient *chela*, was she not? And you shall see—at dawn to-morrow you shall see whether all that glamour of success has or has not dimmed her character by as much as the mist of a man's breath on a mirror."

The Lama looked at Ommony for a long time, repeatedly almost closing his eyes and then opening them suddenly, as if to catch some fleeting expression unawares.

"And when you came, my son, hiding in Chutter Chand's shop. When I knew the piece of the jade had reached your hands. When Benjamin sent word that you were spying on me. Then, it seemed to me that in spite of many faults you might be the man whom I must test. I have tested you in more ways than you guess, and I have seen all your faults, not least of which is a certain pride of righteousness. But San-fun-ho knows how to deal with that. Now think. Answer without self-seeking and without fear, truly. For I offer you my place, as San-fun-ho's protector and servant, to guard her that she may serve the world. My time has come to die."

A man is what he is. He starts from where he is. He may progress, or he may retrogress. All effort in his own behalf is dead weight in the scale against him. All effort in behalf of others is a profit to himself; notwithstanding which, unless he first improve himself he can do nothing except harm to others. There is no power in the universe, nor any form of intercession that can separate a cause from its effect, action from reaction, or a man from retribution for his deeds.

FROM THE BOOK OF THE SAYINGS OF TSIANG SAMDUP.

CHAPTER XXXI

OMMONY sat still. Diana growled and chased some crea-ture of imagination in her dreams. The Lama threw wood on the fire, and watched it as if he were much more in-terested in the outcome of that than in what answer Om-mony might make.

"What makes you think I could do it?" Ommony asked, half stunned by the suggestion, vaguely and uncomfortably conscious that he was being invited to make himself the butt of half a world's ridicule, if of nothing worse.

"A flea—a mouse—a drop of water—a piece of wood—can do its duty," said the Lama. "Is a man less?"

"I will do mine," said Ommony, "if I can see it. But good God, man—how can I take *your* place?"

"She—and they—can go to India very easily, my son, without you. They are all provided for. They will never lack for money. It may be you are not the right man to be my *chela's* friend and in that case it is better for you, and for her, and for the world that you accept no burden you can not bear.

"Do not deceive yourself, my son. There will be no per-sonal ease, no basking in the stupifying rays of flattery. You will be accused of all the evil motives that lurk in the minds of your accusers. Lecherous men will accuse you of lying when you say she is your niece; and you can not prove the relationship. Thieves will accuse you of theft. Am-bitious men will denounce your ambition. Traitors will accuse you of treachery toward the human race. Bigots will charge you with unpatriotic scheming. Men of out-wardly unblemished aspect, but whose secret thoughts are viler than the froth of cess-pools, will accuse you of

secretly immoral practises. They will leave you not a shred
of reputation. They will try to impoverish you; they will
try to prove you .insane; they will try to put you in
prison.''

''Very well,'' said Ommony. ''I will do my best.'' He
nodded, thrusting his stubborn jaw forward. The Lama
could have said nothing better calculated to persuade him.

''And you will find,'' the Lama went on, nodding back
at him, ''here and there are men and women, who will
accept what San-fun-ho can teach. Some of those will be
traitors, who will try to learn in order that they may set
up themselves as teachers and accumulate money and
fame. Those will be your most dangerous enemies. But
some will be honest and steadfast, and they will encourage
others; for the West is moving forward on a cycle of
evolution; and moreover, it is growing very weary of its
own creeds and politics and competition. It begins to be
ready at last to put the horse before the cart, instead of
the cart before the horse as hitherto. There is a great
change coming—although this is Kali Yuga, and it is
not wisdom to expect too much. The harvest takes care
of itself—none knows how many generations hence. This is
a time for the sowing of the seeds of thought on which a
whole world's destiny depends. I have sown my handful.
I can sow no more.''

''What makes you so sure you are going to die?'' asked
Ommony.

''The Ahbors, my son, will attend to it, for I have
broken their law. I made them promises which I intend
to break; I knew that I must, when I made the promises.
There is that in me that blinded me to any other way out
of the difficulty, and although I did my duty, that does
not preserve me from the effects of wrong-doing. The
Ahbors have their rights. This is their country. They
protect this monastery and its secrets. They have protected me. Of my own free will I have availed myself of
their protection and their law against admitting strangers.
Do you remember Socrates, who broke the law of the Athe-

nians, although he did his duty? He might have escaped
after they condemned him, but he refused, although his
friends insisted. And Socrates did well, my son; he had
no right to avoid the consequences of his own acts; it was
enough that he had told the Athenians some great truths,
for he knew those truths, and it was the proper time to
tell; if the Athenians had a law against telling the truth,
that was their affair, not his. Socrates drank his poison,
which was a simple little matter, and soon over with. Does
it appear to you that the Athenians have even yet finished
suffering from the injustice they inflicted?"

"But the Athenians could think. These Ahbors are mere
savages," said Ommony.

"The Ahbors have their rights," the Lama answered.
"They work out their own destiny. I work out mine. If
I had been a wiser man, less blinded by my lower nature, I
could have found a better way to save my *chela* than by
deceiving the Ahbors. But I *was* blind, so I took the only
way I could. When I return to earth again, I am convinced I shall be less blind; and at least I shall owe no
debt to the Ahbors, for I will pay it now."

"Why not leave all that to destiny?" Ommony objected.

"My son, there is no other judge in whose hands I *can*
leave it! But destiny judges a man's unwillingness to
pay, as surely as it judges his mistakes—as surely as it
rewards his hidden motives and his honesty. There is no
thought hidden from the Higher Law, and no escape from
rebirth, time and time again, until each individual learns
wisdom by experience. The Ahbors will learn wisdom,
some sooner than others; but they will not learn it by being deprived of opportunity to use their own judgment.
If they choose to kill me, they must inevitably suffer; but
I would rather they should kill me than that they should
have killed that child, and for more than one reason. They
can do very little harm by killing me; the wrong will not
amount to much, because I bear no resentment. If they
had killed her, they would have robbed the world."

"You have *your* rights," Ommony objected. "You're worth more than the Ahbors."

But the Lama's eyes twinkled humorously. "My son, you argue ignorantly, meaning well enough, but reckoning without the facts."

"For instance?"

"You would not understand. My course is necessary—never mind why, my son. It was entirely necessary for you to come to this place of your own free will; otherwise it would have been impossible for me to open your mind. I could have talked to you for ten years in India, and you would never have understood. But it was also necessary to provide for your admission to the valley, and for your safe return to India after I am dead. You were admitted because I told the Ahbors about your talking dog, and because I gave my own life as hostage, saying they might slay me if you should ever escape from the valley alive. I did that, knowing they would slay me in any event, when they should learn that San-fun-ho and the others have left the valley for ever. You see, my son, it is necessary I should die, in order to consume as soon as possible the consequences of an untruth. As for the Ahbors; they are very ignorant, but faithful to their valley and their own law, generous toward this monastery: it is better that they should kill me, than that they should be faithless to their laws and to their trust. I will do all I can to minimize the consequences for them."

A monk came in again with food, and once more the Lama amused himself by feeding Diana. "Make her do tricks," he insisted, and rewarded her with handfuls of food after each performance, he and the monk laughing as if it were the most interesting and amusing business in the world. The sun had gone down over the mountains and there was a gloom within the chamber that affected Ommony's nerves, for it seemed to foretell tragedy, but the Lama apparently had not a trouble on his mind. The moment the monk had gone Ommony began questioning:

"Does Elsa—I mean, does San-fun-ho know anything about your plans?"

"Enough, my son. A little. She understands she has a destiny. She understands she is to take you with her into India."

The Lama rose to his feet, as if to avoid further conversation; but Ommony shot one more question at him:

"Does she know you expect to be killed?"

The Lama did not answer. His wrinkled face became expressionless.

"Where is she now?" asked Ommony.

"Come."

The Lama led the way, in deepening gloom, along the wooden gallery that overhung the ravine, and through a door into the monastery, which appeared to be a patchwork nest of caves and buildings connected by passages hewn in the rock. Some of it appeared as old as time, but parts were medieval; some was almost modern. There was an air of economically conserved affluence and studied chastity of design—beauty everywhere, but less laid on than inherent in proportions and the almost exquisite restraint.

Pictures were hung on the plastered corridor walls at widely spaced intervals, apparently all drawn by the same hand. The Lama stopped for a second in front of one of them, done in pastel on paper: a study of an eagle soaring, balancing himself to catch the uplift of the changing wind. It might have been done by a Chinaman a thousand years ago, it was so full of life, truth and movement and, above all, so superbly beautiful.

"My *chela!*" he said, and smiled, and passed on.

At one place, where the corridor turned at right angles and a lamp hung in chains from the ceiling, there was another pastel drawing, a portrait this one, of the Lama himself.

"Wrinkles and all!" he said, chuckling.

He stood beside Ommony and studied the portrait for more than a minute; it seemed to amuse him as much as it astonished Ommony, who caught his breath.

"My God!" Ommony exclaimed. "That's—"

"Yes," said the Lama, chuckling. "That old person was my God once. It takes us long to learn. But San-fun-ho drew the picture, and I saw myself through the eyes of my *chela*, which are very interesting. Notice, my son, how affectionate she is, and yet how truthful. Not one hidden foolishness escapes her; and she sets it all down. Yet she is as gentle as the rain on dry hills."

He passed on, opened a door, glanced in, and motioned Ommony to enter.

"School-room!" he said, and chuckled again, as if remembering a chain of incidents.

It looked about as much unlike a school-room as it would be easy to imagine. There was nobody in there, but it was lighted with kerosene lamps as if visitors were expected. Across the full width of the room at one end was a stage, provided with curtain, footlights, wings and painted scenery. There were comfortable seats and small, square, solid tables on the floor for twenty or thirty people; and there was a gallery, at the end opposite the stage, for twenty or thirty more. The place was scrupulously clean and tidy.

"Life, my son, is drama. Why teach how to drug the mind, when the purpose of life is to render it alert and active? Shakespeare was right. You remember? 'All the world's a stage.' No learning is of any value unless we can translate it into action. Bad thoughts produce hideous action; right thinking produces grace and symmetry; and the audience is almost as important as the play. Let the child act the part of a villain, and it learns to strive to be a hero; let the hero's part be a reward for genuine effort, and lo! sincerity becomes the goal. There have been plays enacted here that would have thrilled Shakespeare to the marrow of his manhood. San-fun-ho wrote most of them."

"Who were the audience?" asked Ommony.

"Monks—Ahbors. The stupider the better. Let the actors strive to act so simply and sincerely that even monks and savages can understand. There have been plays acted on this stage that I think would have converted even Christian missionaries from the error of their own self-righteousness.''

He led the way out again along the corridor, and now he began to hurry, striding with the regular, long movements of a mountaineer. He had suddenly thrown off fifty years again, in one of those strange resurrections of youth that seemed to sweep over him at intervals. Ommony, with Diana at his heels, had all he could do to keep pace.

However, there were pauses. He opened doors here and there along echoing corridors, giving Ommony a glimpse of rooms, each one of which had some connection with the beloved *chela*. There was a bedroom, as plain and almost as severely furnished as a monastery cell, only that every single item in it was as perfect as material and craftsmanship could contrive, and the proportions, the color, and something else that was indefinable, produced an atmosphere of unconditioned peace. There was nothing out of place, and no unnecessary object in the room. The walls were pale daffodil yellow; the Chinese rug was blue; the bed-spread was old-rose. There were flowers in a Ming vase on a small square table, but no other ornament.

''These walls will not forget her,'' said the Lama. There was an agony within him, as his voice betrayed.

He led the way along a corridor, opening doors of rooms where the *chela's* companions had slept, making no comment. Those other rooms were more ornate than the *chela's* and vaguely, indefinably less beautiful;—there was more furniture—less character—but tidiness and cleanliness beyond belief.

The monastery was honeycombed into a limestone mountain's heart. It was enormous. There was possibly accommodation for a thousand people, with perfect ventilation and no dampness, although how that was contrived did not appear. Nor was there any sign of its inhabitants, nor any sound, except the shuffling of Ommony's loose shoes and the solid thump of the Lama's bare feet as he

strode with bowed head and the skirts of his long robe
swinging.

They descended a long, hewn stairway presently and
emerged, through a door a foot thick that was carved on
both sides with dragons, into the open air. The rush and
roar of water pouring into hollow caverns greeted them.
They were now on that side of the monastery that Ommony
had first seen, with the terraced amphitheater below them,
but it was too dark to peer into its depths. The stars
blinked down above a rim of mountains. "There will be
a full moon," said the Lama, a propos, apparently, of
nothing.

He led down into the dark amphitheater, by paths and
steps that linked the circling terraces, and turned, midway,
into a tunnel whose dark opening was like an ink-blot in
the shadow of rocks and trees. Ten yards along the tunnel
Ommony heard him fumbling with a lock; a door swung
almost silently; the Lama took him by the hand and pulled
him forward, closing the door but not locking it. Then, in
such utter darkness that all the senses were almost swallowed by it and Diana whimpered, the Lama led, pauseless,
holding Ommony's hand as if it were a child's. The old
man's grip was like a swordsman's, as if his vanished
youth, reborn for the moment, were burning him up.
The strange thrill that was consuming him communicated
itself to Ommony through the linked hands.

At the end of an immeasurable distance—(there was no
sense of time or space in that impenetrable darkness)—
they emerged into gloom under an oval patch of starlit sky,
on a ledge, an incalculable distance down the inside of a
limestone pit—somber, irregularly circular, enormous. The
Lama sat down on a mat that somebody had placed for
him—signed—and Ommony sat down beside him, on the
same mat.

"Let the dog not wander away. Bid her lie here," he
said, in a normal voice.

As Ommony's eyes grew gradually used to the gloom
he discerned that they were very near the bottom of the

pit, whose almost perpendicular flanks rose so high that
the stars appeared like bright dots on a dark-blue dome that
rested on the summit. His own breathing seemed abom-
inably noisy in the silence.

In front of where they sat there was a sheer drop, but
the bottom did not seem to be more than fifty feet below;
and somewhere in the midst of the almost circular space
into which he gazed there was an object, bulky, of no
ascertainable shape, and apparently raised on a platform
of rock so as to be almost on a level with the ledge on which
they sat. Diana lay still, sniffing, one ear raised; there
were humans not far away.

Presently there was a sound below—apparently a footstep, and Diana growled at it. A lantern appeared, but it
was impossible to tell whether the individual who carried
it was man or woman. There were several more footsteps,
and one word in a clear voice—instantly recognizable—the
chela's. There began to be a prodigious phantom movement in the gloom. Something—a great black cloth apparently—was pulled by many hands and the shape of the
object in the center changed. The lantern-light was reflected in a sea-green pin-point that spread and increased
as the moonlight spreads on water, but much more fiery,
and full of weird movement. The lantern suddenly went
out, but the peculiar green glow had made such an impression that with his eyes shut, Ommony could still see
evolving, glowing green.

"What is it?" he asked.

"The Jade of Ahbor."

The Lama's voice was solemn. He seemed almost to
resent the question. However he went on speaking in a
low voice.

"That fragment, that was broken off and stolen by an
Ahbor, has been set back, but there is none nowadays who
knows how to heal the break. There is a blemish. Thus one
ignorant fool can spoil the product of a thousand wise
men's labor. But that Ahbor was no better and no worse
than they who ruin reputations, to possess an hour's self-

righteousness. Others who should know better, will try to break my *chela's* spirit when the time comes—some for their own amusement, some for profit, some because they hate the truth. But she is made of stronger stuff than stone.''

His self-control was not so perfect as it had been. The last few words were in a tone of voice that fought with overwhelming sadness.

Ommony was about to ask a question when the Lama spoke again:

''My son, remember *this*: the highest motive is of no avail without proportion and a sense of fitness; because these are the life of wisdom. Time is a delusion. All is the eternal Now. But in a world in which all is delusion, of which time is a controlling element, there is a proper time for all things. We can not mount the camel that has passed us, nor the camel that has not yet come. Neither does the water that has gone by turn the mill-wheel. He who feels the force of destiny within him, waits, as birds wait for the sunrise—as the seed waits for the spring. It is not enough to do the right thing. If the full moon shines at midday, what does it accomplish? If the drum beats out of time, what happens to the symphony? To discern the right time, and to act precisely then, is as important as the knowledge *how* to act. But discernment does not come by reason of desire; it comes by observation of essential truths—as that the sun, the moon, the stars, the seasons and the tides keep their appointed path, and when they fail there is disaster. This is an appointed time. Mark well.''

The somber silence and the ragged flanks of the pit, that towered upward through a million shapeless shadows to the star-pierced oval summit, combined to inspire dread— but of what? Ommony could feel Diana trembling.

The Lama spoke again after a long pause, as dispassionately as a big clock ticking in the dark—asserting measured, elemental facts.

''Remember. Remember each word, my son. I speak

with death not far from me. At dawn the Ahbors go to
the northern end of the valley, by the Tsang-po Falls, to
await my coming. At noon I meet them.''

He was silent for many minutes. Not until the silence
had grown almost unendurable did he go on speaking.

''Lest the Ahbors harm themselves by slaying more
than me, who am responsible, I have sent into Tibet all
but a few of my monastery people. At noon I will try to
reach agreement with the Ahbors, that if they slay me, for
having broken their law, they shall permit the others to return to the monastery, and a new Lama to be sent to hold
authority. But as to the outcome of that I know nothing.
It may be that the Jade must be hidden by the Tsang-po
waters. There is a time for all things; it is not my province
to know the time for that; there are others whose province
it is.''

He stared into the dark in front of him. When he
spoke again, at the end of five minutes, his voice sounded
almost as if he had left his body and were speaking to it
and to Ommony.

''Remember every word. Those few, who have remained, are chosen men, who know the secret way. They
will take you into India—you, San-fun-ho and all the
European *chelas* to Tilgaun—the Tibetan *chelas* into Tibet
by the route that leads through Sikhim, because *they* have
a destiny that they can best fulfill in Tibet.''

Followed another tense silence, broken by the long-
drawn howl of an animal somewhere on the ledges half
a mile above them. It sounded lonelier than the wail of a
forgotten soul.

''I am not the guardian of Hannah Sanburn. Even as
you and I, my son, she governs her own destiny. But she
is good. No harm can come if she should leave Tilgaun,
because she has done her work there, and it is another's
turn. There is one who will take my place as trustee; he
will present himself; I have written his appointment.
There is one who will take her place; perhaps she is that
one at whose house you were in Delhi; but that is Hannah

Sanburn's business. There is one who will take your
place; but that is *your* affair. No man is indispensable.
He who clings to the performance of a duty when the
work is done and another waits to carry evolution forward, is as the fungus on the living tree. He rots. The
tree rots under him.''

Silence again. A wedge of silver, creeping down the
western side of the pit, dispersed the shadows and threw
great fangs of limestone into high relief; but that was
very far above them. Where they sat it seemed darker
than ever.

''Remember every word, my son. I speak in the portal
of death. I do not say that Hannah Sanburn shall go
with you to the West. That may, or it may not be. I
do say, tarry not in Tilgaun, because this is an appointed
time. Three of the lesser *chelas* will go with San-fun-ho
to the West. Let *her* select them. Let the others stay in
Tilgaun, where as much awaits them as they have the character to do.''

The beast in the dark loneliness above them howled
again. Ommony sat watching the forerunner of the moonlight chasing shadows down the pit-side—wondering.
After nearly a quarter of a century in India he and Hannah Sanburn would be almost as much strangers in the
West as San-fun-ho would be.

''There is a fitness in all things and a time for all
things,'' said the Lama, as if he had read Ommony's mind.
''But a great faith is required, and a sincerity that like
the temper of the steel turns faith into a ready weapon
and impenetrable armor. Hannah Sanburn has nobility.
It may be, she may help you to serve San-fun-ho. But
beware, my son, of the snare of personality. If ye two
seek to serve each other, ye are like the two sides of a
triangle that has no base, nor any purpose. But if ye
both serve San-fun-ho, and she the world, the triangle is
perfect.'' He paused again, then slowly turned his head
and looked into Ommony's eyes. His own were like blue
jewels burning in the dark.

"Without you," he said, "or without her, San-fun-ho
will find others. She is my *chela,* and I know the power
that is in her. But beware of being false! Better for you
never to have been born! Better to die ten thousand
deaths than to betray her through self-seeking! Let her
alone, my son, unless you can follow all the way! Then,
if she should lead you wrong, that will be her affair; in
after lives *you* will have *karma* of sincerity, and *she* the
fruit of false teaching—if she *should* teach falsely.—But
I know my *chela.* She will lead upward, as an eagle, and
all the enemies of light will spread their nets for her in
vain!"

As he ceased speaking the whole western wall of the
gigantic pit became suffused in silver, as the moon's edge
crossed the eastern rim. Wan, scrawny crags of limestone yearned like frozen ghosts toward the light. The
pit's awful nakedness lay revealed, its outlines dimmed
in shadow, as mysterious, as silent and as measureless as
the emotion born of gazing.

Suddenly, as the moon's disk appeared, there shone a
green light in the midst of the pit—a light that swirled
as if in moving water, and increased in size, as if it multiplied itself within the substance it had touched. It grew
into a pool—a globe—a sphere—an ovoid mass of liquid
green light, all in motion, transparent, huge—afloat, it
seemed, in black precipitated silence, two, or perhaps three
hundred feet away. Slowly, very slowly, it became apparent that the egg-shaped mass was resting on seven upright stones, of the same color as itself, that were set beneath it on a platform of dark rock that rose exactly in
the middle of the pit.

As the full moon floated into view the enormous mass of
jade so caught the light that it seemed to absorb all of it.
And suddenly a figure stood before the livid jade—a
girl's; she was the Gretchen-girl, with whom Ommony had
spoken on the night when he first saw San-fun-ho's companions on the stage. She was draped in white, but the
stuff glowed green in the jade's reflection, and as she

peered into the enormous stone she held the end of the
loose drapery across the lower portion of her face, like a
shield, with her elbow forward. She gazed for about a
minute, and then disappeared. Another took her place.

"It is only San-fun-ho who dares to look into the Jade
for long," said the Lama solemnly. "It shows them all
the horror of their lower selves. *They* look by moonlight.
They must drape themselves, for they have much to overcome, and there is magic in the Jade. None but my *chela*
—none but San-fun-ho—dares to face it in the full light
of the sun."

One by one the seventeen girls appeared, looked deep
into the Jade, and vanished into darkness.

"They are not bad," said the Lama. "Not bad, my
son. There are not so many better women. Do *you* dare
to look?"

But Ommony sat still.

"Better so," said the Lama. "In curiosity there is no
wisdom. He who can not look long enough to see his
higher nature shining through the lower, had better have
seen nothing."

There commenced a chant, of women's voices, rising
from the fathomless darkness below the Jade. It began
by being low and almost melancholy, but changed suddenly into faster tempo and a rising theme of triumph, ending in a measured march of glory. There was no accompaniment, no drum-beat, but the final phrases pulsed with
power, ending on a chord that left imagination soaring
into upper realms of splendor. Then, in silence, as sub-
limely as the moon had sailed across the rim of the dark
pit, the girls emerged out of the black night as if they had
been projected by a magic lantern. No sound of footfall
or of breathing reached across the intervening gap as,
with restraint that told of strength in hand and limitless
lore of rhythm, they danced their weaving measure seven
times around the stone, as lovely to the eye as Grecian
figures, cut in cameo on green and conjured into life. It
was sheer spiritual magic.

There was not a wasted motion, not a step but symbolized the ordered, infinitely beautiful evolving of a universe; and as they passed behind the glowing jade their figures seemed to swim within the stone, as if they were nymphs afloat in moonlit water. But there was no sign yet of San-fun-ho.

"They shall remember this night!" said the Lama.

The fire within the Jade grew dim and died as the moon's edge passed beyond the crags. The girls vanished in black darkness.

"And so, you have seen the Jade. Few have seen that," said the Lama. "And you will find that there are very few who will believe you have seen it; but that is no harm, because *most* of those who would believe are merely credulous, of the sort who hunt miracles and seek to make themselves superior by short-cuts. Whereas there are no short-cuts, and there is no superiority of the sort they crave, but only a gradual increase of responsibility, which is attained by earned self-mastery."

Suddenly a voice came from the pit beneath them, clear and confident,—the *chela's*:

"O Tsiang Samdup!"

The Lama answered with a monosyllable, his body rigid with emotion. His dim outline was like an eagle's startled from his aerie in the night.

"O Tsiang Samdup, the Ahbors have come for a conference. They ask for word with you."

"Cover the Jade," he answered.

There was presently a phantom movement, shapeless and billowy, as if a huge black cloth were being hauled back into place; and then the rain came, softly, steadily, until the air grew full of music made by little cataracts that splashed from rock to rock. The Lama sighed and, for a moment, his outline seemed to shrink as old age claimed him, but he threw that off and stood up, motioning to Ommony to move back under shelter of the rock.

"Wait there," he commanded, and vanished. Ommony could hear him climbing down into the darkness—and

presently two voices as he talked in low tones with the
chela. Then silence, for a very long time, only broken
by the music of the rain and a weird wind sighing on the
upper ledges until wind and rain ceased, and there was
only the tinkle of dripping water.

The dog crept close to Ommony for warmth, shivering
at the loneliness. Ommony tried to memorize the Lama's
conversation. He had almost forgotten the Jade. It was
nothing as compared to the tremendous issues that the
Lama dealt in. Thought groped in an unseen future.
The sensation was of waiting on the threshold of a new
world—waiting to be born. The past lost all reality. The
world he had known—war—selfishness—corruption—was
a nightmare, wrought of hopelessness and full of useless
aims. The future? It was his—his own—immensely personal to him. He was about to be born again into the old
world, but with an utterly new consciousness of values.
He knew he had a duty in the world; but he could not
formulate it—would not know how to begin—only knew
it was immensely dark and silent on the threshold.

The Lama's voice broke silence, speaking to the *chela*
somewhere in the pit below:

"The first duty of a *chela* is obedience!"

Silence again. Not even wind or rain to break the still-
ness. At last the Lama's figure, like a shadow issuing
from nothing, approaching along the ledge and sitting
down near him—but not near enough for conversation.
Then, after a very long pause, the *chela's* voice, resonant
and clear from somewhere in the distance:

"O Tsiang Samdup! I obey. And *they* obey *me*. May
I wait until the dawn? It is not long."

The Lama gave assent—one monosyllable—then groaned,
and came and sat closer to Ommony.

"My work is done," he said. "There is a limit to endurance."

He glanced up at the sky, but there was no sign yet of
dawn.

A low chant came from the distance—almost like the

humming of a swarm of bees, but the Lama took no notice of it.

"She will go with you, thinking I come later. You may tell her in Tilgaun, and she will understand. She will be brave then. She will not forget she was my *chela.*"

There was only the sound of humming after that until the crags around the rim of the great pit grew faintly luminous before the coming of the dawn, and the stars grew paler. Then the hum swelled into song, whose music sounded like the mystic evolution of new worlds; they were all girls' voices, thrilling with courage and exultation. Ommony strained his ears to catch the words, but the distance was too great. Somehow, although he could not penetrate the darkness, he felt as if a veil were lifting.

The song ceased, and in the hush that followed Tsiang Samdup rose to his feet.

"I go," he said quietly. "I am old, my son. I can not bear to say good-by to my beloved *chela.* May the gods, who guard your manhood, give you strength and honesty to serve her. She will ask for me. You may say to her: 'The first duty of a *chela* is obedience.'"

He turned into the tunnel, walking swiftly, and was gone. A silver bell rang, over in the distance, opposite, seven times, slow and distinct; then a pause, in which the overtones spread off into infinity; then seven times again. And as the last note faded into silence, dawn touched the crags with silver and the *chela's* voice rose young and glorious, intoning the oldest invocation in the world:

"O my Divinity, blend Thou with me . . . that out of darkness I may go forth in Light."

Daylight spread swiftly down the crags until it touched a ledge on which the *chela* stood, and all beneath that was darkness, like a pool of ink. Her right hand was raised. The other girls, beneath her, were invisible. Dawn glistened on her face.

Her lips moved and her breast swelled as she drew breath to intone the Word. And then, in chorus from the mist and darkness that enwrapped her feet, and from

her own lips, came the magic, long-drawn syllable that
has been sacred since before Atlantis sank under the ocean
and new races explored new continents—the Word that
signifies immeasureable, absolute, unthinkable, all-com-
passing, for ever infinite and unattainable, sublime and
holy Essence—the Beginning and the End.

"O-o-o-o-o-o-o-o-om-m-m-m-m—"

It rose, and rose, and died away among the crags, until
the last reverberation echoed faintly from the upper levels
and there came an answer to it, sonorous and strong, in
a man's voice, from a crag beside a cave-mouth three hundred feet above the ledge where Ommony stood, nearly
midway between him and the *chela.*

"O-o-o-o-o-o-o-o-om-m-m-m-m!"

The Lama raised his right hand in a final benediction,
turned into the cave and vanished. Then the *chela's* voice
—calling to Ommony as dawn sank deep into the pit, re-
vealing her companions on a ledge below:

"O Gupta Rao—change your name now! Wait for me.
I am coming—Tsiang Samdup bids us go forth together!"

THE END

After-word

After-word
by Brian Taves

Imagine an adventurer, just past forty, who comes to California for the first time. As a boy he left Rugby to spend nearly a dozen years in India and Africa, experiencing both the heights of mystical Indian teaching and the depths of a jail sentence for poaching in British East Africa. Named as the co-respondent in a divorce case involving the English nobility, he is unwanted in his homeland and heads for the New World. He arrives in New York and is immediately robbed and severely beaten. Recovering, he discovers a talent for writing and in a few years becomes an acclaimed novelist. After a journey through the intrigue of the post-World War I Middle East, a Hollywood contract takes him to the West, where he will undergo the fundamental philosophical and religious awakening that he has been searching for all his life.

Just south of Los Angeles, on the peninsula that forms the harbor of San Diego, he found a spot where East truly met West. There, long before "Shangri-La" had become a popularly accepted myth, a vanguard movement was promoting the alternative of the wisdom of the Orient. At Point Loma, a community had been founded in 1897 by an intrepid and determined woman, Katherine Tingley (1847-1929), which by the 1920s had attracted some five hundred residents, including many prominent artists and scholars.[1] The group was inspired by the Theosophical Society, originally founded in New York in the 1870s by an expatriate Russian, Helena Petrovna Blavatsky. Her book, *The Secret Doctrine*, was subtitled "the synthesis of science, religion and philosophy," expressing the Movement's aims. It promulgated such concepts as reincarnation and karma, and was based squarely on the idea that Oriental beliefs were superior to those of the West. These were radical assertions in an era characterized by the smugness of European colonial activity, but the activities of the Theosophical Society around the world helped spawn a curiosity and thirst for knowledge about Eastern thought that has given rise to numerous other groups over the last century.

The background of the adventurer who had become the writer we know as Talbot Mundy provided an authentic initiation into the type of philosophical and religious discourse which were the concern of the Theosophical Society. Born in London in 1879 to a middle class, Church of England family, he rejected this heritage by running away, first to Germany, then to India, where he spent two years meandering from the northwest frontier to the plains of Tibet, then went to the Far East, Australia, the Persian Gulf, and Africa before he came to the

United States in 1909. By 1911, his literary career began, and he quickly became one of the top writers for the most literary of the "pulps," the highly praised *Adventure*, remaining one of the magazine's top writers for the next twenty years. Many of his early stories were of British India and strongly reminiscent of Rudyard Kipling. But Mundy soon turned out more enduring, literary books, such as *King—of the Khyber Rifles* (1916) and *Guns of the Gods* (1921). Both told of a devious Indian princess scheming to carve an empire for herself, and illustrated his talent for combining adventure with an exotic sense of intrigue and sophisticated power politics. Mundy had a mind capable of developing extremely complex, convoluted plots, and a potential for colorful characterizations. Among his persistent qualities was a marvelous ability to describe a locale with a convincing touch of authenticity, combining the knowledge from his travels with a vivid imagination, leaving the reader unable to discern where the former left off and the latter began. Mundy discusses this ambiguity in his article, "An Author's Characters," *New York Times* (June 30, 1929), Sec. VIII, p. 4.

Through the Theosophical interpretation of Katherine Tingley, Mundy found a way of thought which gave meaning to his personal contact with the Orient, confirming impressions he had long had. During his travels he had become intensely interested in native magic and occult teachings, making observations that later provided the basis for his writing. He already believed in reincarnation even while in Africa, fifteen years earlier.[2] For Mundy's literature, Theosophy added a broader, more serious dimension: whereas previously he had explored the physical and material mysteries of India, his writing would now expand to encompass its metaphysical, spiritual, and philosophical realm. The 1920s became not only his most prolific decade, but one which would produce the best of his literature as well.

Tingley was impressed with Mundy, recognizing a man whose talents, properly developed, could make a formidable champion of the Theosophical cause. At the same time, a deep friendship sprang up between them, despite the vast difference in age; they shared in common a searching background, including obscure, rebellious early years and unsettled private lives, each having had three marriages and two divorces by this time.[3] One of the Mundy's attractions to the Theosophical Society may have been the fact that it had been both founded, and was now led, by a woman. His life and writings make clear that he never felt either threatened by or resentful towards women, and was a lifelong believer in complete equality between the sexes.[4] Frequently women were the leading players in his stories, ambitious, manipulative, yet also likeable, invariably out-thinking and dominating any man. Tingley, even at age seventy-five, was like the typical Mundy heroine: strong-willed and commanding, with a charisma that captivated and over-whelmed her male followers.

Actually, Theosophical-type thinking had begun to manifest itself in Mundy's writing even before his arrival at Point Loma.[5] From the beginning, a regular feature of his most important books became the brief inserts at the beginning of chapters, in the form of verse or proverbs, often credited to such non-existent sources as "The Book of the Sayings of Tsiang Samdup." While admitting the phrasing was his own, Mundy would claim their ideas derived from the "Ancient Wisdom" common to the beginnings of all religions.[6] Similarly, Mundy had already found the archetypal plot he would use in *Om*. In his 1922 novel, *Caves of Terror*, the shrewd British hero of *King—of the Khyber Rifles* finds himself an outcast from his race for deciding to investigate the supernatural in India. *Caves of Terror* originally appeared as *The Gray Mahatma* in the November 10, 1922 issue of *Adventure* magazine and was later retitled for American paperback and English hardcover editions. He encounters a wise "Mahatma" who reveals to him secrets, never before seen by Western eyes, of the Indian religious philosophy—both its vast possibilities and the pitfalls into which many of its adherents fall. The tale was a fictional explication of Mundy's belief "that, while many of the native magicians are frauds and charlatans, some of them really possess occult' powers that truly come under the heading of magic—in the sense that science has not yet explained them or explained them away."[7] Surprisingly, this serious exploration of Eastern religion, deviating from the norm in *Adventure* by being cast in the fantasy genre, was readily accepted, readers voting it their favorite novel of the year.[8]

On New Year's Day, 1923, Talbot Mundy was admitted to membership in the Theosophical Society, and by the fall he had accepted Katherine Tingley's invitation to take up residence as a guest in her home, the Society Headquarters, where he occupied a room in the northwest corner of the second floor. The next year, Mundy bought a large home, overlooking the Pacific and near the Society Headquarters, and married a young widow, Sarah ("Sally") Teresa Leach Ames, (1886-1963), whom he had been courting for five years. Mundy became a prominent and highly respected member of the Point Loma community, and Tingley appointed him to her cabinet, a position of honor with advisory and supportive duties, and he regularly attended their meetings. In the evenings he often read aloud passages he had written to local friends, listening to their reactions. A tall, broadshouldered, charming man, Mundy became one of the most popular and persuasive speakers in the Society, and was called upon to make numerous addresses on occasions varying from the informal to the ceremonial. He could be especially entertaining because of the clever use he made of his reminiscences of India and other exotic lands, which were bound to have a special appeal to theosophists. He spoke out in support of such Tingley favored causes as universal brotherhood and the social theory of crime, and against capital punishment, vivisection, colonialism, and the League of Nations, the last a reversal of his previous position. He later joined privately held studies of *The Secret Doctrine* led by Gottfried de Purucker (1874-1942), Tingley's protege and leading intellectual of esoteric philosophy; Mundy continued to attend intermittently until 1927. The influence of the society was readily evident in the long series of articles and poems he contributed to in almost every issue of *The Theosophical Path* for some three years. He attempted to convince his publishers, Bobbs-Merrill, to issue theosophical works, Tingley's in particular. Even *Adventure* felt Mundy's growing philosophical interests and willingness to commit himself to causes, publishing over 10,000 words of his letters on such subjects as Indian magic, the Great Pyramid, the lost tribes of Israel, the Lia Fail, and the Ark of the Covenant.

Theosophy's influence on Talbot Mundy was most strongly evident in his 1924 novel *Om: The Secret of Ahbor Valley*. The serialization in *Adventure* from October 10-November 30, 1924 and British book edition were called simply *Om*, and the subtitle, *The Secret of Ahbor Valley*, was added for American book publication. The original title, *Om*, has a tripartite meaning: first, signifying the famous mantra; second, as an abbreviation for the title character, Cotswold Ommony; and third, symbolizing his transformation as a European who adopts the ways of the East and is initiated into its mysteries. Indeed, Mundy hoped to add theosophical visual accompaniment to the text, unsuccessfully proposing illustrations for alternate chapters by Leonard Lester, a Point Loma theosophist. However, one of Lester's unique etchings, in the style of Reginald Machell, was used as the first of the two dust jackets Bobbs-Merrill issued for *Om*.

Tingley's hospitality in providing lodgings for Mundy, together with the intellectual activity of the Society, provided a creative atmosphere and allowed him to write *Om* at a more leisurely pace for the first time in years. Such conditions made it possible for Mundy to turn away from the hasty writing of "pulp" novels that had been a staple of much of his output in 1921 and 1922. In *Om*, Mundy created his most distinctly literary book, surpassing earlier novels in choice of language, plot structure, theme and depth of character. Although in later years Mundy may have matched *Om*, he never exceeded its standard. *Om* is also his strongest fictional statement of philosophy, with the sole exception of his his last novel, *Old Ugly-Face*.

Not only was *Om* written with greater care, it was meant to be taken more seriously. Mundy authored a long letter in the October 10, 1924 issue of *Adventure* to introduce *Om* to readers.[9] He emphasized the reality of the Ahbor Valley and its inaccessibility, his reasons for believing in the "Masters," and the nature of his characters. He had gained the latest information on the Ahbors directly from Sven Hedin the previous year, during the explorer's visit to Point Loma.

In *Om*, adventure, drama, humor and an unusual philosophy are blended masterfully; in a letter to his publisher, Mundy described the book as "soaked with sound philosophy and stirring mystery, plus dangerous adventure."[10] The decision to write such a story would have daunted a less courageous writer; Bobbs-Merrill was concerned about Mundy writing a novel with "philosophy," and the poor sales of *The Nine Unknown*, his less esoteric novel of the previous year, provided apparently discouraging evidence regarding the popular interest in Indian occult novels. Probably only a writer of Mundy's established stature and popularity could have succeeded in taking such a story as *Om* to widespread popularity and publication. Even editor Arthur Hoffman felt obliged to issue a declamatory notice for *Adventure* readers, nodding to Christian sensibilities by indicating he in no way endorsed Mundy's views, adding that there was no intention of starting a religious debate in the magazine's pages.

Om describes picturesque cities, regions and customs, and beneath it all a stratum intimating the supernatural. These aspects are portrayed authentically and sympathetically, and the descriptive power of Mundy's prose as the reader feels the very pulse of India.[11] Mundy's facility for expression, incident, and atmosphere is so compelling and immediate that the story is easily invoked in the mind's eye, as if it were a movie. Moments of danger become transformed into opportunities to create destiny, making the events seem very real, and many of the details and philosophy of life in India remain visible today.[12] The verisimilitude and validity of the descriptive portions becomes a crucial support that allow Mundy's didactic teaching and philosophy to win acceptance.

Om opens with a fascinating panoply of India, as a seemingly inevitable series of bizarre incidents grow into a tempest on the streets, triggering an accidental roadside pile-up—a vivid, materialized depiction of the same Karmaic law of cause and effect that also governs the

souls of Mundy's characters. Mixed with these events is the news of the
departure of the English guardian of India's forests, Cotswold Ommony,
a hero of previous Mundy novels making his final appearance. He is
utterly unlike the standard depictions of British colonials by other
writers, leaving behind the stereotypical confines of such a character.
Ommony is not just curious, he is a student, an explorer of the east and
its traditions. As one who believes the British should leave India, is an
outcast from his own race.

Ommony is a believer in native magic, who has encountered a
mysterious, broken piece of jade that reflects its observer's thoughts. He
seeks the answer to its riddles in the shop of a nearby jeweler, Chutter
Chand. There he meets a lama, Tsiang Samdup, and Samding, his chela
(student). The encounter confirms Ommony's desire to seek the mysteries of which he has learned so many tantalizing fragments, as well as
solve the disappearance of his sister into the inaccessible Ahbor Valley
two decades earlier.

These threads grow into the subplots along Ommony's journey: the
mystical Samdup and his chela, the search for Ommony's sister, and the
pursuit of the jade. All these elements fuse to lead to Ommony's
discovery of a philosophy, labeled here as "the Middle Way," to
credibly explain that most profound of questions, the mystery of life.
Like Theosophy itself, the Middle Way eclectically incorporates the
best of both philosophy and religion, avoiding the pitfalls of extremes.
The Middle Way proves to be not only a philosophy Samdup practices,
but also a material road for secret communication, a type of "underground railroad." Secret paths in India open, close and change constantly, through which the actors pass furtively from town to town.[13] It
is only these scenes, some of which seem rather protracted and slow, that
cause the pace of the novel to sag during the long trek in the center of
the book.

The final chapters, set inside the Ahbor Valley as Ommony hears
Samdup's remarkable story, become Mundy's essay. The jade is revealed as actually part of a scientific instrument made by the savants of
a long-forgotten ancient race, to reflect the best and worst traits of
whomever looks in it, forcing them to undergo a trial of self-revelation.
Ultimately, Ommony faces the entire jade himself. Afterwards, he is
sent out into the world once more to face his destiny. As Mundy wrote
in one of the proverbs of *Om*,

"He who would understand the Plains must ascend the Eternal
Hills, where a man's eyes scan Infinity. But he who would make use of
understanding must descend on to the Plains, where Past and Future
meet and men have need of him."[14]

In Samdup's words, "No learning is of any value unless we can translate it into action." [Mundy, *Om*, 380.]

Unlike some Mundy books, in *Om* characterization is definitely a strength, with a fascinating array of vibrant, authentic individuals splashed across its pages. As Austin Adams wrote, Mundy's *Om* more than withstood comparison with Joseph Conrad, ranking *Om* alongside E.M. Forster's *A Passage to India*, finding that Mundy paints "his portraits of real people . . . almost as convincingly . . . ."[15] Mundy's Indians are incredibly diverse; he spins an endless web of such figures, all equally vivid and arresting—whether the wise Samdup, the blood-thirsty and duplicitous Tsering, the double agent Singh, or the nervous but knowing merchants Chutter Chand and Benjamin.

Ommony's companion traveling back to India will be Samding, revealed to be his niece, the daughter of his late, long-lost sister. Samding has been protected and reared all these years by Samdup as foster-father and teacher. Since she was born in the Ahbor Valley, the natives exact the price of Samdup's life when Samding departs, a sacrifice the Lama willingly makes because he has intentionally tricked them. Ommony, in turn, is to become Samding's chela, assisting and protecting her as she brings wisdom to the West. However, Samding is not, as some interpretations have suggested, a "savior," but merely a wise teacher, one of many who will be needed to convey Oriental wisdom to the occident. In Om both cultures must be brought together, and Samding has the unique combination of a westerner reared in the East—qualifications Mundy hints will be required for the wisdom of the East to be transmitted to the occidental world. Similarly, the westerner H.P. Blavatsky was said to have learned from the "Masters" in Tibet to receive the inspiration to found Theosophy, and the idea of such a figure as Samding was likely based on this conception. As well, Samding is a woman, like so many of Mundy's teachers—H.P. Blavatsky, Katherine Tingley, and Mary Baker Eddy. The novel's visit to the mission school at Tilgaun is clearly modeled on Tingley's own Raja-Yoga principles of education in the Society's academy at Point Loma.

Many Point Loma theosophists thought they recognized Tingley's own teachings in Samdup's sayings and character.[16] Indeed, Mundy acknowledged the debt when he wrote to Tingley, "What wisdom [Om] contains was learned from you, and its unwisdom is my own. Without your teaching, patience, and encouragement I could not have 'imag-ined' either the wise old Lama or his chela."[17] In the words of Pervin Mistry, Katherine Tingley does stand out as the figure of the Lama in *Om*. She represents the character of the wise old Lama for she had all those qualities herself. But it is also true that just as the Lama teaches his audience through plays, analogy and sayings, Mundy himself plays the very role of Tsiang Samdup as personified by his own qualities and innate wisdom. It would have been impossible to create the Lama and the Chela as "living characters" as Mundy has portrayed them to perfection, if he himself did not possess their qualities.[18]

In Om, Mundy vastly enlarges the archetypal character of the wise old sage who had appeared in Caves of Terror two years previously. The Ringding Gelong Lama Tsiang Samdup of Om is far more likable than the Gray Mahatma of Caves of Terror. Samdup is wise yet whimsical, compassionate, perceptive, humble, a man of incomparable serenity even when facing death.[19] Mundy based the character of Samdup on the teachings he learned at Point Loma and elsewhere over the years, but also on the lamas he had met while in India. To Mundy the Lama was a living individual; years later he would tell his last wife, Dawn, that when he was half through with the first draft, suddenly Tsiang Samdup came to see him. Samdup "seemed to be whisking through a wall, and standing in front of him. 'He just looked at me,' Talbot said, 'and said "My son, that won't do."'" Talbot dropped the manuscript and put a fresh piece of paper in."[20]

Samdup's instruction in the Middle Way is partly didactic, but more often by example. In the words of the Lama, "Drama is the way to teach.... By allegories, parables and illustrations men learn easily what no amount of argument will drive into their understanding."[21] By contrast, the British police only understand enough of Samdup's play to claim it is seditious. Ommony, in disguise, follows Samdup as he leads a theatrical caravan toward Tibet, performing small plays wherever they go. In this way philosophical lessons are taught to the audience in the form of stories. Not only is this a reflexive analogy on Mundy's part for the role of his own tales as conduits and illustrations for teaching philosophy, it is the most successful form he ever devised to convey abstract ideas in a comprehensible and practical manner—while still managing to entertain. Mundy's narrative strategy proved fruitful: he "succeeded brilliantly in making philosophy the very life-blood of a most absorbing story ...."[22] More effectively than in any of his other work, Om strikes a delicate, unique balance between the descriptive, the narrative and the didactic, while still retaining the guise of the story-teller.

Samdup's technique may have been inspired by Katherine Tingley's own theatrical background and presentation of widely attended and critically praised performances of Ancient and Shakespearean plays in the Thesosophical Society's Greek Theater. Mundy was attending and reviewing such performances while writing the novel, even enacting a bit part in Tingley's Grecian drama, *The Aroma of Athens*. In *Om*, Ommony plays a series of roles: those he performs on stage, together with the identity of the Bhat-Brahmin actor he assumes in the vain hope of concealing his presence from Samdup. Similarly, Samding wears male clothes to facilitate her passage through India.

Between each chapter are philosophical poetry and proverbs, adding profundity and transcendance to the novel. A number of the poems and sayings included in *Om* had previously appeared in *The Theosophical Path*, and Mundy had doubtless incorporated the suggestions and reaction of Theosophists to them as his outline of the story grew. The fact that Mundy cloaks his philosophy within the guise of authentic Eastern authorities, as fragments "From the Book of the Sayings of Tsiang Samdup," indicates his determination that the reader accept the validity of Oriental wisdom. The sayings themselves are rich and sometimes obscure, changing in meaning for the reader over time; like the Jade of Ahbor, they give the impression of never quite staying the same. Om becomes a journey that can be oft repeated and never leaves the reader unaffected, a book which, perhaps more so than any other by Mundy, richly rewards re-reading.[23]

Mundy used the generic universe of Indian adventure as a vehicle to advance a personal assimilation of Eastern teachings, as understood through Theosophy, but even more by his own experience and study of the Orient. This background gave him a talent for making the fantastic seem plausible so that, while admitting that he allowed his imagination to transmit and vitalize this philosophy to his readers, Mundy offered far more. As critics have noted, "No one, not even Kipling, came closer to India's underlying reality than Talbot Mundy;" *Om* has a "grasp of the English in India and on the Indian philosophy that is substantial and powerful."[24] In Mundy, as in his character Samding, East and West synthesize without clash or disharmony, and the twain must and shall meet.

For *Adventure* readers and other laymen, *Om* could serve as pure entertainment or an introduction to Eastern thought, providing escapism mixed with Theosophy for the unsuspecting. For Theosophists, on the other hand, *Om* is a reaffirmation, fictionalizing and revitalizing their teaching in novel form. In offering Eastern philosophy, *Om* inevitably subverts many of the West's traditional values and beliefs, in favor of evolution, selflessness, a belief in destiny, a search for inner merit at the expense of pride, and an acceptance of the deceptiveness of materialism. There is no ultimate threshold where trial and progress end, either a heaven or a nirvana; the cycle of reincarnation and evolution is unceasing, climbing ever upward, no matter how slowly, never evading Karma. "Because you are doing well, it would not be good to believe you can not do better," Samdup advises; "The road is long, and there are difficulties; but ye *must* face it."[25]

Writing such a book as *Om* was a risky venture for Mundy; he chose to diverge from the conventional commercial path and deviate from the formulas of adventure fiction. While using the structure of the genre, the interpretation was entirely different from previous writers because of Mundy's profound respect and knowledge of Eastern thought. In *Om*, more strongly than in any of his previous fiction, Mundy firmly established the literary pattern of looking to the East, not only for exoticism, but for wisdom and an alternative mode of living that might be superior to western habits. Mundy crystallized the archetype of the westerner who quits the dissatisfying colonial life to disguise himself as a native and search for the wisdom of the east. In this way *Om*, and later Mundy works such as *The Devil's Guard, Black Light, Full Moon* and *Old Ugly-Face*, reinvigorated and revitalized fantasy-adventure literature.

As the *Saturday Review of Literature* said of *Om*, H. Rider Haggard's "stories are thin beside Mr. Mundy's story which is enriched by what is clearly a first-hand knowledge of India . . . ."[26] The same comparison could be made with Kipling's *Kim*, to which *Om* is sometimes likened. Noting that Mundy places the Lama, Samdup, at the center of the story, as the ultimate hero who teaches the main western figure, theosophical author Kenneth Morris remarked that *Om* contains "a character and a plot, which are absolutely new in the whole field of fiction."[27] Mundy, unlike Kipling, foregrounded the Indians, along with their religious and cultural traditions, conscientiously denying western assumptions of superiority. Mundy resented his book being called a "second Kim," since his interpretation of a lama is totally different from that of Kipling, and indeed *Om* is arguably the better work, and certainly the more timeless.[28] The Lama in Kim is fundamentally a passive, impractical figure, hardly a "Master"—in Mundy's words "as untrue to life, as stupid, effete, impossible and missionary-ignorant (to coin a phrase) as a character could be . . . [*Om*] is the only piece of fiction ever written that gives a true view of the inner, that is esoteric philosophy of the Lamas, and a real inkling of who the so-called Mahatmas [Masters] really are."[29]

Om was perceptively and ecstatically reviewed by Gottfried de Purucker in December 1924 in *The Theosophical Path*, emphasizing the novel's psychological power.[30] Theosophists quickly took Om to heart, since it perfectly expressed their deepest beliefs in a popular context.[31] In March 1925, Mundy's novel, described as "profound truths in the guise of vivid and fascinating fiction" was placed in the book list of standard Theosophical Literature. [32] Theosophists the world over immediately began translating Om into a number of languages, including German, Swedish, and Dutch, and the book was commercially translated into Slavic and French.

Although proud of his work, Mundy had expected *Om* to be criticized outside the theosophical community for its favorable portrayal of Eastern ideas. He was surprised when the book became a bestseller and proved equally popular abroad.[33] A typical mainstream review of Om appeared in the Manchester City News:

"The volume contains a wealth of Oriental lore, and is the product of a well-stored and scholarly mind. Those who want philosophy and . . . a work of fiction entirely out of the common may be safely commended to this work . . . The Lama's impressive teachings produce a deep impression . . . Mr. Mundy has produced a literary and philosophical masterpiece." [34]

Among those who spoke highly of *Om* were California's Progressive Senator Hiram Johnson, along with Alice Roosevelt Longworth, a regular Mundy fan, daughter of former president Theodore Roosevelt and wife of the Speaker of the United States House of Representatives.[35] During 1925 and beyond, The Theosophical Path joyfully reprinted excerpts from the stream of praise Om received in letters and reviews from around the globe. [36]

Tingley's confidence in Mundy seemed more than justified. Many other prominent and more senior members of the society were passed over in favor of Mundy for the honor of writing the introduction to Tingley's new book, *The Wine of Life* (1925). Tingley to call on Mundy for a sequel to *Om*, and he promised to try, later deciding to provide instead a new, hopefully better work. [37] This became The Devil's Guard (1926), which carried the search for the teaching of the "Masters" from the Himalayan plateaus where *Om* left off, through an agonizing journey into Tibet. *The Devil's Guard* was serialized in *Adventure* magazine as *Ramsden*, and published in England under this title. *The Devil's Guard* was actually the third volume of a tetralogy that had begun with *Caves of Terror*, continuing with *The Nine Unknown* in 1923, and concluding with *Jimgrim* in 1931. In these four titles Mundy abandoned the literary dignity and didactic, meditative style of *Om*, opting instead to convey Eastern concepts through the depiction of a dream-like realm of nightmarish quest, where souls are governed by psychic forces.

Meanwhile, Mundy was beginning a new series, one entirely

different from anything he had tried before: a series depicting the ancient world. In 1923 he conceived a massive historical novel centered on Cleopatra, which eventually required a dozen years and three volumes to complete: *Tros of Samothrace* (serialization in 1925, book publication in 1934), *Queen Cleopatra* (1929), and *Purple Pirate* (1935). Cleopatra, doubtless partly inspired by the example of Blavatsky and Tingley, is pictured as not only a wily politician but one who revered the teachings of the ancient religious tradition, to such a degree that Mundy's publishers demanded the theosophical implications be toned down. The saga eventually became equally the story of a heroic fictional explorer and philosopher, Tros, who fights the tyranny of Julius Caesar and imperial Rome. Many readers in the 1920s were shocked by an anti-classical, revisionist depiction of Rome, but eventually a consensus sided with Mundy, and the approach Mundy pioneered has now become commonplace.

Queen Cleopatra proved to be his last novel written under the Point Loma influence. Gradually, he drifted away from the Society; he lacked the long-term personal discipline necessary to maintain a leadership position. As well, Mundy was investing enormous capital and time in a Mexican oil-drilling venture that promised wealth and came heart-rendingly close to success. Discovering that he had been defrauded by his business partner, and surrounded by debt, Mundy found the shame unbearable, and in 1928 abandoned his wife and home, moving to New York. Tingley and de Purucker hoped that he would return, and Tingley visited Mundy the next year on her way to a European tour, but only a few months later she died.

Although Theosophy could still be found in later Mundy books, other influences were increasingly apparent as he continued his own personal quest. He was briefly involved with spiritualism, an encounter reflected in his novel *Black Light* (1930). While continuing his interest in comparative religion, never again was Mundy's genius as a writer so frequently apparent: the 1930s marked a steady withdrawal from the type of rigorous intellectual climate that Point Loma had provided. The problematic depression market discouraged him from being too experimental, and he returned to more traditional short stories, serials of adventure and only an occasional outright fantasy, the best of which was *Full Moon* (1935; titled *There was a Door* in England), a testament to his enduring belief in the supernatural in India. In his very last novel, *Old Ugly-Face* (1940), published the year of his death, he again treated the mysteries of Tibet, but in a far more modern style. Mundy's final thoughts on Theosophy were revealed in his only non-fiction book, *I Say Sunrise* (1947). Initially authored as *Thus Spake the Devil* under a pseudonym in 1933, it had repeatedly failed to sell. Posthumously published seven years after his death, it was drastically edited by his widow, Dawn, but nonetheless reveals the most important influences on his life to have been Theosophy and Christian Science, to which he had been an adherent in the decade before moving to Point Loma.

Mundy's association with the Theosophical Society was meteoric, but the timing was also fortuitous. He had a virtually guaranteed outlet in *Adventure* magazine, allowing him an extraordinary freedom to interject Oriental philosophy into his stories. In turn this policy was made possible by the booming business in "pulp" magazines, of which *Adventure* was the prestigious leader with a readership that reached 300,000, publishing 200-page issues as often as three times a month in the 1920s. "[38] At the same time, the Theosophical Society had adopted a thoroughly populist tone under Tingley's leadership, encouraging Mundy's effort to place theosophical ideas into the context of fiction that would be palatable to a large audience. After Mundy's departure and Tingley's death, the Society's focus shifted away from the secular appeals she had pioneered toward de Purucker's more academic style. Simultaneously, the Great Depression hurt sales and made magazine publication much more difficult to obtain. These two circumstances caused Mundy and the Theosophical movement to separate, although both had a lasting impact on each other.

Mundy never achieved the universal popularity of a Kipling or Haggard because, as Elmer Davis pointed out, his interests and theosophical bent were not shared by many readers. At the same time, Mundy's foundation as an author whose works often first appeared in the "pulps," albeit the best of them, rendered him suspect from a conventional critical viewpoint. Together, these factors deprived Talbot Mundy of the literary recognition he deserves.[39] However, Mundy was more than a mere writer of adventure tales; he was engaged, through his literature, in a lifelong discourse on philosophy and religion. He used his stories for much larger purposes than either Kipling or Haggard; for Mundy, as with Joseph Conrad, exotic locales served more than decorative functions.[40] Instead, the atmosphere Mundy so effectively vitalized provided an appropriate background for the treatment of serious, metaphysical subjects in the context of Oriental thinking. He adapted such an approach, especially between 1922 to 1930, in several different ways, using both mass-audience and literary types of works, depicting the ancient world and the fantastic mysteries of the modern Far East. With his own experience in the far-flung corners of the world and the aid of the theosophical influence, Mundy was able to effectively translate Oriental ideas through the filter of his own experience and Occidental consciousness into a western idiom. Few if any other authors have so successfully reconciled such seemingly contradictory ingredients, and the harmonizing of adventure and philosophy was all the more remarkable because the theosophical bent was unfamiliar or alien to most readers.[41] Mundy proved that it was possible to fully integrate the offbeat philosophy of a minority religious group into popular fiction and maintain a wide readership. Simultaneously, his stories were, and still are, hailed as valuable teaching by the Society; Mundy won the approval of both audiences, the already converted as well as the public at large. Thus Theosophy, through Mundy, affected the entire literary genre of Oriental fantasy and adventure, and *Om* stands as a classic monument to the achievements of both a unique writer and Point Loma's Theosophical community.

Brian Taves is a film historian with the Library of Congress and earned his Ph.D. at the University of Southern California. He authored *Robert Florey, the French Expressionist* (Scarecrow, 1987), *The Romance of Adventure: The Genre of Historical Adventure Movies* (University Press of Mississippi, 1993), and edited *The Jules Verne Encyclopedia* (Scarecrow, 1993). Taves is currently completing *Talbot Mundy, Philosopher of Adventure*, a literary study of the writer.

[1] Paul Kagan and Marilyn Ziebarth, "Eastern Thought on a Western Shore," *California Historical Quarterly*, 52 (Winter 1973), 5.

[2] Talbot Mundy, "As To Capital Punishment," *Theosophical Path*, 29 (December 1925), 523-525.

[3] For a further discussion of these traits in Tingley, see J. Stillson Judah, *The History and Philosophy of the Metaphysical Movements in America* (Philadelphia, 1967), 110.

[4] Talbot Mundy, *I Say Sunrise* (Los Angeles, 1963), 53, 92.

[5] Richards Leach Ames, interview with the author, September 1, 1984; Donald M. Grant, *Talbot Mundy: Messenger of Destiny* (West Kingston, RI, 1983), 142.

[6] Talbot Mundy, "Foreword," Tros of Samothrace (London, 1934), xiii.

[7] Talbot Mundy in Stanley Kunitz and Howard Haycraft, Twentieth Century Authors (New York, 1942), p. 997.

[8] *Adventure, 40, (May 20, 1923), 178. See also Grant, Talbot Mundy, p. 147.*

[9] "The Camp-Fire," Adventure, 49 (October 10, 1924), 181-183; reprinted in The Theosophical Path, 28 (February 1925), 194-197 and The Eclectic Theosophist, No. 61 (November-December 1980), 1-3.

[10][2] Pervin Mistry, "An Appreciation of 'Om,'" The Eclectic Theosophist, No. 73 (January-February 1983), 10; Talbot Mundy, Letter to D.L. Chambers, January 8, 1924, Bobbs-Merrill mss.

[11] Austin Adams, "Austin Adams Gives Highest Praise to New Book by Mundy," unidentified San Diego newspaper clipping, Richards Ames Collection.

[12] Talbot Mundy, Om—The Secret of Ahbor Valley (Indianapolis: Bobbs-Merrill, 1924), 267; Pervin Mistry, "From Letters Received," The Eclectic Theosophist, No. 64 (May 15, 1981), 7; Nirmal Singh Dhesi, "Mundy's 'Om' a Psychic or Spiritual Journey," The Eclectic Theosophist, No. 77 (September-October 1983), 8.

[13] Mundy, Om, 89-90.

[14] Mundy, Om, 14.

[15] Austin Adams, "Austin Adams Gives Highest Praise to New Book by Mundy," unidentified San Diego newspaper clipping, Richards Ames Collection.

[16] G. de Purucker, "'Om, The Secret of Ahbor Valley,' by Talbot Mundy: An Appreciation," The Theosophical Path, 27 (December 1924), 607; "Talbot Mundy's 'Om' Much Appreciated," The Theosophical Path, 28 (April, 1925), 391.

[17] Talbot Mundy to Katherine Tingley, November 1924 in Mundy, Om: The Secret of Ahbor Valley (Indianapolis, 1924), notation in copy at the Theosophical University Library, Altadena, California.

[18] Pervin Mistry, Letter to the author, July 3, 1986, 7.

[19] "Om," Milwaukee Evening Telegram (February 22, 1925), clipping in Richards Ames collection.

[20] Dawn Mundy Provost, interview with the author, April 1, 1980.

[21] Mundy, Om, 371.

[22] Cian Draoi, "Book Reviews," Dublin Magazine, 2 (May 1925), 683.

[23] Claire Walker, "Book Reviews," The Eclectic Theosophist, No. 78 (November December 1983), 9, reprinted from Journal of the Academy of Religious and Psychical Research, July 1983.

[24] Clyde B. Clason, "Foreword: Talbot Mundy—An Appreciation" in Talbot Mundy, Old Ugly-Face (Philadelphia, 1949), vii; See also "Story of East Pictures Way of Life," unidentified newspaper clipping, Richards Ames collection (private); Nirmal Singh Dhesi, "Mundy's 'Om' a Psychic or Spiritual Journey," The Eclectic Theosophist, No. 77 (September-October 1983), 8.

[25] Mundy, Om, 179, 222.

[26] "The New Books: Fiction," Saturday Review of Literature, 1 (November 29, 1924), 330.

[27] Talbot Mundy, letter to publishers, February 24, 1924.

[28] Clyde B. Clason, "Foreword: Talbot Mundy—An Appreciation" in

Talbot Mundy, Old Ugly-Face (Philadelphia, 1949), vii; Christmas Humphreys, "Book Reviews," The Eclectic Theosophist, No. 66 (November-December 1981), 5, reprinted from Buddhism in England.

[29]Martin Green, Dreams of Adventure, Deeds of Empire (New York: Routledge & Kegan Paul, 1979), 271; Talbot Mundy, Letter to D.L. Chambers, May 2, 1924, Bobbs-Merrill mss.

[30]G. de Purucker, "'Om, The Secret of Ahbor Valley,' by Talbot Mundy: An Appreciation," The Theosophical Path, 27 (December 1924), 607-609.

[31]For an example of how Om was used with the children of Point Loma, see Aunt Esther, "Our Brothers of Forest and Veldt," Raja-Yoga Messenger, 22 (September 1926), 233-234.

[32]Book List of Standard Theosophical Literature," preceded only by the writings of H.P. Blavatsky and Katherine Tingley. "Book List: Standard Theosophical Literature," The Theosophical Path, 28 (March 1925), back cover.

[33]B.K., "Point Loma's Lure Induces World-Traveled Author To Stay Here and Establish His Permanent Home," San Diego Union, February 15, 1925, 9; Claire Walker, "Book Reviews," The Eclectic Theosophist, 78 (November-December 1983), 8.

[34]"The Way of Life," Manchester City News, April 25, 1925, reprinted in The Theosophical Path, 28 (June 1925), 602.

[35]Talbot Mundy, Letter to H.H. Howland, Labor Day, 1924; Mary Converse to Talbot Mundy, March 9, 1925; Bobbs-Merrill mss.

[36]"Miscellaneous Headquarters Notes," The Theosophical Path, 27 (December 1924), 603; "Talbot Mundy's New Book 'Om,'" The Theosophical Path, 28 (January 1925), 92; "'Om' Delights Everyone," The Theosophical Path, 28 (February 1925), 185-186; "The Wine of Life," The Theosophical Path, 28 (February 1925), 192; "More Words of Praise for 'Om,'" The Theosophical Path, 28 (March 1925), 284; "Talbot Mundy's 'Om' Much Appreciated," The Theosophical Path, 28 (April 1925), 391; "The Way of Life," The Theosophical Path, 28 (June 1925), 602, reprinted from The Manchester City News, April 25, 1925; "'Om,'" The Theosophical Path, 29 (August 1925), 200; "News from Nurnberg," The Theosophical Path, 33 (October 1927), 386.

[37]"Talbot Mundy's 'Om' Much Appreciated;" Talbot Mundy, "Apology," Theosophical Path, 30 (January 1926), 19-20.

[38]"No. 1 Pulp," Time, 26 (October 21, 1935), 40.

[39]Elmer Davis, "A Loss to Fiction," Saturday Review of Literature, 22 (August 17, 1940), p. 8.

[40]See also Austin Adams, "Austin Adams Gives Highest Praise to New Book by Mundy," unidentified newspaper clipping, Richards Ames Collection.

[41]Clyde B. Clason, "Foreword," in Talbot Mundy, Old Ugly-Face (Philadelphia, 1950), vii.

MORE TITLES ON
MYSTICISM
FROM PILGRIMS PUBLISHING

www.pilgrimsbooks.com

For Catalog and more Information Mail or Fax to:

PILGRIMS BOOK HOUSE

Mail Order, P. O. Box 3872, Kathmandu, Nepal
Tel: 977-1-4700919   Fax: 977-1-4700943
E-mail: mailorder@pilgrims.wlink.com.np

Cotswold Ommony
John McGregor
Mr~~Lady~~ Cornock - Campbell

Chuttar Chand - second hero

• Tsiang somdup - Lama
  Samding - disciple
• dawa Sering - Hillman - Spithi
• Benjamin - ~~Jewish~~ shop keeper
         Business agent for
         monastery - Arbnn.
         Agent for the Lama

maitraya - actor strutting
Vasantasena - all is vanity

Dianne - precursor to Snowy
         - Tintin

Prabhu - Singh - so x Rajah